Frankenstein's MONSTER

A Novel

SUSAN HEYBOER O'KEEFE

THREE RIVERS PRESS
NEW YORK

Copyright © 2010 by Susan Heyboer O'Keefe

Published in the United States by Three Rivers Press, an imprint of the
Crown Publishing Group, a division of Random House, Inc., New York.
www.crownpublishing.com

THREE RIVERS PRESS and the Tugboat design are registered trademarks of
Random House, Inc.

Library of Congress Cataloging-in-Publication Data

O'Keefe, Susan Heyboer.
Frankenstein's monster : a novel / by Susan Heyboer O'Keefe. — 1st ed.
    1. Frankenstein (Fictitious character) — Fiction.
        2. Psychological fiction. I. Title.
            PS3565.K415F73 2010
                813'.54 — dc22
                2010005583

ISBN 978-0-307-71732-0

Printed in the United States of America

Design by Lauren Dong

10 9 8 7 6 5 4 3 2 1

First Edition

For Steven Chudney,
for joining me in a leap of faith

Frankenstein's

MONSTER

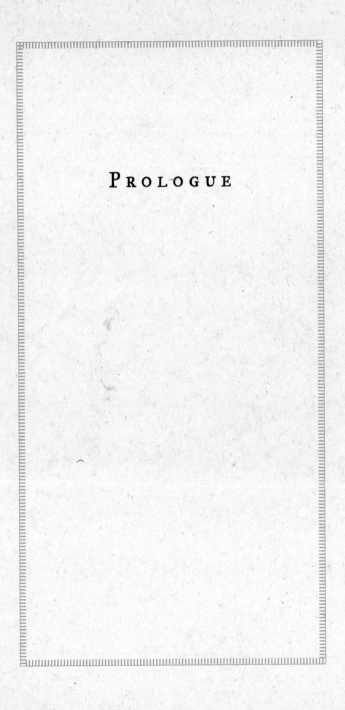

PROLOGUE

Near the Arctic Pole
October 13, 1828

Captain Robert Walton. Private log.

Behind me, stiffened with frost, lie the remains of Victor Frankenstein.

It is so cold I expect ice and not ink from my pen. Hoar en-
crusts the inside of the porthole, icicles drop from the hinge,
and over this page my breath hangs like a cloud. Should
I turn, I might find even the corpse in my bed to be dusted
wholly white.

I must write quickly, for my log may be all that survives me—
but—O Margaret! How can I describe what has happened
without appearing to be mad?

I said I would keep a true record for you of all events occurring
during our separation. You imposed on me exile; I would have
turned that exile into an occasion of grace. If I had succeeded in
discovering the North Pole, I would have enlarged man's knowledge of our Lord's sovereign majesty—and you would have welcomed me home; for could I have been thus favored as God's
servant unless He also deemed me worthy of forgiveness?

The answer is no. Now I have been exiled by God as well.

My hand trembles with more than cold, and these words,
which only you have the power to comprehend, condemn me with
their wavering letters and great blots of ink.

Some weeks ago, I rescued a man from the ice. Though half-
dead, he should not have been alive at all. Resolve had fed him
the scalding food of obsession, giving him a fiery strength to
survive.

He said his name was Victor Frankenstein.

He said he had discovered the secret of creation.

Ever since I rescued that poor man, he told me over and over a story both fantastic and profane about a huge creature made by his own hands, which then rose up against him and destroyed all he loved. Realizing his folly, Frankenstein pursued the thing till he had tracked it to these desolate regions.

His words were those of a man driven mad by the elements, for, in truth, who could undertake what he had claimed, much less imagine an act of such presumption? Yet, despite his madness, there was between us a wild affinity that pulled at me as the North pulls at the needle and that made me listen day after day as he unfolded his tale. I finally understood that he was clearly the friend denied me all my life. You know how I have suffered in this regard, Margaret; how I've believed myself fated to solitude, alone but for you. Yet even knowing my anguish, you can only guess at my admiration for him and my hunger for his fellowship and love.

Already I envisioned the pleasure of your meeting, already grew jealous of your too-generous affection for each other.

But the evil that has isolated me still grips me in its jaws: my rescue came too late for Frankenstein to regain his health. The clear weather failed, and so did he. He died yesterday before dawn as the icy wind keened in mourning. I do believe the sweetest part of me died with him.

It was strange to have found my twin in one whose desires were so blasphemous as to turn the natural into the unnatural. And then he died . . . I became afraid to look in the mirror. Whose face would I see reflected? If I pulled back the blanket from the corpse, whose face would be there?

I have not truly repented.

Oh, Margaret, dare I put such thoughts onto this page you may yet read?

Frankenstein's last thoughts pursued his delusion to the end.

"Must I die," he asked, "and my persecutor live? Tell me, Captain Walton, that he shall not in the end escape."

I could not refuse comfort to one so disconsolate, and I said, thinking my words meaningless, "He will not."

"You shall take up my burden? O swear it! Swear you shall take it up—for the sake of all men, for the sake of your dear sister, swear to me you shall hunt down the creature and destroy it."

"I give you my word."

He pressed my hand, then once more I was alone.

I lost all count of time standing watch over him, until at last the crew grew fearful at my grief and sent two men to bring me above deck.

Death followed me, matching my pace, tread for tread.

Later, a noise drew me back to the cabin. Hanging over the corpse stood a manlike form, gigantic in stature, distorted in proportions. Its face was concealed by long locks of ragged black hair, and one vast palm was extended toward the body. When the creature heard me, it turned, and I saw its face. Never have I seen a vision of such appalling hideousness. Involuntarily I flinched and shut my eyes. Then, all at once, I remembered, dear Sister. All at once, I believed.

Frankenstein, my dearest friend, had not lied. There truly lived a creature that had been created by man.

"I am a wretch," it said.

Its voice was soft, lovely, and beguiling, which made it all the more horrible to hear such evil words uttered by its black, scarred lips.

"I have murdered the lovely and the helpless; I have strangled the innocent as they slept; I have grasped to death his throat who never injured me." He turned back to his creator. "He, too, is my victim. I both pursued him and enticed him to follow until he fell into irremediable ruin. Now there he lies, white and cold and unmoving."

"And finally free from your power to torment him!" I cried out.

"Am I free from his? Like any man, I desire fellowship and love. He has cursed me to a lifetime of hatred."

"Like any man?" I repeated. "Do you mock me? Do you mock him?"

It tried to straighten but the small quarters prevented it from doing so.

"Is it mockery? There is no place, no one, for me—here, or anywhere—as he surely must have known. Now he is dead who called me into being."

Its expression grew decisive.

"I, too, shall be no more, for where else can I rest but in the death I was born from? Mayhap my spirit will find the peace that my body never had."

Having said this, it rushed past me and up to the deck, leapt from the ship, and landed on an ice raft that lay close to my vessel. It was soon borne away by the waves and lost in darkness and distance.

Can a man change so quickly, Margaret? We are promised that, by grace, salvation can come in an instant; I already knew condemnation could be as swift. Suddenly there was something at work in my soul that I did not understand.

What did the creature's existence mean? What did it mean to me? I had pledged my word to destroy what I thought did not exist—a pledge empty of all intent save to comfort my dear brother.

Then I saw it, Margaret. Then I heard it speak.

In a single moment, my empty pledge became a solemn vow. Naught else mattered but its fulfillment.

I ordered the ship to change course away from the main passage to follow what I alone had seen. The creature had said it would destroy itself; it had said it would return to death. But what were lies to a murderer?

I had to see the vow fulfilled, Sister.

I had to see the thing dead.

Midmorning, as the passage ahead narrowed, the sails fell slack. No wind lifted the canvas, no cloud drifted by to be mirrored in the flat glassy water. The world was still, lifeless, and white, the only movement the subtle encroachment of ice both before and behind me, too slow to be seen, yet always present at the corner of my eye.

I set a watch to climb the rigging, to line the rails, to peer out over the ice, searching—for what? For anything that should not be, I told them. For hours, for days, the crew watched in silence. Boards creaked though no one walked the deck; ropes slapped though no wind stirred. In the distance, cracking ice roared. The men leaned forward and stared, so still for so long, their clothes, their very beards grew thick with frost. Even their eyes seemed glazed as they stared unblinkingly.

On the third day, on the third watch, all the crew cried out at once: in the near distance, a thin curl of smoke. Next to it stood a black blot against the white. It appeared all at once, as if our eyes had been enthralled until the thing wished to be seen.

I slipped a hunting knife into my belt and ordered the dinghy into the water. Two men rowed me to the large floe. I bade them to return to the ship and then walked toward the smoke until I reached the end of the ice, where it broke off in sheer angles to the black waves beyond. There, at the very edge, the creature had made its camp.

It sat amid a pile of strangely shaped, upward juts of ice, a king in a ceilingless cave, making its throne among stalagmites. Neither the sharpness nor the rawness of the ice seemed to bother it. Indeed, the fire that had attracted me burned several feet away—and the fuel that fed it was the thing's outer garments. Clearly it had no need for warmth.

With indifference, the creature watched me approach, regarding me with that visage so horrible I did not know how I might look on it and live.

Priests are advised not to address the Devil when they mean to exorcise it. Why did I speak? Why did I listen? I should have leapt upon it at once and slit its throat.

"You said you'd return to death." My breath came hard and fast, my body spewing out the too-frigid air. "Instead, you still live. You could have disappeared. I would not have known. You could have gone to the very pole and stolen my only other treasure—and I never would have known my loss."

"Who are you?"

"Robert Walton, captain of the ship."

"You're angry."

Its dispassion infuriated me.

"You murdered my dearest friend. Now he is gone. And you still live!"

"I spoke in unexpected grief. He was my father."

"Father?"

Ripping off my gloves, I pulled the knife from my belt and threw myself at it. It was like throwing myself against stone. At once it seized my throat and shook me. In its giant fist, I was as small as a child. I slashed wildly; my blade raked its neck. With its dreadful features drawn up in rage, it threw me to the ground, kicked my arm, and sent the knife skidding toward the water. I scrambled after it. What power would I have without my knife?

The creature flung itself at me. For the first time I knew its full enormity, as if a mountain had fallen on my back, breaking every bone, crushing the meat of every muscle to pulp. I stretched out my arm but was able only to brush the tip of the knife; it spun like a compass needle gone wild, skittering closer to the water with every revolution.

The creature seized the knife and with its own huge hand stabbed downward at mine. The blade pierced both skin and bone and severed my middle finger. I screamed, Margaret. Even before my shock dissolved, I screamed at the sight, so much like a woman I am ashamed to remember it.

Blood sprayed across the ice. I dragged myself to my knees. Numbly I thought, how strange that my finger is so far away. And not only the finger, Margaret: the blade had wedged between the knuckle of the fist and the gold band you had given me years ago. Now both lay apart from me, the one still encircling the other.

With a flick of the knife, the creature knocked my finger into the water. The pale, slim shape sank quickly—a flash of white, a glint of gold, then black. A howl tore from my chest.

Without speaking, the creature stood up and walked away, as heedless of the climate as it was of me. It could go where no man could, to the very pole if it wished.

Ignoring the fire that engulfed my arm, I pulled on my glove and tried to staunch the bleeding by pressing the cloth of the empty finger down into the wound. Cradling one hand with the other, I began to walk back to the ship. Both gloves were soon soaked with blood. I grew dizzy, reeled in circles, and collapsed. My men found me and cauterized the wound right there. One man brought out the tinder box he is never without, another tore his own gloves to threads in order to feed the feeble blaze, a third held a blade to the flames till it glowed.

I had not thought the pain could be worse till they pressed the red brand against my flesh.

On ship the surgeon had to reopen the wound to remove the splintered bone down to the joint, then recauterize it.

Last night I tossed between a sleepless horror of all that had happened and feverish dreams in which over and over a glint of gold was swallowed by darkness. This morning I shook pitifully with just the slight effort of pulling myself up through the hatch, my hand useless, throbbing with indescribable agony. On deck I was startled to see that the landscape had shifted dramatically. At first fury deadened my pain: while I had slept, the crew had mutinied and turned the ship from its northern course. Then I realized we had been hemmed in by peaks of ice. Inch by inch they crept closer. All day I waited on their slow dance of death. In the early afternoon, a fog lowered, plunging the world into madness, for within the misty white hid the more dreadful stony white that would kill us.

Then, Margaret, not two hours ago, the whole ship shuddered and jerked! Wood screamed as an iceberg ground against us. Men flew to the side to try to push away the ship; their desperation gained us an inch relief. Before coming to my cabin to write this, I inspected the damage and watched the line of men with buckets. It is not a bad leak, but more than can be bailed in the time needed to repair it. If we stay, we shall drown by teacups. I share the ship's humiliation: little by little it bows, forced into submission by Nature. The prow will be the first to dip, the lovely figurehead, which reminded me of you, the first to taste the waves.

I had thought to bury Frankenstein at sea, shrouded in canvas. He shall still be buried at sea, but now in the coffin of my ship. Water is his grave; ice, my keep. Eternal Justice has prepared this place for the rebellious; here my prison is ordained in utter whiteness, and my portion set, as far removed from God and the light of Heaven as from the center thrice to the utmost pole.

There is one chance left. The crew has begged me to give up my goal—only for now!—and try to make our way south on the ice till we reach either land and a settlement, or open water and a venturesome ship. I have ordered the line of bailers reduced by half to free up men to unload such supplies as can be carried. I will add this log to the pile. A pallet is being hastily built for me, but I must find the strength to walk. I would not burden my men. *Only a quarter may survive the trip, Margaret, and those by God's grace alone.*

God's grace . . .

I no longer know what that means.

I still see, burned into my eyes as if I had stared too long into the sun, the dull glint of gold ever beyond my reach.

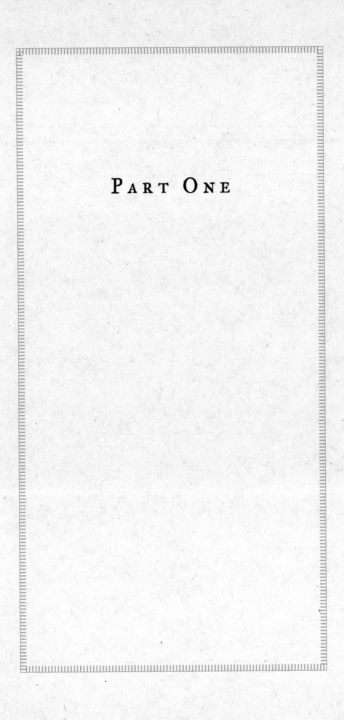

PART ONE

I killed my father again last night.

It was the same dream as always, my father and myself pursuing and pursued till I no longer knew who he was, who I was; indeed, if there were any difference between us.

In the dream my father chases me over a stretch of the Arctic, as he did in the weeks before his death. Once more I flee from his wrath and at the same time lure him on. I drive the sled dogs wildly. As the dogs pant, their spittle freezes and is swept backward by the wind to hail needles against my face. Fog rises from the ice and clings thickly to the dogs: I am pulled along by white devils from Hell.

Devil. Was that not his very first word upon seeing me rise up? What had he wanted from his labors that I proved so poor a substitute?

In the dream, as in life, he chases me endlessly. As it cracks wide, the ice beneath us roars like a wounded behemoth. Huge white blocks are shoved upward in nightmare architecture. At last I abandon the sled and cross the broken ice on foot. Greater and greater are the blocks I must climb, the gaps I must leap. Black water laps at the edges of ice. My father is nearby. I hear him mutter "fiend" and "abomination." His face appears, framed by white mist; it mirrors my own horror and hatred. I reach out. My fingers curl around his throat, as his reach out to mine. He laughs. I wonder if my face shows the same delight. That is all I remember before waking. I know that I have killed him. I do not know if he has killed me.

It has taken me these ten years to be able to recognize that Victor Frankenstein was my father. If he had lived, might he have learned to call me his son?

April 16

Walton is coming. I feel it in my scarred flesh like an old rheumatic who aches at the coming rain. He is close by, but not here in Rome, not yet. How much time do I have?

April 18

I have been here in Rome so long now I almost dare think of it as home. The dream is a warning that I must never grow comfortable. Rome must be like any other city, simply one more place where Walton will track me down.

A city as magnificent as Rome reminds me more brutally than usual that I am only a distant witness to life, and I wonder if I should have done as I had said long ago and rid the world of my unnatural presence. Was it cowardice that stopped me? Can I be so human as to claim that defect? No matter. I did not do it. Although I be a created thing, an artificial man, I cling to my existence.

April 19

My premonition spoke true: Walton has found me again. I flee Rome tonight.

April 20

I am safe for the moment, having taken shelter in one of the catacombs just outside the city. Tonight I shall slip away and travel north. From there I will decide my next destination. For now, I sit watch among my dead brothers. The candlelight flickers over their noble skulls and is swallowed by the blackness of their eyes. If the ratlike scratching of my pen disturbs them, they voice not their complaint. Once I was like them, peaceful and still, the life that animated my bones long forgotten and blown to dust. Then my father, seeking a frame upon which to hang his evil art, claimed me as his own.

How many lives had I lived before being brought together as I am? As many lives as parts? Was I man, woman, animal? My two hands, my two feet, are so mismatched they clearly come from four separate people. My brain, my heart, each had separate hopes and ambitions. What had I seen? What did I know? Do I know it still even now?

How uncannily Boethius wrote:

For neither doth he wholly know,
Nor neither doth he all forget.

My father robbed me of more than he knew, orphaning each part of me of its past.

Enough! With Walton on my scent, I must make new plans.

I had foolishly thought myself safe in Rome and had settled among the dark alleys of that city within a city, the Vatican. My face was always covered with the hood of my cloak. To hide my true height, I remained at all times crouched, knees bent as I sat on my haunches, and even walked thus, my body twisted and stooped like a hunchback's; the girth created by my shoulders and knees and elbows made it appear as if a head had been stuck on top of a boulder. My dead limbs could hold the position for hours. Only in Saint Peter's did I rise up to stand. My dimensions were more suited to the grandeur of the basilica than the dwarfish men who had constructed it. I spent my nights there; by day I sat on the steps out front and begged alms, a dented cup before me with a few coins in it.

For what? The coarseness of my body allows me to thrive

on the meanest food: in the countryside, roots, nuts, berries, an occasional animal; in the city, the refuse of others. A slice of fresh warm bread rubbed with garlic and drizzled with olive oil, the taste of which the poorest Roman knows intimately, is to me ambrosia.

No, it was sustenance of another sort I found upon those steps: I glutted myself on the sight of Rome's women as they hurried to market or strolled to an assignation. How easily I was swept up by their beauty.

Just last week, while I was begging in St. Peter's Square, a woman ran by. Although she was clearly distressed, her face and form were so exquisite I had to gaze on her awhile longer. Her complexion was pale and her hair, fair; I imagined her not a native but a visitor from a Nordic clime, come here, perhaps, for the sake of true love. I wondered how a virtuous and refined lady came to be wandering the streets of Rome alone. What possible complaint was so ignoble as to sully those graceful features? I fancied that only I could alleviate her suffering, if she would but let me.

> *Such is thy beauty, how*
> *Should my heart know*
> *To frame thy praise and taste thy godly pleasure?*
> *Take not thy image hence.*

At a discreet distance I followed the blonde woman to a street where potted plants adorned windowsills and gave each house a cheerful air. At one such place she stopped and rapped sharply on the door. A servant answered. Immediately my beautiful lady accused the girl of stealing a plum when she had accompanied her mistress to the blonde woman's house yesterday. Bright spots of anger mottled her queenly face, her eyes grew ugly, and, as with a rabid dog, foam gathered in the corners of her lips. She struck the servant forcefully; the girl would have fallen if she had not held on to the door frame.

"No!" I cried, rushing forward.

I felt as if I had been in a museum, staring rapturously at a portrait of ineffable beauty, only to have a stranger slash it with a razor. I drew a coin from my cup.

"Replace the plum with this," I said. "It was only a little thing, and the girl may have been hungry. Only do not frown so."

The woman turned to me. Her expression changed from fury at the girl, to haughtiness at a beggar's impudence, to astonishment and fear. Her eyes fixed on my hand. I looked down, thinking the coin had been transformed into a spider. I saw what she saw: I had reached out so far from under my cloak that I had bared my wrist and thus exposed the ugly network of scars where my huge hand had been attached to my arm. Would that my father had been a neater surgeon!

At that moment the mistress of the house came from within to inquire about the disturbance. Terrified, the blonde woman ran into her friend's house and bolted the door behind her. But before I could slip into the alley, even before she told her friend about me, she had regained her shrill tongue and continued to berate the servant for the eaten fruit.

I do not know when to act and when to be still.

I cannot help but equate beauty with greatness of soul. My own self validates this: I am a monster, in both appearance and truth. So when I see a beautiful woman, I think I must be seeing an angel.

The men of Rome, too, gave me sustenance. I was fascinated with the priests and brothers, the professors and their young students. Scholars visited from around the world, and, as in every city I have ever passed through, I often heard as many as five different languages in one day. Through the years I learned them without thought, much as a greedy child devours cake: one minute the cake is on the outside; the next, it is on the inside; and the child not once had to think of how to chew or how to swallow.

But in Rome, it was so much more than mere words: it was what was said. Close to the Vatican, the men filled the air with dizzying talk of history, literature, mathematics, natural philosophy, art, and, of course, their curious theology. It is one thing to read a stolen volume of Augustine—so easily acquired in this city, as are writing implements; it is quite another thing to be so close to conversations about original sin as to be fanned by the gesticulations of argument. How I longed to join in, to pose one of the many questions that have plagued my solitary reading.

Yesterday they argued about body and soul:

"What are you saying, Antonio?" an elderly priest asked, his breath hard and earnest with the topic. "That the soul is just the motor of the machine?"

"He's right, Antonio," agreed another priest. "That's Descartes, not theology. The soul is an act. It does more than inhabit the body; it creates the body."

"The body is penance," said the beleaguered Antonio, a young man with a wispy beard, clutching a pile of books to his thin chest.

"It is not. Only while the body is inhabited by a soul can it be called human. The arm of a corpse is no more human than the arm of a statue."

"The body is our punishment for original sin," Antonio insisted.

"From Descartes to Origen!" said the elderly priest in exasperation. "No, no, no! The universe—the whole universe, along with our bodies—was created out of pure goodness. The body is the servant of the soul. It may even bring good to the soul that animates it."

I sat mute, breath held. What if at this point I had slipped off my hood and said, "I have no soul, merely some animating galvanic energy; even this body isn't mine. I've been created from dead pieces—each no more human, as you say, than a marble statue. So what of me?" Would the elderly priest have nodded solemnly and said, "My friend, this is a theological knot"? Or would those men of God have feared me as the incarnation of Satan?

It is too late now. Yesterday, as I sat in the square by the double colonnades, leaning back for a moment into the cool shadows cast by the great stone pillars, Walton passed not fifty feet from me. His wild black beard, streaked with gray, gave him the look of a desert prophet calling down a rain of fire. His mouth was tight. His clothes were as severe as a monk's. The same fierce, other-worldly fervor smoldered in his eyes.

It has been ten years since my father died; ten years since I struggled with Walton on the ice. I had walked away from him with no thought of the future, or that mine would be woven with his from the same thread.

We had first met over my father's corpse. It was months later when I saw him next. The man I had left on the ice was gone, never to return. Illness had ravaged his face and form, and revenge had fixed itself in his mind. My father's last words were spoken to Walton. What vow had my father extracted, and then made irrevocable by dying, that had transformed a ship captain in search of the pole into a tracker obsessed with my destruction?

In just those few months, Walton was so changed I did not recognize him. It was after midnight, and I was in a poorly lit alleyway in Minsk. A stranger charged me like a bull, with a dagger instead of horns. Assuming he was a courageous though stupid thief, I took the knife away and swatted him aside. He charged again. This time I slammed him against the wall and would have rid myself of his nuisance; then he spoke: "You do not know me, do you?"

Having expected a stream of Russian curses and not English, I loosened my grip and peered at the man's face.

"It makes no difference," I said, my own English heavily accented.

"I know *you*. I know what you have done. I know what you are. You do not have the right to pass as one of us. You are not a man."

"Who are you?" I tightened my grasp round his throat.

"Robert Walton." He held up his hand as if it were a means of identification and, indeed, it was, for it was only when I saw the scarred gap between the fingers that I remembered. "It was on my ship that you destroyed Victor Frankenstein, my one true friend, my brother. You destroyed me." Walton smiled. "Frankenstein's last wish was that I rid the world of you. Now it's my last wish, too."

"Why? For your finger? My father could have sewn on a new one."

I flung Walton to the ground. He sprang up, drawing a second knife from his boot.

"I spoke only so you would know that I will have my revenge if it must be from Hell. Next time I will not stop to speak."

He slipped away to seek some later, more opportune, moment.

What stayed my hand that first night and the others that followed? That Walton was the sole person who knew the truth of my existence? That he was the sole link left to my father? I do not know. Over the subsequent months and years that he tracked me, each time that I did not rid myself of him made it that less possible to kill him. Now it is unthink-able. I doubt I shall ever fully understand his reasons for re-venge, for his word was true: he has not spoken to me again in all this time. We meet and struggle in silence, usually in the night; sometimes we spill our blood onto the ground; we part, knowing we shall meet again.

Thus it has been for nearly ten years.

The candle now melts to the stone, and its flame grows dim. While there is still light, I shall put away my pen and take out my book of poems by Cavalcanti. Although I pick-pocketed it only last week, I have read it so many times—for lack of anything else—that the words are now my own. Once I thought every book a true history. Now I know the decep-tion of art. Cavalcanti deceives twice over: he writes love po-etry. Even so, he has been my companion on this part of my journey.

Tonight I shall read him aloud. The skulls here have not heard poetry in too long and are eager for diversion.

Venice
April 30

Venice, city of freaks, city of death. I have disappeared into its watery Byzantine labyrinths. In Venice I can stand next to the carved walls that line the narrow alleys and be just one more gargoyle whose features excite disgusted admiration. Like me, nothing here is symmetrical. The once-gorgeous palaces totter with rot. Only their proximity to one another supports them, like a one-legged cripple leaning against a leper with no face.

Dwarfs, hunchbacks, idiots, and other oddities haunt the backstreets like cats. The Venetians tolerate, even patronize, such unfortunates, being fascinated with decay and deformity. Such a vice will be a virtue if it allows me to dwell here for a time.

I landed in Venice as a stowaway, sitting cramped, knee to chin, in the ship's hold. I shared the quarters with crates of moldering cheese and some curious rats. Together they made a fine meal. In the morning, I climbed out of the hold while it was still dark, dropped a rope over the side, and silently slid into the Adriatic. The ship's wake boiled around me, and my sodden cloak was a millstone. As if in concert, they tried to pluck my fingers loose, but I clung to the stern like a barnacle. At last there was a final swell as the sea rushed into the lagoon, and all was calm.

The water of the lagoon had a milk white pall, while the city was gray and pink; in the dawn it shimmered like a dream dissolving. Fishing boats wore the tree of life, omniscient eyes, and other cabalistic signs painted on their prows. Only the stench of garbage and human waste—dumped into the canals and awaiting the tide—belied the fairy-tale wonder of the vision.

I stayed in the water all day as the ship was unloaded, all evening as sailors and merchants came and went about their business. At last, night descended and the docks were empty. It was so quiet I could hear the soft padding of feet as a cat walked by.

I let go of the rudder, swam to the side of the ship abutting the dock, and pulled myself up. For a few minutes I crouched in the shadows. Water puddled off my cloak and dripped through the planks like a fall of rain. I did not move. I had waited all day in the lagoon, lump of flesh that I am; on a dry dock I could wait forever.

In the distance a bell began to strike. Before I could count the hour, another bell, and another, and still another rang, till the air vibrated first with striking gongs, and then with their echoes. I left the dock and crept onto shore.

In the canals, the water gleamed blackly like oil. Once, as I was getting ready to cross a bridge, railed with wrought iron, instinct pressed me back. I stood still in the darkness. Seconds later a gondola sliced through the canal. Up front a uniformed officer stood with a lantern held aloft, searching on either side. I remained motionless till the last trace of light had faded and the sharp laps of water against the bulwarks were replaced by silence.

I soon found a half-tumbled-down campanile, whose heavily rusted bells still lay amid a pile of bricks at the bottom of the tower. First I made certain that the structure was not shelter to someone else, then I settled down in its most secluded part to rest.

It is dawn. Men are already about on morning business. Voices outside the campanile complain about the city's occupation. After a thousand years of glory, Venice has begun to change hands as often as a weary old whore. The Austrians claim her now, not for the first time. Arguing over who is worse, the Austrians or the French, the voices at last move away.

My clothes and boots are still wet, my cloak still soaked, but the oilcloth I keep wrapped around my few belongings has once more kept my treasures dry. A candle, a flint, my precious journal, pen and ink, and my current book—each is safe.

May 2

Sometimes Fate offers me gifts. No matter how small, I count each one a treasure.

This morning, before dawn had stolen the safety of the lingering shadows, I found a man facedown in an alley, his expression beatific, his cheek comfortably resting on a pillow of dung. And there—by the fool's hand—a book! I have read the Cavalcanti five times over. A new book was more welcome than usual. I picked it up, wiped it on the man's shoulder, and slipped it into my cloak, still wet after its bath in the Adriatic. There the book bumped against the volume of poetry.

I was nearly to the next street when I turned and walked back. A fool with a book is less a fool for having one, given most fools and most books. I gave him the Cavalcanti in exchange for his and hope he finds some wisdom in it.

My new prize is *Sorrows of Young Werther*. It was one of the first books I ever read, along with *Paradise Lost* and Plutarch's *Lives*, and had such a profound effect on me that I hesitate taking it up again. Then, I had read it as my introduction to the entire race of humans. I believed all men to be like Werther: deep, sensitive, overwrought, noble, suffering with the agony and isolation of sheer existence. Now I hope to read the book as a cautionary tale against emotionalism, against the dangers of believing oneself to be accepted—nay, more seductive, against the dangers of believing oneself acceptable.

May 3

"Light a candle," said the voice, and a candle was lit.

"Light another," the voice repeated, and another candle was lit.

On and on the voice commanded, until a full candelabra blazed in the darkness.

In the dream, I wrote in my journal by the candles' radiance, breathing in the thousand spices of Venice: not the stink of the rotting hulk in which I now dwell, drained by centuries of extravagance, but the incense of ancient Venice, jewel of the sea.

On waking, I eagerly dwelt for hours on every detail of the dream, burning each into my mind as a memory of actual life. Such fleeting images, the mere suggestions of printed words, offer me more joy, more consolation, than reality ever has.

May 4

"Alms for the poor and blind!" the little beggar cried out. "Pave your way to Heaven with alms! A coin for me is worth more indulgences than a dozen novenas!"

Today I have met Lucio, master beggar, who gives twice what he gets, though not in the same coin.

The abandoned campanile is a mere dozen streets from the Piazzetta, next to the old Ducal Palace and overlooking the Basin of San Marco. Yesterday I wandered from alley to alley till the sun set. I drank in the light that is so peculiarly Venetian, its luminosity doubled by the water. The facade of the palace deepened from pink to rose. The building seems to be supported by air alone, lacy columns beneath, with a solid angular bulk on top. It is an impossible structure, and for that I feel kinship with its stones.

Today I arrived at the Piazzetta early and settled in a corner, enthralled with the conversations around me. An hour after I arrived, a blind man took up position a few feet away and held out a wooden bowl to be filled. Instead of sitting in silence as I did, he harangued every person who walked by, grabbing at the air to try to catch a skirt or pantaloon if someone passed without giving.

"Alms for the poor and blind," he said coaxingly. "I am blind, my wife is feeble, and our baby is sick. Alms! God hears the prayers of the poor, especially when they pray for their generous benefactors. Alms!" When the coins did not fall quickly enough, his speech became louder and included threats and curses.

Never in a week have I collected half of what he earned in hours. As his bowl filled, I could not help but imagine what I might buy if the money were mine. I could purchase books I truly desired, rather than stealing or stumbling on random titles. For a brief moment I considered his feeble wife and sickly babe, then dismissed the thought. Even if the story were true, he was richer than I simply to possess their companionship.

I crossed to him noiselessly and bent close.

"I have learned to fear the rich," the beggar said. "Must I fear the poor as well?" From inside his ragged cloak, he pulled out a chunk of bread, tore it in half, and held a piece toward me. "If Venice has been that tightfisted with you, my friend, I should not be. It's an unprofitable business all around when beggars must steal from beggars."

Though his eyes wandered slackly, each filmed as if with a caul, he addressed his words in my direction and held the bread before my face.

When I did not reply, he laughed. "You are thinking now, is he really blind? And if he isn't, can I take the money anyway and outrun him?" He gestured again with the bread. "Go ahead, take it, even if you mean to steal from me besides."

Surprise at being openly, even kindly, addressed fixed me to the spot and made me more hungry for the spoken word than the written.

"How did you know anyone was there?" I asked. I sat down and accepted his bread. "*Are* you sighted?"

"I'm blind, but for every fifteen coins that clinked in my cup, one would clink a little away from me. How long have you been practicing the noble art of begging?"

"Not long. I arrived in Venice just a few days ago."

"And not from elsewhere in Italy either, judging from your

accent. Well, you're too silent, my friend. Here, you must fight for every penny. You must speak up. Beg loudly, pray for those in the crowd, curse them, grab them, jeer at them, make them know you are here. They know Lucio's here. That's me. They cannot escape Lucio."

Lucio talked and talked, as though—robbed of his eyes—he had grown two tongues. When crowds moved our way, without a break in breath he resumed his loud beseeching. I began to leave, and he seized my cloak.

"Stay. You will starve without me. How could I sleep at night with that on my conscience? Besides, you are an amiable conversationalist: you say 'yes' and 'I understand' at all the right times." Laughing at his own remark, Lucio asked me my name. I gave him the first one I thought of; so quickly was it gone from memory that I cannot record it here.

When the beggar departed for the night, he earnestly sought my assurance that I would return tomorrow to the same place. He also made me promise that, sometime soon, I would accompany him to the lean-to he considers home and share his dinner.

"It is little more than a hovel," he said, "and the food may be meager, depending on the day's luck, but I promise you the conversation will be filled with sparkling wit! You will do me the greatest honor, my friend, for what could any man want more than the sound of his own voice being listened to?"

Lucio has told me of his wife and their babe of six months: yes, they are real, but neither is sickly. Because of them, his hovel for me would be as grand as a palace. I doubt that I shall go there, however. His wife is not blind.

May 6

I am almost fearful to commit my thoughts, my experiences, to paper. *Experience*—what a strange word for one such as I who lives too much in the mind. Something has happened. I have had an *experience*.

To Lucio's sincere delight I returned to the Piazzetta. The little beggar touches a place in me I did not know was there. He talked and talked, and, when it came time to appeal to the crowds, he included me in his rantings, asking for alms for the "poor devil beside me too dimwitted to beg for himself."

It was a day such as I have never had, and my story has not even begun.

At sunset Lucio left and I remained. The city quieted down around me till I could hear only the gurgle of water from the nearby basin and the rats as they crept out of hiding. Despite the peaceful night, I began to feel tense anticipation. I grew restless, yet was reluctant to leave. The dank air pressed in around me and urged me to stay. The darkness thickened as I waited; it held me in and thwarted my attempts to move.

At last a gondola from the basin was drawn close, and men climbed out of it. I edged round the column of St. Mark's Church so as not to be visible. I heard a weak, muffled moan, followed by a rush of whispers.

Two men were dragging a woman across the Piazzetta; she was gagged, bound, and blindfolded. The scene was disturbing enough; the contrast between the men and the woman made it more so. The men were dressed in rich velvets with feathered caps, their plump hands bejeweled with rings. The woman was thin and dirty, wearing cast-off clothes from several disparate outfits. Weeping, she fell onto her knees, only to be kicked till she stood again.

I emerged from behind the column, hobbling and bent low.

"Who's there?" one of the men challenged. I was enormous, yet to him, still just a lame, hunchbacked beggar with his alms bowl. "Go away. This does not concern you."

"What is your business with this woman?"

He looked incredulous to be confronted.

"I tell my business to no man, much less garbage from the street."

Wine and heat exuded from them in sickening waves. I limped closer till they were within reach.

"What will you do with her?" In answer, they laughed. "Let her go and I will not harm you," I said, which only set them laughing again. With a single movement, I shook off my cloak, stood straight, and grabbed one of them off the ground by his collar.

"What will you do with her?" I repeated.

"It is nothing," he gasped, his eyes wider with shock at my face than with choking. "It is merely a prank. We have bought her and are going to make a gift of her to a friend."

"Bought her?" This I understood, for I had often wondered if I might buy an hour of acceptance. "If you bought her, why does she weep?"

The other man, the drunker of the two and who had not seen me as clearly, chuckled. "She did not want to be bought. It was her man that sold her."

During this discourse the woman, still blindfolded, turned her face from one voice to the other. She made a pleading moan.

Holding her tightly, the drunkard reached into his pocket, withdrew his purse, and threw it several yards away. "Take it and go," he said to me.

I tossed aside the one man to grab the other. He let go of his captive and ran at me, head down like a butting goat. I caught him by the shoulders and shoved hard. He landed on his back. Quickly I stepped on his arm; the plaza resounded with the sharp crack of a branch being snapped. The man's howl became whimpering gasps for breath. He dragged himself to his feet, arm dangling, face oiled with tears of agony.

"Leave her, Camillo," he said, teeth gritted. "I need help."

He staggered into the shadows.

The one called Camillo came up behind me and caught hold of the woman.

"Do you know her?" he asked harshly. "If not, what is it to you what I do with her?" He drew a knife and held it to her throat. At the bite of metal, she choked back her weeping and stood still. "It should mean nothing even if I kill her," he said. "What's one life less on the streets of Venice? A beggar should know that best of all."

"You're right," I said softly. "What is one life less to me? Nothing. Kill her. I don't care. It will give me a better reason to kill *you*."

Slowly he backed toward the dock, holding the woman as a shield. I followed, certain he would try to escape in the gondola. My only question was whether he would attempt to take the woman with him. Instead, he pushed her into the water, then ran, daring to stop to retrieve his friend's purse.

As he must have hoped, I jumped in after the woman rather than pursue him. Bound so tightly, she would never have been able to save herself, even if she could swim.

I grabbed a fistful of her hair, pulled her struggling body to the surface, and lifted her out of the water. Curled on her side, she coughed in violent spasms as I removed the gag, blindfold, and ropes. Eyes pressed shut, she wrapped her arms around herself and lay shuddering. She did not respond to my soft entreaties. At last I enfolded her in my cloak, picked her up, and carried her here to the campanile.

May 7

Mirabella.

Beautiful sight.

That is what I call her. I mean no irony in the name. Surely, after she saw me, she must have understood why I called her *beautiful sight*.

Mirabella.

She is sitting in the corner this very minute watching me attentively.

Who is she? Where does she come from? What were those men going to do with her?

She is plain of face, with quick movements and alert black eyes. She cannot speak: her neck is marked by the jagged red scar of a recent wound. It is no wonder she grew still when the knife was held to her throat. She watches my writing with fascination. When I offered her my pen, she shook her head.

I was amazed at how little she reacted when she saw me that first night.

"I am ugly," I warned her, her face shielded from mine with the hood of the cloak I had wrapped around her. "Uglier than you could ever imagine. But isn't ugliness better than fairness that deceives, like those men who would take you with them?"

She nodded, then slowly pulled back the hood. On seeing me, her features registered not the slightest change. Perhaps simple calculation made her accept me: I had rescued her; therefore, there was at least the possibility that I might be good. If she expressed her revulsion, she might have had to return to whoever sold her to the nobles.

Or, if she expressed her revulsion . . . I might kill her.

To fill the silence I have named her and constructed my

own elaborate story, given her a history of neglect, ending with the kidnapping. In my fancies, I have continued the horror as if I had not interfered, knowing that, without my presence, her misadventure would have ended in abasement. I have embroidered the story with so many dark deeds, I shake that the subject of my wretched dreams actually sits next to me.

What would have become of her? What am I doing with her now?

I spent that first night talking to her, still believing she was capable of telling me, showing me what had happened. I have spent the day with her as well. I do not dare to leave her alone in order to join Lucio, lest she vanish in my absence, but also do not dare to bring her, lest someone recognize her and try to take her from me. It is my own sort of kidnapping, I suppose. I want her for my own, with a desire as base as that of the nobles.

May 8

We have just finished the last of the food and water.

May 9

"Have I harmed you?" I asked Mirabella this morning. "Have I made a move against you in any way?" She shook her head no.

Seized with restlessness, I paced back and forth in the confines of the campanile, still uncertain what to do, what to say. I am more accustomed to writing words than speaking them, am more manlike in my thoughts than in my deeds. Violence and desire make my fingers tremble until action sets them free. I wanted her, but more than the moment's gratification, I wanted her to remain with me.

"And you," I said, spinning round and pointing. "You have made no move against me by trying to leave."

Again she shook her head. Although she leaned easily against the stone wall, her eyes were wary. If I did not calm myself, I would frighten her into escaping.

"I will ask you plainly," I said. "Will you stay with me? We have nothing left to eat. I must go to the Piazzetta to join Lucio"—for I had told her of the blind beggar—"and there I will earn enough to bring back food and water, wine if you wish. I want you to be here when I return, but I do not want to keep you tied up while I'm gone. Will you stay?"

She nodded. And so I left, saying I would see her in few hours. Instead, I slipped to the rear of the campanile and watched her unawares through a window.

She crept to the door and peered out. Apparently satisfied I had left, she began to pick through my few belongings, lingering over random objects I had picked up on the street: bits of colored pottery, a glass bead, a tin candlestick, a length of rope. The glass bead she balanced between two fingers and held out her hand appraisingly as if she wore a ring. Next, she sorted through the rags I had piled up as a pillow, holding each against herself for something wearable. A few of these she kept separate.

At last she stood up and looked around the stone-walled room. She saw it differently than I did because she began to rearrange its contents, moving the pile of rags from one side to the other, sticking the candle stub by which I wrote into the candlestick, setting my book next to it, and propping the largest piece of colored pottery up against the wall as decoration.

She meant to stay.

I hurried off, the sooner to hurry back.

Lucio expressed concern at my absence of the past few

days. He accepted my story of being too feverish to come out, for I was reluctant to tell him so soon of Mirabella. Then he described with great detail all I had missed yesterday. A near riot had provided some rare excitement. Austrian soldiers had combed the city looking for a deserter, as Venetians stood by and jeered. Accusing the more boisterous ones of hiding the fugitive, the soldiers threatened them with imprisonment. Lucio heard swords being unsheathed and shots fired into the air. To his disappointment, the crowd broke up, and nothing came of the posturing.

"It could have been a day of riches for some," he said longingly. "With a little eyesight and a little talent for pick-pocketing, a man could have worked his way through the commotion and come out a prince. Ah, but that's my wife's talent, not mine."

In the past, Lucio's words would have nourished me. Now impatient, I tried to hasten the day with wishing. Before this, all of time had always been the same. Day passed into day, week into week. There was little to anticipate, nothing to hope for. Today, both eagerness and dread gnawed at my soul. Would Mirabella still be there?

As soon as I had enough coins, I pled ill health, bought food, found water, and returned to the campanile.

She was waiting.

May 10

Lucio has moved our post to the palace courtyard. Now we sit on the steps of the Giants' Staircase, which the doges used for their public coronations. Above us loom the statues of Mars and Neptune. How surprised Lucio would be if I told him my stature matched theirs more closely than it matched his.

The begging is the same here, but Lucio insists that the gossip is better. It is gossip of a shared misery. Sadness and regret are in the very air of Venice. He explains that many of the patricians have disappeared since Napoleon's first occupation, as if their families took a suicide pact not to have children. Of the nobles who remain, Lucio speaks with fond familiarity. He cannot see that these men despise him. Those who toss a coin his way, deliberately missing his bowl so that he has to scrabble in the dirt, look on him with hatred. Blindness is not contagious, nor poverty; these men act as if both were.

Even as my anger rises, the sweetness of Lucio's face bids me hold my tongue. What good would I do if I revealed the truth about his "benefactors"? Would his own anger, however righteous, put more coins in his cup? It would steal the bread from his mouth. Nobles prefer their beggars to be fawning and obsequious.

May 11

"I'm looking for a deserter," the Austrian captain said in broken Italian.

The soldiers despised us as much as any Venetian nobleman, jostling us as they marched down the steps in the courtyard where we begged. Their captain sauntered behind them and peered at us closely. He made a move toward the hood that shadowed my face. I half-stood, prepared to strike him down and flee if I had to. My size even at a crouch warned him off, and he pulled back his hand.

"Speak up! It's a crime to harbor a fugitive."

"Yes, a very serious crime," Lucio agreed. "Such a great crime that there might be a reward if this fugitive is returned?"

"It is patriotism to turn in a deserter."

"For an Austrian, sir." Lucio shrugged. "For a blind Venetian beggar it is business."

"And do you have business to transact?"

"A blind beggar is easy to ignore. People often reveal too much in my presence."

During this exchange my limbs tugged at me to run. The captain wore a brace of pistols. I too easily imagined him ripping away my hood to see if I was the deserter, imagined him shooting me once he had looked upon my pieced-together face. If I were not killed instantly and managed to slip away, he would follow the trail of blood. He would find Mirabella.

I could not bear the thought of losing her. It has been just a few days since she agreed to stay, yet her ease with me grows by the hour. Only this morning she excitedly led me to one of the windows, a place I avoid for fear of being seen. There she showed me, in the early dawn, a lone flower growing out of the stone wall, its single bud unfurling in the sun. She is like that flower, blooming in impossible circumstances, her caution and reserve slowly dissolving. If I only had light to offer her and not the darkness of hiding . . .

And so, when the captain questioned us, I could not help crying out, "We have nothing to tell you!"

Lucio turned in my direction, surprised at my outburst.

"But we would if we could, sir," he added.

"Your accent," the captain said, suspicious. "You're not Venetian. Who are you?"

"You must excuse my friend," Lucio said before I could answer. He reached out to pat me, missing my arm by several inches. "He's had the fever all week."

Immediately the captain faltered backward and spat in disgust.

"You beggars are worse than the rats in this dirty city," he said. "I don't want to see you in the courtyard again."

Lucio nodded, smiling, until I told him the captain had left.

"That was a very stupid thing to do," he said, the smile dropping from his face. He felt on the ground for his few belongings and began to bundle them up.

"Don't leave."

He could not know how I felt. I had spent my life avoiding attention. Now, when I needed most to be invisible, I had marked myself—and Lucio with me.

"Tomorrow you should find a place of your own to beg, my friend."

A reply choked in my throat. I have stayed nowhere as long as this, nor ever made myself so open and vulnerable. Lucio's companionship has been a miracle, more words said to me this past week than in ten years, and said kindly. But he would be done with me.

Hours have passed since the incident. I sit now in the campanile, writing this entry in my journal. Mirabella is at my side dozing, her head resting on my arm. While a woman's continued presence is more than I ever dared believe possible, Mirabella's silence makes me yearn for the talkative little beggar that much more strongly. If he only knew why I had spoken rashly . . .

Lucio has a wife and child. He is not immune to sentiment. He will understand.

I shall go this minute to explain. He has given me directions many times in anticipation of the supper we will share. I will tell him about Mirabella, then tomorrow we shall find a new corner to beg from—together.

Later

My father was right. I am a vile thing, a mockery of all that is human.

At last, after threading back and forth through alleys and across canals, I found where Lucio lives—in the remains of one of the many buildings destroyed by Bonaparte. I could not tell if it had once been a church or a palace, because only three run-down walls of a little inner chamber stood amid rubble. For a roof, a dozen planks had been laid across the uneven walls, and a tarpaulin over those. More tarpaulin was attached at the front to serve as a door. Now it was rolled up, showing Lucio toward the rear of the hut. Next to him sat a thin, pale woman holding a sleeping baby.

At the entrance, visible through the open flap, burned a low fire, inviting me in to share Lucio's fellowship. I paused, wondering what to say, how much to reveal. Had I not paused, none of what followed would have happened, but I did: I stopped to listen, to witness what I had no right to see.

I crept closer. However dismal their home, it worked a sort of charm on me. My eyes drank it in greedily, and I strained to hear every word of quiet conversation that passed between husband and wife.

"What a lovely day," Lucio began. "Today the winds were sweet. I could smell Rome and Florence in the air." He had said as much this morning; it was more poignant said to his wife, representing all the places he could not take her. He reached forward into what was only blackness for him and waited. "I smelled Paris and London. Saint Petersburg, too."

His wife caught his hand, brushed her cheek with it, then folded it back into his lap.

"Speaking of foreign places, we were out when the ships docked," she said.

"Oh no," he chided. "That's too far. Didn't carrying the baby tire you?"

"I had to try. After all, the Austrians have brought at least one good thing with them—rich, curious tourists." She laid the child down by the back wall, returned to sit by her husband, and began to undo her bun, removing one after another mysteriously placed pin till her hair fell loose and she shook it out. It cascaded in brown waves that caught red glints from the firelight. What a transformation! The curls softened her sharp features, and she became as lovely as any woman I have ever seen.

"And?" Lucio asked, turning his face toward her voice. "Did any passengers have bad luck today and lose their purse?"

She laughed easily, a deep throaty sound that made me realize how little laughter I have heard in my life.

"Their luck was better than mine. I had taken just a stickpin when someone started grabbing Venetians and questioning them."

Lucio sighed. "The Austrians are looking for a deserter."

"No, the man was a passenger from the ship. A priest, I think. He had that look to him, although he didn't wear a cassock. Anyway he made the crowd too wary. By then, the baby needed nursing."

"Such a good mother," Lucio cooed.

His searching hand found her, tugged at her to lie down on the straw, and began to unbutton her dress. She in turn loosened his clothes as well. She moved with delicacy: not one thread of the flimsy scraps was pulled. Lacing her fingers in the hair of his chest, she kissed her husband hard till she at last broke away, breathless.

"Let me pull down the flap," she panted.

"No one is there."

"Someone may come." Half-undressed, she hurried to

the entrance as I moved round to the side. She peered into the darkness for a long time.

"Hurry," Lucio complained.

After she lowered the flap, I crept round the corner to the back. Several bricks had fallen loose, creating a hole a few feet from the ground. I looked inside. Lucio and his wife lay tangled on the straw right next to where I knelt. The glow of the dying fire hid the dirt and bruises of their poverty. To me, they were angels suffused with divine light. At that moment, I still could have left. I still could have prevented what happened.

I did not. I was transfixed by their joined bodies and wanted what they had.

The starving man hungers for even the sight of bread.

I have never known love. I have never felt a caress on my scarred cheek nor the sweet pressure of willing lips on my blackened mouth. I have never had a moment when I did not burn with the consciousness of how ugly I am. . . . No, not just ugly. Even an ugly man can have a wife or lover. He can raise children, make friends, inspire respect, and die contented in his bed.

There came a moment—should I say, of course?—when Lucio's wife turned her face upward and, as the ecstasy of spending abated, opened her eyes. I had pulled away my hood, the better to look through the narrow hole, the better to memorize each pearl of perspiration, each roselike stain on her face and breasts. I meant no harm. I only wanted to see.

Shock and horror and fear passed over her beautiful features; despair, too, as if she suddenly realized that she had brought an innocent babe into a world that held the likes of me; and something more, a primal hatred of all that is alien.

This hatred lashed out and seared my body through the bricks.

Her mouth opened wide. There came from it a harsh choking sound, then she at last found her voice. In her wild tormented scream, I heard the cries of everyone who had ever rejected me.

Thrusting my arm through the hole, knocking bricks out of the way, I seized her by the throat. Her body jerked like a puppet's, and she gasped repeatedly. Lucio beseeched her to tell him what was wrong. Tenderly he felt her struggling body for injury. Shock evident in his face, he touched first a huge arm, then a huge hand at his wife's neck. He shouted and struck at me, trying to break my grip.

Feeling the woman grow limp, I dropped her onto her husband. At once his arms encircled her. As she weakly coughed, he pulled her behind him for safety, bits of straw clinging to his sweaty skinny body. In that moment, my pathetic longings were replaced by rage, and I hated him. His nakedness revealed him as what the nobles saw: a parasite, a blight upon society. His wife was no better, yet she had screamed at the sight of *me*.

What other ruinous mischief might I cause them? My eyes found the baby, swaddled in rags, lying in the back corner. I could rob them of their child and present it to Mirabella; thus might we live—monster, mute, and kidnapped babe—in a grotesque parody of life.

Sensing where the danger next threatened, the woman whispered, "Raphael." Lucio crawled to the back wall, searched for the child, and clutched it to his chest as his blind eyes roamed back and forth.

"The baby is safe," he said. "What happened? Who was here?"

"A terrible thing like a stone gargoyle come alive," she whispered hoarsely, weeping.

Unable to listen further, I left. Mirabella was asleep when I returned.

May 12

> *My breath is corrupt, my days are extinct*
>> *the graves are ready for me,*
>> *and all my members are as a shadow.*
> *I have said to corruption, Thou art my father:*
>> *to the worm, Thou art my mother, and my sister.*
> *And where is now my hope?*

> *We wait for light, but behold obscurity;*
>> *for brightness, but we walk in darkness.*
> *We grope for the wall like the blind,*
>> *and we grope as if we had no eyes:*
> *we stumble at noonday as in the night;*
> *we are in desolate places as dead men.*

May 13

When I woke this morning, Mirabella was gone. Mindless fury overtook me. I shredded the rags she had used for her pillow, crushed the flowers she had gathered from outside, ground to dust the pottery she had set as decoration. These puny efforts could not drain off my anger, and, with a tremendous grunt, I picked up one of the rusted bells that lay on the floor of the campanile and hurled it. The bell cried out so loudly it hurt my ears as it crashed against the wall.

I had wanted the bell to shatter. I had wanted the campanile to fall down around me. Frustrated, I whirled around for something else to lay my hands upon.

Mirabella stood in the open doorway.

"Where have you been?" I demanded. The blood throbbed within my hands.

She pointed behind her to a wooden table. It was old, but its top had a pleasant veneer, and although it had but three legs, if lodged against a corner, it would have at least the appearance of stability. She would have had to go out very early to scavenge such a prize from the streets before anyone else.

Her emotionless eyes accomplished what tearing apart my makeshift home had not, and drew off the passion that had overwhelmed all reason. Overcome, I sank to the floor and covered my face with my hands.

"I thought you had left."

Hand at her throat fingering her scar, she seemed to weigh the circumstances she had left, against those I presented: actual violence, against the potential for a violence beyond measure. Unable to watch these thoughts cross her face, I lowered my eyes. Quick steps hurried back and forth. I thought she was gathering what she could take away with her, then realized she was trying to straighten the mess I had created. After long minutes her footsteps stopped, and I looked up. Tears streaked her pale cheeks and both hands clutched the rags I had scattered about. She gestured at me with these clenched fists: it was useless for her to clean up, useless for her to stay, and useless, too, for her to leave.

May 14

This morning the food and water were gone, and I needed to go out and beg.

Before I left, I told Mirabella that I wanted her to remain with me, but that if she decided to leave, I would not force her to come back. Unlike that first time, I did not spy on her to learn her decision.

I could not return to the palace courtyard or to the Piazzetta. Though there was nothing to connect me with the monster at Lucio's window, I could not bear to hear from him the description of myself that by now must have spread to half of Venice. Instead, I begged aimlessly throughout different streets, wandering till I found a corner I could claim as my own. It was well suited, situated beneath a crumbling facade of gargoyles—what Lucio's wife had called me—just one more Venetian grotesque.

I sat in silence, my cup at my feet. I refused to speak or to lift my cloaked head, even though several times I was stared at for longer than usual. My silent image must have been pitiful enough because I soon had sufficient coins. I bought bread and hurried back to the campanile.

Mirabella had stayed.

Later

Tonight Mirabella unpinned her hair and shook it loose. It may be something she has done every night since I rescued her; tonight I seemed to see it for the very first time. When I realized what she was about to do, I had her sit before the low fire, just as Lucio's wife had sat.

Mirabella's hair caught the glow of the flames and crowned her with burnished gold. Using her fingers as a comb, she spread the hair like a fine veil across her face, then shook it back over her shoulders. Her clothes tightened around the swell of her breasts, the slimness of her waist, as over and over she combed her hair, shaking it back. The movement was both innocent and full of calculated art, and invited my thoughts where they had not been encouraged before.

Only once in my brief life have I had the opportunity for true companionship. Many years ago I had begged my father to give me a mate. Refusing at first, in the end he relented and retreated to the Orkney Islands of Scotland. He did not know, although surely must have guessed, that I followed him close behind from his home in Geneva to Strasburgh. Then I moved from one hiding spot to another while his boat glided down the Rhine, passing islands, rugged hills, and ruined castles. At Rotterdam, he took a ship to London, and there delayed for nearly five months before he finally packed up box after box of medical and chemical equipment and traveled north.

The Orkneys were the most desolate place I had ever been; I had not yet seen the Arctic. While the largest of the islands was habitable, the farthest were little more than wind-blasted rocks that fought both sea and storm to survive. My father's choice mirrored the essence of his task: wild Nature to be subdued and harnessed, wild loneliness to be assuaged.

I stayed outside the rough stone hut where he had set up his laboratory. The wind howled, rain beat down, waves lashed at my foothold, thunder and lightning consumed the air—and I thought myself king. I had found my own country, a land savage and alone, apart from men. Soon I would have a companion like myself—life, where there should be no life—someone, something, that would temper my ferociousness so that existence did not hurt as much.

Horror of what my father had already created in me eventually overwhelmed him. How his countenance sickened each time he touched the body!

Then came that final day. As I had done many times before,

I peered into the window of the hut. His work was nearly completed. By chance he looked up and saw me. Pleased that this would be my wedding night, I smiled—a ghastly sight! Terror, madness, and hatred slashed his face like razors. Trembling with frenzy, he destroyed his incipient daughter, reducing to offal the precious limbs of my would-be bride.

An eye for an eye, his Bible says. So I killed Elizabeth—his sister, cousin, betrothed, and bride—just hours after he and she were wed. It was the act that sent him on the hunt that should have ended with my death, but ended with his.

These unpleasant thoughts have a pleasant end in Mirabella. Just days ago I was in despair because I had lost the friendship of Lucio; as if, without speech, Mirabella could never understand me. Now I wonder if I have underestimated her. I have judged her only by her silence, just as many would judge me only by my ugliness. Instead, I should judge her by the rare charity and acceptance she has shown me. She has seen my face and is not afraid. She has seen the beast in my nature and waited for the man to emerge. If I lay my hands gently on her shoulders or encircle her waist, she does not faint or try to escape.

There is a grim humor in this. How did I choose my mate? She was the only one who did not shriek at the sight of me.

May 15

Last night a disturbing dream: Dressed in swirling, patterned silks, Mirabella walked toward me without coming closer. Her breath was sweet like honey, smoky like incense; I breathed it in like a drowning man breathes in air. A shadow cast its dark hand over her face, then reached out to touch me as well. Filled with dread, I jerked backward and awoke. I must have moaned in my sleep, because I found Mirabella stroking my sweaty brow to calm me. I tried to articulate my emotions to her. Even here in my journal, I find it difficult to put a name to what I feel.

Something haunts my dreams.

Haunts . . .

There is so much death in me I would not be surprised if a ghost had come to lay claim to my heart. Whose heart was it? I had none of my own. A thousand ghosts might haunt me, each one rightfully seeking its hand, its eye.

Some unearthly darkness has crawled out of the night to haunt even my waking hours. I dare not turn around to see.

May 16

Last night, after I finished writing and had closed my journal, I sat back against the wall and fell into deep, moody thoughts. Mirabella sat next to me. Absentmindedly at first, I patted her hair as I brooded. The feel of it was loose and soft, and soon I pushed her down onto the pile of rags. She lay shyly beneath my touch, yet did not refuse me, as if she had been waiting for this; as if her decision to stay with me included her decision to allow such intimacies. Feelings and sensations that have lain dead in me came to life, and I was overwhelmed at their awakening.

When I was done with my kisses and stroking, or I should say when I stopped—to prove to her, to prove to myself, my capacity for restraint—I turned onto my back. She tucked herself under my arm and lay her head on my chest. The gentle rise and fall of my breath was like the rocking of a cradle and she was soon asleep.

I write this by the light of dawn as she sleeps, her face pressed into the warm bedding where I recently lay. My dreams were troubled, but oh, there was the sweetness of waking to her face. Today when I go out to my corner beneath the gargoyles, I shall stay a bit longer, the more coins to acquire. After I have bought bread, I shall buy Mirabella a pretty trinket. I shall give it to her tonight as a wedding present—then take her for my wife.

May 17

. . .

May 20

Mirabella is dead.
   I can write no more.

May 23

Curse this pen! Curse this habit!

May 24

Eight days ago . . . *eight days* . . . Mirabella was still alive. I sat begging, cheerfully for the first time, spinning plans for the night ahead. Cup before me, I kept my head bowed, even when I was stared at. Uncertain whether it was the building's landlord or the Austrian soldiers, I did not look up. Even though the hood cloaks my face, any movement at all might attract attention and cause me to be driven off. At last the person moved away.

   It was fully dark and the streets were deserted by the time I had begged enough, gone to the Piazzetta to make my purchase, and returned to the campanile. At once I called Mirabella to my side. She smiled and nestled within my arms.

I pulled a necklace from my pocket and held it up, suddenly embarrassed by its cheapness. But what a treasure her face was! She was as delighted as if this cheap trifle were her first and only gift. She put it on at once: the chain fit snugly around her neck like a collar, and from it little charms hung down. She tossed her head to make the charms tinkle like bells, then offered her neck to my lips. I held her close and drew her down upon our bed.

I wanted to lose myself in her, to lose sense of my own dark ugliness.

At every moment I held myself back, aware that I had little experience distinguishing between passion and force. She was a small bird that might be easily startled; worse, easily crushed. I was determined to let her responses guide my actions.

Gently, I began to caress her. With excruciating slowness, I kissed away each layer of clothing. Finally her shawl, skirt and blouse, shoes and stockings, and petticoat lay scattered on the floor. She had on nothing but her chemise, a once-lacy cloth now worn thin. Her eyes were cast down, and I thought that the changing nature of my touch had at last made her hesitate. When I paused for several seconds, she looked up into my eyes and nodded, pulled my face down to hers, and kissed me.

There was a harsh shout from outside the campanile and the door burst open.

"There he is! There's your deserter!"

Walton.

Forcing their way in behind him were a half dozen Austrian soldiers, sabers drawn. I knew at once that Walton was the black shadow I had met in my dream.

Mirabella struggled to get up. Perhaps she had not understood the reference to a deserter and thought her wealthy kidnappers had sent soldiers after her.

"Rape!" Walton cried.

The Austrian captain, the very man who had insulted Lucio, drew his pistol.

"Give the woman up," he commanded. His face contorted as he got a better look at me. "This is not my man," he said to Walton, and to me: "Who are you?"

"No. Say, '*What* are you?'" Walton's eyes looked dazed, the fulfillment of ten years' chase at last within his grasp.

I stood. The captain's mouth gaped with astonishment. From the side a soldier grabbed Mirabella and pulled her away. She struggled, striking his face, trying to twist loose.

And in a single dreadful moment: Mirabella's frantic movements distracted the captain. He turned toward her. She jerked free from the soldier and ran back to me for protection. Walton shook off his trance, seized the pistol from the captain, aimed at me, fired, and—

Mirabella fell dead within the circle of my arms.

Horror paralyzed the captain as he stared at her fallen body. Walton leapt in front of him, gesturing wildly.

"Take him now!" he shouted to the captain. "You don't realize what he can do."

"The woman . . ."

"The woman is dead. And if she was his, she deserves death!"

His savage words impelled me to action. I rushed at him, still holding Mirabella. Thinking I meant to flee with her body, the captain yelled, "Don't let him escape!" Instantly his men surrounded me, blocking me from the door, blocking me from Walton. I set Mirabella down and with a cry embraced the battle.

Rarely have I so gladly given myself up to violence: it blinded me, numbed me, deafened me. That night, men wore no faces, only eyes to be gouged, limbs to be snapped as

I fought my way to Walton. He hung back, keeping a wall of bloodied flesh between us, then disappeared once he realized I could not be taken.

As I write these words, faces flash before my mind's eye: Frankenstein's brother, his friend, his bride, he himself worn to fatal sickness, tracking me down; the nameless who, like the Austrian soldiers, unwittingly placed themselves in the path of my rage; even the myriad bodies that comprise my parts. All of these clamor in noisy accusation: *You are death.*

And now Mirabella. I am bruised and beaten, but it is her blood that stains my hands.

The soldiers retreated, forming a loose circle around the campanile to guard me while reinforcements were sent for. In that moment of quiet, I knelt beside Mirabella and cradled her. She was as warm as life. "Wake up," I murmured. "It's just a nightmare. I'm here now. You're safe. You will always be safe with me."

She was the only one who had found gentleness in me, the only one who had waited for me to be gentle. I clothed her as best as I could, not wanting her nakedness exposed to those who would judge her unkindly, and then laid her body on the pile of rags that had been our bed. Tenderly I kissed her lips, eyes, cheeks; the scar on her neck, so like my own. When I kissed her, the charms on her necklace clinked, a soft but brittle noise, as though all their music had come from her and not the tiny bells, and now she was gone. I slipped the necklace from her throat, where it had rested for so short a time, and fastened it around my wrist.

I took my cloak, pen, journal, and book; kissed her one final time; and left the campanile forever.

May 26

What foolishness possessed me to think that I could steal a crumb from life? For ten years, a thin layer of ink is all that has held me back from madness. This time I need to bathe in it, I need a baptism of ink to salvage my spirit. . . .

May 27

I had been so smitten with the prospect of living as a man I had not seen the warning signs. Someone stared at me for too long a time in the palace courtyard, on the Giants' Staircase, beneath the gargoyles when I begged alone. I thought nothing of it. Being large and misshaped even under my cloak, I am always stared at. I did not even lift my head to see who it was. And before that, Lucio's wife reported a stranger, badgering the crowds. I did not hear her words. I saw only her hair in the firelight.

I write this now from St. Mark's Church. Last night, all was dark save for the guttering light of a few candles. At dawn, priests walked down the aisle in reverent silence to say Mass, each at his own side chapel. I squeezed into a pew and huddled on my knees, just another beggar seeking forgiveness. The Latin chant ended, and all of the candles except those in the main sanctuary were snuffed out, yet I remained on my knees till the church had emptied. The side chapels are shadowy. Even though I might be told to leave, no one would think it unusual to find a beggar at the feet of an altar. Perhaps I came here looking for more than refuge, hoping for mercy and consolation, such as the old women seem to find in the unceasing click of their rosary beads.

For me, there is no mercy, no consolation. My only God is my father, and he is dead.

Later

Seized by the conviction that Walton would return that night to the corner where I begged, I threw down my pen and paper and ran from the church. Surely he would be there, at the very spot. At last I would feel his throat beneath my fingers, see his eyes pop, smell his fear; I would hear his last rasping breath.

Down streets and alleys I ran, my feet echoing so loudly I might have been leading a stampede of wild beasts. Nothing remained in me but raw passion.

He was not there. Breathlessly I paced back and forth, possessed by rage.

I was not dead.

Walton was not dead.

Mirabella was dead.

The gargoyles sneered at me. I leapt at the building they adorned and hammered at the face at the corner till skin scraped from my hands, blood mingled with stone dust, and horns and snout snapped off. I clawed my bloody fingers into the tiniest cracks on either side and pulled. The mortar finally yielded, crumbling beneath my touch; the stone slid out. Over and over I ran at the building and smashed the stone against the wall. Though ugly, the face was more comely than mine. I did not stop until it disintegrated into a thousand chips. The eyes, two hollows of darkness, bloodied by the imprint of my battered hands, were the last to crumble.

With Mirabella, I had thought to put death behind me. What foolishness, what pride! Death is my element, my body, my blood. I hesitate no longer. I will kill Walton. I will be the soulless monster he thinks I am. For the sake of one person, Mirabella, I would have made peace with all mankind. He has denied me that. If I am not allowed to inspire love, then I will cause fear. From now on revenge shall be dearer to me than food or light. I may die, but Walton shall first curse the sun that gazes on his misery.

May 29

Blind fury cut short my last words, written with bloodied fingers. Today bids me to take up my pen so I can form a plan.

I do not want to draw attention by staying in St. Mark's by day, and so I slink through the streets like a furtive rat. All the city searches for me, as the story of what happened in the campanile has been told and embroidered and retold. The Venetians long for the sight of the hideous giant that kidnapped a nobleman's beautiful daughter on her wedding day, murdered her, and then, being discovered, broke free from the dozen soldiers that her father had sent to rescue her.

Walton has taken up the hunt once more. I can feel it. To him, I am more elusive than the Magnetic Pole he once sought, and perhaps more powerful. Though he searches for me, I must find *him* to have the advantage. He must have no possibility of escape.

Hours before midnight, the rain poured down in such torrents that I returned to St. Mark's Church earlier than usual. I found this corner and write. Tomorrow I will mingle with the crowd again as a hunchbacked beggar. I need to know what people are saying; more specifically, I need to know where Walton has his lodgings.

The approaching dawn has begun to lighten the stained-glass windows. Usually I find some measure of enjoyment

in the church's statues, enamelwork, gold, and jewels—
today, none. I have unwittingly made my nest beneath the
church's famous mosaic, the story of Adam and Eve illus-
trated in tiny stones and gilt paint. Where was I when God
made man?

May 30

This morning the rain let up, although the sky remained a
dismal gray, as if the clouds would burst open again at any
moment. I left the church and sought out Lucio. Of anyone,
the little blind beggar would have the most recent gossip.
It has been almost three weeks since he bade me leave. Not
knowing if he would speak to me, I thought only to stand
close by, listen to his banter, and thus learn something that way.

He had returned to our old spot in the Piazzetta, this time
in the shadow of the column that is topped by a statue of a
fierce, winged lion, symbol of St. Mark himself. Lucio had a
wealthy old woman by the sleeve and was speaking quietly,
a shock to me because his voice was often the loudest in the
square. Perhaps he was engaged in gross flattery, softly cajol-
ing her into buying a love amulet. Or perhaps he thought the
woman to be younger, although he had never made that mistake before. She threw a coin into his bowl and hurried off.

I walked closer. How he had changed! He was thinner,
and his blind eyes were sunken and darkly circled. His manner was more subdued as if it, too, was overshadowed by
darkness.

"So, my friend," Lucio said. "You have returned."

"And you have given up begging for peddling."

He pulled from his pocket strangely woven knots made
from colored yarn. "The crowd finds them a novelty, at least

for now, and have been filling my bowl more quickly. That's good. These days I hurry home early. My wife is . . . not well."

I would not question him about her sickness, knowing its cause.

"But how are you?" he asked. "I have missed you. Where have you been?"

Such a short time ago his affection would have warmed me.

"I worked another corner, as you asked me to do," I said. Obviously he had regretted his words. I said nothing to soothe him; he had wounded me, and I was glad to see he had been wounded in turn. "Then I fell ill."

"And when you felt better, no doubt the corner was taken by someone else. The Austrians are right," he said. "Venice has too many beggars. We fight for the same paltry coin and hurt only ourselves." He leaned against the column and sighed.

"Tell me what's been happening," I encouraged him. "I've been shut away for so long, I feel as if the whole world has changed while I've been gone."

"Old man Petrocelli was robbed last night. There are rumors it was the giant."

"Giant?" I said, feigning surprise. "What giant?"

The delight of gossip did not bring its usual smile; instead, his face tightened. "If you have not heard of the giant, your fever must have made you senseless."

I listened to the story, which, by now, just days later and in a different part of the city, had been embellished even more. What had been a small, spontaneous attack, instigated by a foreigner who had claimed he discovered the deserter, now encompassed valor, honor, bravery, and such audaciously brilliant tactics that, although they failed, were sure to merit commendations. Lie piled on lie, body on body, until I had killed half a regiment and, with a strength like Samson's, brought down the campanile itself.

Lucio's words cut the most sharply when he ended:

"The worst of all of this . . ." His voice, now beyond his power to control it, began to tremble. "The girl was really not a rich man's daughter, as they are saying. She was just a girl he'd dragged in from the streets, as poor and helpless as we are. The giant raped her in the vilest of ways and strangled her. The soldiers broke in, but it was too late. The girl was hanging lifeless from his enormous hands."

Shame and hatred jerked my body so fiercely I knocked over Lucio's bowl and sent the coins spinning.

"My friend?"

I backed away before he touched my vile, enormous hands, still stained with blood.

His stories had said enough that I now knew where I might find Walton. I would have gone at once but for the silent sadness that had returned to the beggar's face. His words would be like broken glass in my ears, but I asked how he himself had been.

He tried to command his emotions before he spoke:

"Right before the girl's murder, my wife was brutally attacked. I'm certain it was the giant. He invaded our home, but I didn't even know till he had grabbed her!" he cried in anguish. "He choked my wife while I held her in my arms!"

Lucio's voice failed him and he turned away.

"Till that night I never thought I was less of a man for being blind."

Remorse is too pallid a word for what I felt.

"He did not kill her," Lucio continued. "But the shock . . . They tell me her hair has gone entirely white. She won't stay alone, yet won't come with me to the Piazzetta. She does not eat, she does not sleep. She just stands by the window and keeps watch. She must be reminded to nurse the baby, though it cries and cries and her dress is wet from leaking milk. She no longer hears the baby, my friend. She no longer hears me."

"I'm sorry for your troubles," I said, touching his shoulder. I could not bear to listen to him another moment. "Good-bye, Lucio. You have always been kind to me."

"No, I've been harsh. I'm glad you came back. Will you be back tomorrow?" He grabbed at the air to try to find me.

I fingered the little chain of charms that encircled my wrist.

"It depends on my luck," I said, and quickly walked away.

June 2

I write now from a quiet place, whose silent peace mocks me.

After I spoke to Lucio, I returned to St. Mark's and impatiently waited for night. I could not go out until it was late enough that Walton would have returned to his room. Outside, people gathered on every side of the church and created an unexpected air of merriment that crazed me with anticipation. Through this door, prostitutes sold themselves on the steps. Through that one, soldiers patrolled by fours. Here was a couple arguing over infidelities. There was a drunk singing arias from *Così Fan Tutte*. The hours stretched till I imagined it close to dawn, but a bell pronounced it two.

Late enough.

A hush as thick as cotton wadding had settled over the night as I stealthily made my way to the quays at the Fondamente Nuove. According to Lucio, it was near there that the foreigner lived, in a house owned by the elderly Signora

Giordani, in the corner room on the second story: such was the precision of the gossip. When the foreigner was not wandering the streets, he stood in his corner room and stared out at the lagoon, madness burning in his eyes.

Separating the house from the one next to it was a narrow alley. I braced myself between the two buildings and by force steadily inched my way up. When I had gained enough height, I hung on to the ledge and reached around until I caught the sill and was able to climb up. I squeezed through the open window and into the room.

It was empty.

Cursing, I shredded the bedsheets in rage.

Had I come too soon? Had I entered the wrong room? Had he already left Venice?

The room held a desk, chair, book, and candle. After slipping the book into my pocket—for even now I could not ignore a gift from Chance—I saw that beneath it was a letter written in English. "My dearest brother," the letter began. Dated a month ago, it was signed, "Margaret." Was it Walton's? Surely he was not the only Englishman in Venice.

At last, on the floor I saw the large folded sheet that had enveloped it. The letter had come from a Mrs. Gregory Winterbourne in Tarkenville, England, and was addressed, I read with satisfaction, to Robert Walton, in care of an address in Rome. That had been scratched out and an address in Venice written to one side. The letter had taken this long to catch up with him.

I let the sheet drop to the floor, snuffed out the candle, and stood in the darkness, thinking. Should I wait for his return? Where could he be at this late hour?

The door cracked open and candlelight streamed in.

"Signor?"

I moved farther into the shadows.

"Signor? You are restless again. Would you like wine? I know you said you never drink. For tonight only, it would help you sleep. . . ."

An old woman stepped over the threshold. I pressed myself against the wall and whispered, "Yes, thank you, wine."

She stopped. Hesitation, then fear, crossed her broad, innocent face. She backed out of the room, slammed the door, and ran down the hall.

A moment later I left the way I had entered.

A wild shriek came from directly below me as a face showed in a first-floor window.

"Help! Thief, thief!" I dropped to the ground, and the old woman saw me clearly. Her next words were choked. "It's the giant!" she cried, leaning out of the window.

Shutters along the street flew open. A man took up the cry.

"The giant! Don't let it escape! Kill it!"

The cry was echoed by some while others hissed. Shoes flew at me. A boot struck me sharply in the head. With unnameable emotion, I shook back my hood. I had not stood undisguised before so many people in ten years. I had often wondered what might happen if I did, and here was my answer: hatred pouring from every open window.

I stretched my hands out to the night sky. Under the eyes of the crowd I felt tall enough to wipe away the clouds and reveal the stars beyond.

"Look at me!" I demanded of my audience.

What was it that suddenly silenced them? In that brief moment of quiet, my arms still flung upward, I turned to each face, one after another, searching its expression for a clue as to what each person saw, what I was. I was hoping for the thinnest thread of connection. Instead, a wave of movement swept along the street: people making the sign of the cross and dropping their eyes. No one would meet my gaze.

"What do you see? Tell me!"

Would no one answer? Then—

"I see a murderer!"

"Murderer!"

Someone threw a rotten cabbage. With that, every voice started up again, united in one obscene yell like a dissonant chord struck and pedaled and held. The loudest voice belonged to the old woman, who leaned out perilously far.

"Murderer!"

A chamber pot flew at my head. I saw it too late. It was a glancing blow, but it overturned, dumping its cold filth on my face. In it I tasted the heart of Venice.

I seized the old woman by the scruff of her withered neck, dragged her out of the window, and held her up to the crowd, her tiny bare feet dangling like a hanged man's.

"Is it murder you want to see?"

How quickly they had opened their windows to shout at me. Would they just as quickly come to the woman's assistance? No one had come to help Lucio when his wife had been attacked. In that forsaken part of the city, no one had answered their cries.

Again the crowd fell silent. I lowered my arm till the old woman's body rested against mine and I could feel the frail drumming of her heart. Her eyes were closed; her lips murmured silent prayers. Between my thumb and forefinger her skull was as thin as an eggshell.

Whistles blew from a distance, footsteps clattered, and the crowd yelled, "Here! The giant is here!"

I threw the old woman to the ground and ran. At the end of the street appeared the patrol, the men's faces set in boredom despite the double-time of their march. No doubt this was not the first cry of "giant!" they had investigated this evening. At the sight of me, their expressions caught fire and they charged, spreading out and cutting off my escape. I dashed down the nearest alley. It twisted like a tortured snake, dank ruined walls on either side. There was enough pitting and scarring to provide handholds, but my pursuers were close: they would have time to shoot me down if I tried to go straight up.

The alley ended at a canal, wide enough to let two gondolas pass each other easily. I climbed over the wrought-iron railing, teetered on the edge of the brickwork, and leapt to the other side. Footsteps echoed down the streets here as well.

Even the freaks of Venice had been aroused against me. Hunchbacks stoned me, and cripples created a gauntlet of crutches as I ran through the beggars' quarters. Gleeful virulence united them. As long as I existed, there was someone beneath them they could despise.

Through the last hours of the night I was chased in one long mad frenzy, up and down streets, along and over canals, from shadow to shadow. My mind drifted back to those final months when my father had chased me over the ice near the pole, the quintessential description of our relationship. I goaded him ever onward. I would never let him catch me, but I would never let him rest.

Venice was avenging him.

When I made my way back to the Fondamente Nuove, dawn had begun to lighten the overcast sky from black to dishwater. The dreariness gave the water the opaque milky blue of a cataract eye. I immediately thought of Lucio, then of what I had done to him. Fate had robbed me of possibility, but I had robbed Lucio of happiness he already had.

A whistle pierced the air.

"This way!"

I jumped in.

I stayed underwater till my lungs burned and my sight ran red with lack of air. When I could no longer bear it, I bobbed up between two gondolas, gasping. Voices exclaimed excitedly from close by:

"It jumped in here!"

"Did you see it? It was bigger than two men."

"Two? Three!"

"It was hideous."

"There! Did you see something?"

I swam along the dock; just as quickly the voices followed.

Then I saw it: a gondola larger than the others, decorated like a macabre gift from a ghoul. From stem to stern it was draped in great pleats of stiff black and gold cloth that covered both sides of the gunnels and hung down into the water. Midway on the gondola's length to the stern was a large canopy of the same black and gold material. Once more I ducked under. This time, I surfaced between the cloth and the wooden shell of the boat. Now I could keep my head above water without fear of being seen and so outwait my captors.

It began to rain. Drops striking the thick, stiff material muffled the voices, except when someone stood directly overhead.

"It's useless," I heard at one point. "He must have drowned."

More voices from a distance: soft weeping, the sound of arguing, and then, "We have nothing to do with this. Let us pass."

The gondola rocked wildly. A sharp thump and scrape, as if a trunk had been brought aboard and shoved aside, then the footsteps of people settling themselves. I had at last found my escape. When the gondola was pushed off from the dock, I would hold on. If the boat moved heavily, I hoped the gondolier would ascribe it to the trunk he carried.

The trip was far shorter than I had hoped. After the trunk was unloaded and the people had stepped off, the gondola stopped rocking, as if the gondolier, too, had disembarked. The voices faded. After a few minutes I slid out from under the drape. Only one other boat was tied up. The water was dimpled by the increasingly heavier fall of rain. All I could see was a pinkish stone wall lined with cypress trees. I did not recognize where I was.

I swam along the wall and was about to pull myself up when I heard voices and hurried footsteps. The gondolier helped two women and a priest into the boat, then pushed off. In a few minutes two younger men approached furtively. They left in the other gondola and rowed in the opposite direction. Pulling myself out of the water and over the wall, I lay behind some thick bushes, waiting. When I was certain that the area was deserted, I ventured onto the grounds to see where I was.

The tangled bushes gave way to more-sculptured arrangements of shrubs and flowers. Beyond this was a clearing in which stood a church. Fanning out from the church were graves and mausoleums. Some had the smallest of plaques; others, ornate headstones, embellished with leaves and vines and stony-eyed angels. Three graves were open. Not new graves—old ones beneath moss-covered markers. The freshly turned earth scented the air with decaying mold that not even the downfall of rain could erase.

I advanced to the closest open grave. A cart was set next to it, shovels and picks abandoned on the ground. In the cart was a pile of bones, streaked with brown rivulets as the rain washed away years of accumulated dirt. At first I wondered what terrible deformity gave birth to so many bones within a single frame, then my eyes made out the curves of more than one skull. I was looking at the remains of several bodies thrown together like rubbish.

I turned my head, blinking rapidly, caught unawares by

both the sight and the emotion that it produced. And in turning, I realized for the first time that I could see water in the distance. I turned and turned again. Water in all directions.

Life had scorned me once more.

I had escaped from Venice only to be carried to its graveyard, the Isle of the Dead.

San Michele
June 5

> *The sharp rain, drizzling through that place of fear,*
> *Pierces the bones gnawed fleshless by despair.*
> *How dismal, O Death, is the place of thy dwelling!*
> *The grave locks up the treasure it has found;*
> *Higher and higher swells the sullen mound—*
> > *Never gives back the grave!*

Never gives back the grave?

Obviously Schiller had never met my father.

How strange it is: not that I am lying in a burial place, so true to my nature, but that I am writing in the sunlight, undisguised, open to the day! Despite the rare pleasure I take in this, the warmth and brilliance of the sun do not fool me. I cannot pretend I am a fop lazing in a pasture. I am a dead man resting in a graveyard.

I know where I am only because Lucio told me the history of this place. Because Venice was running out of land, Napoleon made a decree that is followed today: Burials take place on San Michele. After a fixed time, each body, reduced by then to bones, is removed and put in a common grave on another island, which is used solely as an ossuary.

When relatives still care about the deceased, they come to

San Michele to accompany the bones to the ossuary. When no one cares, which happens more than civilized men are honest enough to admit, the diggers sometimes commingle the bones here to simplify their work, rather than bring each skeleton separately to the other island.

No one lives on San Michele. The priest who cares for the church is a drunk, but has enough sense, or fear, to return to Venice each night. The gravediggers come on their own gondola. Though the island is small, I am able to hide myself. The mourners do not wander. They proceed from the boat to the church to the grave and return directly.

Earlier today I met the priest. He believes he has met the Devil.

Near noon, believing the last funeral had been held, and the last mourners had left, I came out of hiding only to discover the priest still here. He had collapsed in the bushes by the side of the church and knelt there, retching. My guess is that the gondolier had decided the priest was too ill to travel by water and would return for him later, when the danger of vomit in his boat had passed.

The priest straightened, wiped his mouth, and turned around. He paled when he saw me and pressed his eyes tight.

"Not another drop, sweet Madonna, I swear it!" he murmured.

Roughly I pulled him up by his cassock and propped him against the church.

"How often have you made that promise?" I asked. "How often this week alone?"

"Too often, I know . . . But this time, *this* time . . ." He opened his eyes. Beneath their bleariness was a strange expression of resignation. "It is at last the end, no? You have come for me. It's too late for promises. The Devil has come for me."

I sat back on my heels and laughed. I liked the idea. Why

be some insignificant blot upon nature when I could be Satan himself?

"So," I said, playing my part. "You have been a bad man and a worse priest." He nodded. "Even so, you hope, maybe even secretly believe, that you deserve forgiveness."

Clasping his hands at his heart, he asked, "Can the Devil have compassion?"

He crawled toward me and clutched my leg. His chalky, perspiring skin elicited pity; the mingled smells of wine and vomit, disgust. I pushed him away.

"What if I told you I wasn't the Devil?"

His drunken brain tried to understand my words. "Who are you?" he whispered. He caught hold of my hands: one was larger, rougher, and of a darker complexion than the other. There was no symmetry in me anywhere.

The priest used his thumbs to trace the scars along my wrist.

"It's as though . . ."

When he swallowed, his throat clicked.

"As though what?" I prompted.

"You were . . . saved?" he asked.

"You mean, in the Church?"

"No, saved, rescued from a horrible accident, and"—he gestured toward my mismatched hands—"patched together with the remains of those . . . who were less fortunate? A miracle of medicine, no?"

Slowly I smiled, *evilly* I smiled, and shook my head.

"No. This is how my unholy father made me. I was never a baby, never a child, never a youth, and so never a man." I forced humor back into my words. "Maybe I am a god then, like Athena springing full grown from Zeus's head."

The priest pulled away and dashed off the sign of the cross. Fearing, almost expecting, to be carried off by the Devil, he had developed a measure of acceptance. To be here on earth, helpless before *me,* was something else. He covered his eyes; tears slid through his fingers as he prayed.

"Lord, please, isn't there room in Your infinite mercy, even for one such as me?"

They were words I myself had whispered many nights. I slapped his face. He fell to the ground and covered his head. While he lay there cowering, I dived off the dock. I stayed in the lagoon till at last the gondolier returned and helped the babbling drunkard off the island.

June 6

The rest of the day yesterday and all last night I did not sleep, pacing the graves like a restless ghoul thirsting for something to haunt.

"The woman is dead. And if she was his, she deserves death!"

Walton's words have burned their way through my coarsened flesh: *she deserved death*—because she accepted the unacceptable, showed mercy to the merciless, brought life to the dead.

Did Mirabella's goodness damn her own soul? God is two-faced: overflowing with loving forgiveness, blazing with wrathful judgment. He himself does not know who He is. How then should men? And how do they not go mad, trying to live with such Mystery? Their God is like Walton forever lighting my funeral pyre, while Mirabella forever quenches it with her tears.

Beneath these thoughts lies a single truth: whether Walton acted out of his own evil or as an agent of a vengeful God, he killed Mirabella. Thus, through him, I am her real murderer. I am the real Devil.

Not even the Isle of the Dead should be home to me. I should be borne away by the waves until lost in darkness and distance.

June 10

For days now, only black thoughts.

Walton.

Walton first, Walton last, Walton always.

What long ago brought devastation to Frankenstein, what now has brought devastation to me, will surely bring the same to him: to destroy anyone he might love. The letter in his room is from his sister, Mrs. Margaret Winterbourne in Tarkenville, England. I will seek her out, and anyone else he cherishes, and destroy them first, just as I did with my father, just as Walton has done to me. When he receives news of these accumulated tragedies, he will rush home, knowing that only I could have done this.

He will come home to his own death.

I grin now as broadly as the smiling skulls around me. The diggers here are not too ambitious and often leave a job half-finished, slipping away once the funerals for the day have ended. It was quite easy to collect a dozen skulls and line them up in rows as a mute audience to my ranting.

I gesture to my laughing friends and speak aloud: "If any condemn me—speak now!"

Silence.

PART TWO

> Neptune spoke, and high the forky trident hurl'd,
> Rolls clouds on clouds, and stirs the watery world.
> At once the face of earth and sea deforms,
> Swells all the winds, and rouses all the storms.
> Down rushed the night: east, west, together roar;
> And south and north roll mountains to the shore.
> Then shook the hero, to despair resign'd,
> And question'd thus his yet unconquer'd mind.
>
> With what a cloud the brows of heaven are crown'd;
> What raging winds! What roaring waters round!
> At length, emerging, from his nostrils wide
> And gushing mouth effused the briny tide.

On reaching shore, Odysseus pressed on, while I stop to write.

A short time ago I was in France, at the port of Calais, where the Strait of Dover is at its narrowest. I stood on the top of Cape Gris Nez outside the city and stared across the strait. The fog lay too thickly to be pierced. Still, I fancied that, in the distance, Dover's sheer white cliffs could be seen, a denser white looming just beyond the white of the fog.

In Calais, the weather prevented all ships from sailing, and I was too impatient to wait for it to clear.

"Could the strait be swum?" I asked.

"Absolutely not," said the garrulous seaman whom I questioned.

He explained that what is but a quarter inch on a map has killed some and humiliated more. The waves slap back and forth between the cliffs of the two countries. Sandbanks throughout make more waves. Worse, there are shallows and headlands and breakwaters, and the waves crisscross each other at canted angles. A swimmer could be battered to death from all sides. Even if he survived the waves, he could not fight the tide.

"The tide is much too strong here," the man concluded. "With fog and with the wind up, like today, not even the ships sail." He must have seen resolve in my posture and said, "Don't attempt it today! The water is too cold; the fog, too thick; the tide, all wrong!" Without answering, I tossed him my last coin for his information.

Late that afternoon I stood on the quiet beach. On a chain round my neck, I wore a compass I had stolen in the market. I had already tossed my cloak to the side, refusing to worry how to replace it once I was in England. But my boots! They were something of a prize, and I wanted to keep them. Several years ago, I had happened upon two tremendously tall brothers with matching boots, but of different sizes. Only then was I able to adequately cover my own differently sized feet. I felt, at least from the dry vantage point of the shore, that the boots were worth carrying.

So I took them off and made a slit in each one up near the top. Then I removed my shirt, threaded it through the slits, and tied the shirt around my waist by the sleeves. Thus fastened, the boots sat like holsters on a belt. I tucked the oilcloth with my journal into the toe of one. I had at first thought to remove Mirabella's necklace and pack it with my journal, then decided against doing so. If I lost the boots, I would lose everything at once. Letting the necklace remain on my wrist gave it its own chance of survival.

At last ready, I looked out for a moment toward England, still invisible in the fog. Then I jumped in and began to swim. What I was attempting was sheer folly. Had revenge driven me past reason?

Letting the water numb body and mind, I concentrated on the act of swimming. Stroke and stroke and stroke—my legs kicking, my arms reaching ever forward. The elements became more destructive than my thoughts: the wind, the tide, the waves, the deathlike cold of the water. The fog was an impenetrable wall mere feet away. Its white was the white of the Arctic: a perfect, deadly white. Muffling sight and sound, it annihilated the rest of the world. As the hours passed, I felt that I was the only creature left on earth. If I survived to land on the shores of England, I would find it deserted.

Gradually at first, then, in the end, all at once, the white became soot gray as the sun set. I stopped swimming and looked at the compass. Darkness and condensation obscured which way the needle pointed. I could just make out its direction and realized I had been swimming southwest, for how long I did not know. Left unaltered, my path would have taken me out into the ocean. I needed a more northerly course.

As if to emphasize that I could spare no thoughts, gigantic waves walled me in. The fog hid their presence till the very end: without warning, great blankets of froth crashed down on me one after another. I dived underwater to escape their fierce weight. When I burst to the surface, gasping for breath, another wave would crash down, as if it had been waiting for me with sentient purpose. Time after time, I found myself turned round; time after time, while I stared at the compass, a pounding wave forced me back under.

My precious boots became boulders strapped to my back, but their heaviness only tightened the wet knot of the sleeves tied round my waist, and I couldn't free myself. Do not dwell on these things, I told myself. Not the weight, not the wind, not the waves. Each moment brought me closer to shore; I could think only of that.

Bursting upward yet another time, I surfaced in an area where the fog had lifted enough to allow a ring of visibility a hundred yards across, eerily lit by a gibbous moon. What I saw was so amazing I cried out: the menacing humps of a school of whales. Then I realized I was seeing only hills of water, huge waves that had not broken to foam. I checked the compass, adjusted my direction, and swam.

Something snaked across my face and chest, leaving traces of fire on my skin. Batting it away, I slapped against a spongy mass and found myself entangled in the long stinging tendrils of a jellyfish, and then of another, and another, until a huge swarm, bobbing on the waves, ringed me in with torment. I would have thought myself too numb to feel such pain, but a thousand needles pierced my body—and still the swarm extended before me. The salt water burned my wounds and made me suffer afresh.

From a distance came a weird whistling sound, high pitched and keening. Water whipped away from the tops of the humps. I feared I was swimming into breakwater again. The whistling grew louder, and both water and air slapped me in the face. It was the wind funneling through the cliffs on either side of the strait. The thick dark gray of the fog was soon swept away, replaced by the purer black of night.

Hour after hour I swam until monotony became my new danger. I saw only unending dark, felt only iciness, heard only the ceaseless howl of the wind. Somehow, without knowing it, I had drowned, I thought; I had died and gone to Hell. Sisyphus had his rock; I had the strait. But stroke and stroke and—dawn would come eventually, and I would reach England, as long as I kept swimming north. At last I saw the horizon, a dark sky above the darker sea. On my right were the changing colors of sunrise; before me, white cliffs, like a tremendous ice shelf. I no longer needed the compass.

I pulled myself onto shore. People would soon be about, though I did not care. At the base of the cliffs I found a rotting boat and crept underneath its overturned shell. I fell asleep without bothering to untie the boots from my waist. It was not until I woke that I realized I had lost my journal. Amazingly, the clasp on the necklace had held; the little charms tinkle as I write this.

The loss of my journal so stunned me that my first action was to break into the nearest firm, a solicitor's office. A thin twig or the shaft of a small loose feather—these are always at hand, even if they are annoying substitutes for proper quills, which I am able to obtain only when a bird is large enough, and unlucky enough, to be my dinner. For ink, I have used everything from crushed berries to the water of simmered walnuts, from boiled-away coffee to lampblack. Even a small stoppered phial for the ink can be foregone awhile.

But paper!

A fresh diary is as rare as a friendly face, so I settle for stolen ledgers and account books, hoping not too many pages are already filled with numbers. An extra good in such thievery is this: where there are ledgers, there are quills; and where there are quills, there are phials, providing the convenience of not needing to make ink so frequently.

Despite my good fortune in replacing all these, my old journal has been lost. I have no past except what I create by writing it down. What I created before is now gone. A new journal, a new past. A new man?

I shall think only of murder.

October 8

I carry with me a map of England. I feel kinship with the picture. The divisions of rivers, roads, and boundaries are like the scars on my face: each tells a story of something once separate and divided, now brought together and made one. But where is Tarkenville?

Before I could ask directions, I had to find suitable clothing. I stopped first at a farm and from its stable stole a horse blanket to use as a cloak. Later on my journey I shall fashion a hood for it; now I draw the blanket down to shadow my features.

Nearly shredded by the waves, my shirt proved more difficult to replace. Cloaked but bare chested, I traveled from village to village till at last I saw a man so stout as to serve my needs. I waited by his window till the candle was long put out, crept inside, and found his bedroom. Snoring loudly, he lay oblivious as I searched his chest of drawers and found two spare nightshirts. The fine white cloth—so full and wide to accommodate his girth—fit perfectly across my broad shoulders and chest. Its length, below his knees, was just to my hips. I looked into his armoire greedily and saw a black jacket and blue trousers, both of soft wool. His jacket on me would be a waistcoat, his trousers on me would be breeches. I rolled my treasures under my arm and left.

Now at least, when I ask directions, though my face might be hidden, I can show a clean shirt.

October 9

"Go north till you're in the middle of nowhere," said a man in Dover. "If you hit Scotland, you've gone too far."

Those were my first directions to Tarkenville, which seems to be no closer than Hell and no more desirable. It is not on the map. If a man has even heard of Tarkenville, his advice begins, "Go north," but then provides no other help.

Finally, one man said he thought that Tarkenville is up near Berwick-upon-Tweed, which is indeed north, nearly at the

Scottish border. He did not know to what side of Berwick Tarkenville lay, but it could not be east as then it would be in the sea.

So, for now, until I am closer, I travel north, led by the Pole Star to Margaret Winterbourne and through her to Walton.

Newton Mulgrave
October 10

From my crossing of the strait through today, my experiences provide, not the memoirs of a murderer stalking prey, but the sedate observations of a vacationer. I walked up the North Downs of Kent, remarkable for the tent cities that spring up overnight, temporary housing for crowds from London come to harvest the hops. I crossed the Thames just east of London and made my way into Essex. There, the neatly thatched cottages and fertile farmland made me yearn for quiet domesticity. Then rain turned the red-clay fields to blood, and my thoughts to darker images.

In Cambridge, the colleges reminded me of the heady intellectual swirl I once sought outside the Vatican. There, as in Rome, I found myself so "clumsy" as to bump into one of the students and knock his armful of books to the ground. He would later discover himself missing Spinoza's *Ethics*.

Tired of slipping from shadow to shadow along city streets, I found the steaming bogs in Lincolnshire more suited to my mood: they are said to be haunted. Because of their devils and ghosts and malarial air, I was alone when I witnessed thousands of wildfowl breaking cover from the marshes and rising up as one, their wings beating thunderously. Like a fool pointing out the most obvious event, I wanted to turn to a companion and say in wonder, "Did you see that?"

No one was there.

Farther north the fens have been newly drained to create drier, passable land. I keep to those portions not yet tamed. And still farther, stone manor houses sit high upon the wolds; these I eyed only from a distance. The highest of the wolds rise hundreds of feet up. From the top looking eastward I could see bands of color like an earthbound rainbow: the green of the marshes, a yellow rim of sand, the blue of the sea.

I am currently in Yorkshire, where at every turn there is a river, stream, or brook. After fording or swimming across the Don and the Aire, the Wharfe and the Ouse, and dozens of rivers whose names I do not know, I have come to a sea of a different sort, an ocean of heather. The bluish purple of its rolling waves is broken only by flocks of red grouse. A huge stone cross stands to mark the way—to where I do not know. No doubt its builders thought to dwarf men with its size. I can easily trace the full front of its face, its carved lessons worn smooth by centuries of wind and rain. The sun shines now though, and I have stopped in the cross's shadow to write this.

My thoughts twist ever inward. My father was not a believer. Nevertheless, if he had accepted me as his son, would he have made me learn, even if by rote, the Christian creed? Left alone, abandoned, I made my own creed. In mine, the son does not die as atonement; the father dies. This is as blasphemous as my father's seizing the power of creation—and as unsatisfying. Neither offers me hope, nor does the Church itself, that hoarder of redemption. If there is a Hell, I am probably damned to stand outside that as well.

Berwick-upon-Tweed
October 19

The words skitter on the page with excitement: I have just spoken to someone who at last knows where Tarkenville is. I must retrace my steps, as it is a little south of here. If I had traveled along the coast instead of inland, I would have passed it on the way.

More important, my informant has also heard of the Winterbournes; indeed, he is cousin to a man who works their flocks.

Walton's sister, Margaret, came here years before he began his mad pursuit of me. Although she had had no previous acquaintance with Gregory Winterbourne, she married him only six weeks after her first husband's death had made her a very young widow. Winterbourne carried her and her small daughter up here to wild Northumbria, away from the more civilized south.

Over the years, the pleasant new bride became a morose and suspicious woman. She now believes the whole world is determined to do her ill and imagines a thief or murderer hidden in every shadow. She has grown miserly, too: there had better not be a sock's worth of wool nor a chop's worth of meat missing when the accounts are tallied up.

Never mind the chop, I thought as the man spoke; the murderer that Margaret believes to be everywhere has come to her at last.

Walton's sister has no issue from her second marriage. That there are only three Winterbournes to kill disappoints me. I want to leave so wide a trail of blood that Walton can see it from Venice.

Tarkenville
October 24

I know now why the name Tarkenville is not on the map; it is barely a smudge on the coast, as small as a town may be and still be called a town. The Winterbourne estate is its chief feature: an ugly square on top of the sandstone cliffs by the sea, although set back from the edge. At the bottom of those cliffs is the cave that now shelters me.

As close as I am to the estate, I feel safe. The cliffs are treacherous; there is no easy path down, not even for one as goat-footed as I. The shoreline before the cave is empty of signs of fishing lines, traps, or other human occupation. In addition, a veil of fresh water spills over the cave's entrance, hiding its existence from all but the most curious.

When I made a fire in the cave, I found myself in a chamber that was an uncanny shade of red, too deep to be merely sandstone. The red color comes from a type of moss that paints the cave's walls and ceiling. With the firelight flickering against these crimson walls, I can imagine myself Satan in Hell, plotting against all mankind.

Driftwood for fire is plentiful, and there is an abundance of food as well. Shellfish collect around the rocks of tidal pools, and there are many seabirds, such as oystercatchers, turnstones, and redshanks. I leave the curlews alone; their eerie piping affects me strangely.

Fresh water, food, fuel, a dry shelter: not long ago it was all I asked of life—that, and to be left alone.

Now? In a few hours I will go up to the estate.

October 26

It was near one o'clock in the morning when I began the steep, nearly vertical climb. Knowing it would impede me, I left my cloak in the cave. At once the cold shot through the thin cloth of my shirt. I kicked toeholds for myself, sometimes clinging to no more than an exposed root. The rocks I disturbed tumbled down, rattling against the cliff face till the sound disappeared into the endless rush of waves, the tide eating up the sand, yet remaining hungry. I clawed at the unyielding stone; the wind clawed at my back. Below me, behind me, above me: the gale wind tried to knock me loose.

At last I scrambled over the top and set my feet upon craggy ground. Before me lay a distance of rough terrain, at length becoming a garden that had been imposed unsuccessfully on the land. Immaculately tended, white gravel paths led to stone benches and fountains and statues, but every tree within the garden was gnarled and twisted, beaten into a crouch by the fierce ocean wind. Only scrub survived; it had learned how to bow.

The Winterbourne house was a massive stone block, unadorned by columns or balconies or other decoration to ease the eye. Smaller outbuildings stood a distance away: what looked like a stable and then, set closer, perhaps a summer kitchen, banished to the outside so that, I imagined, the cook's mighty labors did not cause Walton's sister a single sweaty drop of discomfort. Other structures were attached to the house like afterthoughts. One was a greenhouse, perhaps meant to provide what could not be coaxed from the land. Another looked like an observatory, but its foolish placement, low and adjoining the house, would blind the observer to half the sky. Nearest to the cliff, and farthest from the central part of the house, was a chapel, marked by a cross large enough to proclaim the owner's piety.

A slight figure—Margaret Winterbourne?—emerged from round back of the house, wearing a dark cape and carrying a lantern. Behind her were mastiffs and pit dogs, unleashed but rigid with obedience.

Moving behind a statue, as if that could possibly hide me, I stepped on a branch. The dogs lifted their heads, quivering as they waited for a single word. The woman looked up as well. The statue offered little cover, the wind-blasted grounds even less, and I could be seen as easily as I saw.

"Have we a rabbit, boys?"

Her voice was low and throaty, full of quiet laughter at her own joke.

"Go."

The dogs sprang. Brown, black, and mottled fur, yellow teeth, pink tongues in gaping mouths—all blurred into the blood red of the chase. Rabbit, indeed. I would run before them until it no longer suited me.

"Hurry, boys!"

The gasped words mingled with growls and snorts. Amazingly, the woman ran after me, too. Her one hand gripped the lantern; the other gathered her cape and skirt in great folds about her knees. The hood of her cape hid all but her smile, as wide, white, and sharp as a snarl. She did not have the good sense to be afraid, and I grinned back, hoping she saw it.

The landscape grew more desolate and wild. Stunted trees mockingly human greeted me with outstretched limbs. The wind through their empty branches whispered, "Here is a good place to kill her."

I stopped, wheeled round, and waited, my anticipation intense.

At my unexpected halt, the dogs howled. The closest one hurled itself at me. But then the command—"Down!"—and, in midair, the dog snapped its fangs shut. It hit my chest passively, like a thing thrown, and fell at my feet. At the command, the other dogs dropped to the ground, too, mournful complaints half-strangled in their throats.

No longer hurrying, the woman closed the gap that the dogs' speed had created between them. As she walked, she pushed back the hood of her cape. She was young, much too young to be Margaret Winterbourne, and so instead must be her daughter. By the lantern's light, I could see her features plainly: a heart-shaped face, porcelain skin, a wild halo of raven-colored hair. Her beauty, and that it came from Walton's family, mocked Mirabella's plainness and made me all the angrier.

I expected the woman to cry out at the sight of me. Instead, she approached slowly. Her one hand lifted the lantern high toward my face; the other reached out, palm forward. I took the gesture for a calming motion as one might make at a strange dog. When I realized that she meant to touch the knots and seams of my skin, I knocked away her hand.

"Who are you?" I demanded, though it should have been she who asked the question.

"Lily Winterbourne."

Walton's niece.

"You stopped deliberately," she said. "You could have outrun the pack. No one's ever done that before. But you stopped. Why?"

Steeling myself against her face, I focused on her words, spoken as if she chased intruders to the cliff every night, perhaps over the cliff as well.

"I stopped to see who you were," I lied.

She accepted that as if, indeed, all the world should want to know who she was. She was unflinchingly fearless. To be out walking alone at night, even with hounds, gave indication of her character—and then to chase me down to the cliffs and try to touch me . . .

What would frighten a woman so bold? The sight of my face had not. The feel of my hands? The image made my breath quicken, fingers dance. I had come to do murder. I could do worse harm first.

She stepped closer.

"Who are you?" When I did not answer, she said impatiently, "I am mistress here and am not accustomed to asking twice. Shall I let the dogs give you another scar? Attend," she said to them. The animals stood in anticipation. "Who are you?" she repeated.

An idea took root in my mind.

"I know your uncle. Robert Walton. Your mother's brother."

"I have never met him," she said coolly. "He rarely writes to Mother even though she writes him every day."

"Your uncle travels extensively. By the time a letter from your mother arrives, he has undoubtedly moved on, and the letter must be forwarded, sometimes more than—"

"What are you to my uncle? Surely not a friend."

"No, not a friend. Despite that, our paths have crossed frequently. I thought, while I was in England, that I would give your mother news of him."

"And you steal upon my grounds past midnight to deliver your message?"

"I wanted to see the house first, before I decided how to make my approach. I am not welcome everywhere."

"Of course you aren't. You're repulsive."

"I was in an accident," I said, remembering how the priest at San Michele had tried to explain my appearance.

"An accident?" She laughed too merrily. "You must tell me about it. Call on me for tea tomorrow and you can relate your story then, as well as deliver your news to Mother."

"Do not jest with me," I said. "I am not someone who is welcome in polite company."

"I am quite serious," she answered, an edge in her voice I could not interpret. "I want to know the story of every crooked scar. I must warn you, though: Mother will respond with disgust, despite her ecstasy at hearing news of Uncle

Robert. Father will respond with shock, although he will try not to show it. I will enjoy seeing that. I will also enjoy seeing your reaction to them. I want to know what it's like to be hated."

An invitation into the Winterbourne house—with such motives as I could not understand.

"Are you afraid of being taunted?" Lily challenged. "Then do not come for tea tomorrow. Come instead the night after that. It is my birthday and my father is holding a costume ball in my honor. I can invite whomever I wish. The guests will be wearing all manner of masks. Wear one to hide your hideous scars. Or come without one and say your face was made by a master mask-maker from the Continent. You'll be the envy of the party."

"If I do go," I said, "how will I know you?"

"It doesn't matter." Her lips curled back. "Clearly I will know you."

With those biting words she turned to leave, my attendance confirmed in her mind. She spun round. "What is your name? I'll leave it at the door so you'll be expected."

For the first time my namelessness vexed me. Her beauty forced me to seek out what little humanity I possessed, and I took my father's name: Victor.

"Victor. And your surname?" Though it is the usual practice of men, it was too much to say Frankenstein and take my father's surname as well. My hesitation made Lily shake her head. "Very well. I shall simply say I am expecting a foreigner named Victor."

I waited till she was out of sight before I climbed down and made my way to the cave.

Later

One by one I count the charms round my wrist. Twelve little charms. Did I have twelve days with Mirabella? Walton
should know that only a fool takes meat out of the mouth of
a hungry dog.

And now my enemy has unwittingly sent him to his family.
Soon he will have no family, as I have none.

Patiently I wait and one by one count the little charms.

October 27

Tomorrow is the masked ball at the Winterbournes'. Earlier tonight I climbed the cliff—farther down the shore was an easier
route—and saw the preparations being made. A great hall, lit
up, had opened its several sets of double doors to the night. The
enormous room was alive with maids and manservants rushing back and forth. A tall, thin woman roamed about, her eyes
ceaselessly inspecting, always with displeasure, everything from
the room's decorations to a wrinkle in a servant's uniform. Her
words caused fearful looks and a flurry of curtsying and bowing. She is Margaret Winterbourne, I am certain. She shares
her brother's sharply pointed features and look of fanaticism.

I yearn to venture within that room. I have been *invited* to
venture within.

Slowly, as I write, a plan begins to form in my mind. Will
revenge not keep one more day? Tomorrow night offers my
first opportunity to walk "unmasked" among men. There will
surely be queries as to what I am. What if I tell the truth under the guise of a story? I will see how my listeners react. If
they can grant a storybook character its right to exist, perhaps they will grant the same to me. If they say it should be
destroyed, they will be describing their own fate.

October 29

Last night, I heard the strains of the orchestra as I climbed toward the estate. The wind off the ocean beat at my back, tugged at my cloak, and rushed by my ears, but when it softened, music dripped down over the edge of the cliff as thick and sweet as honey. I paused, clinging onto the rocks like a lizard ascending a wall, and lifted my face to the sound. Each note called me closer.

Colored lanterns had been placed on either side of the drive, providing a multihued path for the endless stream of carriages. Jesters and fairies, princes and princesses, animals both real and imaginary, descended from their conveyances. Stern-looking liverymen opened the doors, letting out a rush of light, music, and conversation as the invited guests hurried in. Expecting to be refused entrance, I waited for a break in this line of visitors, stepped out from the shadows, and walked up the drive.

The liverymen spoke quietly to one another as I approached—a huge hooded figure, alone, on foot—but they opened the door for me without saying a word. I gaped disbelievingly at the extravagant sight: dozens of blazing candles, carved lacquer vases as high as my waist, intricately patterned Oriental rugs, silver candelabra, marble busts, bronze elephants, oil portraits, tapestries, and huge potted ferns.

"Excuse me, sir. Are you going in?"

All this was only the entrance hall.

I crossed the threshold, the doors swung gently shut behind me, and I was inside.

"Your cloak, sir," someone asked. There was a quick intake of breath, even a choke of disgust. I did not turn, trying to ape the indifference the wealthy show their servants. I was a guest, I was wearing a mask, of course, and I had every right to be there. I shook the cloak from my shoulders, handed it over, and waited, uncertain what to do.

Just when my ignorance would betray me, another uniformed servant came from an archway to the left. Face blanching, he tripped back in horror, then steadied himself. A scowl darkened his features.

"You are Miss Winterbourne's guest," he said. There was so little surprise in his voice and so much weariness that I understood I was not the first embarrassment Lily had invited home. The blood rushed to my cheeks, but I met the man's eyes.

"Yes, I am."

His sigh was audible. A gentleman would not have accepted such insolence. He and I both knew I was no gentleman.

"Follow me."

He led me down a long hallway past many closed doors, into a large room lit only by a dying fire. So, I thought, I was not to be summarily dismissed; neither was I allowed into proper company. Lily's invitation had been crafted to humiliate me.

"Wait here while I inquire if she will see you."

He closed the door when he left.

One wall was lined with the mounted heads of a dozen animals—deer, bear, and elk—as well as sets of antlers and horns. *You are just one more beast,* their eyes said, *perhaps even more beast than man in your parts. Your head belongs up here with ours.* I could smell their presence, a warm musky odor that lay beneath the room's stink of tobacco.

Books lined the other walls, more books than I have ever seen at once. After running my fingers over their bindings, I pulled out a volume. An inscription bore the date 1832, but the pages had not yet been cut—six years later! How I must plot for each of my books, while here a treasure house went ignored! This, as much as anything, made me despise these people.

From the hall came the sounds of a subdued argument. Without looking at its title, I tucked the book into my pocket. By the time the door opened a moment later, I had stepped away from the shelves and was standing beneath the mounted heads.

Lily stood in the threshold, framed by light from the hall behind her. Dressed as a queen, she carried a gold scepter and wore a gold crown encrusted with jewels. Her gown was purple silk; around her bare shoulders she wore a long, wide silk shawl of darker purple, gathered by her one hand and held in draped folds at her waist. Her feathered mask, dyed to match, covered the upper portion of her face; her loveliness struck me breathless.

"So, this is where Barton hid you!" she exclaimed. Behind her was a tall older man, dressed for the hunt in riding breeches and long boots and carrying a crop. He wore a plain black mask over his eyes.

She turned to him.

"Barton quite exaggerated my friend's appearance, didn't he, Father? This costume isn't as dreadfully shocking as he said. At least it *is* a costume. It shows imagination, Father, which yours does not."

In the dim light, Winterbourne squinted at me from across the room. His face was a study in restraint as he tried to master his reactions.

"You must forgive us for this reception, sir," he said at last. "I am Gregory Winterbourne. My daughter said only that . . . that she had invited someone named Victor. Your surname?"

I could not answer. My silence lengthened beyond awkwardness to rudeness.

Lily's eyes darted round the room, then—and she smiled—they settled on the stag I knew was above me, mounted on the wall. I was certain she had guessed the truth, making me hers to destroy if she so chose. Her expression lost its hardness and softened to one of mere mischief. Displaying her power but not using it seemed enough for now.

"Hart . . . mann," she said, dragging out the words. *Hart* and *stag:* two names for the same animal, but only *hart* was common to man.

"Victor Hartmann. He has news for Mother of Uncle Robert."

"Yes, so you told me. Well, there's time enough later, I suppose. We have been ill mannered enough to Mr. Hartmann for one evening."

The name buzzed in my ears as if a wasp had whispered it. Victor Hartmann. *Hart*-mann. Animal man. Could Lily possibly know? Was she mocking me?

We left the darkened study and stepped into the better-lit hall. Winterbourne's eyes widened, and he tore off his mask, the better to see, revealing his own countenance: black eyes, black hair shot with silver, strong hawkish features. But there was none of the predator in him. Instead he looked like a wise old bird that had gladly abandoned the hunt in favor of serenity. His face was so good-natured that, even as he fought wildly to comprehend what he saw, I knew that his words would not be harsh.

"Sir," he at last burst out, "I beg your forgiveness for gazing at you so intently."

"It is I who am sorry," I said. "If you think I will disturb your guests, I will leave."

My words shocked me. Why had I apologized? Because I had seen a gentleman struggle to accept me?

"Sir, do not leave," Winterbourne said. "And, again, I beg your forgiveness."

"Why?" Lily asked slyly. "Do you think his mask too horrible?"

"His mask?" Winterbourne looked from me to his daughter. "Lily, it is clearly—" He gestured for what he could not say.

"I will leave," I said. "I see now that my . . . appearance . . . is inappropriate."

Winterbourne took a deep breath.

"You are a guest, sir, and are welcome in my house."

"Of course, he is," Lily said. "Now, Victor, accompany me into the ballroom."

The sudden slackening of Winterbourne's face revealed he had not meant his welcome to extend to the party.

"Lily . . ."

"I shall do as I like, Father, as always," she said, slipping her arm through mine. I looked down at her, at her bare neck and the swell of breasts exposed by the neckline of her gown. I felt the heat of her skin and smelled the faint scent of lavender. Did she toss her head back merely to expose the sweeter part of her throat? I could not read her eyes. I knew only that she stood too close. Despite Winterbourne's extraordinary effort to put me at ease, if he had tried to separate his daughter from me, I would have struck him.

The ballroom was so vast it must have run the entire length of the house, and was ablaze with so many candles I wanted to shield my eyes. I did not, lest I miss a thing. The room was a mad whirl of color as costumed couples danced and as servants hurried to and fro with trays of food and drink. Then we entered. Everywhere we walked we created silence. Servants stopped and stared. Musicians abandoned the melody to dissonance. Dancers stopped midtwirl. Only a single serving girl, intent on her duties, continued to pass from guest to guest, until at last she noticed something was amiss and turned. Her silver tray clattered to the floor.

I tried to stare down each pair of eyes fixed upon me.

"Well, we have no need to decide whose costume is the best tonight, have we?" Lily exclaimed shrilly. From a nearby servant, she took two crystal glasses filled with shimmering gold liquid and passed one to me. In my hand, the tiny glass was a thimble. It was an act of will not to shatter it with a simple squeeze of my fingers.

Lily urged me forward, enjoying how the crowds parted before us as if I wore the tinkling bell of a leper. Eventually, a more subdued tune was struck up by the musicians. People gathered behind us in our wake.

Off to one side was a door; Lily steered me through it to a salon. Chairs drawn close together, and cigars left smoking in ashtrays, indicated recent occupants who had gone out to see the commotion. As soon as we were alone, she dropped my arm.

"Why did you invite me?" I asked.

"Why did you come?" she countered.

"To see you again." The truth in my reply softened the violence beneath my every thought.

"Then if you died tonight, Victor Hartmann, you would die a happy man, wouldn't you," she said sharply.

"There you are!"

Gregory Winterbourne entered the salon followed by nervous servants bearing trays of food. Several guests peered round the edges of the door.

"I thought you might prefer to take your refreshment in here. The ballroom is noisy, not a pleasant place."

"Thank you." I appreciated his delicacy of phrasing. "Sir, I do not deserve your attention. Why don't you return to the party?"

"No, my place is with my daughter. It is her celebration. There is the matter, too, of your news from my brother-in-law. My wife has not yet come down to the party and may not even appear at all tonight. I fear that preparing for it has been too much of a nervous strain. Tell me of her brother, and I will tell her."

Selecting the sturdiest chair, Winterbourne bade me sit, which I did cautiously, testing the chair's strength as I slowly lowered myself. The guests who had been at the door stepped inside the room. Soon sitting or standing about me—eyes fixed in wary stares, lips pulled tight in revulsion—were men dressed as a baker, an executioner, two knights, and a mouse. Despite the room being a smoking salon, there was a woman, too—an older woman who wore no costume, just a simple gray gown and a silver mask. She had taken the seat farthest from me.

Winterbourne did not tell the guests to leave, perhaps thinking that whatever news I had of Walton was not of an intimate nature.

Before he could mention him, the baker took up a pipe, pointed with its stem, and said, hesitantly, "Your costume—"

Immediately the others began to question me.

"Is your mask rubber? It moves when you speak."

"Is your face glued on?"

"Why did you dye your hands different colors?"

"Are you wearing stilts?"

Even as the guests edged closer, their features grew more distressed, as they left the real question unasked.

"Who are you meant to be?" asked the baker.

I sat back and steadied my hands against the armrests. This was what I had planned: to check my murderous intent and use this opportunity to hint at my true nature, then to judge the reactions of those who heard. Yes, my face is terrifying; I will never be able to change that. But if people knew, if they could understand, could they move beyond their fear? Or would they condemn me? Drive me out of the house? The world had changed much in recent time. Centuries ago, advances like gaslight, chloroform, and the telegraph, even a friction match, might have brought denunciations of witchcraft. Now they were science. And after all, what was I but a product of science? Should society not take responsibility for what it had produced?

I decided to present my life as mere fiction and let their response to it determine the rest.

"There is a legend in my country," I began, "so famous that, had I appeared at any party there, I would have been recognized at once. I assumed the tale had traveled this far. I can see by your faces it has not."

Revulsion transformed into enthrallment as my audience listened. I suddenly realized that so famous a creature would have a name, like France's La Velue, Denmark's Erlkönig, or even Yorkshire's Jack-in-Irons. My eyes searched the room for inspiration, then moved to the ballroom beyond the open door. There! A jester in motley—and suddenly I had my name.

"It is the legend of the Patchwork Man."

Heads nodded, eyes stared more intently at my face. My first few words, combined with my hideous scars, had hinted at what was to come without diminishing the audience's expectations. Now I had only to fulfill their horror.

"Many, many years ago," I said softly, "there was a young man, a student more of philosophy than medicine. Many have questioned his character in an attempt to understand his actions. No satisfactory explanation exists. I will leave his character to others and merely describe what he did.

"This young man, after innumerable experiments, discovered the secret of life, the secret of creating life from inanimate matter. And having discovered the secret, he of course sought to create the highest form of life there is—a human being."

The guests sat forward. A half smile played on Winterbourne's lips as he lit a cigar. Lily stood behind my chair, her presence a shadow over me. I wished to see *her* face as I spoke, yet could not bring myself to turn around.

"The student worked in solitude," I said, "for to whom could he tell his secret? He must have felt many doubts, many fears, and yet, too, an overwhelming sense of triumph. To create life was to cheat death itself. It was the power of God. Had the student truly discovered that power? Or was he able to steal it only because of an unholy pact?"

"An unholy pact," laughed the executioner as he relit his cold cigar. He blew a thick cloud of smoke overhead and slapped the mouse on the back. "Now we're in your territory, Reverend Graham."

"Hush," urged the older woman. "Let him continue."

"The student worked, as always, on the darkest of nights, and, on one such night, his experiment proved a success: he was able to animate a man of his own creation. When the thing rose up out of the oblivion of nonexistence, the student was struck with dread. He ran out of the laboratory and wandered the streets of the city in a near-trance. What had he done? When he returned, the creature was gone."

"Gone where?" Winterbourne asked.

I did not answer him immediately. I had never spoken of my origin to anyone. To frame it now in such fairy-tale language made it more fantastic. My father, around whom my thoughts orbited crazily like moons knocked loose from their bearings: Was that all he was, a student playing at science? Had I imparted too much meaning to his role in my life? However purposefully he worked, I was an accident.

"The creature was simply gone," I said at last to Winterbourne. "Never to be seen again, or so they say. They also say in my country not to walk the streets alone late at night. If you do, you may hear slow, heavy footsteps and, if you dare to turn, you will see the creature itself, the Patchwork Man, wandering the night, looking for his creator."

A murmur rippled through the crowd, and the guests sat back in satisfaction.

Reverend Graham struggled to remove his papier-mâché mask, yanking up the mouse head so quickly his sweaty hair stuck out like spikes on a mace. He had a weak chin, a timid face, and the frantic look of a real mouse caught in a trap.

"'A man of his own creation'? What do you mean? How does one make a man?"

Lily edged closer, half-leaning on my chair. I still could not see her face. She slipped her finger inside the collar of my shirt and unerringly traced the heavy scar that circled my neck.

"Yes, tell me," she said, a tremor beneath her challenge. "How does one make a man?"

"The creature was . . . assembled . . . from the inanimate."

Reverend Graham froze. I softened my voice as I explained, or admitted, the nature of my birth: "Parts of dead bodies, both human and animal, were stitched together to form a whole."

"Abomination!" he cried, jumping up and knocking the papier-mâché head to the floor.

"It's not an abomination," argued the baker, thinking the word a comment and not an epithet. "It's a new Adam. You'll have to tell that story to the bishop, Reverend."

"Christ is the new Adam," the reverend said, with agitation. "You—your Patchwork Man—are the Devil!"

He backed out of the room slowly, as though I might attack him if he turned.

"My, he took that quite seriously," said the older woman.

"He took it quite *theologically*," said the executioner.

"And was theologically offended," said one of the knights. "What we don't understand offends us."

"Such a fuss!" the older woman said. "All for a story, something to frighten little children to behave. After all, if one truly believed that such a creature existed . . ."

"Yes?" I prompted her eagerly. "If such a creature did exist, if one truly believed . . . ?"

She looked inward; what she beheld there caused her to shudder.

"I could no longer feel safe in this world."

The executioner nodded vigorously. He withdrew the cigar from his mouth and blew its smoke toward me as he spoke, its odor heavy and rancid. "There is merit in what Mrs. Eliot says. A creature made from the dead could have no respect for life."

"Or, could appreciate it more keenly," I suggested.

"No, it would have no understanding of what it means to be human."

"It would want to know. I think it would want desperately to know."

My reply put a stop to the discussion. In the silence I turned to Lily behind me. It was her reaction, above all, that I wanted.

"What do you say, Miss Winterbourne? Have I told too gruesome a tale?"

She shook her head, yet without explanation rushed from the room, her hand pressed to her mouth. The crown toppled from her head and clattered loudly on the hardwood floor. I made to follow. Gregory Winterbourne pressed me back into the chair.

"My daughter has been skittish of late, sir. Do not presume your story to be the cause of her discomfort. I myself found what you said more interesting than you could know. I would speak with you about it," he said. "Tomorrow at tea?"

"I would enjoy that." My thoughts spun giddily. "Now, I must excuse myself."

"Of course."

Winterbourne gestured and a servant appeared. I followed him to the back of the salon, where I could exit without passing through the ballroom. I meant to leave, but Winterbourne—and, thus, his servant—had misinterpreted my words. The servant led me down a corridor, left and right, and at last to a door, lower and narrower than the others and discreetly designed to look like part of the wall. The servant motioned to it, then stepped back. Dipping my head, I entered and shut the door behind me. It was a water closet, a room dedicated solely to private comforts, such as I had read about in books.

Behind a screen stood a prettily decorated commode, too small and delicate for me to ever use. The rest of the room was a wonder. Greedily, my eyes took in everything in a single moment: The room was painted in pale green and beige, depicting figures from Greek mythology, who reclined in leisure in a meadow. A chaise longue and three chairs were arranged in a corner, each seemingly too fragile to hold a doll. A console was set against one wall, its top covered with an assortment of perfumes, soaps, creams, and oils. The console itself had a dozen drawers, each with a small brass handle. The drawers held medicinals: smelling salts, salves, unguents, and more.

Everywhere I turned, there were candles. Everywhere I turned, there were mirrors. And everywhere I turned, there were lilies: tiger lilies and panthers, goldbands and trumpets, madonnas and Novembers and pink arums—names I knew, names I guessed at from books—bowl after bowl of cool waxy petals, their fragrance thick and heady like overripe fruit. What far-flung countries had they been gathered from to then be forced to bloom, just for the sake of caprice?

I leaned against the wall and closed my eyes against the glamour of these things, which were just more sources of confusion.

I was at once gladdened yet disheartened by what had just occurred in the salon, so much so that my face refused to obey me, as if all its former owners were reasserting their separate claims: my eyes and lips trembled, cheeks prickled, ears twitched. I had sat in polite company, conversed with party guests as one of them, entertained them with a tale. I had been extended and had accepted a return invitation.

And had been called an abomination.

Made an old woman shudder.

Forced Lily to run from the room, gagging.

She had touched the scar around my neck. It was not until minutes later that she fully understood that it meant a severed head had been attached to a headless body. Only then had she run from the room. Who would not be disgusted?

Mirrors are an unwanted luxury: I seldom see myself, nor want to. I studied my reflection as dispassionately as I could. My lips are as black as my hair. My face has a slight undertone of gray, as though the blood had returned to the flesh too late to hide the color of death. But the scars joining the various strips of skin are no longer violent red. I could even fancy that the thicker scar around my neck made it appear I had barely escaped the hangman's noose or had been near-mortally wounded in battle. But it is more than just scars that inspires dread. Do people look at me and see horror lurking just beneath this tattered skin? Or is it the reverse? Do they see that something is missing, the spark of divinity that makes a life human? I am a void, a chaotic abyss, that would swallow up the world.

Outside the water closet, the servant waited to lead me back. He walked to the rear door of the smoking salon. Instead, I moved toward the ballroom to look inside.

I had expected to leave; Winterbourne expected me to rejoin him. I needed time to . . .

The ballroom was a living thing unto itself. The gaiety, the colors, the music! Silk rustled, satin flashed. Faces smiled or laughed or nodded slyly. Eyes winked or flirted; shone with fondness, pride, shyness, love; yearned for a life as wonderful as a perfect party. Hearts that were sad or envious or hateful could not abide such joy and had fled, for the moment, into the shadows.

Guests noticed me and backed away, though I had not even crossed the threshold. Their apprehension prompted an ever-widening circle of uneasiness that spread through the room. My melancholy burned off, leaving the dross of anger. Who were these people? What frightful things would be revealed if *their* masks were lifted?

Inciting me further, I saw Lily, well recovered from the disgust I had caused her. She spoke animatedly with several young men. Each was dressed like a king. Perhaps they had learned of her costume beforehand and had wished to be her partner. As she and the men spoke, she looked around carelessly—nothing they said was of consequence—then she saw me, and her eyes clutched onto mine.

Her careless expression yielded to . . . I knew not what. Dismissing the group, she pushed her way through the crowd. Guests detained her at every turn to exchange courtesies or, glancing at me, to share their worries. She nodded at each and slipped away, moving ever toward me. Her lips were pinched white. I braced myself against what she might say.

She reached out and pressed my hand gently, took it in both of hers.

"I am sorry, Victor," she said, startling me with her words and her express of concern. "I truly did not think you would come. I never meant to—"

A scream ripped through the waltz, through the conversations, through the tap and thump of feet and the bell-like tinkle of glass. Music, speech, movement—all stopped; the scream endured, ripping through even the sudden silence it had caused, as brutally as a sword piercing a white veil.

Margaret Winterbourne had seen me.

She said no words. She did not point. She no longer saw at all: her eyes were opaque with terror.

"Margaret!"

Winterbourne's voice, the speed with which he burst from the salon, the path he frantically cleared to rush to his wife, broke the ballroom's silent tableau. Guests rushed toward Winterbourne with curiosity, while others tripped backward from me, for surely *I* was the reason Margaret Winterbourne had been stricken.

Winterbourne stood on one side of his wife, supporting her limp frame. On her other side stood Reverend Graham, whispering urgently—to Winterbourne, to Margaret?

Where was Lily? Should she not have hurried to comfort her mother, too? She was nowhere in the ballroom. She had left as soon as her mother screamed.

November 3

> *I know not who put me into the world, nor what the world is, nor what I myself am. I am in terrible ignorance of everything. I know not what my body is, nor my senses, nor my soul, not even that part of me which thinks what I say, which reflects on all and on itself, and knows itself no more than the rest.*

Would it have profited Gregory Winterbourne to have cut the pages of his book and read Pascal's words? Does it profit me now? I know who put me into the world, I know what I am, I know what my body is. But of my senses, my soul, "that part of me which thinks what I say, which reflects on all and on itself"—of that I am no less ignorant than any man.

I sit in my cave by the fire, reading these words that earnestly attempt to elucidate the human condition, all the while waiting to climb the cliff to do murder. At the party, more guests were inimical to me than not; more cowered like Lily's dogs than overcame their revulsion to at least speak with me. Margaret's shriek of horror, even despair, had turned the whole room against me.

She forces a quick end to things. I must act before she flees. But if I kill her, how can I not kill Lily, who is also Walton's blood? If I kill the two women, how can I not kill Winterbourne himself, who calls them wife and daughter? And if I kill Winterbourne, how can I not kill in me the soul that should be there?

November 4

After midnight, I slipped around the outside of the Winterbourne house. From the distance came the howling of dogs, but the sound came no closer. I quietly tried each window till I found one unlocked, which opened onto a room decorated with ruffles and lace. On either side of the room, velvet settees, piled high with pillows, were flanked by tall panels lavishly embroidered with Oriental splendors. On a dainty writing table stood a pen and inkwell and blank sheets of pale yellow paper—the yellow stationery I had seen in Venice. This was Margaret's desk. Also on the desk was a small, uneven pile of dirty gray sheets and scraps of paper.

Stepping closer, I scanned the top one and saw "Your brother, Robert" scrawled at the bottom. These pages I folded into my pocket to read later. Then I crept down the hallway and found my way to the main staircase. I paused on each stair to make its creak long and soft, no more than the breathing in and breathing out of an old house at night. My own breath was ragged.

At the top of the stairs, I turned right and passed glowering portraits, heavy tapestries, overstuffed chairs, little footstools, vases of dried reeds, wicker birdcages with no birds, tall wooden clocks that did not tick—an increasingly senseless array of goods. The rooms here were furnished in rich splendor, yet none were occupied.

Returning to the staircase, I now proceeded to the left. The first room was filled with books—a *second* library? The books drew me inside like iron to a magnet, although I knew I should not tarry. Shelf after shelf lined up to dazzle my eyes with even more treasures than were downstairs. The room held two large leather armchairs, a massive desk and chair, a telescope set up near the window, a globe, and a narrow table on which sat glasses, liquor decanters, and humidors. Cigar smoke lingered in the air, embedded in the rugs and drapes.

Easily I imagined all this my own, reading every book on every shelf, writing in my journal every day, no want ever of candlelight, no want ever of paper and ink. I would finish one journal, and another would be waiting to take its place. I would burn a candle not halfway down, and dozens more would appear.

But not even paper and light equaled the wonder of the desk. It beckoned to me. A fine place to read and to write! Overcome with desire, I sat down; the immensity of the chair, the desk, fit me like a close embrace. I stroked the wood, smelled the oils used to polish it, bent my cheek to its cool surface.

"It is beautiful, is it not?"

Winterbourne laid his candlestick on a table, pulled one of the leather armchairs toward me, and, as if he were the visitor and not I, sat.

"It was my father's desk." He brushed his fingers along one edge. "He often said a man needs a solid place from which to make solid decisions."

Again, as on the night of the party, I had the sense of both Winterbourne's power and his peace. I was also filled with overwhelming confusion. To do what I must, I needed to create an idea of a Winterbourne who was worthy of hatred. The idea fell before the man.

He leaned into the silence, a peculiar expression on his face.

"I had asked you to tea, Mr. Hartmann. I was disappointed when you did not come."

"You still expected me? Truly? Tell me, how is Mrs. Winterbourne? Did she wish to take tea with me as well?"

"I'm sorry. You finally come to us for help and—"

"Help?"

"Of course. Why else would you be here, except for my brother-in-law? I confess I did not realize who you were at first because I have so discounted Robert's fantasies. The

Waltons have a family tendency toward mania. My poor wife suffers from it. My daughter, too, already shows signs, I fear. And, of course, Robert. But I never imagined that his fixed ideas sprang from reality, that he was tormenting an actual person. You see, I know who you are. Or at least, I understood it when you told your tale of the Patchwork Man."

"You know who I am?"

Winterbourne knew, *he knew,* and still he sat and talked to me! After the wonder of how he treated me at the party, his respect here was almost too much for my spirit to bear.

"Yes, you are the unfortunate whom my brother-in-law has pursued these many years. I apologize, however little recompense that is. I mean, it's surely misery enough for you to have suffered through the unspeakable calamity that left those scars. And then, besides, to have had a, a *madman*—there, I have said it—create his own frenzied explanation for those scars and hunt you down because of it." Winterbourne paused to calm himself, disturbed by what he perceived as my situation. "Mr. Hartmann, it is beyond human understanding how you have not become as deranged as my brother-in-law. I promise you: I will do whatever I can to make him stop. I only wish I had learned of your existence earlier."

I nodded, too disappointed to speak. I was made of such obviously mismatched pieces that I had silenced an entire ballroom and would have sent its occupants into a stampede had Lily not been on my arm. Despite this, Winterbourne had prettified the monster into the victim of an accident. By doing so, he no longer flinched at the sight of me and, thus, was able to discourse with me as an equal.

That in itself was as dizzying as strong wine, and for that, I would accept his ignorance or the lie that made it possible.

He pulled his chair closer. "Obviously, Mr. Hartmann, you

related the story of the Patchwork Man to reveal to me who you were. It is Robert's mad invention. Still, as you told the creature's tale, I sensed sympathy in your voice."

"It has been ten years," I said. "I've worn the Patchwork Man's identity so long I have become the thing I am accused of being."

"I understand." He stood up to pour two glasses of liquor. Opening a humidor, he asked if I smoked. When I shook my head, he took out a cigar for himself, then set a glass before me on the desk. "Men often become what they are told they are," he said. "If you repeatedly tell a man he is a slave, he will eventually forget how to think as a free man, although I am optimist enough to hope that there is something in a man that will always remain free."

"And if you repeatedly tell a man he is a monster?"

Winterbourne took the still-unlit cigar from his mouth and studied it.

"Mr. Hartmann, you did not come for tea as I invited you. Why tonight, like this?"

"Calling on you is impossible." I took the glass and cupped it between my huge hands. "Besides, I'm more used to the darkness."

I sipped the liquor and let it warm me. How easily I had become a man.

"Still, I might have come in here with my pistol," Winterbourne said, with not threat but curiosity in his words. "I might have thought you were a thief."

"Why didn't you?"

"Because you had much to say that had not yet been said, and I sensed that you would appear at an unexpected time to say it."

"I would speak with your daughter again, too," I said carefully. "I offended her."

"You wish to apologize?" He dismissed my request with a curt wave. "Regarding my daughter, it is best if you neither take offense nor think that you give offense. I would say nothing to a suitor, but to you who know her uncle, I may speak the truth. Her erratic behavior may be from the family weakness. It may be from her own overly strong will. The result is the same: she is uncontrollable. She gives me much cause for worry, yet should I lock her room each night? I believe she would climb down the trellis to have her freedom."

"I find her fearlessness admirable." It would also give me, I knew, sufficient opportunity to take her when the time was right.

"It is not admirable. It is foolish and unseemly. Women have been put in Bedlam for far less." Winterbourne shook his head in sadness. "There are other ways she reveals that she is not well. Nightly she runs with the hounds past exhaustion. When she returns, she is wild eyed, as though she had been chased by demons. She brings home strangers of all sorts. Men who are dirty beggars."

Like Lucio? I thought.

"And beggars of another sort as well—men with no income, not even dignified employment. They have nothing to show but their poor breeding."

"Which is all I can show."

"Mr. Hartmann!" Winterbourne exclaimed, mortified to remember that I, too, was part of this group. "You are not like the others. But Lily met you as a stranger, while alone, and invited you, as a stranger, to her party. You told her you know Walton, but I assure you, it would have made no difference if you hadn't. She still would have invited you."

"Perhaps she acted from kindness," I suggested.

"When you walked into the ballroom, did you feel that

she'd been kind? She possesses a coldness of heart I find disturbing." He shook his head with vehemence. "She also believes herself mistress here. See how she even dressed as a queen for the party."

I thought it harsh that he would invest so much meaning into a mere costume.

"As I have told her many times, she will never inherit this." He encompassed the house with a single gesture. "She is not a son. She is not even a natural daughter. The property is entailed. Without a son, I have only a life estate in it. On my death, everything passes to my nephew. And while I'm alive, I am restrained even in the property or revenue I may give her. Despite this, she believes that the house is hers, in fact, is hers already, even though I have told her many times it is not and can never be."

Closing his eyes, sighing, Winterbourne let go of the forcefulness in his speech and spoke more gently.

"It is one thing for me to cancel orders and repeatedly return goods, but she has also, on numerous occasions, engaged servants without my knowledge. What then? I cannot maintain her every hire, but these are hardworking people who have left good situations to come here. What is to be done with them? They cannot be treated like a divan about which one changes one's mind."

Winterbourne had already redeemed his life many times over. Now his last statement tormented me with how much suffering my revenge would cause him.

"Your daughter's behavior," I said. "You attribute it to the same illness that makes Walton pursue me?"

I could not excuse the man that easily.

"Yes, and that bedevils my poor Margaret as well. I'm sure the inconstancy of my wife's affections adds to Lily's own flightiness; thus, the illness feeds on itself. At times Margaret treats her daughter with such fierce jealousy as to defy understanding. Other times, she acts as if the mere sight of the girl grieves her, as if she were an object of censure. And she *will* be, if the truth is ever revealed."

Again Winterbourne had to calm the heat in his words.

"Illness or not, I blame everything on Walton," he said stiffly.

"Have you ever met him?" I asked.

"Once. And I do confess that, although I have the deepest affection for my wife, if I had met her brother first . . ."

Sensing Winterbourne's reluctance to say more, and his possible regret that he had already said too much, I stood up. Sitting so long in a chair was new to me. The discomfort was pleasing.

"I thank you, sir," I said, "for speaking with such candor. Your mere welcome has been more than I ever thought I would receive."

"You deserve much more from us than hospitality, Mr. Hartmann. Whatever you need, I will see that it is yours. If you need funds—for you must find employment under such conditions impossible—I will give them to you gladly. I only wish I knew I had been funding your tormentor as well."

He turned away as if his next words embarrassed him.

"And then, too, there is your face. . . . There is something in it that elicits a reaction from me I cannot explain. With so many scars, with your features rearranged, your expression has gone quite beyond human feeling."

"I do feel," I protested.

"I do not deny it," he said. "It's just that I see no sign of it. Neither do I see signs of condemnation or of judgment of any sort. It was as easy to speak to you as if speaking my thoughts out loud in an empty room."

I stepped toward the door.

"I've offended you," he said.

I held up my hand lest this good man apologize to me once more.

"No, you haven't. But the hour grows late. I should leave before our speech wakens your wife or daughter."

"Tell me first what I may do for you."

"I must have time to think."

Perhaps there is a solution here I did not see, a solution to my entire life.

November 5

Tonight I heard the hounds baying close by. Knowing Lily would be with them, I climbed the cliff and walked toward the house. The dogs soon caught my scent and led their mistress on.

"Victor *Hartmann*. You left my party without dancing with me."

"You ran from the salon, physically sickened. I thought you were running from me. I thought you might run from me now."

"It was nothing. That nauseating cigar smoke made me ill."

"And not my story?"

"Should I care so much about anything you could say?"

"Tell me"—for the question had been in my mind since the party—"later that night, you said you were 'sorry' and that you 'never meant to'—but you weren't able to finish your words. What were you sorry about? What did you never mean to do?"

"I am never sorry," Lily said, her eyes defiant. "And whether I have done something or not, then I meant to."

"Why did you rush out when your mother screamed? Another daughter would have hastened to her mother's side."

She laughed, it seemed with anger.

"So many questions! And from someone who has no right to ask them."

Would I ever have such a time and a place as this? I grabbed her upper arm more roughly than I intended. My fingers extended beyond the edge of her cape and were shocked by the feel of her soft, bare flesh. She did not try to pull away.

"Have you not considered the dangers of being out late alone?" I asked. Menace must have been in my voice; the dogs growled.

"You are too like my father!" she said with annoyance. The comparison to Winterbourne, while my heart nursed such evil, sent a flush to my cheeks. "What can befall me here?" she asked. "If misadventure strikes, it is only because I have invited it and am willing to pay the price."

"How dear a price are you willing to pay? An expense to your own person?"

"Even more than that." She bared her teeth as the hounds had.

I pulled her closer. "The story you heard that night, the scars round my neck that you touched . . . What would you think, what would you feel, if I said that is truly what I am?" I tightened my grasp lest she recoil.

"I have heard the tale many times from Mother," Lily said, gazing up at me. "You are the Patchwork Man, Victor Hartmann. You have been created from the dead."

There was no horror in her eyes, no fear, yet neither acceptance nor understanding. She might have just said, "You are very tall, Victor Hartmann."

I dropped her arm and, while thoughts of her father still protected her, said she should return home at once.

November 6

You are the Patchwork Man, Victor Hartmann. You have been created from the dead.

If only I had not discovered my father's journal!

I was still unable to read when I discovered it. I did not know what reading was, nor words, nor letters. I did not know that meaning could be captured in seemingly insignificant marks, nor that it could transform one's life forever. Not knowing any of this, I should have thrown away the journal.

I did not.

How different my life might have been if Gregory Winterbourne had been "a student more of philosophy than medicine." He would not have abandoned me. He would have trained me with patience and affection in the ways of life and instilled goodness in my soul. He would have helped me recognize that I am free.

November 7

Tonight I climbed the cliff to speak with Winterbourne again. On my way to the house, I passed the site where I had last met Lily. There, wedged in the fork of a tree trunk, was my cloak. I had left so abruptly the night of the party I had forgotten it, and now there it was. I had passed over my previous opportunity to take Lily and now had missed another entirely. I could no longer hesitate, I told myself, even as I sought out her father.

It was eight o'clock. Staying downwind of the dogs, I circled the building quietly, but did not catch sight of Winterbourne. Then I smelled the lingering scent of a cigar and followed it to the garden. The man whose company I desired stood by a bench, one foot up on the seat, looking out across his estate with great satisfaction.

He turned when I cleared my throat.

"Is that you, Mr. Hartmann?" he said without surprise. "It's a pleasant night, is it not, despite the incessant wind. I see your cloak has been returned to you. Good. Lily said she would put it where you were sure to find it."

"I would have preferred that she returned it in person. I have not seen her since her birthday," I lied. "Has your daughter spoken of me?"

"Beyond the matter of your cloak, no, she has not spoken of you. Don't feel slighted. She treats all men heartlessly, including her loving father."

"Is that, too, a family characteristic you fear? Or is it merely the frivolity of any young woman?" I spoke as if I were well accustomed to the frivolity of women.

He smiled and gestured for me to join him as he walked along the white graveled paths. "Though my mood tonight would have me say it lightly, Mr. Hartmann, do not minimize the cruelty that flows in Walton blood. You of all men know this truth too well."

I nodded. "Yes, but my own mood is also light."

Winterbourne turned to me eagerly. "Then you've decided how I may help you?"

"No, I have given it no thought. I am pleased enough to have your conversation. However, what you might do is tell me the circumstances of when you met Walton. It may give me insight into his behavior."

Winterbourne said he met Walton years ago while he and his wife were touring the Continent. They had never had a proper honeymoon, delaying it so long that he began to think of it as a gift for their first anniversary, then for their second, then for their third—with not a single plan ever made. At last, Winterbourne made his resolve and saw to the details that would allow them an extended stay, including arranging for an additional governess for Lily, who would remain behind.

Margaret was overly excited about the possibility of meeting her older brother, as she had not seen him since they lived together with their family. Winterbourne had the impression that Walton had been sent away in disgrace just weeks before his sister's marriage to her first husband, Mr. Saville, and had been forbidden to return home. Their father had vowed to kill him if he did. Margaret refused to explain further, although Winterbourne asked several times. Later she angrily denied saying even this.

Walton had gone to sea a novice and advanced with incredible speed until he was captain of his own ship. Margaret's good opinion of him and her affection were all that really mattered. He somehow became convinced that, if he were the first to discover the North Pole, he would redeem himself. Again, when Winterbourne asked her about it further, she angrily denied saying anything about redemption.

From what Winterbourne could piece together, Walton lost his ship to an iceberg, lost his men to exposure, and, in a way, lost his own life to the journey itself: even though he was rescued from a floe by another ship, he was never the same. He suffered a long febrile illness, which gave birth to his new mission: his "sacred debt to his truest friend to rid the world of a monster."

With a shrug, Winterbourne smiled his apology to me.

"Thus, knowing all this family history, I prepared to meet my brother-in-law."

Margaret sent Walton their itinerary as soon as it was decided on. Over the years, despite her many letters, he rarely wrote back, so when he responded to this, she was beyond joy. His reply was terse: *September 13. The whaling museum near Mainz. Three o'clock. I will not wait for you. If my quarry flees, I must follow.*

What new absurdity was this? Winterbourne thought. Whales in the Rhine? Margaret wept with such happiness that he said nothing.

Since the Winterbournes would be in Mannheim on the twelfth, the extra day's travel to Mainz was no hardship, and they arrived in late morning. Winterbourne hesitantly asked for the whaling museum. To his surprise, it existed. A local boy had broken his father's heart by running away to sea. Two decades later, he returned as a captain, laden with mementos. The father was overcome with emotion at the reunion and had a cottage museum built just to exhibit them.

"Whales on the Rhine," Winterbourne muttered.

Despite himself, he was captivated by the museum's contents: a ship's helm and compass; a reconstruction of the captain's quarters; harpoons and wicked-looking knives; a whaleboat, oars up, ready to plunge into the sea; scrimshaw and ambergris; and, the most precious piece, a jawbone from a whale from which not a single tooth had been taken for ivory. On the walls hung maps, drawings of the son's ships, and sketches of the son's wife—his sweetheart from his tender youth—and their many children.

Winterbourne tried to coax in Margaret for a look. She was anxious that, if Walton did not see her at once, he would not look for her, and so she refused to leave the street. Winterbourne even had to bring refreshment out to her from a nearby tearoom.

Walton arrived at sunset. The two are forever linked in Winterbourne's mind: a molten ball above the horizon, and then suddenly a man with such burning in his eyes he seemed to have caught fire from it. Tearful introductions were made, the molten ball set, and Winterbourne saw before him not an ascetic but an unkempt vagrant in shabby clothes.

At dinner, his wife's eyes never left her brother's. She, who had always been fastidious, hid his dirty hand in her lap, from time to time clutching it to her cheek. Winterbourne was more unsettled by her behavior than Walton's. A door in her soul had been thrown open, and he knew not how to slam it shut.

"Where is the creature now?" she asked.

For one so lean, Walton had a greedy appetite. While his one hand was still captured in Margaret's, his other roamed over every plate, picking out the choice parts.

"An hour from here," he said, his mouth full.

Margaret gasped. "Are we in danger?"

"No, he has fallen into a ravine and can't escape. I've tried shooting him from the top. To jump down and confront him would mean my certain death, and so I wait."

"For what?" Winterbourne asked.

"For the right plan. While I think, several men guard the ravine. I promised to pay them on my return. I'll need money to do that, of course."

"Of course," Margaret whispered, grateful to contribute to her brother's quest.

Winterbourne was irritated. To please his wife, he had already discharged the remaining debts that Walton had incurred with his failed Arctic voyage.

"After you capture this poor devil, will you turn him over to the authorities?"

"No, sir. I will kill him, as I pledged my brother I would."

This alarmed Winterbourne, but he was not sure how to frame his objection. Instead he asked Margaret, "You have another brother?"

"He means Victor Frankenstein, his brother in spirit," she said impatiently. "The man he rescued on the journey to the pole, the man who was the thing's creator. I have explained this to you many times since we've been married."

"So you have. Tell me, Robert," Winterbourne said to bait him, "how is it that the creator, who should bear the greater blame, is your friend and brother, while the creature, who had no choice in being brought to life, should be your enemy?"

I turned away as Winterbourne told this part of his story, pretending to admire one of the many statues that stood along the white graveled paths. *The creator was more responsible than the creature.* Winterbourne gave me hope that I might confide in him and find sympathetic understanding.

"What did your brother-in-law answer?" I asked.

"That his friend had had only goodness in mind when he unwittingly created pure evil. As soon as he realized it, he abandoned his life of privilege to pursue the thing, just as Walton had done, just as I would do, once *I* had seen it." Winterbourne looked away. "I confess, Mr. Hartmann, it embarrasses me to repeat his words."

Returning to his tale, he said that later, during the meal, Margaret cried out, "Robert, your ear!"

Walton brushed back his stringy hair and revealed that the lobe was missing.

"Sliced off in a knife fight," he explained. "Madrid."

"With the monster?" Margaret asked.

"Not directly. But he was behind it."

Winterbourne at last had to admit his brother-in-law was mad. He pushed his uneaten dinner away and said, "Come, Margaret. Your brother has urgent business elsewhere."

"I cannot leave him. Not again!"

"Your brother's life is one of"—Winterbourne sought inoffensive words—"of constant motion. He must be free to travel at a second's notice."

"I have a splendid idea!" Walton said, slapping his palm

on the table. "Come with me now and see the ending your-self!"

"We will only hold you back."

"Sir, to you I am a stranger who needs to prove himself, and to you, Margaret"—Walton's expression twisted—"Margaret, I fear that even you have had misgivings."

"No, never! Tell him I never doubted him, Gregory!"

"She has always believed in you."

Both brother and sister became so agitated Winterbourne was reluctant to refuse them. He had a carriage brought round. During the ride, they sat side by side, hands clasped like children, until Walton banged on the coach ceiling for the carriage to stop.

"From here we must walk."

By the time Winterbourne had taken the driver's lantern, Walton and Margaret were in the woods, trampling over bushes and rocky ground. At last Walton turned and laid a finger on his lips. He covered the remaining yards alone at a silent creep. Then—

"Where are the guards?" he cried out, dismayed.

Fury overcame him. He grabbed the lantern, ran to the edge of the ravine, and hurled it down to light the blackness below. The glass shattered; sparks swam up to the sky.

"Where are you?" he screamed. Dropping to his knees, he beat at his head. "I never should have left! Why did you ask to meet me, Margaret?"

"My wife has no blame in this," Winterbourne said sternly.

"No," she whispered. "I never should have distracted him. He is right. I am at fault. Whatever that thing does from now on rests on my head."

"I will not let you castigate yourself for Robert's sake. Having caught the creature, he decided to come to Mainz anyway."

She would not be consoled.

"I forgive you." A tight smile thinned Walton's lips. "See how easily that was said? And how quickly! You won't feel the torment that I have felt. I forgive you, dear Sister."

She pressed her fist to her mouth and wept.

The cloud in Walton's eye lifted for a moment, and he said to Winterbourne, "Take better care of her than I have." He fled into the woods. Margaret cried the whole journey back and for hours into the night.

After this, she daily grew more concerned about expenses. She insisted on seeing every bill, adding up their accounts over and over, poring over scraps of paper while they were at museums and at the theater. She pointed out how, if they took an extra roll at breakfast and hoarded it for lunch, they would save so much in a week. At first Winterbourne thought she regretted how much her brother's debts had cost him. Then he realized the truth: she meant to send her brother the savings in order to help him in his quest. Only when the creature was dead and her brother back at her side would her guilt be expiated.

"I sent Robert money monthly after that, for her sake," Winterbourne added. "He never acknowledges it. He thinks it's his due. Since we met, his mind has greatly deteriorated. He was mad, yet he spoke with a madman's logic. His few letters over the years show that even that small measure of logic has disappeared."

Winterbourne sat on one of the stone benches set along the graveled paths. Whether from cold or restlessness, he leapt up in a moment.

"My poor wife . . . she was most amiable and affectionate when I first met her, Mr. Hartmann. You would not know her as the same woman. Even though she had just suffered the loss of her husband, Mr. Saville, she was strong willed and did not trouble others with displays of sorrow and tears.

Then, just shortly after our wedding, she no longer seemed to be ... herself ... although we had married so quickly that I cannot really say what her true self was. Perhaps I should not have married her so hastily. She wanted to marry; she did not want to wait. But perhaps all of this was set loose because she did not let herself grieve long enough for Mr. Saville."

Winterbourne had begun to pace during his last words, then abruptly set off down one of the paths. I said nothing as I walked at his side, waiting to hear if he would say more. Finally, sighing, he did: "No matter what the cause, my poor wife changed, bit by bit. At first, it seemed like nothing, like pulling a single thread off a jacket, and another—but the next unexpectedly unravels and the jacket begins to fray. Then she reunited with her brother. It was no longer threads unraveling, but someone taking scissors to the same jacket. Never could I have predicted the swiftness or the sharpness of her transformation. I finally had to admit that there would be no reversal in her health.

"I have reconciled myself to our life together, but I cannot reconcile myself to the same life for Lily. As a result, I find myself doing things like promising her the costume ball—even though it cost Margaret endless worry. The poor woman repeatedly asked, Why must it be a masked ball? Costumes are only an added expense. Why must there be eight musicians? Would not four or perhaps three make as loud a noise? And why did some guests have to stay two, three, four nights? That stole extra food from the larder. Could they at least bring their own provisions, say, a few eggs?

"I tell you, Mr. Hartmann, it sounds like a point of humor to hear that my wife was worried about eggs. Her worry leads to tears and unfounded accusations and long weeks of a black mood. If it had been a party on my behalf, I would have canceled it at the first sign of her distress. But it was for my daughter and I would not go back on my word.

"You may say that, in indulging Lily, I have only denied the mother. But I too clearly see Lily's future in her mother's cheerless present, and so I try to give the girl what happiness I can while she is still capable of enjoyment."

We had reached a corner of the garden. Winterbourne paused and let his gaze sweep from the cliff, past the wind-roughened land, to the great stone square that was the house. He had regained control of his face, and I watched his features keenly. Through his eyes, even the stunted trees must have had nobility; what others might have described as gnarled and bent must have been, to him, courageous and enduring.

These were the same eyes that looked at me.

He gestured that we should continue our walk. The path led to a low wall. Unevenly carved on one side, the reverse revealed a marble bas-relief of the Three Graces. The carving faced the house and was thus protected from the grinding wind. I stopped to admire it: three women of great beauty, each with one arm entwined with another's, one arm outward, offering the viewer figs, pomegranates, and apples. The faces of the women were tranquil, gentle, and mild—as sweet as their divine gifts.

The Graces were like Lily in their beauty, unlike her in their peace.

"You have no hope for your daughter then?" I asked.

"I pray every day that I am wrong."

"Your wife and your daughter . . . You are buffeted from both sides," I said—poor phrasing of the sympathy I felt. "My appearance was a terrible shock to your wife. I am her nightmare, her brother's nightmare, hideously enfleshed. And so you've suffered with her." *That* was my concern: how I had unwittingly hurt *him*.

"It was a shock," he agreed, "but the final blame is mine. If I had known that beneath the delusion lay truth, that someone's life was being stolen from him day by day, I would have had commitment papers for Walton drawn up long ago. Again, my sincerest apologies."

I shook my head as if the past ten years had been nothing.

"Please, suffer not on my account," I said.

"Well, my cigar is spent, Mr. Hartmann," Winterbourne said, smiling, "and you have still not told me what I may do for you."

"On another night, perhaps."

Bowing as I took my leave, I walked toward Tarkenville as if I were staying in town.

November 8

Having heard about Walton, it is time to read what he has written. I had taken the handful of letters from Margaret's desk days ago, meaning to gloat over them when my work here was done. But I am no longer certain that my original intention best serves me.

Margaret has read and reread the pages so often that the folds in the paper are translucent with wear. Walton's deterioration is clear, as Winterbourne said.

March 2, 1824

Dear Margaret,

My spirits have been low of late. All men dream, all men have a dream, all men want a dream . . . I have none. What shall I put in its stead? I do not know. Melancholy is my only companion, and she does not dream either.

I can no longer endure this bitter separation. Please

speak to Father on my behalf, but I will return whether he allows it or not. I will make my home under your roof, where he cannot touch me. Saville would not refuse you this; no good husband would.

Tell Lily I am coming. She will surely be pleased to meet the hero of the many adventures you have told her. How grown she must be by now! It is strange to miss so much a child I have never met.

I shall see you soon, dear Sister. Each hour shall be as the last, and then, on a day no different from the others, I shall be at your door!

Your brother,

Robert

October 11, 1824

Dear Margaret,

I find myself offering you condolences and congratulations in the same greeting. Your new marriage chases so closely after death it may trip on its heels.

I had thought to be with you by now, but Fate has kept me at sea. This must be a sign to continue my life's current voyage and not attempt a change of course. Because of this, I will once more ship out with the most promising venture. I must find out why Fate keeps me alive.

Fondly,

Robert

August 21, 1828

Dear Sister,

I write to you with great excitement! Nature has forgiven me my late departure and has held back the cold. Now, within my grasp, is that near-mythical place where the *compass needle spins in confusion. I can already feel my own magnetism imposing order on it. I will stop the needle's frightened twirl and compel it to point to me.*

I am so close to my goal that, even now, you should prepare for my return.

I stop my words here, because we have met a southward-bound ship. Its captain, with his uncertain mind and cowardly fear of the weather, has already given up his own quest. He has agreed to post this letter as soon as he reaches land.

Sister, think of me often. I will be home soon!

> *July 17, 1829*

Dear Margaret,

Though you are silent on the subject, I could not return even if you begged me. While the thing lives, I cannot.

How can I convey my burden to you without your having seen the creature for yourself? What I once wanted shames me—to have wanted something else, anything else, while it exists.

Frankenstein was my friend, my brother, my twin. Yet, I must plainly say he was consumed by unholy lust. He took the natural and made it unnatural. And succeeded! Yet my holy quest was denied.

Why? The answer must become part of my search.
Robert

The undated letters became disjointed. I read the brief letter summoning Margaret to the whaling museum; in what must be the next one, he blamed her for letting me escape:

It has been ten months since you let it go free. I forgive you. I have said as much, have I not? Just as you said you forgave me. Do words have meaning? Sometimes I fear I have deliberately put this thing between us. What would a conventional life be after such pursuit? Deadly dull and boring—and more terrifying a thousand times over. Do you hate me? I say over and over that I do not hate myself. I pile up reasons to hate him.

This, written on a scrap of paper:

I must never forget my true aim: I am the compass needle, circling in bewilderment, not because I have conquered the north, but because I haven't.

Finally the letter that set me trembling:

She is dead, Margaret! His slut is dead! Now his rage will force him to make a mistake. Not that he feels for her: it is only that he has been deprived of satisfaction. From now on I must look at all women with new suspicion. Guard yourself! Even you could become prey to his gross carnality.

November 11

I have not left the cave in days. Both sorrow and wrath consume me afresh.

At night I hear the hounds and know that Lily is out running. She has been harsh to me, she is Walton's niece, and the callousness of his letters urges me to act. Still, I pace the length of my hellish red cave.

Why do I procrastinate? I must take my revenge or quit this place at once.

I do neither.

November 13

Tonight, after hesitating hours at the top of the cliff, I walked to the house.

It was past midnight. Stalking the grounds, I saw Lily hurrying to the stables with the unleashed dogs. Both she and the dogs panted heavily. Winterbourne was right. She was running herself to exhaustion.

I waited for Lily to return from penning the dogs. She saw me at once, as if she had been waiting for me. She was beautiful, like one of the Three Graces in the garden statuary, her hair undone, her pleasure genuine; and, like one of the Three Graces, about to give me a gift.

"Victor!" she said. She touched my arm, my chest; gently took my hand, turned it this way and that, and looked at it with wonder. "It's been so long I was beginning to think I had dreamt you."

"A week's passing is enough to turn me into a dream?"

"Merely a week? I've been ill. I did not realize how little time had passed."

I took the lantern from her and held it up. She did not look ill; indeed, her color was high from running with the hounds. But there was sadness and resignation on her face.

"Are you well now?" I asked.

"No."

"What's wrong?"

Pulling her cape tighter, she spoke in a frightened whisper: "How shall I describe it? A worm eats at me from the inside."

"What do you mean?"

"A parasite. It feasts on me."

"I've seen these things bleed life from even the strongest

of men," I said, greatly troubled by her words. "Did you send for a doctor?"

"Should I be seen by a man, so that later he may boast of it? No, I went to see old Biddy Josephs. She gave me all manner of physic, but . . ." Lily shook her head. "Today my father at last saw I was sickly and called the doctor himself. The doctor was delicate for my sake and called it a mere illness. Then he closeted himself with my parents. I fear the words that will be spoken tomorrow." Her eyes grew unfocused. "It is too late. My time is short and my life is no longer my own."

I had come to England to kill this woman. An illness might do the work for me. If it did, Gregory Winterbourne would be beyond sorrow.

And what of me? What would I feel if I lost her?

"Your words grieve me more than I can say."

"Can I have such power over you?" Her mood lightened and she laughed. "I must devise some test of this power to see if you speak true. Kneel before me, knave!"

I knelt. She traced the scars on my face, softly at first, then with growing firmness. I submitted to the exploration, remembering she had tried to touch me the same way the night we met, before we ever spoke. For the sake of her beauty I allowed it, for the sake of her illness, for the sake of the sudden ruttish thoughts that had not crept into my mind since Mirabella.

Apparently satisfied, Lily leaned close. I took her arms; her flesh was soft and yielding beneath the cape.

"Speak the truth, Victor Hartmann," she said. Breath like perfumed silk warmed me to desire. "What does it feel like to be dead?"

I pushed her away. She clung to me, holding me down, as if she had the strength to do it.

"We all die," she said. "*I* will die. It is surely coming, but I cannot comprehend it. You have already been dead. You come from death. What does it feel like?"

She asked the question not with fear but fervor. I finally saw in her the disease of which Winterbourne spoke; finally saw the emotional disease, just as I learned of the physical. She was being devoured in mind and in body.

"What does it feel like?" she repeated.

It felt like death to come from death. There is no faculty left untormented: for smell, there is the breath of mold; for sight, the opaque blackness of the grave; for sound, the gnaw of teeth on coffin wood; for touch, the jelly of corruption; for taste, the bitter rot of one's own body. This was death. And she was eager to know it.

She shook her head, impatient at my silence.

"Answer me."

Bringing her face closer still, she shook her head again, this time slowly, letting her hair brush my cheek in exquisite torture. Seconds after her words had repelled me, I would be a man after all, full of denial and with a memory no longer than my last sensation.

From behind us came a faint sound, like dry twigs whispering against each other.

"Someone's there," she said and tried to pull away.

"It's the wind," I said softly. I would not release her. She smelled of roses; her skin was as soft as their fallen petals.

Again from behind us, this time closer: a faint sound, like dry scrub rustling.

"Let me go. I tell you: someone's there."

"You wanted to know what death feels like. Would you leave before I tell you?"

Sadness and resignation returned to her face.

"There are many ways to know death, Victor Hartmann.

Many times, many places. We each find our own. We each are found."

Now, when she pulled away, I let her. As soon as she was free, she picked up the lantern and blew out the flame.

November 14

All day I brooded on Lily's words: her time is short and she will die. Is her illness that serious? Her father will suffer so! And what of me?

I decided I could not wait to wrest the truth from her; indeed, I may not succeed in doing so. Under evening's first shadow I walked down the shore, climbed the cliff at another point, and, cloaked and hooded, entered Tarkenville.

The town was nearly deserted, despite the early hour, and I saw no one who might tell me where Biddy Josephs lived. As I turned down another street, staying in the shadows I heard a thunderous voice come from the church: *"When the wicked man turneth away from his wickedness that he hath committed, and doeth that which is lawful and right, he shall save his soul alive."*

I cautiously peered inside. Clothed in full vestments, Reverend Graham had just read a scripture verse to a nearly full church. After this forceful declamation, his voice unexpectedly dropped to a soft tone. His expression was one of loving adoration, which surprised me. From his manner at the Winterbourne party I might have expected harsh words on behalf of his harsh God. But his face was at peace. The gentility of his prayers, the murmured responses, the shuffle of feet as the people stood and kneeled and stood—all of these lulled me into a moment of quiet. I leaned against the wall beside the window and listened. It was not what they said, but how they said it that beguiled me. Too soon, it seemed, the prayers came to their end: *"Lighten our darkness, we beseech thee, O Lord;*

and by thy great mercy defend us from all perils and dangers of this night."

I left quickly before the church began to empty out.

At last I came upon a man who told me that Biddy Josephs lived outside of town, deeper in the woods and far from other houses. I approached the lone cottage slowly. Both it and the large shed nearby were well lit, windows open to the night. Inside the shed, bundles of plants hung, leaves downward, from the rafters—some still fresh green, others a straw so brittle that a sharp glance might break it. Slices of long woody roots were threaded together and also hung to dry. Tables along the walls held more leaves spread in a single layer. A strange though not unpleasant mix of odors wafted out on the air.

The door to the shed was kicked open from the inside and a woman emerged. Though white haired and very old, she was tall and solidly built and moved with a brisk step, carrying a large jar made of glass too dark for me to see its contents.

"Shut the door, but don't douse the fire. I have more work to do."

I waited for whomever she was addressing.

"You there," she said, half-turning. "In the shadows. Did you hear me? Or have you come to have your ears candled?" She walked to the cottage, banged on the door with her foot till it swung open, and entered. I shut the door to the shed and followed her to the threshold of the house.

"I hope you didn't come alone," the old woman said, setting the jar down before shelves full of more jars. "Or have you not heard? There was murder done last night."

Murder.

I froze. I was guilty before I had done the deed: the very word condemned me.

"A young boy was beaten to death. Jonathan Ridley. Did you know him? That's why I say you shouldn't walk alone in the woods. As for me, there are few that would bother the witch woman."

"Biddy Josephs?" I asked.

"A man. Your quiet step deceived me." She began to rearrange the jars, not bothering to look toward me as she spoke. "What can I get for you this evening, sir? A nice mix of valerian and hops to help you sleep?" She opened one of the jars and sniffed it. "Or devil's bind to loosen your bowels? Be careful there: too much and it does indeed bind you."

She looked my way and though my face was hidden, I stepped back.

"No, I think not devil's bind after all," she said slyly. "What brings a gentleman to Biddy Josephs in the shadows of dusk and keeps that man outside where I may not know him?" Turning back to her jars, her fingers paused lightly on several as she named them. "Coriander, fenugreek—these can be powerful aids for male potency. Hmm . . . The green shell of the walnut would be better."

"It is not for myself that I come."

"Your woman, then."

It was strange to hear Lily so named.

"She is ill. She said she came to you already without finding relief."

"Who is she?"

I hesitated.

"Have no fear, sir," Biddy Josephs said. "I tell no one who visits me."

"Lily Winterbourne."

"So beautiful. Yes, she was here."

"What did you treat her for?" I asked. Perhaps it was not as serious as Lily had intimated. Perhaps there was hope for her yet and solace for her father.

"What did she tell *you* was her illness?"

"She said she had a parasite, an evil worm."

"Indeed, it was wormwood I gave her. That and pennyroyal, hedge hyssop, shepherd's purse. Some ergot would have been good, though I can work only with what the season and good friends bring me."

"She said it is with her still."

Biddy Josephs shook her head, her expression thoughtful as she stared into the shadow of my hood.

"Your voice, sir. I've never heard your accent here, have I?"

"I've been in Northumberland less than a month."

"So short a time, and already you are in love with Lily Winterbourne."

Love? I have never spoken the word, not even to Mirabella.

The old woman's brow creased more deeply.

"There is nothing for you to do, sir. Go home and wait. Perhaps she may still recover. And if she doesn't, you will have an opportunity to prove your love."

She had confirmed the worst.

I returned to my cave. Earlier I had planned my supper to be a nice plump turnstone I had surprised when sunning itself. I have lost all appetite. Instead I have been writing until it is late enough to climb the cliff up to the estate.

Will Lily be waiting?

My foolishness cannot be measured.

November 17

Every night I have roamed the Winterbourne estate, hoping to find Lily.

I feel her more in her absence than in her presence. Everything is black without her. And yet, with her? She is too dark in spirit to be the sun. Still, she shines. She is, thus, the moon—although now, in her illness, the moon waning.

I come from death. She goes toward it.

Tonight there was a letter from her, wedged between the branches of the tree where she had left my cloak.

Dearest Victor,

I am still not well. Please come to the house tomorrow night at eight. I wish to see you while I am yet able to. My mother knows that I feel for you some affection and that my father holds you in regard. Also, my father has explained to her your situation and how her brother has persecuted you for years. She does not agree with all that was said, but she has seen for herself that pursuing you has given her brother no peace.

She knows you will be reluctant to come because of her behavior at the party, but asks for your forgiveness. She wants to hear whatever news of her brother you may have.

Therefore, speak with her tomorrow night at eight. She will wait for you in her sitting room. Enter through the veranda doors, as you did before. And then, if I am feeling better, I will come downstairs afterward to see you.

Do not fail me.

Fondly,

Lily

Lily regards me with some affection? She addressed me as "dearest" and closed with "fondly"? Have I ever seen evidence of these feelings? Perhaps, in my inhumanity, I have simply not recognized them. Or perhaps, in her changeable mood, she has created another occasion for torment. I am fool enough to try to discover which.

If she speaks the truth, what of Margaret's more wondrous desire to speak with me? She says she wants to judge me on my own merit and not on lies. I hope Winterbourne will be at our interview to be my ally. It is his continued acceptance I seek more than hers.

In a sudden single moment, I fear total betrayal of my plan for revenge and yet understand it as the best vengeance of all if Margaret someday writes:

"Robert, we have met your monster at last . . . and happily call him friend."

November 21

The night after I had received Lily's letter, I approached the sitting room I had entered two weeks ago. Margaret Winterbourne was already there, wringing her bony hands, then pressing them to her chest as if her heart might burst with dread. Just a few candles were lit, throwing the room into shadow. In the dim light, my scars would look less fearsome—Winterbourne had probably suggested it—but she seemed terrified of the dark itself, startling at each anxious turn of step. Although her husband's presence would have strengthened her, she was unaccompanied. Perhaps it was a test: her willingness to be alone with me as she heard me out. I was disappointed Lily was not there, even though the letter said she would see me afterward only if she felt well.

I knocked on the glass door. Margaret jumped and held up a hand to ward me off.

"Mr. Hartmann?" With her hand still half-raised, she lowered her head and averted her eyes to the left. She could not endure the sight of me. "Come in."

I took one step inside, frightening her so badly that she half-fell, backing away. Her breath came in gasps, and she edged toward the door leading to the rest of the house.

I pulled up the hood and said, "I will come no closer. How is your daughter?"

Margaret's features passed through lightning changes, none of which I could read.

"As you might expect," she answered.

"I expect nothing and fear the worst. She said only that she was ill."

"Did she? But where . . . where are my manners?" she said. She gestured toward a stout chair far from where she stood.

"I will stay here. You are discomforted by my presence."

"I am." Her eyes darted away from me again, but there were too many shadows to give her peace: behind the velvet settees, behind the tall embroidered panels, beneath every chair, and within every corner. The cold fireplace itself seemed a tunnel from which evil might slither.

"Perhaps we should speak at another time."

"No! I won't have the courage!" She steeled herself, clenching and unclenching her fists. When the steel at last entered her eyes, she said, "You have seen my brother more often than I. *You!*" She did not attempt to hide her outrage. "Tell me, when you last saw my brother, did you leave him well?"

When I last saw Walton? How innocuous he appeared: his clothes shabby, his face dreamy, his eyes dazed. I might have felt pity did I not know that a second later he murdered Mirabella. Now I stood alone with his sister. My fingers burned to grab this woman's skinny wattled neck and choke her.

"Did you leave him well?" she repeated. "I know there is . . . unpleasantness between you."

"Unpleasantness?" I laughed bitterly. "He's robbed me of ten years of life, trying to kill me, and then robbed me of even more. The last occasion I saw your brother is best left undiscussed."

"Is it?" Her thin voice grew shrill: "What *will* you discuss? Why you stole his letters from me? How long you've been in Tarkenville? *Did you leave my brother well?*"

I stepped forward, wondering if I should call Winterbourne to calm her. At my movement she flattened herself against the wall, her eyes struck with horror. I backed up to the veranda door.

"What of your daughter?" I asked from that distance, hoping a change in topic might distract her. "She said we might meet tonight."

My words provoked Margaret to turn her head aside with disgust.

"You would see my daughter? Very well," she said tightly. She tugged on the bellpull and waited. Moments later Lily appeared. She wore a loose dressing gown and was very pale, very thin. Her eyes burned with fever.

Hand extended, I walked farther into the room to greet her.

"Now! Seize him now!" Margaret shrieked.

From the veranda, from behind the screens, from the door behind Lily, rushed brutish men. Two grabbed me; several pressed clubs at my head; one carried an axe. I could have thrown them off, but Gregory Winterbourne—the man who had made me believe that *I* might be a man—tore into the room, shielded his wife and daughter, and aimed a pistol at my heart.

"There!" Lily crowed. "Did I not tell you he'd come at my word?"

"You were a guest in my house!" Winterbourne waved the gun so wildly the men who held me flinched. "You listened to my confidences!"

"And *you* spoke to me as one man to another. For that I am truly grateful."

"'As one man to another'? You're a monster!"

"We talked of this. I am only what men have said I am."

"You're a *thing*!" Margaret cried out with hatred. "My brother was right. He has always been right!" She turned angrily on her husband. "You thought Robert was mad. You ridiculed him. You sneered at me for believing. You're a fool. You've always been a fool. You've—" What she could not say strangled her.

"Lily, what does this mean?" I asked. Perhaps in her coldness she could explain to me what her father in his heat could not.

"Don't you dare address my daughter!" Winterbourne's passion overwhelmed him; spittle appeared at his lips as his mouth worked over words that would not come. He gestured again with the gun and said, "I was kind to you!"

"Was I not kind in return?"

Kind? Because I had not murdered him? Blood rushed to my cheeks. I remembered Biddy Josephs: she spoke the language of men, whereas I did not, so I said, "Sir, I love your daughter."

"Love?"

He would have thrown himself at me had his men not held him back. One of them said, "Leave him for the sheriff, sir."

"The sheriff? What's my crime?"

"Murder."

"That's the least of it!" Winterbourne shook the gun at me.

Murder? Biddy Josephs had mentioned murder.

"I've harmed no one."

Another of the men holding me spoke: "You beat the

stable boy so badly we had to identify him by a birthmark. It was Miss Winterbourne who found him, isn't that right, miss? It was a terrible shock."

"I shouldn't have taken the dogs out," Lily said softly. "*He* was out, too. I saw him leaving the stables. When I brought the dogs in to pen them . . . that's when I found the body." She sagged against Margaret's narrow chest.

Lily and I had heard noises that night, a faint but persistent sound, like twigs and scrub rubbing against each other. She had said someone was there, but I did not believe her. Could she have heard the murderer? Had she walked in his very footsteps? It seemed that death stalked her on all sides. But—

"I wasn't in the stables," I said to her. "I was with you."

"Never!" she cried, near swooning. "You were never with me!"

Margaret led her daughter out. The men tightened their circle.

The accusation in Winterbourne's eyes scorched me with shame. How could he possibly believe that *I* was capable of murder? Laughter bubbled from my lips.

"He does not even attempt to defend himself!" Winterbourne said.

"An innocent man needs no defense." I drew myself up and said, *"Conscious of his own purpose, such a man does not deign to manifest the wrath that righteously seethes within him."* Into the following silence I added, "Alfieri's 'The Free Man.'"

Winterbourne hammered my face with the pistol butt.

His men pulled him off me.

"Sir, that's too bloody to be a gentleman's job," one said. "Stay here while we take him to the sheriff. If you want, sir . . . we don't have to reach town."

Winterbourne hated me enough to hesitate.

"No!" I cried out.

Blows pounded my neck and shoulders. A club cut me down at the back of my knees, forcing me to the floor. While the axe kept guard, Winterbourne again beat me with his pistol.

All along, I had held back, certain I would be allowed to explain. Now, blinded by my own blood, I exploded from their hands and grabbed the axe. In my last act as a man, I yanked the head from the handle and hurled both aside lest I turn the axe on every person there.

Two of Winterbourne's men struggled to keep him away from me. The rest attacked with a viciousness reserved for diseased vermin. Instead of subjugating me, they beat me into fury. I kicked shins, kneecaps, thighs; punched ribs and jaws. Bones snapped like castanets; I would dance to their rhythm. Seeing Winterbourne break free of his men, I scattered mine like a boy bored with his tin soldiers. I lunged. Winterbourne aimed and fired. With scalding pain, the bullet chiseled a crease into my temple.

Blackness hovered.

"Quickly, while he's stunned!"

From behind I heard the whistle of wood. Driving back the dark, I twisted round, stopped the club on its downward swing, then charged bull-like through the circle of men. Someone had closed the windowed doors to the veranda. With a contemptuous laugh, I shielded my face, burst through the glass, and landed on the flagstones. Blood flowed heavily from my forehead and temple and now, too, from my hands, scored by glass shards.

I scrambled to my feet just as Winterbourne cried out, "The hounds!"

The first one leapt at me from the side and knocked me on my back. It snapped at my wounds and encircled my throat with its teeth. I seized its head, clapped my knees around its rib cage, and wrenched its neck. The dog slumped to my chest. I regained my feet just as the other hounds arrived. I swung the limp body by its feet, slamming the other dogs away as they came after me again and again. The dead animal's head battered their heads, while its dead blood mingled with mine. Soon the dogs cowered and whined at this thing that only looked like a man. I threw the hound's body, terrifying them: years of obedience were erased in moments.

Bleeding, throbbing, reeling, I had to find shelter before I passed out. The cave was useless now. I would be too easily tracked, too easily cornered there. On buckling legs I made my way into the woods and began to cross and recross creeks and brooks and rivulets to weaken the trail and wash off my blood. My pace slowed to a stumble. Splashing my way up a large stream, I tripped, lost all strength, and collapsed. My floundering efforts to climb out of the icy water attracted the notice of a horse and rider. I waited for the pistol shot.

"Do you require help?"

A moment's stay. I nodded, trying to recall where I had heard that voice before.

"Come out of the water. Or are you too drunk to stand?"

The Reverend Graham.

"No, I am not drunk," I gasped. "I've been attacked."

I stood halfway. Graham's breath whistled out.

"You!" As if sharing his surprise, his horse reared. "You murdered that boy!"

Pain split my forehead, my sight darkened, and I swayed on my feet. In the distance a hound bayed. I tried to appeal to him using his religion. "I am accused falsely," I said, "as your Jesus was."

"That's blasphemous."

"Is it?"

Graham's head dipped forward as if he were straining to see better.

"Were you really created by a man?"

I gestured, took one step, and fell back. After a long hesitation, Graham dismounted and led the horse down the embankment. The horse bucked and whinnied at my touch. Graham patted its flank and steadied it for me to mount, a giant on a child's pony. Walking the horse out of the water, he held the very end of the reins, as if fearful of my reach. He did not know how weak I was, too feeble even to form a plan. The ache in my head drove out all thoughts, and exhaustion tried to drag me to sleep.

Right before we would leave the woods and enter the town, the reverend stopped. His thoughts were transparent: should he lead me to his church or surrender me? At last he turned toward the shadows at the rear of the parsonage.

"Thank you."

He turned to me in openmouthed amazement. My profanity had not shocked him as much as my gratitude did. The talking dog was full of surprises.

By now we had reached a small barn, which stood on a side street; the church fronted the main avenue. He helped me down.

"I spoke with Mr. Winterbourne this afternoon," he said.

"Winterbourne." The very word scratched at my ears.

"He told me that Lily was ill, that you had killed the stable boy, and that they feared you had murdered Mrs. Winterbourne's brother as well."

"I did not kill her brother. I did not kill the stable boy." I could scarcely stand and had to grip the stall door for support.

Unsaddling the horse, Graham felt the animal's trembling side.

"She's overheated from carrying your weight. I must cool her down at once."

Did he put his horse above me, the natural above the unnatural? I slipped to the floor, then knew nothing more.

It was not sleep that had overcome me, but my head injuries. For three days I lay unconscious. Unable to move me, Graham cared for me in the barn. What torments he must have suffered. Was I guilty or not? Could he offer the sanctuary of the church to something that may not be a man? Did sanctuary extend to the church's outbuildings?

My criticism does him a disservice: he saved my life when I expected otherwise.

At last I awoke. I pulled off the damp cloth that covered my head, my cloak that covered my body. My first action was to check that my journal was still on my person. Graham might have searched me during those three days and read it. I think not. My words confess to such heinousness that he would have summoned Winterbourne and allowed him to kill me while I lay helpless. Did Graham grant me the dignity of privacy? Or was he simply loath to touch me?

On weak and trembling legs, I walked outside. It was late afternoon. Graham was in the church, prostrate before the altar, arms thrown outward. I cleared my throat.

"No, no," he said, jumping up, alarmed. "You should not be in here!"

"If a dog wandered in, would you at least not treat it kindly?" I asked, hanging on to a pew. "It does not realize it offends, after all."

"I'm sorry. I spoke too brusquely."

He quickly moved to my side and opened the door to the pew so I could sit. I had to twist my body to get into it and even then sat with my knees squashed up to my chin. But the seat was steady where my legs were not. I had walked too far too soon.

"I'm truly glad you have recovered," Graham said, sitting in the pew ahead of me.

"Are you?" I asked. His eyes were swollen and red. Had he wept on my account? "You have been agonizing over what to do. My death would have forestalled such a decision."

His cheeks flamed. "I wish no harm to any man."

"But you don't think I am a man." I felt as if, during my long black sleep, my mind had been considering the same question. "Then what am I? Someone at the party said I was the new Adam. Am I a new type of man?"

"A new species?" He shook his head. "God made everything once and perfectly at Creation. If matter developed on its own . . ." The sentence was too dreadful to finish.

"*This* matter," I said, gesturing to myself, "did not develop on its own. I was created by a man."

"You may be no more than a machine." Graham turned away at the lie. "The Luddites destroyed machines they said would replace us. What would they have done with you and your like?"

"There is nothing to fear on that account. I'm the only one. But what am I? Do I have a soul? You must decide."

He stared up at the cross as if waiting for his God to answer him. At last I could no longer watch his suffering. I gently touched his shoulder. He flinched.

"If you cannot decide," I said tiredly, "can you at least give me a little bread? Even an animal needs to be fed."

"Yes, of course."

He brought me soup and bread; also a book of prayers, although he set it down without speaking of it. Perhaps he thought it would be sacrilege to proselytize an animal and so left it up to me to convert myself. I took the book with weary greed.

The days since I was attacked have passed as a blur: my vision, my insight, has been blinded. I have set down the incidents here, writing quickly in case my mind becomes again disordered, but I find no relief. Sometimes words are merely something to be rid of, like washing hands of filth.

Beneath my pain and confusion simmers black rage at Winterbourne. I burn with rancor. His rejection is far worse than the hate others have always shown me; he taunted me with something I had never before felt: hope. I want to rip him apart for being falsely kind. I want to ravage his world and all those he cherishes.

November 23

Graham has decided nothing about my nature, or nothing he would reveal.

Day by day I grow stronger; day by day, more agitated. I have moved into an upper room in the church. The sexton cleans only that which can be seen: both the upper room and its loft overlooking the nave have been neglected for years. His negligence benefits me.

Now that I have occupied the church, I know more of the town's business. Besides the conversation from the street below, I hear gossip from the sexton, who is also the town apothecary. For him, each medicinal has a dark meaning, which he gladly interprets as one of the seven deadly sins. This one was in for a bromide of ground seashells—gluttony! That one, a poultice for his son's infected back—anger!

Although Graham tries to silence him, he also prattles on about the stable boy's murder. It is a favorite topic in town. The Patchwork Man is real! It stalks the night! Hurry home! Lock your doors! But even that may not be enough. . . .

After the sexton left this morning, Graham climbed the staircase and, fixing his eyes on me in an unwavering gaze, said, "Swear to me, for I must hear it from you again: are you indeed innocent of this murder?"

"I do swear it. I would have you believe me with certainty, and then share that certain belief with Winterbourne. I . . . I am innocent."

"You hesitate."

What should I say? Graham is a public proclamation for a religion that swings erratically between forgiveness and condemnation.

But truth has value in itself.

"Of *this* murder I am guiltless," I admitted at last. "But other blood stains my hands. More would have, had not circumstances intervened."

"Shall I tell Mr. Winterbourne that as well?" Graham asked sharply, my response obviously not the one he wanted. A new Adam? I had already fallen and been expelled from Eden.

"Everything I did, however wrong, I believed necessary to protect myself."

Without meeting my eyes, Graham crept back down the stairs.

November 24

It is done and it cannot be undone; I have had my revenge after all.

So much to set down that I will run out of ink!

Late afternoon, a carriage was driven into the churchyard. Spying from the loft, I saw Winterbourne alight. He hurried into the church.

"Graham!"

No matter how enraged my earlier thoughts, they melted to nervous optimism. Perhaps here, in this place he must hold sacred, Winterbourne would at least listen to me.

The reverend hurried in. Winterbourne seized him by the arm.

"I must discuss a matter of urgency," he said.

Glancing toward the loft, Graham led him out of the church and beyond earshot. At first he listened, but soon he was shaking his head vehemently. Winterbourne tightened his grip and would not let him go. Words poured out on each side. At last, the reverend nodded curtly, pushed him aside, and with obvious distress ran back into the church. Winterbourne followed.

"Speak no more of it!" Graham yelled, again glancing upward. "I've agreed under the strongest of protests, but I won't hear another word! Wait while I gather what I need."

"You need nothing. Come with me this second."

Would Graham not take at least a moment to speak on my behalf? My thoughts must have been forceful, for he addressed Winterbourne more civilly.

"One moment, sir. Surely you can wait one moment more."

"What is it?" Winterbourne asked impatiently.

"I heard that you attacked the Patchwork Man, as he called himself."

"That vile thing?" Winterbourne's brow darkened, almost as with blood, and his voice grew harsh. "After all these years, I am finally sympathetic to my brother-in-law's obsession."

No! I clutched the railing of the loft.

Graham turned to the altar, to the cross, and spoke softly: "I found him in the woods that night, gravely wounded. I . . . aided in his escape."

"Are you mad?"

"Sir, remember that you are in church. I assisted him because he swore he was innocent."

"If this thing is capable of murder, Reverend, surely it's capable of lying."

"I believed what he told me. Also, I believe he . . . is a man."

I pressed my forehead to the railing, shuddering with the desire to weep. Graham's voice held both his belief in me as well as something of the price he paid for it, exacted from his religion.

Winterbourne breathed hard with anger, too furious to speak; breath by breath, his reaction bled me of all gratitude and replaced it with hatred. The reverend continued: "The creature—I mean, Mr. Hartmann—wanted me to tell you he is innocent. And if I myself came to believe it, he wanted me to tell you that as well."

"Mercy has made you a damned fool!" Winterbourne said. He grabbed his arm and dragged him through the door. "But fool or not, this day you'll play your part for me."

By the time I ran to the window, Graham had shaken himself loose, run to the sexton, and whispered into his ear. The man's eyes grew round with wonder. Winterbourne pushed the minister into his carriage. At once the sexton ran into the street, gossiping with each person who passed.

I wore down the floorboards with pacing, besieged by wrath, humiliation, comfort, puzzlement.

Nearly two hours later, the sexton at last entered the church. Bloodlust clouding my eyes, I jumped over the railing and grabbed him from behind.

"What is Graham's business with Winterbourne?" Had Lily's health worsened that quickly they had called for the reverend? When the sexton did not answer, I squeezed tighter till his eyes bulged. "Tell me."

"Wedding . . . Miss Winterbourne . . . Stuart Hawkins."

Lily married? My prize danced a little farther beyond my reach. Just weeks ago Winterbourne had spoken about "any man" with whom he might arrange a match. Now there was a groom.

"Who's Hawkins?" I asked.

The sexton could not answer. I loosened my arm.

"Has money. Does this and that. Import and export. Some whaling. Shipbuilder. Why, you never saw so strange a sight as a frigate sailing down a cobbled street on its way to the—"

I tightened my arm to shut him up.

"Matches are made every day," I said. "Why does this one cause so much gossip?"

"Hasty weddings cause talk."

"Hasty?"

"This evening. No banns, no license. Extreme poor health."

Would Lily not live the three weeks to announce the banns?

"If Miss Winterbourne is so ill," I asked, "why bother marrying?"

"Miss Winterbourne?" The sexton talked boldly, perhaps thinking gossip would earn him freedom. "It's Hawkins who won't last, what with him being old enough to be her father and coughin' up blood. They'll get the license afterward and pray he lives that long."

"How does marriage benefit *him*?" I asked.

"He'll die happy. Maybe even get an heir. Doesn't take but the once."

Gritting my teeth, I stifled him. *Get an heir?* So, no one knew of Lily's illness.

"How does this benefit Winterbourne?" I asked, relaxing my arm again.

"His property's entailed. If the daughter becomes Mrs. Hawkins, she needn't fear ruin when Winterbourne dies. Nor need his wife fear it. He's just seein' to his duties. He made Hawkins change his will first. The price of flesh."

The price of flesh. The words incensed me. I squeezed the sexton's neck until his struggles became annoying, then let him drop to the floor. I paced up and down the church's center aisle.

"Winterbourne," I complained, "has caused me more pain than anyone in existence, with the exception of his brother-in-law. More so! Walton never deceived me. But this man invited me into his house—only to attack me!"

"Such injustice," the sexton agreed, wheezing from my last assault, but all the while crawling away. "You do not deserve to be ill treated."

"I swear, I will have my revenge after all!" I cried. "I was a fool to put it off."

The sexton was nearly at the door. I grabbed him by the feet and yanked him back. He squealed over and over till I slapped him into silence. Propping him up against the base of the pulpit, I held his sweaty face so that he might at last look at me.

"Why are you leaving?" I asked. "You have to prepare the church for the wedding."

"The wedding isn't here." His quavering voice once more broke into that piglike squeal. I raised my hand; he clapped his own against his mouth. "Do not kill me," he whispered from behind his fingers.

"Give me no cause to do so. Where is the wedding?"

"The Winterbournes' private chapel."

A single blow rendered him senseless.

The chapel's stained-glass windows, lit from within, were vibrant against the black sky. Although the small building was attached to the house, it sat at the end of its own drive leading through the grounds. Even with the ceremony's haste, there were guests, perhaps the result of the sexton's gossip. Horses were tethered nearby to iron stanchions, their carriages still engaged, but only two of their drivers stood by.

I circled round from the far side. The chapel had double wooden doors with a great ringed handle on each. The iron circles rattled as one of the doors opened and a servant with a lantern emerged from within. He set the lantern between himself and the two drivers.

"It was faster'n lightnin' to get 'em into the church," the servant said. "Now it's slower'n a snail to get 'em out. I never saw such prayin' in my life."

"Still, they'll run outta breath sometime," said one driver. "And I want my chance to eat before that. Go call Tim and Charlie and the others back from the kitchen. It's their turn to watch the horses."

The servant took the lantern and headed toward the main house.

"And hurry," called the other driver. "They've had time enough to eat three times over."

Silently I moved from the shadows. My presence made the horses skittish, which distracted the men. In just seconds I dragged their unconscious bodies to the side. I kicked at one of the empty stanchions till it loosened and then yanked it from the ground. When I hefted it, its weight as a bludgeon was satisfying. I shouldered it like a club and entered the chapel.

The first set of double doors led into a dark vestibule. Seeing a second set of doors, I set my eye at the crack.

Lily wore a white lace dress and veil, with a jeweled barrette in her hair that caught the candlelight. Next to her stood a slight, sickly man who leaned heavily on a cane. The ceremony was over. Margaret was congratulating the groom, although her movements were jerky and fearful. Winterbourne's face wore a peculiar smile. The crafty hawk was pleased. He had married off his daughter, done his duty, all the while successfully deceiving the man, as he deceived me.

But Lily! Her pale cheeks and fever-harsh eyes had been replaced by ineffable beauty. What cruel illness could paint so lovely a portrait? My anger thickened. No matter how Lily had teased me with intimate talk, I could never rightfully purchase such a prize. I did not have the price of flesh. Her husband could take from her by law what I could take only by violence—even though he and I were both corpses.

As if to agree, Hawkins was gripped by a terrible cough that wracked his body and stained his handkerchief. Graham, Winterbourne, and Margaret at once turned to help. Ignoring both the choking noises behind her and the good wishes offered on both sides, Lily walked away from the altar toward the closed double doors.

Yes, I thought, still peering through the crack, a more able bridegroom awaits you here. With growing hunger I gazed on her as she approached. When she was a few yards away, I burst through the vestibule doors. Men leapt up, some to flee, some to do battle. Matrons shrieked. Margaret fainted.

Lily stood motionless, staring at me, her expression neither frightened nor comforted. I grabbed her around her waist. Only then did she come to life and begin to fight.

Winterbourne rushed down the aisle to his daughter. I swung the stanchion to fend him off and, when he still advanced, slammed it against his upper arm. Screaming, he fell to his knees. I raised the stanchion over his bowed head.

"No!" cried Reverend Graham. "If you would be a man," he begged, "if you would have a soul . . ."

I lifted the stanchion higher.

"So, this is how you replace your slut."

From the corner shadows stepped Walton.

Why was I surprised? Had he not followed me everywhere before this? He was cadaverously thin and unkempt; his eyes burned like hot coals set into a skull. There was a murderous ease to the man, as if triumph were already within his grasp.

A moan drew my attention to Winterbourne's imploring face. He whispered my name.

In a mocking tone, Walton said, *"If you would be a man . . ."*

I looked from one to the other, then dragged Lily backward through the doors.

Outside, I slipped the stanchion into the ringed handles, thus bolting the chapel from the outside. Then I freed the horses. Panicked by my strangeness, they scarcely needed my slap before galloping away. I shoved Lily into the last carriage and drove off.

It was a phaeton, its top folded back. I had chosen it for its lightness and speed. Also, I could drive the span of horses with one hand and hold on to Lily with the other. If I had had to sit up on the driver's seat of an enclosed coach, I believe she would have flung herself out. As we raced over the countryside, she slapped and bit and kicked at me. Her protestations were so steady and vigorous that she soon slumped at my side.

Seeing how exhaustion had made her submissive, I pulled off the road and drove the phaeton to where thick shrubbery provided shelter. There I stopped. I had fanned the horses into a great lather and they needed to rest. I gagged and bound Lily with strips torn from her veil. She twisted and thumped on the bottom of the carriage, but at least would not be able to cry out to any who might pass. At one point she fell into a light, uneasy sleep. When she woke, her eyes moved unfocused across the night sky. Then they filled with memory, and her expression held such abhorrence and loathing, such malice, I could see she was clearly her mother's daughter, her uncle's niece.

I took out my journal and candle stub and now sit here writing. I needed to think and have always done so through my pen.

Walton.

Because of him, the woman who would have stayed with me was dead. Because of him, the woman I had taken would hate me forever.

Thoughts flash through my mind more quickly than I can write them—lightning in a night sky, instantly illuminating the darkness of my desire. I know what I must do.

Later

I led the horses back onto the road. Earlier, as the animals rested, riders had passed in the distance, and galloping hooves joined with the baying of dogs. Another group rode out later in a different direction, also with dogs, and later still, a third. Once quiet had returned, I reined the horses back onto the road and drove to a place near the top of the cliff, where I knew the path to be gentle. I secured the phaeton and shouldered Lily like a sack of flour. She kicked me and banged her head till I came to the edge of the cliff. Then she pressed against me tightly as if her slightest movement would push me hurtling forward. Once on the shore I trotted north, set her deep within the cave, and covered her with my cloak. Her muffled cries echoed as I left her in darkness and went back up to the Winterbourne estate.

The house was a beacon, every window lit: a lighthouse to guide their missing daughter home. Winterbourne had foolishly sent out too many men to hunt me and kept too few behind to guard so large a house. They stalked the grounds, armed with rifle and musket, cudgel and axe, and yet it was nothing for me to wait, hidden, until one had passed by, then to creep forward and wait again. Apparently all the mastiffs had been sent out as well. My presence triggered no howling response. And since I had used the phaeton to escape, the only scent they could track would be my footsteps leading back to Reverend Graham's church.

I began to circle the house, from window to window. I did not see Walton. It was as if he hurried from one room to another just before I peered within. What did his child's game matter? I would be the dog here: I would find him easily, following the stench of frustration, baseness, and corruption. He spoiled all that he touched and left behind nothing but blowflies.

At last: Winterbourne, his wife, and Walton, together in a sitting room. The sleeve of Winterbourne's jacket was empty, his arm beneath it bound in a sling, his hand limp and floppy. His other hand clutched a glass. The butler Barton brought in a fresh decanter of liquor and took away an empty one. Where was Lily's groom? Tucked away in bed, spinning bloody drool, like a spider spins web?

Though I could not hear the conversation, I understood that Winterbourne was trying to persuade his wife to go to bed. She refused as he gestured again and again toward the door. Finally Walton took his sister's arm and led her out. Winterbourne poured himself a fresh drink, downed it in one gulp, poured another, and sat, the decanter within reach. He drank himself to unconsciousness, slumping forward in the chair, then rolling to the floor. I slipped into the room and snuffed out the candles. By the banked fire I studied his slack, snoring face. My hands stretched out. In the air between us, I could feel the warmth of his drunken flesh and the pulse of his jugular.

No. I would wait till he could be roused and could see the face of his executioner. I had come here to kill Walton. In the end Winterbourne's betrayal made him deserve the greater punishment.

Beyond the sitting room drifted murmuring, which I followed to the top of a small stairwell. What worthy gossip I had given the servants!

Upstairs, the door to a bedroom was open. Margaret slept fitfully in a chair drawn to the open window to keep watch. I passed her for now; she would be easy enough to take later. In this wing no other room appeared to be occupied, but at the end of the next corridor, an open doorway spilled light. I inched close. Although candelabra burned on either end of the mantel, and candles illumined a book on the vanity, the room was empty. I was about to continue down the corridor when I noticed a dirty black coat on the bed and, beyond the bed, a door leading to an inner room. As I approached it, my fingers, moving on their own, closed upon the book and pocketed it.

A noise behind me from the corridor . . . and without a word, without a cry of alarm, Walton hurled himself on me like a rabid wolf, leaping upward to grab my throat. He held on, feet dangling, years of hatred compressed into his grip.

The viciousness of his attack forced me back against the mantel. Flailing, my hands found the lit candelabrum. Immediately I pressed it against his face. Red flames kissed his sunken cheek, and hot wax dripped down his neck. Madman that he was, he did not loosen his hold, nor even scream. He simply gritted his teeth and butted the candelabrum with his head until I dropped it. His hair shriveled, dry weeds for kindling, and then caught fire. Red tongues crowned him like a martyr. Smiling, he pulled himself up closer and leaned toward my face: rather than let go, *he* would be the tinder to make *me* ignite. Instinct fought insanity: for the first time in all these years, I truly battled rather than merely eluded him, and I battled for my life, not revenge.

I swung round in place and slammed him against the mantel. At last he let go and fell to the floor. While we had fought, flames from the dropped candelabra had licked the bottom ruff of the bedclothes and then shot along its full length like a fast fuse. The charge flashed: the entire canopy and hangings were ablaze. The rush of fire startled me. For one thoughtless moment, I backed up and shielded my eyes, and in that moment, Walton leapt from the floor and threw himself on me. Soon we struggled within a burning circle. His madness proved the equal of my strength.

As my one hand grappled with him, the other sought a weapon. Again and again I picked up a glass or porcelain trinket, smashing each down on his blistering skull without effect. Finally I found a bookend and he crumpled to the floor. The room was a contrast in searing white flame and deadly black, and I could not see him for the smoke. I stumbled out into the hallway, but the fire had outpaced me.

Swallowing ruffles and doilies, drapes and rugs, the flames had already eaten their way through the room and were beginning to flicker along the bottom edges of tapestries lining the walls. A crazed chuckle broke from my lips. Besides the tapestries, in just this corridor alone were carpet runners, upholstered chairs, needlepoint pillows, lace tablecloths, wicker stands, and so much more. I had spoken of kindling; *this* kindling would burn the house, purging Winterbourne of his excesses, the foolish source of his pride.

With more merriment than I could have anticipated,

I ripped down one of the burning tapestries and dragged it behind me. It lit my path, but the path I had come from, as if I only had hindsight. Everything accepted the fire eagerly. Its life had withered long ago. For decades it had awaited the mercy of the funeral pyre: peacock feathers overstuffed into vases, Oriental fans arranged like bouquets, useless oil portraits painted for useless men, silhouettes scissored from black paper, and white paper quilled into pastoral scenes.

Winterbourne had decried me as a thing? His other things, in their absurdity, were no more deserving of life than I was. I laughed with forced gaiety lest I howl.

I rushed to his study, grabbed the liquor decanters, smashed them onto the huge lovely desk, the desk behind which I never should have sat, and held the burning tapestry to its edge. The puddle caught at once, and a sheet of flame spread from corner to corner. A man needs a solid place from which to make solid decisions? Winterbourne should have decided to love and not hate me. He should have decided to be honest and not deceive me.

I watched the fire burn, and in that brief moment of inaction was almost overcome with heartsickness. To drive back the feeling, I snapped the leg off a straight-backed chair, wound a length of drape around its end, soaked the cloth with brandy from another decanter, and lit it. I carried the torch past the staircase to the other wing. There I weaved in and out of the empty rooms, laying it on everything. I would burn it all, every meaningless prize, every forgotten pleasure. I would burn the life that in its narrow provincial fear would not give me even the shade beneath its boot. Some future winter, when I was alone on a January night, memory of this fire is what would keep me warm.

My lungs burned with every breath. Sweat sizzled off my brow. Cinders kissed my hands and left love bites.

Suddenly—as if the numbness swaddling my mind burned away, as if I myself needed first to burn—I realized, *the books*! I was destroying what was most precious to me. In the past, when I had no people, I always had paper flesh. When I heard no voices, I always had paper words. Now all of it burned, and I had set the fire myself.

I tried to fight my way back to the study. Some of the books could be saved, at least one or two—*must* be saved! It would be worth every new scar. I dropped to the floor and slid on my belly, but, like the snake, I was blocked by fire and could not return to Eden. Close to tears, I had to forsake the library. I found the main center staircase and crawled down, the railings on either side solid tracks of fire. At my back, crackling flames chattered maniacally, ever louder until their roar deafened me to all other sound.

Near blind, I made my way to the outside. After the smoke, the fresh air needled my lungs like angry wasps.

Margaret lay on the ground, coughing, her hand pressed to her chest, a servant at her side. Here and there stood the men who had been set as guards against me, their clubs and knives and muskets dropped to the ground. A small group of servants huddled together, dressed in gowns and robes and nightcaps; their faces upturned, their eyes so mesmerized they saw nothing else. I wondered at the handful of them: surely, so large a house would employ more than these few?

A man's shape crossed one of the blazing windows on the second story. He pounded on the glass with outstretched palms and then with balled fists. With amazement I recognized the tall, thin shadow as Walton's. How had he survived being at the heart of destruction?

Over and over again he hammered at the glass, clawed at it, struck it with his shoulder. His figure slipped to the floor, then stood up a second later holding a chair, which he flung full force at the windowpanes. With a terrible shriek, the wooden frame buckled outward. Glass fell in a silver shower. Like a scarecrow struck by lightning—head, body, and limbs bright with flame—Walton jumped out onto the flagstones below.

Margaret, who not seconds ago appeared too weak to move, scrambled to her feet, ran to her brother, and smothered the fire with her own body. The crumpled figure did not move. Her wail pierced the roar of the conflagration.

Walton was dead.

I felt no triumph, only overwhelming exhaustion.

Glass shattered as window after window exploded.

Winterbourne! I had left him on the first floor, drunk and unconscious, meaning to save him as dessert to a meal of rage. I would not let the fire claim my right to destroy him.

Eagerly, I circled the house, but Barton was already dragging his master's lifeless body from the smoking building onto a white-graveled path. The servant looked up. Tears washed white lines down his sooty cheeks.

Death had cheated me, but I was not angry at death. I was not angry at all. Still, why could I not breathe? What angry thing choked me?

Walton was right: I was flawed, I was perverse, I was unnatural. I should not have been. I should not be. For the briefest of moments, I had been a man. Now Winterbourne was dead, and I was a man no longer. It was not enough that I had killed the father given me by Fate. I had killed the father I myself had chosen.

It was shame that suffocated me.

I fled before Barton's sad, cruel eyes.

I ran at a crouch until I was some distance away and then sat until my heart was some distance from bursting. At last I turned. Having finally created a mirror large enough to reflect me, I comprehended my whole life in one glance, a revelation of what I was and what I did, of what I am and what I do, and so I stole words from what man calls his Book of Revelation and made them my own:

> *I was a star fallen from heaven upon the earth. And there was given to me the key of the bottomless pit. And I opened the bottomless pit: and the smoke of the pit arose, as the smoke of a great furnace; and the sun and the air were darkened by reason of the smoke of the pit.*
>
> *And lo, the sun became black as sackcloth of hair, and the moon became as blood; and the stars of heaven fell unto the earth, and the heaven departed as a scroll when it is rolled together; and the kings of the earth, and the great men, and the rich men, and the chief captains, and the mighty men said to the mountains and rocks, Fall on us, and hide us. For the great day of his wrath is come; and who shall be able to stand?*

The insistent clanging of a bell informed me that a fire brigade, belated and futile, was on its way from Tarkenville. I left.

Halfway down the cliff, spasms of grief, shame, and disgust nearly shook me loose. I stopped and clung tightly to the sheer rocky face.

What if I simply let go?

The moment passed, and then another moment, and then . . .

I no longer wanted to die. But how would I live?

A single madman had searched me out before. Then I left my place among life's outcasts and dared to walk among civilized men. Now, spurred by their civilized hate, they would hunt me down with more thoroughness and method than Walton had ever possessed.

They would comb the cities, thinking I would seek the anonymity of crowds. They would comb the country, thinking I would go to ground like a badger. I needed to go beyond both to a place so barbarous it would repulse even those who would kill me, a place where *I* might rule.

My spasms broke into laughter and I again pressed myself closer to the rock lest I fall. Had I not already been shown my empire? Was there any site more wild?

Eagerly I scrambled down the rest of the cliff, rushed into the cave, and scooped up Lily. From behind her gag, she screamed. Ignoring her struggles, I carried her down the shore and back up the cliff where the carriage was tied. There she saw the flame-lit sky, with its glowing bits of ash like fireflies on a mild evening.

Still this was not enough. I drove the horses onto the Winterbourne property. I held Lily's face toward the fire and said, "You have nowhere to go now but with me." I took up the reins and whipped the horses into a gallop.

There in the north, in a place storm-lashed and sterile, my father once shaped a creature to match my ugliness. His nerve failed him. Mine will not. I have my mate, my bride, my harlot, my whore. As the worm eats her, her fairness will turn foul and fouler. When she is more worm than woman, and her ugliness rivals my own, I shall crown her my queen consort. For I take her now to my nation, a land under my dominion, and there in the Orkney Islands I will claim my throne as king of the monsters.

PART THREE

Lily escaped . . .

After urging on the horses till dawn, I had pulled the carriage off the road to hide it as I rested. I was still in England, having driven southwest from Tarkenville through the night. As dangerous as this was, I would have been more vulnerable if I had attempted to go north at once to cross the River Tweed. I planned instead to roughly follow the border down the Cheviots and to cross into Scotland at a lower point. From there I would travel directly up to Stirling and at last over the Highlands to the coast, and then northeast to the Orkneys.

Lily had been strangely docile. Bound and gagged, she lay on the bottom of the carriage, having toppled off the seat after I had driven over a rut. As we raced through the countryside, she did not seem to see the clouds or trees that overhung us; her dazed eyes were filled with images of burning. At last she fell asleep, disturbed by neither the carriage's breakneck speed nor the sudden cessation of movement when I pulled over to rest.

I stretched out on the ground next to the horses, which made them skittish. What creature was it that had driven them, rather than wear a harness like their own? I closed my eyes and began to drowse.

The sudden thunder of galloping hooves shattered the quiet. Though the riders were not visible, I leaned into the carriage and kept my hand by Lily's mouth lest she, too, wake and try to call out. She did not. I sat watch till exhaustion forced me to true sleep. When I opened my eyes too many hours later, the sun marked late afternoon.

While I lay there, light slanting into my eyes, I noticed the flutter of something white caught on a bramble just beyond my reach. I realized what it was and jumped up.

Lily was gone. All around, clinging to rocks and brambles, were the strips of wedding veil I had used to bind and gag her.

In the distance a white-clad figure moved toward a speck on the horizon that might have been a town. I had suffered too much with no pleasure as reward to let her escape. That first night, Lily had hunted me. Now *she* was the rabbit.

Even from here I saw how slowly she ran. I followed at an easy loping rhythm. She looked backward, still expecting me to be asleep, and nearly tripped when she saw me. Her feet were shod in thin white slippers, which offered no protection against the rocky soil and forced her to run awkwardly, as if barefoot. But my presence proved inspirational: she gathered the skirts of her gown and, despite the slippers, ran faster.

I could have overtaken her at once. Why did I hesitate? Was I considering letting her go because of her illness, her fear of me? Why should I care about her illness, as long as it did not mar her beauty? Why should I care about her fear?

At last I ran alongside her. She tried to dart ahead. I held out my hand to slow her. She knocked it away, again and again, till I grew tired of the game, and grabbed her, and forced her down onto the ground. Her panting breath was hot against my eyes, the lace of her gown unexpectedly rough when I pressed my blackened lips to her throat. I caught the cloth between my teeth and ripped it, kissed her where the blood beat closest to the skin. She fought and twisted and tried to throw me off. My mindless body was soon aroused, her strug- gles like the urgent fondling of a hasty lover.

When I thrust my hand under her skirts, she fell slack against the earth. I pulled back, thinking she had died of fright. Then I saw her eyes. Her fear had been replaced with something else. She looked at me directly and in a soft voice said, "My father is dead, is he not? Or why else would you have said I had nowhere to go but with you? You killed my father."

She could not have calculated a remark more damaging to desire, and I rolled away.

Taking my silence for assent, she continued: "The estate is mine then, what is left of it."

"What?" I was shocked by the serenity on her face.

"The house is mine."

"Should you not ask about survivors? Your mother was alive when I left."

"So? Was it you who rescued her?" Anger painted her cheeks. "Do not invent meaningless good deeds after nearly destroying my house!"

"Walton is dead." The words should have dripped from my lips like honey; instead they tasted bitter and unsatisfying.

"I did not know him," Lily said. "But what of my hounds?"

I dragged her toward the carriage. Luck had granted me this day while I had slept too long. I could not be so foolish twice.

"You killed my father. And my uncle too."

"You do not understand what was between your uncle and me."

"I understand enough." She dug her heels into the ground. Though her gesture was nothing to my strength, I stopped and faced her. Her eyes narrowed. "It involves a whore, my uncle said. And you would replace such a base person with me?" She pointed to Mirabella's necklace, which I still wore round my wrist. "Did that belong to her? Such trash. Not like my jewels." She fingered the barrette in her hair. "The whore forgot her trinket one night and now you hold it dear. She keeps no souvenirs of you, I warrant."

"She is dead, as you shall be if you do not keep still."

I lifted her into the carriage and drove back to the road. "Get out," I said, shoving her from the phaeton. She tumbled out and sat in the dirt. "Wait here. There will be riders along tracking me and, if not them, those who use the road for commerce. Tell them there is a reward for your return—although *I* would not offer one—and they will bring you back safely."

"To what?" she said, getting up. "To a smoking shell where I shall sweep cinders all day?"

"What about your husband?"

"I have no husband. I'm sure his solicitor has already written up annulment papers and had him change his will at once. My virtue has been compromised," she spat, alluding to the very thing I wanted from her. "You have seen to that!"

She tried to climb back into the carriage. A light shove—and again she was sitting in the dirt.

"What of your mother?"

"My mother loves no one but her brother. She will not miss me. I am a drain on her monthly purse."

I could have simply ignored Lily and driven away, but her gross illogic in trying to get back into the carriage puzzled me.

"You were my prisoner. Not an hour ago you tried to escape. Now you would come with me willingly?"

She grinned. A bit of Walton madness glittered in her eyes.

"You do not want me now, which is why I shall go with you," she said. "I hate you far too much to do as you wish. Moreover, you have destroyed my house. It is only right that you should care for me till it is once more inhabitable."

Did she think I would act as her protector? That her house would be rebuilt merely because she wished it so? Did she believe I would later return her at her command? I had already tried to take her. What might I do with time?

With amused wonder I bowed and welcomed her back. She carefully brushed the dirt from her wedding gown, then pulled herself up into the carriage. She was with me by choice now. For the moment I would allow it, for the sake of curiosity and for the sake of her beauty. When I next tried to take her, it would be at my ease and not when my eyes must forever scan the horizon. Till then I would keep her like an overbred pet.

"I shall drive," she said, positioning herself daintily. "You are much too slow for someone being hunted for murder."

There was a tremor in her voice. Perhaps she plotted to turn the phaeton around. Perhaps she was only cold, clothed in just her lace gown. When I dropped my cloak over her shoulders, she shrugged it off with haughtiness. I gave her the reins and pointed down the road toward the southwest.

To my surprise, she drove the horses with a fury that surpassed my own. The whip sat familiarly in her hand. With unseemly coarseness she cracked it high in the air over the horses' heads, low against their flanks till blood ran with their sweat.

"Easy with them," I said. "They must run tomorrow as well."

"Tomorrow we shall have new horses!" she cried, lashing out again. Pink foam flew backward and splattered her face. She wiped her cheeks and, smiling, showed me her reddened palm.

She drove the horses faster and took curves recklessly. One horse fell lame. Its limping gait yanked the other horse back as the phaeton shot forward and bumped both animals, nearly overturning us.

Lily jumped from the carriage and beat the lame horse. She turned just as viciously on me and scourged my face. I seized the whip away, broke its handle, and flung it aside. Twisting her arm, I pulled her close. I should *wait* for this harridan? No, I should take my pleasure, snap her neck, and dump her body. Taken now or later, she would prove the same insubstantial meal. And she was no longer protected by my foolish thoughts about her father.

The image of Gregory Winterbourne rose up, like a haunt that appears at the mention of its name. It was the face, not of the irrational man who had struck me, but the wise contented bird who had spoken fondly, foolishly, of his daughter. Who would take care of her, now that he was dead and her marriage—even the roof above her head—was in ruins? With one blow, I had both destroyed her life and taken on its obligation, all for the price of a glass of brandy and an hour of talk.

I dropped her arm and turned away.

The horses reared and grew frantic when I approached. In their panic they tangled themselves in their traces and reins. Fortunately the lame horse had not broken a bone, so I did not have to put it down. I undid the knots and set it free. It limped off as quickly as it could while I soothed the other animal and reharnessed it to carry the carriage alone.

As I worked, I felt wetness on my cheek. My fingers came away bloody from where the whip had fallen.

"What's one more scar on your horrible face?" Lily taunted.

Lingering thoughts of Winterbourne subdued me. For the violence I had done him, for the violence I would have done his daughter, I said nothing.

It is morning again and we are lodged in a hut. The shepherd to whom it belongs unwittingly obliged us by leaving us gruel, encrusted on the sides of a pot, but still warm. After eating a mouthful, Lily wrapped herself in a blanket and fell asleep on the floor, while my mind returns again and again to her father.

He was the rich man I expected to despise, who in a single evening became the father I hoped to love, and in another, my betrayer. Was he so filled with contradiction, or did I simply not fathom his full nature? My grief mingles with guilt.

Winterbourne made me believe I was his equal in many ways. Perhaps in death, I will be. I never was in life.

November 26

While Lily slept, I pulled from my pocket the volume I had taken from Walton's room the night of the fire. Instead of print, I saw the same writing as on the letters from Margaret's desk. Walton kept a journal, the same as I. Some dark night we may have sat at the selfsame hour to write of our mutual torments. I felt unsettled: he is with me still, his journal lying against my heart. He is with Lily now, too, his blood in her veins, his madness in her eyes. Walton joins us, an unseen ghost, on every step of our journey.

Less than half of the journal has been filled. None of the entries are dated. I can read only a few at a time; Walton's anger fills me with too much of my own:

Margaret does not, can not understand. Would I have her see me as I now am? She would not recognize me. She claims to be in despair, yet has roused herself enough to act and take solace in another, too readily I think. She says it is for the girl's sake she goes north. I had thought she would always keep the light in my old bedroom lit. But now in the north, there is no light lit for my return.

❖

The monster has been spotted! This time I will not fail.

❖

Some days I am the Hand of God, carrying out His will. Other days I am the creature's shadow, following it in doomed mimicry.

Once I was a reasonable man. I have found there is an end of reason.

◇

My face is setting itself into a mask of insanity, for it is far easier to present that mask to the world than what lies beneath. I am a wretch, unnatural and forsaken by God. I cannot destroy the unnatural in me and so I turn it outward. That is why I pursue this thing, and pursue it mindlessly lest I take a second to think. It is as much a wretch as I am, and perhaps in more-innocent ways. I should have pity for it, but pity would weaken me.

November 27

Detouring southwest to go to the Orkneys grates on me, but yesterday I found my decision justified. It was sunset, and we were about to leave the thickly wooded area where we had spent the day. Hearing whistling, I crept to the road and saw a man walking in my direction. Before I could attack him and take his purse, several men on horseback overtook him and demanded to know: Had he seen a young woman in a white lace gown? Had he seen a huge, terrifying freak?

The man answered no, though his curiosity was stirred.

"He cannot still be ahead of us," said one rider to the others.

"Perhaps he intends to try for London," said another.

"From this far west? I think he's taken one of the smaller roads."

"No. He waits for us to give up and will try to cross the Tweed."

Two riders decided to continue south and later separate to search the smaller roads. Whipping their horses, the others returned north to post extra guards along the Tweed.

I crept back to the carriage.

"We will remain here for the night," I told Lily. "There are riders both north and south of us on this road. They are still searching for you."

"No. They are bent on catching *you*, not rescuing me. They presume I am dead, and rightly so, given that you are such a beast."

"You must be tired of provoking me. Here is your opportunity to leave. Take it. *Go*."

"I was going to do that very thing," she said. "But since you bid me leave with so much enthusiasm, I will not."

Containing my aggravation, which would only guarantee that she would never quit me, I led the horse through the trees. About half an hour later, Lily pointed.

"Through there, Victor!" she commanded.

We had come to a village. I refused to bring the carriage farther.

"We cannot stop in the woods," she complained. "I am hungry. You have only given me dug-up roots and water from a spring."

"You could not have been so hungry, for you did not eat even that."

"I am not a savage like you," she retorted. "I need a sweet pudding or perhaps cake with citron and currants."

"You only want those things. What you need would have been well provided by the turnips I'd found."

"Then you have forced me to beg."

She stepped from the carriage, took my hand, and tried to walk toward the lights. I held back.

"Come with me," she sweetly coaxed. "Protect me."

Her lightheartedness was both vexing and confusing. Did she wish to entrap me or did she really not understand the danger?

"Together we will attract more attention," I said.

"Then I will go alone!"

She smacked the horse on its flank. While I restrained it from bolting, she ran from me toward the village. A lone man was walking down a path and she hailed him.

It is over now, I thought. He will have heard of us. He will know at once who she is. My muscles tensed in anticipation of flight.

I could not hear what Lily asked. In answer, the man pointed toward one of the thatched houses. She hurried to the front of it and knocked. Apparently ignorant of who she was, the man continued on his way down the path.

After tying the reins, I crept closer. I was unable to hear what pitiful tale Lily told; I only saw great gesticulations on her part and a baffled expression on the face of her audience, an older woman with white hair, arms floury to her elbows. The woman shut the door. Lily stamped her foot and knocked at a second cottage. Again she was refused.

"They are a selfish lot," Lily said, seeing me. "What is a slice of cake to them?"

"Come, before they make a public complaint."

She knocked at a third house before I could leave. The door opened so quickly I could scarcely step to the side. For the first time I heard her story.

"I am so sorry to trouble you," she said, anxious and apologetic. "My friend and I are part of a group traveling to London. We became separated in a terrible storm. Until we catch up with them, we have nothing. Might you spare us cake?"

While her story was one of woe, her voice and face conveyed near hilarity. I no longer wondered why doors had closed on her. What was this strange mood?

"What sort of group was it?" asked a young voice.

"Oh!" Lily waved dramatically. "A theatrical group! Actors and acrobats, magicians, sword swallowers, singers, dwarves—and a giant! Please? My friend and I are very hungry."

"Your friend? I see no one else."

"He's very shy." Lily waved to me. "Victor, come here," she urged. I peered round the corner of the house. Peering back was a young woman; a girl, really. She had a broad blotchy face and tangled brown hair, and she carried a child on her hip. From within the cottage came the whimper of an infant.

Even from the shadows, my cloaked figure made the girl's eyes pop, so that she resembled a strange bug.

"The giant?" she asked.

"Him? Oh no," Lily said scornfully. "He's just one of the actors. A very bad one. He seldom gets a role."

"But he's so tall!"

"He's nothing compared to our giant."

"Why is his face covered?"

"He's so handsome he attracts too much attention. It's wonderful on the stage—no one notices his acting then—but it's quite a nuisance the rest of the time."

I stood mute with incredulity.

The girl stared at me openmouthed. Then she sighed and her eyes grew distant. "I always fancied myself on the stage," she said, her face turning deep pink. "I sing."

"Do you?" Lily asked pleasantly.

"Oh yes, but . . ." She lifted the child up as explanation.

"Well, we would enjoy listening to you," Lily said. "Perhaps over tea and cake?"

The girl shifted the child from one hip to the other. Her face was a transparent working of opposite emotions. Clearly we were strangers of questionable status, not to be trusted, perhaps not even to be talked to . . . and yet . . . she understood, she thought, our ragtag actors' life. Decision settled over her features.

"There's a cottage in back," she said, the words tumbling out. "Just the one room. I've been meaning to bring Mum up from Spennymoor to stay with us, though Harry says we'd be better off letting it out, profitable, you see, and quieter too, for Mum likes to talk, but I guess it would do no harm if you wanted to stop the night there—if you're very quiet—and get a bit of food too and—and—"

"Hear you sing?" Lily asked.

The girl smiled a gap-toothed grin.

"And Harry—will he cause me trouble?"

"Harry will—" The girl's mouth closed, her cheeks darkened, and her eyes slid to the side. "There'll be no trouble, only you must be quiet," she whispered. "Harry's not the sociable sort. I can sing for you now because he's not home, and besides I'm always singing to myself, like. But he's not fond of company. I won't even mention you're here when he comes back, and then he won't know, will he? Because you'll be quiet?"

The girl was so clearly without guile, I did not fear a trap, only that she might speak a loose word. But each time she referred to Harry, there was something in her bearing that assured me she would mention us to neither him nor even her neighbors. Slowly I understood how much she was risking to have her song heard.

The cottage was little more than a hut with a dirt floor with a smell that indicated animals had been kept in it. But it did have a fireplace and was warm and dry.

While Lily used the privy, the girl returned with bowls of steaming stew and chunks of bread; I pocketed the latter for tomorrow. Setting down the tray, she stammered, "I'm Cassie Cooper. I mean, Cassie Burke, Mrs. Burke." Misery was plain on her face. She was as young as I had supposed, perhaps sixteen, but her waist was thick, her skin was rough, and deep creases showed on either side of her mouth: life had already set its mark on her.

"I am Victor . . . Victor Hartmann." I was no more familiar with my name than she was with hers.

She nodded that quick bobbing nod.

"Sir, you are really the giant, aren't you? Why does your friend tease you?"

"I don't know why she says such things."

Cassie nodded again, with as much feeling as one might put into a nod, as if she, too, did not understand what caused people to act.

"And"—her glance up at me was furtive—"you don't wear that hood because you're too handsome, do you?"

I shook my head.

The words burst from her: "Once, Harry said he'd put an oat bag on my head before he'd let me in bed. That was my fault, you see, because I cried so hard at a sad story I once heard and had just remembered after years and years, and it made me all red and puffy."

Twisting her apron, she stopped speaking as suddenly as she had started.

"Even a queen cannot cry without reddening her eyes," I said.

"The queen?" Cassie at once forgot her distress. "Have you seen her? I don't mean, have you seen her cry, for she never does, she mustn't! But have you seen the queen at all? Oh!"

Lily had appeared at the door. Perhaps recognizing the arrogance in her posture, the girl half-curtsied.

"What tales are you telling, Victor?" Lily asked. "Of your many audiences with the queen?" Her voice was now sullen and mean-spirited.

"I brought you something to eat, miss," Cassie said.

Lily settled on the floor. She prodded at the bowl's lumpy

contents, pursing her lips with distaste. She pushed the bowl aside.

"I asked for cake. I cannot even give this a name."

"It is food from her children's mouths," I said tightly. "Thank you, Mrs. Burke."

"Oh, your dress is so beautiful, miss," Cassie said, rushing into the silence. "Why, it puts me in mind of a wedding. You must have been playing at being a bride when the storm came, and that's why the dress is dirty and torn. You'll need a new costume when you meet up with your group again, while this one is being repaired."

Lily said nothing. Under her stony eyes, the girl dropped her gaze. She stood before us without moving, fingers knotted in her apron. Her expectation was obvious and full of hurt.

"Would you like to sing for us now?" I asked.

Cassie sighed gratefully, but before she could open her mouth, from the house came a loud crash and a louder caterwaul, followed by a thin whimper.

"I cannot stop being a mum to blink!" she said, running out.

There were cries, more screams, a slap—abrupt silence that yielded to sobbing. I did not know if it was Cassie who wept or the child, as both their faces were wet when she returned. On one hip she held the child we had seen before, now squirming and blubbering; on the other hip, a squalling infant whose cheeks and neck bore inflamed boils ready for lancing. There was also a rapidly forming bump on the infant's forehead.

Ignoring both children, the girl strode determinedly to the center of the little room and began to sing.

She should have had a voice as sweet as her nature, making her presence in this town like a rose growing in a dung heap; alas, she did not. Her voice reminded me of a drunken barmaid's I might hear at night passing an inn. The older child twisted and kicked as she sang, begging to be let down. When Cassie ignored him, he struck her hard across the mouth.

The girl's lips trembled, then she burst into a fit of weeping and ran out.

"What ugly mewling brats," Lily said, her beautiful face drawn into disgust. "They should have been drowned at birth, the way you'd drown a litter of kittens."

She leaned against a wall and shut her eyes.

Late that night, a staggering step and mumbled curses warned me that Harry had at last returned. I prepared to leave. His angry words were followed by blows and crying, a sound I had heard too often these past hours. I put my finger to my lips to silence Lily and quietly walked outside.

The substance of Harry's argument was that his dinner had not been kept waiting for him.

"It would have dried to paste," Cassie said between hiccuppy sobs. "Let me cook you a meal right now. It won't take a minute."

"It'll still taste like paste," Harry growled. "Where is it? I'll eat it all the same."

"I—I gave it to a stray dog. I knew you wouldn't have wanted it and the dog was so hungry—"

"You gave my dinner to a dog? Damn you! Every time I turn my back you find another way to steal me blind!"

I made a scratching noise just below the window.

"There's the cur now, still hungry after your cooking, I'll wager. I'll show it what it will get here from now on!"

The shutters were thrown wide. Through them emerged a large hand clutching a boot, then a muscular arm, then a bearded face that turned this way and that. Harry Burke was tall and thick with a mean swaggering expression and downturned lips. Before he could spy me, I grabbed him by the throat and yanked him out of the window so forcefully he broke a shutter coming through. Loose thatch spilled over both of us as I slammed him against the wall repeatedly until he howled. I did not fear alarming the neighbors; they were accustomed to violence from this house. I grabbed the boot and, using its heel like a hammer, struck him full in the face and broke his nose. He gurgled a bloody plea.

From my right a mouse squeaked. I backed up, Harry still in my grip, and saw Cassie framed by the open window, her hands pressed to her mouth. Her forehead bore a fresh lump to match her infant's.

I pulled back my fist and held the pose, an archer taking careful aim, till Harry's eyes gaped. Then I shattered his jaw with a blow. Broken teeth flew out, his eyes rolled back to white, and he lost consciousness. Tossing his body aside, I smiled at the blood where his teeth had scraped along my knuckles. Then I thought, was it for *this* feeling rather than Cassie's protection that I had struck him?

Harry would blame her for this, too, I realized, if only because she had seen it happen.

From behind me Lily rushed up.

"Come with us," she said, grabbing Cassie's hands through the window. "This very moment. Do not stop to think."

Cassie looked back over her shoulder deeper into the cottage.

"The children," she whispered.

"Leave them! They are a millstone waiting to crush you. You can come with us, but you must leave now and you must come alone!"

A single tear slid down Cassie's cheek, all the sorrow she had left.

"Come," Lily urged her again. "You cannot think on it. The doing is always easier than the thinking."

The girl shook her head.

"Then you must tell Harry we were thieves," Lily said. "Say there were five of us, so that he will not have his mighty pride offended by being overcome by just one. Turn his pockets inside out, take his purse, and ransack your house for hiding places. But do not spend a halfpenny of whatever you find or he will know. Even if you wait for months, he will know! Bury the money where no one—*no one*—can see you do it. Where no one can ever find it. Save it for when you run away, which you must. If you have a third child, you will never escape. And never, for a moment, let him think a stranger was trying to save you."

The girl nodded, the understanding between them shockingly immediate.

I ran back to the woods, slowing only after I had stepped within the shadow of trees. Later I felt Lily's touch on my shoulder, letting me know she had returned.

Confused beyond reason, I did not ask how it was that she in her callousness had done more good than I in my attempt at compassion.

Drexham
November 28

"What's wrong?" I had asked Lily earlier at noon.

"The worm," she whispered.

She had scarcely touched her food. I thought at first it was our journey that stole her appetite. Exhaustion, too, played its part, as we had walked since morning, the second horse having also fallen lame from her abuse. At noon she gazed longingly at each mouthful I ate, while her own hand shook when she tried to bring to her lips the bread I had saved from yesterday. Her eyes filled with tears, and she dashed the morsel to the ground.

"The illness is still with you?" I asked.

She pulled her lips into a thin smile. "Did you think you had destroyed that along with everything else of mine? Would that you had." Her grin grew more dreadful. "It is eating me alive."

"We're close to the border," I said. "I had meant to bypass Drexham before we cross to Scotland. But I see that I'm wrong. Drexham is a city. There should be doctors in Drexham better than the one you had in Tarkenville."

"Doctors . . ." A strange light came into her face. Was it hope at last? "You're right, Victor. All I saw was the one, and who's to say he was capable? Drexham is a city. It will have many doctors." The light faded. "But I have no money for his fee."

"You could pay with your barrette," I said. "If it is very valuable, pry loose just one of the stones."

Lily's thin hand closed over the hair clasp, a last remembrance of her wedding. She darted me a look of hatred.

"You cling to your whore's necklace. Give it here and I'll pay with that, since it seems to have such value."

More sharp words sat on her tongue, but she did not say them. At last she shook her head and pressed her hands to her stomach, wincing.

It was dusk when Drexham appeared on the horizon, and night when we entered the city. We stayed close to its outer edge, as if the more easily to escape. Neighborhoods worsened, buildings sagged, alleys tightened. There was debris everywhere, from rotting garbage to such broken furniture as Mirabella had once salvaged for us.

Four poorly clad roughs slid from the darkness and blocked our path.

"You put yourself in more danger than you know," I said, having no wish to fight.

"Did you hear that, Jack?" one of them said to a thin,

weasel-faced man. "He's a bleedin' gentleman, givin' the four o' us the opportunity to run from the one o' him."

Jack signaled to them to circle us.

Lily pointed to a nearby crate. "I'm tired. May I sit while I watch?"

Her request surprised him into a laugh and he nodded. As she sat down, the shepherd's blanket she had been wearing as a shawl fell aside.

"Eddie, look at the white dress!" Jack said to the runt of the group, and then to me: "I know who you are. There's money on your head." He pointed to Lily's barrette. "And *that* is not paste." I could hear his greed coagulate into thought.

The four of them rushed me at once.

A few easy blows drove off two of the men, but Jack enjoyed the fight, and Eddie possessed annoying tenacity. They took my own restrained swipes as a game, insulting me playfully as they tugged on my cloak until I turned and swung at empty air.

"What is wrong, Victor?" Lily taunted. "You fight as if you're blindfolded."

My next blow landed sharply, and she applauded.

Jack jumped me from behind and dragged my hood away. Eddie backed up in wonder.

"No wonder he's got to steal his women." Eddie shuddered. "It makes me crawlylike even to think about it." With a grin, he said to Lily, "We're doin' you a tremendous service, miss." He picked up a loose board from the debris and swung it like a bat to test its heft.

"Have a go at him, Eddie." Jack bowed with a great flourish, then withdrew to Lily's side, familiarly slipping his arm around her shoulders.

These men were gnats and did not know how easily they might be squashed.

Eddie swung and poked and prodded with the board. I moved as quickly as he, yet only to block his blows. I pushed him away again and again till luck allowed him to slam the board against my ear. The breath whistled from my lips. I snatched the board away as from a naughty child and shoved him down with my palm flat on his chest.

Jack was less careless and much faster. He leapt in and out beyond my reach, peppering my body with a dozen differently aimed blows till he thought he had found a weakness in my lower torso and hammered at the point. Each blow stoked my temper.

"Victor, I shall lose my honor to them at this rate," Lily said, feigning a yawn.

Eddie joined in the attack but complained, "The trouble is, he's so tall. From where we stand, he's all body and no head."

"Still you have bested me," I said, gritting my teeth against the struggle to strike back. I clutched my side dramatically. "I will piss blood for a week."

"'Bested you'?" Jack repeated in a simpering voice. "There's no reward for 'bestin' you.' You are dead already, only you don't know it."

"Yes, he does," Lily said, with such mirth that I turned. Eddie grabbed the board again and raked it along my face. I knocked him down so hard he lay senseless in a puddle.

"What was it that spurred you just then?" she asked, jumping up. "The memory of what you are? Then think on it once more, for the last ruffian will not give up. And if my laughter is not enough, look at the brute and see our little songbird's Harry. Imagine his heavy hand against her pimply face. Think on that and on what else Harry is doing to her this night for what you did to him the last."

Sharp pain in my lower back so coincided with her words I thought they had cut me. Fire flashed up my spine and down my leg and made my foot jerk. I reached around. Jack's hand was beneath mine, gripping a knife handle.

Lily gasped.

"Victor!" she said in a hushed voice.

The rage locked up inside me rushed out through the open wound, faster than blood and just as mortal—rage at this thief who stupidly sought out his own death; at Harry Burke, who, though as cruel as I, could live as a man; at Lily, who spoke such tormenting words of truth; at myself, who had felt dark enjoyment last night at the feel of bones being crushed—so much rage I trembled. The blood within me boiled to a dance that shook each limb.

I grabbed Jack's wrist, jerked him so viciously his arm popped from its socket, and held him, dangling, his body supported now not by a joint but by tender muscle and skin that threatened to rip beneath the weight. He lifted his weasel face to the night sky and screamed. Around him decaying walls echoed both his agony and my answering laugh.

"It is enough," Lily said firmly.

I looked down. She had come to stand beside me, an act far braver than she could ever imagine.

Like a savage inarticulate beast, I shook the body to indicate I was not done with it, causing Jack to howl again.

"It is enough," Lily repeated, very softly, touching my hand.

What should she care, I thought, about my actions or their consequences? Defiantly I snapped Jack upward again. His scream wound down to a whimper that so annoyed me I at last swung him by the arm against the nearest building. His face striking the brick at last silenced him.

"Come with me, Victor. He will bother us no more."

"Come with . . . you?" I said, trying to let the overflow of anger spill out through my panting breath. Blood beat in my ears, and my limbs throbbed. "Did you not goad me to act?"

"To do what was necessary to keep our freedom."

Was this freedom?

Lily reached up and touched my chest.

"You are hurt, and the knife still sticks from your back. But he stabbed you through the cloak. Perhaps it is not deep."

I reached round for the blade's handle.

"Let me," she said. "You must sit first. You're too tall for me to pull it out straight. Sit there, where I was before."

I would have made tinder of the crates had I sat. I used the sturdiest as support and knelt, sucking in my breath with the effort. Lily leaned her shoulder against my spine for leverage. The knife burned as much going out as going in and I had to steel myself against turning on her.

She unfastened my cloak, let it drop, gently pulled up my shirt to examine me.

"He stabbed you just above the hip, too close to the side to do the damage he intended. Either that, or all your insides are in the wrong place. Perhaps tonight you're fortunate to be a monster."

Reaching beneath her dress, she ripped cloth from one of her undergarments, wadded it up, and pressed it tightly against the wound to staunch the bleeding. Then she guided my hand to where hers had been and told me to keep it pressed there. When I twisted round with the movement, again my breath whistled through my teeth. She ripped the rest of the undergarment into strips that she tied round my waist to secure the bandage.

"When we find the doctor, you must see him, too. You may need stitches."

With her continued display of concern, I could not trust what words might come from my lips. As if knowing how she perplexed me, she said, "Do not mistake what I do for affection. I still hate you. Yet I could not manage without your protection. I will go north with you to the islands you mentioned. When my home has been restored, you will escort me back. Till then I must, at the least, keep you alive."

She spoke of her hate as sweetly as if she gave compliments, smiling to show a dimpled cheek. And why not? At her wedding, had not her cheeks shone beautiful and fair while the worm ate at her guts?

Yet I understood. I myself was no more than a trained horse that could strike the ground and thus appear to do sums. I write, having only the words of men and none of their feelings.

Lily was too tired to go farther, so we are resting in a sheltered corner. I grow tired of writing, so I pull my other book, Walton's journal, from my pocket and read.

She writes: Did I think of her today? No, I did not. This morning I saw the creature's spoor, I smelled where it marked its territory, I heard in the forest's stunned silence that it had passed just minutes before. Should I see a pile of dung and think of her? I cannot understand her.

Did she come to Germany, come to show off her new husband, to torment me? "See how well I have lived my life without you," she seemed to say. I thought the girl would be there, too. She said no, she must have this time alone with her husband. What shall I do? I need to see if the girl . . .

My head is bound with a band of gold, wound ever tighter like a clock spring, tighter and tighter, till I think it is a crown of thorns I wear.

I played the madman for Margaret's husband—the fool!— though she herself did not seem to notice. What does that signify?

*That I am not so mad as I thought? Or that I was mad before,
and that is why she never noticed? He actually gave me money
when we parted, as if he could buy her from me. How much is a
sister worth? How much a wife?*

◇

*I re-read the above. So many months have passed! Could
I have written such blasphemy? I do not feel the time, I do not
feel the changes in me. I had thought to play the madman for
her husband, but the player has become the role. I am becoming
mad.*

Later

Walton's insane portrait was a mirror into which I dare not
look. Just the thought of it made me restless, which woke
Lily. Even though it was too late to ask for a doctor, and no fit
person was awake to ask, she insisted that we leave our rough
shelter and walk through the city. As she followed me, her
mood became silent.

We came to a part of Drexham that sat along a river. The
water churned with an awful, deliberate sound and ran muddy and
opaque. No breath stirred, save the frost from our own mouths.
The odor that had accompanied us since the woodshed thickened and hung rank and pungent in the motionless air.

A terrible sound tore through the night—a long, low groan
that hitched up into a high squeal, then just as suddenly was
silenced.

Jack had cried so with *his* pain.

Nodding to myself, I walked with more purpose.

The building where the cry had originated was not surrounded by others the way the tenements were crowded
together. It stood apart, backing directly onto the river.

Despite the hour, dim lights shone in the first floor; and an open door cast a pale yellow square onto an empty stretch of fenced-in yard.

"The sound came from there," Lily said. She lifted her head and sniffed. "The smell, too."

I strode to the gate, entered, and crossed to the open door. The yard was wet and sucked at my boots.

The wide doorway led just inside the building to a bare room floored in stone that had been heavily tracked with mud. The smell was painful, as of something gone rancid in the hot sun. Inside the room was a small wooden pen, about chest high to a man, that opened onto the door of a second room. Lily stepped into the pen to see better.

"Oh, my God!" she cried. I followed, anticipating what she had found.

The second room was awash in blood, as was the short muscular man who stood before us, holding a dripping blade. Bits of gore clung to his clothes, his beard, his fleshy though pale face. He wore a leather apron to little effect, as his entire front, both shirt and trousers, glistened red as though splashed with paint. At his feet lay a steer, its slit throat gushing a steady stream onto the already-drenched floor. Behind him skinned and gutted carcasses hung from wooden frames, their bodies still draining. Strewn about the floor, sometimes half-covered in blood, lay severed animal heads, their watchful eyes adding to the nightmarish scene.

The cry had led us to a slaughterhouse.

After twin nights of brutality, what more fitting place for me to consider my nature?

The blood-covered butcher scowled and waved the knife.

"You gave me a start!" he said. "It wasn't enough I didn't knock it out with the first blow." He pointed toward a sledge-hammer leaning against the pen. "Now you made me jump and I didn't get a good bleed. A month from now some guv'ner will get a tough piece and blame me. And will I be able to blame you? No!"

He bent over and skinned the animal with a sureness and an economy of movement that were frightening to watch.

"We British must have our beef. Biggest beefeaters in the world, don't you know. Give a man a steak and he can conquer the most savage tribe, eh?" He gave us a glance. "Still, it's not often I get customers at midnight, and as strange as yourselves. Although, perhaps, that's not why you're here?" He gestured with his butcher's knife in a way that emphasized its deadly efficient blade.

"I need a doctor," Lily whispered. "But . . ." Her eyes darted wildly from body to bloody body.

"But you're curious, huh? Let me show you."

He returned to work, folding the steer's skin and laying it atop a pile on a wooden table. He quickly sliced off the head, knocked it aside, and dragged the flayed body toward an empty frame. To the animal's rear legs he attached metal fasteners that dug into the bone; these in turn were attached to ropes that led to the top of the frame. He meant to pull the carcass up to let it hang neck downward like the others. Straining against the weight, the man's pale face mottled with the effort.

I walked across the slippery floor, took the ropes, and with one long pull hauled the body up by myself. The man tied it off quickly. Not quickly enough—my stab wound burned. If the bleeding had slowed, it no doubt started up again now.

"That's right gentlemanly of you, sir," he said, tying off the ropes. "It's properly a three-man job but with my boy sick and the other one—well, the laggard was drunk again. But I'm not so grateful as to be foolish. Men have been killed for far less than a good piece of meat." He took up the knife again.

"The woman spoke the truth. She needs a doctor."

"And how did you decide to be askin' such as me for a medical reference?"

"Look at me!" Lily said impatiently. She took off her blanket, holding it high so it did not drag on the filthy floor, and stepped closer to one of the lanterns. Its flickering light emphasized her ghoulishly thin face and shadowed eyes and showed how loosely her bride's dress hung on her frame. "And look at him!" She jerked her head at me dismissively. "Should we stop a carriage in the park? Should we ask a Beau Brummell or one of his admirers?"

The sight of what would have confirmed another man's suspicions seemed to finally erase the butcher's.

"My name is Bishop. Slaughterin' Bishop is what they call me."

He extended his hand to me. Fresh blood hid neither the network of scars that crisscrossed his skin, scars enough to rival mine, nor the missing top joint of his thumb. Seeing me stare, Bishop laughed and held both hands up for Lily to see as well. On his other, the forefinger was also missing its first joint.

"A butcher's hands, without doubt," he said proudly. "The Masons have their secret shake and we have ours: wiggling our nubs against each other." He fingered what was left of the thumb. "As long as there's enough of a stump to rest the handle against, I won't be without work."

He crossed to his set of knives and picked up the largest.

"This is what you do every day?" Lily asked. Another woman, a man even, might have fainted at so much blood. I did not know whether to admire her ability to be unmoved, or to fear it.

"Yes, miss," Bishop said, "and, as you can see, many a night, too."

He dragged a large tin tub to the newly hoisted carcass, took the knife, and split the carcass down the middle of its chest. With one seamless motion he grabbed the flow of entrails with his left hand; with his right, he reached inside toward the back to free up the liver and pull it away. Using the knife again, he sliced through the diaphragm to loosen the heart and lungs and let the whole mess spill into the tub.

If Jack had been more clever with his knife, I wondered, what would he have found in me? Suddenly the room grew dark and tilted, and I had to grab the wooden frame that held the carcass for support. Bishop mistook my leaning close as my own interest and said: "Those that know, know it's an art of sorts. One little nick"—he pointed at the intestines—"and you've poisoned half your customers. Course I'd deny it, say it was a storage problem."

"What do you do . . . ," I began, still dizzy. "What do you do with the rest of the body?"

I made myself step closer to the tub. I had brutalized two men when a few strong blows would have achieved the same end. Perhaps I had been led here to be reminded of what I am.

"Oh, most everything gets used," Bishop said. "The fat makes soap, heads and feet go for glue, skins get tanned, bones get ground for fertilizer. The bits that are left get swept out that hole there and washed into the river."

Flipping back my cloak, I forced myself to plunge both hands into the tub's sticky, already-cooling mess, not caring that it bloodied the sleeves and front of my shirt beyond cleaning. I drew out the enormous heart, still attached to veins and arteries. I half-expected it to start beating.

"What call do you get for organs?"

"Some are considered delicacies. I've a mind you're leading me to something else."

Lily laughed, though not cruelly.

"Yes, tell where you're leading him, Victor," she said, "where you're leading yourself. Tell Slaughterin' Bishop what sometimes happens to the organs. Show him."

Bishop backed away and held up the knife.

Dropping the heart into the tub, I took off my cloak. I gave Bishop a moment to consider my face, then I pulled up my shirt to display my chest. I could not see whether the bandage at my back had soaked through.

"I've been laid open and filled up," I said. "Some days I wonder with what."

Bishop whistled appreciatively and grinned. "Sloppy work, that is. Still, I'd like to meet the butcher that did that."

"'Twas no butcher, sir," Lily said. "'Twas his father. A medical man. Or so Victor says. Is it possible? Or does he lie just to be sweet? Some men have the strangest way of courting."

Bishop frowned.

"I know nothing about courtin', miss, and as for your question—well, I guess anythin's possible when you're as ignorant as me."

He picked up the steer's heart and held it appraisingly. "Might be too big, though, even for you. Hogs, now, there's a thought."

"Hogs?" Lily laughed. "Oh, Victor, you shall make your fortune hunting truffles!"

I looked at my hands, and then at the bodies, the heads, the eyes that looked back with their own questioning gaze. I had come here to shock myself, to turn the truths I had only read about in my father's journal into bloody reality, to discover—what? What would Winterbourne have thought if he had been present tonight? What would he have thought of me?

Abruptly I pulled down my shirt and threw on my cloak. Its bottom edges were now soaked in blood.

"It's past time we left," I said.

"Is it?" said Bishop. "You never did tell me your business here."

"We did! You never answered!" Lily cried. She clutched a fistful of the white lace at her abdomen. "Do you know a doctor?"

The butcher stared at us, his eyes moving from Lily to me and back again.

"None as would be happy to see the two of you at this hour. Go down three blocks to the Fightin' Cock Tavern. Tell 'em Slaughterin' Bishop said to give you somethin' to eat and a place to stay. Tomorrow noon go to High Street and ask for Dr. Fortnam."

I nodded my thanks and gestured to Lily. When she left, Bishop grabbed hold of my arm and pulled me close.

"Tell me," he asked urgently. "What really happened to you?"

"I do not know."

He grinned. "Well, it was a good joke, just the same. A hog's heart, indeed."

The shed behind the Fighting Cock, where we are now, holds a straw mattress, a blanket, and even a candle stub. There is no basin, no water to wash my bloody hands, but there will never be water enough to wash them clean.

In the corner, Lily sleeps as peacefully as ever, influenced by nothing. Still, her continued presence is becoming an unexpected comfort even beyond its novelty.

Though she has no understanding of the place's significance, she has said she will accompany me to the Orkneys. We must fly there all the faster.

Later

At dawn we were wakened by a loud knock on the shed and found a bowl of oatmeal and a tankard of ale outside the door. Lily gagged on one spoonful, and I ate the rest.

Outside she asked a passerby for Drexham's market. As in Rome and Venice, I hunched beneath my cloak and drew the hood low. Lily distracted merchants with sharp criticism of their goods while from behind I raided the cash boxes on their carts. Toward late morning Lily thought we had payment for the doctor.

Soon after, we found Dr. Fortnam on High Street. The building, the very avenue, had a look of such propriety even beggars seemed to be intimidated: there were none to be seen. While I considered this from the alley, Lily darted away from me, undoubtedly confident that her true station in life would be instantly recognized despite her appearance. She was admitted to the surgery, only to emerge minutes later, angry, holding a slip of paper.

"He could not have examined you in so short a time," I said.

"No, he would not see me at all. The woman there said that he treats the *poor* and the *unfortunate*, but separately from his respectable appointments. I was to leave at once. He will see me at eight o'clock tonight"—she held out the paper—"at this address."

That night, in a run-down neighborhood, we stood before the building designated on the scrap of paper; it was entirely dark, then a lamp flared on the second floor.

"Does your wound require a doctor's care?" Lily asked, not wanting to go alone.

Without looking, I said, "No, the bleeding has stopped."

I was unwilling to be confined in so small a place as that upstairs room.

There was silence as she looked at the light.

"He will leave soon if you do not go," I said.

"There are so many kinds of death," she murmured, as if she had not heard, "and I fear each one." She started toward the door, then ran back. "Here." Removing her barrette, she thrust it at me. "I have his fee in coin. He shall not get a penny more!"

At great length she reappeared. Teetering in the doorway, she grabbed the jamb. Her eyes glittered wildly; her mouth was set into a ghastly smile.

"I am too far gone," she whispered. "There is nothing he can do." She pounded my chest and cried, "Coward!"

"Coward?"

Fury quickly spent, she slumped against me.

"I am a coward, else I would end this thing myself. End it now, for my suffering has not even begun."

I held her close in silence until I felt her composure return. She straightened her back and stiffened her manner. In a few minutes she pushed me away. "Do not hold me so tightly," she complained. "There is a horsy odor about you that makes me long for a whip." She brushed herself off as if I had befouled her. Her expression was indifferent; her hands trembled.

"What is it?" I asked softly.

"Should I tell *you*?" she asked, her voice rising. "That would be like telling one of my hounds. What can an animal know of a woman's pain?"

"Obviously as little as the woman knows of the animal's."

Dumfries
November 30

Scotland at last! Crag gives way to bog, black woods to glen—the ever-changing landscape of the Highlands. The Scottish weather, as sharp as my thoughts and just as changeable, seems to bring me salt in every breath I take. The sea is just beyond the moment, and beyond that, the Orkneys!

I feel an optimism today I did not feel yesterday: perhaps my spirit knew the exact moment it trod on Scottish soil. Given the enmity between the English and Scots, I no longer fear pursuit. I move of my own will now. I hasten toward, rather than from.

Shrouded by last night's visit to the doctor, Lily does not share in my good cheer. She is more tired, as if the doctor's confirmation somehow made her illness more real.

She is being eaten by a worm. . . .

I shudder at the thought, while knowing it is the fate of all men. How curious that I, not a man, was food for the worms before I ever breathed.

These thoughts are morose!

No longer will the smell of burning itch my nose, or the stain of blood sully my hands. No longer will I see faces in the shadows, from my father, who would deny my existence, to Winterbourne, who would reproach me with what might have been. I will create my own life just as I was created: apart from the natural order.

And if I am able to leave my past behind, perhaps Lily shall, too. Beneath her paleness, she is still beautiful; beneath her cross words, she is still my companion by her own choice.

December 4

Lily spoke little, ate less, and walked more and more slowly. Just lifting her gaze from ground to sky seemed to exhaust her. That she did not dispute my every decision was the surest proof of her fatigue: she had not the strength to complain.

I sought out a place more comfortable than the ones I had been choosing. About eleven at night, I broke into a small barn, set a distance from a cottage. The barn held an ancient horse, a lean cow, and scraggly chickens, as well as hay, feed, and a few farm implements. I spoke gently and stroked the horse. When it calmed, so did the other animals.

I made a bed for Lily at the back of the barn, behind bales of hay, and laid her down. I planned to nap a few hours, but to give her as much sleep as possible. Instead, I myself slept through. Shortly after dawn, voices from outside the barn woke me, but Lily did not stir. I crept closer to listen.

An older man was sharply giving instructions to a youth regarding the care of the cottage during his two days' absence. His commands seemed endless. Finally a carriage pulled up and took him away. Not five minutes later, I heard the voice of a boy. The young man passed to the boy his just-assigned chores of milking the cows and feeding the chickens so that he, too, could be off. He gave the boy a coin and promised another on his return.

"If I find you did nae keep still, but went braggin' round your kith how you run the farm in my stead," he said, as sharply as the older man, "I'll give you a beating *and* get my money back."

"I'll tell no one. You know I mean it."

The young man hurried off, whistling a gay tune.

The boy performed his duties quickly, letting the animals out into the fenced yard and throwing feed on the ground.

He brought out a bucket, hurriedly milked the cow, then took the milk away with him. Lily slept through everything.

The cottage was simple enough to break into; a loose shutter gained me entrance to the bedroom. Inside were a clothespress, washstand, chamber pot, and a straw bed piled with quilts. The kitchen held a table and chairs; cooking utensils hung over the fireplace. At one end of the room stood a wooden deacon's bench, a hooked rug before it on the puncheon floor. Just outside the kitchen was a larder with steps leading to a root cellar. The cellar held potatoes, carrots, turnips, onions, and a barrel of meat covered with foamy brine.

If alone, I might have done no more than raid the larder. But Lily was undoubtedly still tired. I unlocked the cottage from the inside, woke her, and explained that we could use the cottage till the next day. We need only keep out of sight when the boy came to milk the cow that evening.

Together with her long hours of sleep, the idea of using the cottage as our own enlivened her. She cooked a quick meal of eggs, then set about preparing a chicken for the afternoon, early enough so the chimney would no longer smoke by the time the boy returned. She surprised me by scraping carrots and potatoes, then taking an axe and killing the chicken herself. Her blow was not clean, but from lack of strength, not nerve. She repositioned the dying animal at once and delivered the final stroke. For a moment I thought the exertion might be too much, for she seemed dazed as she stared at the rivulet flowing from the neck.

"It's always easier than you think it will be, isn't it? You need only do it."

She tossed me the bird to pluck; a spray of blood arced through the air.

Earlier she had set pots of water on the fire to boil. Once the meal was simmering in a Dutch oven, she declared she wanted a bath and told me to drag in from the barn the wooden tub she had spied there. I pushed back the table and chairs, carried in the tub, and pumped bucket after bucket to fill it halfway. Lily added boiling water till she found the temperature tolerable, then shooed me out. She hummed as she bathed, her voice carrying outside to where I sat below the shuttered window.

An hour later she showed me her transformation: she was not only clean, and her hair washed, but also in fresh clothes taken from the press. From a pair of trousers she had cut off length, and in a belt she had punched a new hole. The cottager's tucked-in shirt bunched thickly at her waist. She still wore her hair swept up with the jeweled barrette.

"Now it is your turn," she said, unbuttoning the throat of my shirt. "You are more filthy than I was. I will not let you sit down to dinner without a bath. The tub is cold, but the kettle is still steaming, and so is this pot. Go on now." She ran outside and shut the door after her.

I undressed slowly, aware that just an hour ago she had undressed in this very spot; aware, too, of how lighthearted she was today. How long would her mood last? How far would Lily play the wife?

I picked up her wedding gown that lay forgotten in a corner, breathed in her scent, and brushed the lace against my lips. The lace had felt rough that day I had tried to take her. Time and travel had worn it smooth, perhaps had done the same to Lily. She was not a woman to be forced in the dirt. Neither would she be snared by domesticity; yet, surprisingly, it had its power on me.

Before me stood the tub filled with her bathwater. I did not add any warmth, as if to do so would dilute whatever of her might remain. The tub was too small for me. I lowered myself and sat in it anyway, feet on the outside, body wedged against the wood. I cupped the water and washed my scarred face; cupped the water and let it spill over my scarred body. This water had touched her skin; now it touched mine.

I imagined approaching her with subtlety and delicate enticements; I imagined a drawing-room seduction. But imagining, too, Lily beneath my hands, I felt crude passion rise up instead. I could expect no more: *I* was crude, crudely fashioned, with raw, unpolished thoughts and abhorrent desires. I did not have a man's sensibilities, nor could I fathom a woman's heart. Lily was right: what could *I* know of humanity?

Chastened, I finished my bath quickly and once more put on my same soiled clothes. There was nothing in the clothespress into which I might change.

Bound by this ill humor, I threw open the kitchen door and tipped over the tub. From the yard where she had been waiting, Lily called me to stop. "You should take more care," she said. "The boy will become suspicious if he sees a puddle by the door."

I thought she knew of my desire but understood not to speak of it. I thought she . . .

She served me dinner, touching my arm lightly as she passed back and forth between the hearth and the table, brushing my knuckles as she reached for the saltcellar. I barely tasted the food but was pleased to see her eat.

"It is just this once, since I cooked it."

"Then perhaps we should stay here forever," I answered.

The afternoon grew late. I washed the dishes, put out the fire, made sure the barn was as I had found it, and locked the cottage from the inside. We waited in the kitchen in silence. Lily sat on the deacon's bench restlessly and from time to time crossed to the window.

"You are anxious," I said.

"I do not wish to be made to leave."

"You can see yourself here?" I asked. "In such a place?"

"Can you?"

"If it were as today, yes."

"Was today so wonderful?"

Today I had seen a small promise of what life might be, but could not say the words.

"Hush," I told her. "There's the boy."

Lily peered out through a crack in the shutters. "He's wearing boots," she said, considering her own feet. With her wedding slippers worn to scraps, she had put on a pair of the farmer's shoes but they were ill fitting. "Perhaps his boots will be more comfortable than these." She reached toward the latch, then pulled back.

"We'd have to leave at once. Tomorrow when he returns will be soon enough. We have the night before us."

"Yes, the night."

She sat on the bench, I at her feet, both of us listening as the animals were brought into the barn. Her face grew thoughtful, her eyes distant. Something made her unhappy; perhaps the talk of a simple domestic life emphasized her own uncertainty. The worm ruled her. What manner of future, if any, would it allow her?

As the sun set, red light glowed through the crack where the shutters did not meet, dividing the shadows with a single stripe of rose that moved across Lily's face. She must have seen the same on mine for she bent forward and stroked my cheek.

"You are all pink—like a flower, like a sweet William."

I caught her palm and kissed it.

"Now I must call you sweet Victor instead," she murmured.

A rattle at the door made me leap to my feet—then a

second rattle, as the shutters were tried and found locked. The boy was securing the cottage for the night.

Lily also stood up and faced the cold hearth. Placing my hands lightly on her shoulders, I felt what my eyes had not perceived: all her softness was gone. I had already seen her stomach's bloat of starvation; now I felt how her softness had wasted to the thinnest pad of flesh. Despite that—whether because of the sunset's forgiving shadows, or because of my own need for her not to be sick, at least for this one night—she was more beautiful than ever.

Standing behind her, afraid to see her face, I offered her my hand. Between us lay a chasm of immeasurable depth and width, unfathomable thought and desire. She reached up across the blackness, placed her hand in mine, and turned.

"Victor," she whispered. She did not look up.

"Yes, Lily."

"I'm sorry."

"You have done nothing. It is I who am sorry. I have naught to give you. Instead, all I've done is take."

"When we met," she said, "it was already too late. Everything precious had already been thrown away. There was nothing left for you to take. I am sorry for that as well."

Stepping away, she tried to free her hand.

"Shhh." I would not let her go.

At my touch, she relaxed and let me pull her close. I bent low, nuzzled her hair, brushed with my lips the bare skin of her neck.

She broke my clasp gently and, without looking at me, walked into the bedroom. I heard a flint strike, the clothes-press open and shut, the shoes softly drop, the straw mattress tick—then another sound, unfamiliar, a quiet *shush* repeated over and over.

I stepped through the open door. Lily sat on the bed facing away from me. She was dressed in a white nightshirt worn to a whisper, her clothes on the floor in a pile. The candle stood on the washstand between us, casting our separate shadows on separate walls.

The unfamiliar *shush*, repeated over and over, was the sound of Lily brushing her hair. The raven curls were knotted, their color had dulled, and yet—something about the gesture moved me in ways I could not understand. For eons, women have brushed their hair at night while their men watched. It seemed that all of time had led us to this moment.

Lucio's wife had unpinned her hair and combed it with her fingers before she and Lucio made love.

And Mirabella . . .

I moved to Lily's side. She knew I was crossing the room— I saw her hand pause in its downward descent at the sound of my footfall, saw her look up at the wall where my shadow covered hers—but when I came to her, pulled her to her feet, and embraced her, she shrank back. At first all I could see were her tears and the inexplicable anguish in her eyes. There was nothing else, nothing more important to me. What made her cry like this? And how could I comfort her?

"How dare you touch me!"

Despite her tears, her mouth writhed with repulsion.

"Dare?" I repeated, not understanding. I clutched her. Every struggle sent sensation roaring through my body. "Was I not invited to touch you? When I kissed your palm, did you not call me 'sweet Victor'?"

"I say the same nonsense to the hound that licks my foot!" she cried, striking my face with the hairbrush. Cheek stinging, I knocked the brush to the floor, grabbed her arms, and wrenched them behind her back.

"I was led by the open door to your bed," I said, fighting

to hold her tighter. "What man would not be teased by such an invitation?"

"A man, yes. I would not have teased a man."

"You also should not have teased a monster!"

I seized her face and pressed my lips, as black as ash, against hers. Twisting her mouth away, she spat and wiped her mouth.

"A monster? Is that what you think you are?" she asked. "At best you are only some freakish animal."

"Animal?" The word penetrated to the heart of my fears and echoed Walton's accusations.

"Yes," she said lightly. "An animal. You can be no more than the parts from which you claim to be made, can you? In the end, you are like some great hound given too much license, who eats from the table and sleeps on the bed."

My hold on her loosened as passion was replaced by violence. She slid from my grasp. Instead of running, she stood not inches away as she continued: "You are not a man, Victor. Neither are you a monster. You are nothing."

How quickly every drop of lust turned to blistering madness.

"You do not know the danger you put yourself in," I said.

"You would give *me* the same warning as those street ruffians? At least that is more than you gave Harry Burke!"

Of itself my hand tightened into a fist and struck at her. At the last moment I turned an inch and slammed the wall next to her eye. Plaster fell to the floor in chunks. Lily jumped at the blow, but did not move from the spot. She laughed and cried at once, as though, in her lunacy, she was confused by what she wanted.

"Can't you see how pathetic you are?"

She lifted her chin and held her arms wide. She was so close to me, so close and small, like a porcelain doll; so close, so eager to be hurt. I seized the washstand and smashed it against the wall. Bowl and pitcher shattered, threw shards against her bare feet. The candle dropped, sputtered, smothered the room in black. Blindly I reached out. I grabbed her by the hair and dragged her to me.

"Do you know what my father thought of you?" she asked, voice tight. "My father thought your existence meant the end of all meaning in the world. But you are nothing so grand. If my father saw you now, all he'd see is a dog eager to lap cunt."

Crying out, I knocked her aside, stumbled from the cottage, and ran into the woods.

I was not a man? I was not a monster? At best I was an animal? Then I would be one fully; she would not take that little from me: I would glory in it. Piece by piece I shed my clothes, that poor disguise of humanity that I had worn always in vain; piece by piece I shed the mask till I ran naked. In the thick underbrush, stickers and branches made a gauntlet that would flay me of this skin, stolen from men to hide the beast beneath. I ran mile after mile, deeper and deeper into the woods, until, at last, they claimed me for their own, and I was no longer not a man, no longer not a monster; I became in my mind an animal in truth, a wondrous, undiscovered species.

If only the woods had been magic as in a child's story. . . . The illusion would have been complete: the forest could have woven enchantment about me and grown me hooves to cover the soles of my feet, fur to preserve my limbs and body. Imagining these, wishing for these, I felt my senses, ever sharp, flood with a beast's thousand perceptions: I thought I smelled in the wind the next town. I thought I heard the breathy snores and muttered dreams of men, tasted a dozen women sleeping in their dozen beds.

The path before me tightened on either side with cruel

thorns and jagged twists of brambles, yet both gave way like silk against my imagined fur, caressing me into feverish pleasure. On and on I ran. At a point determined by instinct alone I turned and burst through the arching branches that formed the overgrown path. I found myself in a clearing where a herd of deer had been at rest. At first paralyzed, they rose up as one and leapt away, tails flicking as they scattered to the left and right.

Setting my eyes on a young doe, I rapidly closed the distance between us till her hooves snapped at me with each vault. I matched her leap for leap till I sensed her spirit flag under my ceaseless pursuit. Only then did I quicken my pace. I reached out, grabbed her from behind by the thighs, and forced her to slow. Her hooves battered my knees, then she reared up in front to try to shake me loose, but I held on until she stopped running. I grasped her firmly along her flanks till her kicking quieted to fearful shudders, and then lifted her up to meet me, to join with me as no woman ever willingly had. She panicked and once more I gentled her, this time with a low shushing moan. I was kind to her, though it was not kindness that had led me to such desperation.

At the last moment I cried out from the pain of knowing there had been no one human to accept me.

I was Victor Hartmann. Hart-man. Animal man. Lily had named me well.

Exhaustion overtook me. I woke hours later, naked. A thousand cuts scored my flesh, and my whole body ached and stung: that was the truth, not an imagined metamorphosis. I stood up and slowly retraced my path through the woods, piece by piece reclaiming the poor possessions I had shed, piece by piece again disguising myself as a man.

Walton alone understood me. Walton alone knew what I am. Now he is dead. What am I without him?

Dawn had just begun to pinken the sky when I could see in the distance the cottage's thatched roof.

Oh that my heart had—

I stopped. The words had no sooner whispered in my ear than I realized my habit of poetry was only a trick, a novelty, a trained response: instead of feeling, I have learned to echo someone else's feelings. On command, the parrot sings, and I quote a verse.

Last night I had fled the violence that awaited me in this place. In fleeing, did I truly choose against violence? Or did I simply choose a corruption deemed, in men's eyes, much worse? Perhaps that is why I walked back to the cottage, for only by returning, and seeing Lily, and not being enraged, could I learn the answer.

She sat outside the door of the cottage, already prepared to leave, dressed in the shirt and trousers she had taken from the clothespress after her bath. Over these she wore a heavy jacket. Beside her lay my cloak and a small bundle, perhaps of food.

She stood at once at the sound of my step.

"I am sorry," she said softly, her head low. Her eyes, fixed on the ground, were red and swollen; she was still crying. "The words I spoke . . . were not true. Nothing I said in that room was true. *Nothing.*"

Even so small a reference to last night summoned up each poisonous remark. The blood beat in my temple, the skin there jumped, the heat rushed to my face. How might I answer such an apology? How might I regard the evidence of her tears?

I said nothing, fighting for self-mastery. On tiptoe, she reached up and for a brief wounded moment laid her palm against my scarred cheek. Her hand, cool in the morning air, quivered like a butterfly's wing. All I could see was how easily it might be crushed.

"My father's opinion meant much to you, did it not?" Her ability to cut to the heart of me was unerring. "The words I claimed were his . . . those were my uncle's words." I still did not reply, and she said, "In the beginning, my father spoke well of you. He thought you had shown courage and restraint given my uncle's treatment."

"And later," I said, speaking at last, "what did your father say later? After he had discovered the truth and tried to kill me? Before I then killed him."

"Later, he spoke very little." She risked a glimpse at my face, so swift a look I felt myself to be Medusa. "He was disappointed in himself for having reacted with such severity."

"And you, Lily, are you disappointed in yourself? Will you now tolerate the freak and treat it as a man? Perhaps it does not matter. I'm certain you could hate a man just as well."

"You are not a freak," she said.

She touched me lightly on the arm, although her eyes did not meet mine, and she seemed to curl in upon herself and grow smaller. But I was not to be appeased.

"If I am not a freak, what am I?"

"I'm sorry," she repeated, as though that answered my question.

"I think your sorrow is another lie. Your words of contrition are as deliberate as the words you spoke last night."

This time her glance was sharp and direct.

"I am not my words," she said, with a faint smile, as if to say that included the apology she had just made. "Here is my deed instead: I will stay with you."

"Where is the benefit in that?"

She would have spoken again, rashly I think, but in the end

decided to keep still. I, too, kept still, till my blood beat more softly and my face felt cool in the dewy morning air.

At last I bent down to pick up my cloak and the bundle. I saw, for the first time, that Lily wore not the shoes she had yesterday taken from the cottager but a pair of boots, new and unmarked, save for a dark stain on one toe.

December 7

Three days without writing . . . My memories of the cottage and the woods were so painful, should I have used blood for ink? So short a time ago I had written, *I hasten toward, rather than from.* I did not know that within my mind hid another hunter.

With one step I vow to abandon Lily. Another step, and Winterbourne rebukes me for endangering the daughter I stole from him. A third, Walton gloats at my solitude. A fourth step, and I count the days with dark satisfaction. Another, and Lily says something that makes me fear for the future.

Yesterday morning, seeing a city in the distance, she said, "Oh what gossip I'll inspire when I return home! Tarkenville will turn out, eager to see both my new house and me!"

Her eyes danced, but in sockets ringed with purple shadow. Daily she grows thinner, but she yields to her illness not an inch of her ferocity. Later in the day, she stuck two fingers into her mouth and yanked out a back tooth.

"It has been loose awhile now. The worm has found a way to eat even when I do not. Clever worm," she said. "Soon it will suck the marrow from my bones."

She tossed away the tooth, a pearl with a bloody stump.

During the night, the false excitement in her eyes was replaced by something softer, and in the morning:

"Life has not treated you fairly," she said, over a breakfast she did not eat. "And neither have I." There was no sarcasm in her voice, just a sad, dreamy concern. She smiled. "I am all extremes, without moderation. Perhaps that is what holds us together."

And more of Walton's journal:

This morning I found blood on my pillow and thought, "Somewhere he bleeds." Panic made my heart thrum like a netted bird's: I was again being cheated! I had been robbed of everything— robbed now, too, of the last triumph left to me.

I realized with relief that such a small spill of blood, like a finger tracing a mysterious word, could not signify his, our, death; no, if such a thief comes in the night, I will wake in a scarlet sea, I will gag on great mouthfuls of clots, and that is how I will know he is dead.

He lives still, and for the moment, so do I. In my doubled soul, I envy the sliver of glass, the sharpened blade—whatever licked him with its cruel cutting edge.

December 10

The groan of wagon wheels, a clank of metal, a hushed voice.

I touched Lily's lips to be quiet. The night was damp and fell, with blinding fog and a frost so heavy I breathed ice. We were standing on the steps of a church, where I meant to stop for shelter. The building had coalesced from the mist, sudden, tall, menacing—its spire swallowed whole by grayness. Next to it was a graveyard. The stones in what must have been its older section canted at dizzying angles. The newer tombstones beyond disappeared in the fog, ghostly soldiers marching off to a ghostly war.

A whinny, another clank.

"Someone's coming," I whispered. "Be still."

Now I heard the horse's hooves as well. Their slowness, combined with the late hour, suggested someone who desired stealth as much as we.

At last: a smudge of bobbing light and then a man's face, lit by a sickly yellowish cast. He walked in front of a wagon, a lantern held before him to mark the road. His expression was one of unsteady nerve, and he whispered to himself as he walked. The wagon followed the edge of the graveyard. After a few minutes, there sounded a metallic bang like a bell tolled and then damped. My mind had scarcely understood, when I doubled over with mirthless laughter.

"What is it?" Lily asked, who had trailed behind me.

"Everywhere I go, life seeks to teach me a lesson," I said. "I asked the question, 'What am I?' and now life will answer. Or rather, death."

I led her through the thickening fog. For the first time I felt resistance from her.

"What is that noise?" she whispered, holding back.

"You don't recognize it? Of course not," I said, chuckling. "Your life has been much too sheltered to have been exposed to the commonplace. It is the sound of my birth pangs."

I pulled her into the graveyard, using the distant lantern as a beacon. As we approached, the fog muffled the light in hazy confusion, blinding us to, rather than illuminating, the surroundings.

The noise grew louder: a metallic scrape, a soft shush, scrape, shush, in a tireless rhythm. Realization widened her eyes. For a moment she refused to walk. I tightened my hold and urged her forward. Then she stuck out her chin and ran ahead, as if to say, "This, too, is just something else to see." She caught her foot on a headstone and tripped.

"Who's there?" asked a quavering voice.

"Friends," I called out.

Hearing a sudden scramble, I rushed toward the light.

The lantern stood among the graves next to a shallow hole, out of which a man was clumsily trying to crawl; next to him lay an abandoned pick and shovel. At my hurried approach, the horse became skittish and trotted off. I hauled the man out of the hole by his collar. As he turned his fearful face toward mine, I was assailed by the reek of liquor. I patted his coat till I found a hard bulge and drew out a flask.

"The night's work requires courage, does it not?" I let him go and handed over the flask. His hands trembled as he tipped it to his lips.

"I do nae know what you mean," he said, his burr hoarse.

"Tell me, sir," I said. "I'm a foreigner here. What's the prevailing rate for bodies?"

"A grave robber!" Lily said.

The man peered at her in surprise.

"She's a woman!"

"Is she?" I asked with bitterness. "I think she's a sexless wretch. Still, it's no matter that she is not a woman, since I, after all, am not a man."

The false merriment in my words stung; I stifled what might have been a laugh—just as easily a moan—stepped into the hole, and picked up the shovel with feigned relish.

"Let me finish for you. I did say I was a friend, and I have some experience in this work, although I do confess it was from a different angle." I undid my cloak and tossed it over a headstone. "Look at me, sir, and guess where your night's work might lead."

The man's lips pulled back. "I do nae understand," he said in a low voice.

"Nor should you. If you did, you would run away, babbling senselessly."

I began to dig at a furious pace.

"Victor," Lily pleaded, hugging herself. "I do not wish to stay here."

"But think of the story you can tell at your next ball!" I said cruelly. "Remain here, if only for the anecdote."

Perhaps emboldened by the liquor—or else convinced I was just a hallucination caused by it—the grave robber became increasingly calm. He seemed as much fascinated by me as by my assistance and looked on as I worked.

"We are much too far north to be of use to the medical school in Edinburgh," I said to him.

"S'for a young doctor up in Malverness," he answered. "Says he needs more trainin'."

"And how many times has he asked for 'more training'?"

"This is the third. But if he do nae know a head from a toe by now, I would nae bring my cat to him." He stared at Lily with open curiosity. She edged away, wrinkling her nose. The only sound was the rhythmic digging of dirt. Into the silence I quoted:

> *Our course is done! Our sand is run!*
> *The nuptial bed the bride attends;*
> *This night the dead have swiftly sped;*
> *Here, here, our midnight travel ends.*

"What a fine voice for recitin'," the man said. His tone was tenuous, as if he wasn't sure whether to attempt conversation. "Is it a song?"

"It's a poem about a young girl who curses God when her lover does not return from war," I answered. "One night, he appears on horseback! To her delight, he carries her off: she is at last to be married! She does not know that she is riding on a nightmare, and that her lover is already dead."

Metal screeched against wood; both Lily and the grave robber jumped. I cleared the dirt off the coffin. I felt myself sink into the poem's doomed hopelessness, and yet continued: "The dead man urges the horse on furiously until they arrive at his grave. There he tells the terrified young girl, *that* is her wedding bed. The young girl looks around and sees—"

Thin, sheeted phantoms gibbering glide
O'er paths, with bones and fresh skulls strewn,
Charnels and tombs on every side
Gleam dimly to the blood-red moon.

Picking up the spade again, I broke the coffin lock, bent down, and wrenched off the lid. Lily clapped a hand over her nose and mouth, but stepped closer to look.

"What happens to the girl?" the man asked.

"She at last sees her lover for who he really is:

Lo, while the night's dread glooms increase,
All chang'd the wondrous horseman stood,
His crumbling flesh fell piece by piece,
Like ashes from consuming wood.

"But it's too late," I concluded, fixing my eye on Lily. "The dead lover descends into the grave, and howling spirits drag the woman down to join him."

Death itself lived in the poem; it lived here in the graveyard, too, though with less art and more stink.

Slowly I unwrapped the winding sheet. Instead of a beautiful woman, before me lay a stout matron of fifty, her fleshiness slack as a deflated balloon, her ashen face spotted with black. I stared at her blank visage. If she had had a soul once, if any human had one, it was gone now. What was left was as stupid and unyielding as the dirt. How could I expect any share in humanity when assembled from such as this?

I grasped the woman under her arms and began to haul her up like an unwieldy sack of flour. The task should have been easy for me, a second's effort. I breathed rapidly, even panted, as if I had just dug a million graves. I left the body propped halfway out of the coffin and paused to quiet myself.

"Well," the grave robber said. "It's a great favor you've done me, but I don't think you'll be shoulderin' the corpse all the way to Malverness. Let me see what's happened to the wagon." He wandered into the fog.

"Just leave it, Victor," Lily urged when we were alone. Ignoring her, I once more put my arms around the body and lifted. This time I easily pulled it up over the edge and onto the ground. The same perversity that had brought me here tonight—that bid me grab a shovel and quote poetry—now made me sit at the hole, feet dangling, and gather the corpse up close. I balanced it on my lap as one might hold a child.

How could something so cold not be ice itself? The body made my flesh shudder in fits and strained my arms. I should have been loath to touch it. Instead—nerves throbbing, tears pricking my eyes—I smoothed the woman's gray hair, cupped her chin to tilt her face up, pressed my lips upon hers, and with feigned fondness said, "Mother!"

"You cannot know her, Victor," Lily said.

"There were many like her who helped form me."

Whatever fear or hesitation Lily showed before was driven out by impatience.

"Yes, many like her," she said, "and a whole herd of cattle as well!" She stamped her foot imperiously. "Now lead me back to the church, Victor. I am cold."

I threw the body to the side, grabbed Lily by the back of the neck, forced her to her knees over the corpse, and pressed her head down till her face rubbed the dead woman's.

"Cold, yes, but not half so cold as she!" Delirium ringed round my mind and began to dance. I gave Lily a final push and threw her onto the corpse. With a choked cry, she scrambled up, bumping into headstones, tripping on rough ground. I did not care whether she returned to the church or fled down the road; it was with both malice and kindness that I had shocked her.

I felt raw, as if my nerves had been sewn outside my skin, yet again I pulled the corpse onto my lap. However appalling it had been to thrust my hands into a tub of cooling animal guts, knowing mine were the same, it was more appalling to hold the human dead, knowing it had been violated to make me. Human life was sacred. I had come to recognize that, though I neither possessed what was sacred, nor could understand its secret.

Presently the grave robber returned without the horse and wagon.

"A wheel is stuck in a rut, and the horse is shakin' behind a gravestone, like it heard your poem and did nae like it." He raised an eyebrow at how I and my new acquaintance sat so familiarly.

"Come join us, sir," I urged, unwilling to leave. The longer I stayed here, the more distance I would put between myself and Lily. "Sit with us and tell us your story, for surely there's one behind your coming here tonight."

"I'll wager yours is more interestin'." He sat down, but at several arm lengths away.

"I know mine," I answered. "First, your name."

"I'm Ailbert Cameron," he said. "Cam to my friends, and

any as what digs graves for me." He pulled his flask out of his pocket and was polite enough to offer it to me before taking a drink himself.

"I don't drink," I said, remembering that exceptional evening in Winterbourne's study.

"Never?" His mouth gaped. "With a face like yours?" He gulped and turned as gray as the fog, perhaps realizing how much offense his words could cause—and not knowing if my temper matched my face.

"I did try it once . . ."

He so eagerly asked me to share the tale—which would distract me from his insult—that I could not refuse him. I pulled the corpse closer and tucked its head beneath my chin. What had seemed dreadful a short time ago had lost its ability to make me giddy with horror.

It had been about five years ago, I told him. I was in Spain, about twenty miles north of Barcelona, on a rainy night after a rainy day. I was soaked through; indeed, I could have wrung out my cloak and had enough to wash with. I came across cultivated land and a curious set of buildings; a second group was set up higher. I broke into one of the large buildings lower on the hill.

"I went inside," I said. "My nose was assaulted: yeasty, then vinegary; fruity, then sour and rotten. Sweat covered my face, attracting tiny bugs that itched madly. Wandering around in the dark, I bumped into a huge wooden panel. It startled me, as the wood possessed the warmth of a living thing. It was a vat, just one of many—fermenting vats."

"And in them?"

"Wine."

"Nae to my likin', but we each want death to taste a certain way. So there you were, vats on all sides. Were you brave?"

"It was an honorable match, though I was bested in the end."

The corpse slipped, threatening to roll down and unwind its sheet back to the grave. I caught its neck in the crook of my elbow, stretched my other arm round its hips, then pulled the body onto the ground next to me.

Cam encouraged me to continue. I began to drink, I told him, and was soon flushed with wine, but shivering with the wet. I made a fire using empty casks. I was not drunk, I told myself, otherwise I could not have had the sober thought of keeping the fire on the stone floor and not the wooden one.

He nodded. "It's the sober thought that's most cunning."

"I stripped, laid my clothes out to dry, opened another bottle, and fell asleep. I was wakened by a shriek. I tried to lift my head. Somehow it had tripled in size. After great difficulty, I succeeded in opening my eyes. I looked down and saw two gigantic bare feet, which greatly alarmed me until I recognized them as my own. Then I looked up. Before me stood a line of nuns. They had come to hear Mass and had smelled the smoke."

Cam slapped his knee appreciatively. "It would reform any man, a sight like that."

"When I tried to cover myself, the floor rolled beneath me like storm waves.

"'Keep still,' one of the nuns said, 'or we'll be cleaning up puke. And don't clutch yourself like that. You've nothing we haven't seen before, though not quite so . . .'

"'So big, María Tomás?' one of the older nuns offered."

At this I stopped talking. Cam poked me.

"And then?"

"Then Sister María Tomás sobered me up and told me to go and drink no more," I said, forcing myself to smile.

I stopped my story there. Cam's lips moved noiselessly as if he were already adding a more comic conclusion to the tale to suit his retelling. At last we both stood, the corpse still on the ground between us. I lifted it up and swung it onto my shoulder.

"You best find your woman now," he said. "It's late."

"I wish I could persuade her to remain in the church. Let her plague whoever first comes to pray in the morning."

"You'd be rid of her then?"

"She is mine neither to leave nor take."

"Well, this one is," he said cheerfully and patted the dead woman's rump.

He led me to the horse. After I put the body in the wagon, I threw my cloak in the back next to it and lifted the wheel out of the rut.

Lily must have been nearby the whole time, for she rushed out of the fog.

"You cannot leave me, Victor," she pleaded. Like a child, she pulled at my sleeve.

Silently I climbed into the wagon and helped her up next to me. Cam nodded, a satisfied expression on his face.

The ride was long and bumpy: Cam in front; Lily, myself, and the corpse in back. After a while, Lily leaned her head close and, with her eyes cast downward, whispered: "Your words to me in the graveyard . . . I have always believed your story of being the Patchwork Man, but seeing you there holding the corpse, and knowing you are the same . . ."

There was something in her voice I had never heard before and could not identify, something soft and at the same time unsettling. Perhaps the graveyard had revealed to her not just my past, but her own immediate future.

Remembering my father's journal, I said, "Book knowledge is never quite as vivid, nor as bloody, as experience."

She found my hand and traced the scars where it was joined to the wrist. "You were trying to frighten me in the graveyard, weren't you? So that I would not stay?" I shook her off. "I will not be frightened, Victor, not by what you are or by what you were."

As if to prove her words, she lay down and, using the bundled-up dead body as a pillow, fell asleep.

December 11

Cam left us at the edges of Malverness, the better to slip unseen into town with his illegal delivery. It was just before dawn. By the time I found the market square, morning had fully come. The place was busy with peddlers, farmers, housewives, and servants, all haggling over the prices of buttons and lace, eggs and butter, turnips and beets. Hunched over, I watched the crowd, wondering whether it would be better to beg or to steal something for Lily. She would not be able to eat it, but I would rather waste the food than have none for her if she asked.

Lily snatched the hood from my head and showed my face.

"Stand up! Let them see who you are!" she said fiercely.

I thought she mocked me, yet no smirk deformed her mouth.

I stood in the middle of the market square, as good as naked. I could not read what thoughts lay behind the widely opened eyes as people gasped. Lily, too, stared as if seeing me for the first time. But this was not a party for the gentry. This was business—food on the table, and clothes on the back— and so, in a few moments, business went on, even if conducted at a wary distance.

It is late afternoon as I write this at the side of the road, my face once more covered, even though there is no one here to see it. Just a few minutes ago Lily approached shyly, holding an oatcake.

"You should eat it," she said, offering me her own sparse meal. "I'll only gag on it. Cake?" She tucked it into my hand. "I think they call it that to tease children."

"Why did you bare my face?"

"Was I foolish to have done it?" She turned away, her expression remorseful. "I have been foolish all along."

She ran across the road and into the field. What new trick was this? Did she expect me to go after her? Raw with uncertainty, I remained where I was.

Only now do I remember that in this last town I did not look for another place where I might leave her.

December 12

There is no word to describe Lily's behavior. Against expectation she has been sweet and mild and neither morose nor giddy. She speaks softly, touches me with a light, lingering hand, and stands so close as to insinuate herself into my every breath. More astounding, she looks grieved when I pull away.

It was easier living with her hatred than expecting deviousness. It was easier knowing I could leave her at any time than wondering if she may hold something for me.

At such moments I fear that the world has shown me more compassion than I have ever known, but that Walton had so poisoned my mind I could not or would not see it— and perhaps never will. Lucio, Reverend Graham, Winterbourne . . . the people in the market who stared but did not attack me. Even years ago, there were those who saw and did not turn away.

Since talking to Cam, my mind has wandered again and again to that part of the story about the winery I had not shared, the part about Sister María Tomás.

Sister María Tomás was a plump woman of middle age in whose red-cheeked face one could see both the dazzling beauty of her youth and the bare skull of her inevitable death. Her wit was sharp, her criticism sharper. She spoke and laughed and walked more loudly than anyone, yet was given to such meditative silences she could not be roused.

When I had first awakened in the winery, I could not lift my head from the floor. The nuns stood fixated. Finally, María Tomás shooed them into action—the ones who were not in a faint or had not run off—sending them to Mass with the instruction that someone rush back with the abbess, the abbot, and Brother Mateo, who acted as physician for both communities.

Waiting for them, Sister María Tomás removed her veil to let me cover myself, which still left her head and hair swathed in a white wimple, snug around her face and neck. She sorted through my clothes to see what had dried. Each effort of my own made the room tilt, so she tried to pull on my breeches for me. The movement was too much. Quickly she knocked over an empty cask and rolled it to where I lay. I vomited till I sank to the floor, trembling and weak. When I opened my eyes, I saw the abbot, the abbess, and Brother Mateo looking on.

Brother Mateo was the oldest of them and the shortest.

"This must be the monster the man spoke of," he said calmly.

"What man?" asked the abbess. She stood just inside the door, clearly troubled by my presence.

"Late last night a man knocked at the gate and wanted to know if we'd seen a monster." As he spoke, he tried his own luck with my breeches. "The thing would murder us in our sleep," the man said, "so we must give it up at once."

The abbot's brows drew close in a frown.

"What should we do?" he asked the abbess.

Before she could answer, María Tomás blew out a derisive breath, grabbed the breeches from Brother Mateo, and shook them impatiently.

"What should we do? We should wrap the poor creature in a sheet and care for him right here till he can dress himself." She quickly dipped her white-capped head. "Forgive me, Reverend Mother, Father Abbot," she said, without a trace of apology in her voice. "I speak out of turn. As always."

"Well, Father," said the abbess. "I'm glad the visitor is relying on your generosity and not mine. However"—her mouth stretched thin in a tight smile—"I suspect there'll be more vomit to clean up. I offer you Sister María Tomás for help."

Attacked by nausea, headache, and dizziness, I did not realize my vulnerability until later. Walton had been just yards away, while I had been drunk, dulled to threat, at times unconscious and snoring. The lesson was quickly taught to me again. Walking on wobbly legs to the monastery's sickroom, I heard that the strange man had returned that morning.

"What did you tell him?" I asked Mateo, at last able to speak.

"Brother Porter answered the door. He said there was none beneath our roof whom God did not love."

"Brother Porter has not seen me," I said, smiling grimly.

Other monks visited throughout the day, one by one peering into the sickroom. The rule of silence was helpless before me, and my presence was debated in forbidden whispers: I was a drunkard. A murderer. The Devil himself. I was a portent. A prophet. A test of faith.

The next day, the abbot and the abbess explained their dilemma: They could not endanger their communities' safety. They did not want to endanger mine. They could not allow their contemplative existence to be disturbed. They did not want to expel a soul in need. No one spoke for an unbearable length of time, and then they left.

Sister María Tomás was the only other nun I saw, as women never entered the monks' living quarters; indeed, even in the church, they remained behind a screened-off area. Her heavy footsteps, direct speech, and boisterous laugh echoed throughout the monastery halls, despite her entering and leaving from the outside directly into the sickroom. Brother Mateo, who might be at my side praying, would frown as if his ears hurt and slip out before she arrived.

She was not always full of noise. Sometimes, she would spend an hour doing no more than studying my face.

"You are like a tremendous quilt of God's people," she said, her words uncannily close to the truth. "There must be a story in each stitch, and a lifetime in each seam. Will you not tell me what happened?"

"I did not know that nuns were confessors," I said.

"We are not, but we're just as curious!" Then, hearing someone in the hall, she scooped up a book and read aloud an edifying tale of martyrdom.

María Tomás told me why she was allowed such freedom with me. She was often intolerant of her sister nuns. The abbess thought that caring for someone as extraordinarily "different" as me was a providential opportunity for María Tomás to learn acceptance.

Had I been dropped back in time to the Dark Ages? When and where else might a monster appear at the door and thought to be didactic? Her own attitude was more earthy.

"I believe Reverend Mother is hoping you *are* a murderer," she said cheerfully. "You will save her the trouble of strangling me herself."

"You have not learned to be more accepting then?" I asked. She laughed, because she always laughed.

"You are beyond ugliness," she answered. "But you are neither willfully stupid nor willfully mean-spirited, unlike some of my sisters. Therefore, I doubt that you can teach me—at least not the lesson Mother hopes I will learn!"

I malingered, relishing each extraordinary moment. My fourth morning there, María Tomás entered the room with an expression that told me everything before she spoke.

"You must leave," she said. "No one here fears you," she lied. "It is that strange man. He will not quit the grounds. Just now he tried to force his way into the convent itself and almost became violent."

I nodded and stood up to leave.

She had hastily arranged a plan. At that very moment, the abbess was arguing with Walton and would finally allow him to search the convent buildings—with several brothers accompanying him, of course—while all the nuns gathered in the chapel. He could search the monastery as well, she would say, although she had no authority to allow such a thing. While he searched the convent, I would sneak out on the far side of the monastery and flee.

"The plan is too obvious!" María Tomás sighed. "But there's no time to be clever."

She put together some items to take with me: enough bread and cheese for several days, candles, two blank ledgers for journals, and a Bible. Patting the wrapped package, she said, "The ledgers were my idea, the Bible was Reverend Mother's. She hopes you will find in it the road to Godliness."

"What do *you* think I'll find, Sister?"

Her expression softened to a saint's smile, holding within it a saint's sadness.

"Good stories. Consolation. I hope much more. For many, Heaven and earth themselves are there to be found."

As we parted, she took me by the cloak and pulled my face down to hers.

"My prayers will be with you," she whispered, "for I fear the life you must lead."

She kissed my lips, both cheeks, my closed eyes, and my forehead. Her mouth was sweet and as soft as a blessing against my skin. What manner of lover might she have made, what manner of mother, if she had not chosen her present path?

I stepped through the door from the sickroom to the outside and felt, as keenly as a razor's slash, the difference of those few feet from inside to outside. María Tomás grabbed my cloak again.

"Remember this," she said fiercely: "*'And God created man to his own image: to the image of God he created him. And God saw all the things that He had made and they were very good.'*"

I roughly jerked away and left.

December 13

I must learn that Walton's hatred lived in his heart alone. And though Lily is Walton's niece, what she feels is *hers* alone. Over time it might turn to genuine warmth, just as mine toward her is softening.

I think these thoughts and write these words, but do not understand them. Are men as baffled by emotion as I am? And if they are, how do they live their days in such confusion?

December 14

Tonight we stopped to rest in a barn. Instead of making her bed yards away, Lily lay down close, although not close enough to touch me.

"I have been unkind to you, Victor. At the butcher's, in the graveyard."

I held my breath, afraid to nod.

"And I . . . I was not kind to you in the cottage."

Tears hovered on her lashes, and her voice was nearly inaudible.

"Have we *ever* been kind to each other?"

Desire stirred within me; also distrust. I was certain there would be another word from her—because there was always another word, the single word that upturned her kindness to cruelty—but she said nothing more.

I lost all desire in the waiting. In its stead I found fear.

I was afraid.

I made my bed in the farthest corner of the barn.

Walton's diary. I no longer understand what moves him:

Here in Dhallatum death hangs in the very air. Cremation ash drifts down like black snow.

The women were young and beautiful, ripe for marriage. Why would all of them have taken their own lives? No one here could say.

Only I know the truth. He was here, had come for them in the night. By dawn they saw, felt, knew they had been violated. In taking their own lives they showed such bravery as I had not thought possible of savages.

He has done this terrible thing to spite me. He shows off his strength, knowing he has rendered me helpless. I had thought it lost, my finger, my ring, but now believe he must have returned for it and now carries it like a souvenir. And why not? Why should the blackest sea be an impediment to him when nothing else has been? Like a diver searching for pearls, he plumbed the depths and found the heart of me.

One girl was not touched by the madness, the people say. She had been away from home visiting a cousin and thus was not here when the others took their lives. I say she is a coward! Or else she lusts for more than life. I see clearly how my duty has for the moment changed.

I never jumped into the sea for Walton's finger.
I never heard of Dhallatum.
I never traveled to India.
How much evil has he wrought in my name?

December 15

Last night Lily and I took shelter under an old stone bridge. Quickly I gathered a pile of downed branches, each coated with frost. At last a smoky fire grew under my practiced touch. Steam hissed from the damp wood. The flames grew bright and sent my shadow dancing against the bridge's stone supports.

She sat close to the fire, hugging herself.

All day my feelings for her have swung between desire and rage, compassion and callousness.

I began to pace, my steps short, my turns abrupt. Rain poured on us a baptism of misery. My steps slid on the slippery ground, provoking my temper. I pointed at Lily, who sat dreaming, and roared, "You know nothing of me!"

She leapt backward at my outburst. Sparks flew in a white arc to her lap. She batted at her breeches to extinguish them.

No sharp reply, only a whisper: "I *cannot* know you, Victor."

I lifted my face to the night sky. The rain could not cool my thoughts, even though it was changing to sleet. Again I pointed at her as if she had hotly disputed my every utterance.

"I took you to the slaughterhouse," I said. "I took you to the graveyard. My every bone, my every muscle and vein and organ was selected *separately*—from some *one*, some *thing*—and assembled like a block city put together by a child. Do you understand?"

I stretched out my hands for her, my two different hands. In the firelight every huge joint looked dissimilar, as if every finger, too, had had its separate source. I could feel the pull of a thousand souls clamoring at me.

"When the parts were fit together, I lay waiting in brine—for what am I but a piece of meat?—waiting for what my father called a 'life spark' to leap from the living to the dead. He tortured healthy animals to animate me."

I crouched by the fire, blown low by the wind, seized Lily, pulled her face close to mine.

"I am just a twitch, a shudder. What animates me is the mute cry—for he must have muted the animals first, don't you agree?—the mute cry of a burnt paw, a scratched cornea, a flayed udder, a severed fetlock. Now all this pain is my own and I can never let it go. It is the very thing that gives me life. *Do you understand?* How can you then speak of kindness?"

Lips parting, Lily closed her eyes and leaned back. For a moment, her expression resembled that of Lucio's wife in the moment of spending. I grabbed her chin and tilted her face till she looked at me again. Her eyes did not show the ecstasy I expected. The drops on her cheeks were not rain.

I shivered and told myself it was the wind.

"Why do you stay with me?" I asked.

"So neither of us will be alone."

As I squatted, throwing twigs and branches into the flames, she touched my leg and rested her head against my thigh. The night was too lonely; her words, her gesture, too intimate. I no longer tried to resist her. I sat against the bridge's stone support and pulled her shivering body within the folds of my cloak. I had held the corpse thus.

"Has there ever been anyone for you?" She rested her face against my chest, her hand by her mouth balled in a fist.

"What do you mean?" I asked. Suspicion flared up. "Have you so quickly forgotten my whore, as your uncle called her?"

Lily fingered the charms of the necklace I wore on my wrist. She shook her head.

"I mean, were there other creatures like you? A creature . . . *for* you?"

I was surprised by anguish as the images rose up, so real as to be a waking dream—my father's face distorted with repulsion; *her* face, that of his other creation, lifeless, but full of *coming* life.

I told Lily the story, whispering the words close to her ear as the wind keened and whipped the fire to darkness. I whispered how I had begged for a companion and, in the telling, once more felt the tears of my youth. I whispered how my father put off this task over and over until he at last fled his home. *I* was "born" in Ingolstadt. For this new horror, now that he knew what he was creating, a barren, storm-lashed rock in the Orkneys was better suited.

"The Orkneys!" Lily said, now understanding something of what drove me northward.

Following him, spying on him, I saw how he created her— my sister, my wife—how he must have created *me*. I saw how he destroyed her. Why had he been so violent? Why not simply stop, refuse to grant her life? She was already dead. Why destroy the body before my eyes, hacking it apart with savagery?

He was too cruel. Yet I was the monster.

"What did you do?" Lily asked.

"I swore I would be with him on *his* wedding night. And I was."

A long, low sigh escaped her. She buried her face against my chest and breathed rapidly as if in great distress. When she was quiet, she looked up and, with feathery touches, stroked my face, the scars on my cheeks; she lightly shut my eyes, she traced the outline of my lips.

"He ended your life there, the life you might have lived. Take me there. Take me to the very spot, Victor, and I will give you back your life."

Slipping her hand behind my neck, she drew my face down to hers and kissed me. Her thin lips were raw and chapped beneath mine, wet with sleet. Hungrily I pressed her closer. I wanted her now, not so much for herself, but because tomorrow she might hate me again.

As I expected, she said, "No," and tried to pull away.

"What difference can a few days hold for you?" I asked.

"Not here, Victor," she insisted softly, kissing me a final time. "You would have had your wedding night there, and there you shall have it still."

Who was this woman? Was she so unnatural she would of her own volition lie with me? Did that make her mad? What blame for it must I take?

And do I care, as long as she does as she says?

December 19

Four days since last I wrote. I am like a man possessed as I travel northward. If I were alone, I could make the journey in seconds, propelled by lust, but I must keep pace with Lily's ebbing strength.

Tomorrow I will steal a horse for her.

December 21

Lily has not spoken of her intentions since promising herself to me. Tonight, roasting a rabbit I knew she would not eat, I tried to approach the subject by asking how she felt.

"I am weary of travel," she sighed, rearranging her jeweled barrette to push back her hair.

"Oh? Since I stole the horse, you have held it to a gallop."

"I thought perhaps . . ." She searched for words, then clenched her fist. "I am weary! I need say no more."

"What more could you say?"

"Is that not enough?" Her eyes narrowed. "It is the worm, isn't it? You would make sure it does not cheat you of your prize." She pressed her stomach. "Galloping away, I have one moment of forgetfulness and you bring this evil to my mind once more. Don't worry. I am still with you, am I not? Content yourself with believing you know my reasons."

"Why? Have you lied to me?"

She chucked me under the chin. "You would not know if I lied, would you? You wouldn't allow yourself to know. I could tell you anything and you would believe me."

My face must have betrayed the danger to her, for she let her hand linger on my cheek. This time when she spoke her voice was soft: "Silly Victor. Believe me if you must, for belief is good for you. I can see how it soothes those high-strung nerves that must have once belonged to a fine racehorse. In the end I will do as I want. Neither you nor I will know what that is until the time comes. So believe, and I will believe, too."

Anger ran through my veins like floodwater through well-worn canyons carved over time. I forced myself to remember: *I am not my words.*

That is what I will believe.

And from Walton:

Once I understood life. I knew my place in the world and, though that place seemed to slip lower and lower, I could recognize what led to my decline and still had hope of lifting myself up.

Now I ask who I am, where I am, what I am doing, why, and the answer frightens me: There is no longer a why, a where. There is no longer a who.

December 25

"What day is it?"

Lily has asked me that all week, her eyes overly bright with the question, her lips smiling at each reply.

Today, when she asked, I said, "December twenty-fifth."

She clapped her hands.

"At last! Merry Christmas, Victor!"

"Christmas?"

I looked around us. All day, the mountains had loomed, slate gray against a dreary sky, like hostile giants lumbering toward us. We were in a treacherous stretch of bog: oozing swamp, slime-coated trees, rushes and sedges—every puddle a possible deathtrap, hiding quicksand. The place oppressed me beyond my ability to fight it.

"No, Lily," I said softly. "Christmas does not come to such places as this."

"Yes, Victor, it's Christmas! We shall have goose and bread sauce and Brussels sprouts! Mince pie and roast apples and pudding in brandy!"

Grimacing, she clutched her stomach. When the spasm passed, her eyes glittered.

"And we will have a Christmas play from the Mummers! *The Plowboys*—that's the best one for today. The Fool is killed by his children, but do not worry," she whispered, a finger to her smiling lips. "He is resurrected at the end. There are fancy costumes and sword dances, singers and pipers. There is even something special for each of us: For you, there is so much verse, in the end you will feel like a child sick on trifle. And for me, there is a character called Wild Worm, who jumps in unexpectedly to frighten the audience." She began to sing:

> *Come in, come in, thou bonny Wild Worm!*
> *For thou hast ta'en many a lucky turn.*
> *Sing tanteraday! Sing tanteraday!*
> *Sing heigh down, down with a Derry Down A!*

"Shhh." I cupped her chin with my hand and brushed my thumb over her mouth to silence her. "We will celebrate later, Lily. But for now, as soon as the ground is firm again, we will stop so you can rest."

On the other side of the bog, I tied the horse, lifted her from the saddle, and sat with her on my lap so the damp ground did not chill her. She leaned against my chest and slept. I thought her mood would pass, but when she awoke, she sang, very softly: *"Sing tanteraday! Sing tanteraday!"*

I wanted to stop up the words, but if I did, would they not

just remain in her, growing and festering like the worm itself? I let her sing herself to exhaustion and she slept once more.

This time when she woke, she was calmer.

"Today is Christmas, Victor. Christmas comes to every place, no matter where. I made you a gift." She reached inside her clothes and pulled out a plait made from long thin stalks. One end was finished; the other, not, with many inches of stalk left unworked.

"I made it from dry cattail stems," she said. "All week I was certain you'd see me making it but you didn't. That both pleased me because of the gift and vexed me because of your inattention." She spoke the words with no vexation at all.

I fingered the fine braid.

"Thank you, Lily. What is it?"

She wrapped the plait around my wrist. It was not long enough. Quickly she plaited the unworked stems until the braid fit me, then she worked the ends securely into the rest.

It was a bracelet.

She slid her fingers beneath the cuff of my shirt, found Mirabella's necklace, and smoothed the two side by side. I jerked my wrist from her. I wanted to cry out that Mirabella was dead and so she must not put her gift next to mine. But she would only smile and say that she was dead, too.

December 26

The sea! We are just outside the town of John o'Groat's from which we will arrange passage to the Orkney Mainland. And from there . . .

December 29

Though from John o'Groat's to the Mainland is only twenty miles, crossing proved difficult. We offered our stolen horse as payment but were refused, once with a gesture to ward off evil. The superstitions of the land are a trifle to those of the sea: Lily and I were simply too strange to bring aboard.

I had come so far only to be stopped within sight of the islands! I dared not put a boat in the water myself with Lily as mate. In an instant we could be struck by a wild winter gale, and she might drown.

In the end it was a gale that set us back on course.

Two days ago, near dusk, the sky lowered, showing an unnatural orange beneath the gray. In minutes the wind doubled, tripled in strength. Everywhere people raced to secure their boats, fasten shutters, collect children, herd pigs and chickens into their homes. Doors slammed at my request for shelter till only Lily and I were alone on the street.

The rain was a sudden driving onslaught that washed the color from her face. Hail flew sideways with the wind, beat her cruelly, and made her stagger beneath its force. I tied the horse to a fence and hammered against the nearest door till its wooden lock splintered, then I pushed Lily inside and stood her shivering body before the fire. Squawking chickens and an old woman in a corner chair were the only occupants. At our violent entrance, the woman grabbed a knife.

"Help! Help! Murderers!" she cried, her voice too thin to be heard over the storm. With the latch broken, I set a bag of grain before the door as a stop for the wind.

"I mean you no harm," I said. "No one else would help and the woman is ill. Surely you would not send us back out?"

"Murderers!" the old woman repeated, now less with fear than sly delight. Her tiny black eyes shone, and she shook the knife. From the kettle at the hearth, I ladled out a bowl of soup for Lily. The old woman leaned forward.

"And thieves, too."

She said nothing else, not even when I removed my cloak to dry it before the fire.

For hours the storm battered the cottage. The wind whipped smoke down through the chimney so often I put out the fire despite the cold. Hail and sand pelted the shutters and drove through the tiniest cracks to sting my face. From outside I could hear our horse fighting its confinement till I heard a snap, then galloping.

At last, the storm passed, giving us several quiet hours before dawn. Lily slept, while the old woman and I eyed each other. I asked her name, where we might find passage to the Mainland, and whether she preferred her murderers beheaded or hanged.

"Is it over?" Lily asked, waking. "Can we make it to the island today?"

"No one will take us," I said, slipping on my cloak. "We'll have to go up the coast."

"Ask for Doughall MacGregor," the old woman said, startling me. "Tell him his granny says to take you over as a favor."

"Why?"

"For nae murderin' me." She grinned, showing a single tooth.

Though the horizon was just beginning to pale, the town was awake. People busied themselves setting right the damage; even more hurried to the shore with baskets. MacGregor was one of them. Large and muscular, black haired and bearded, he possessed the same beady eyes as his grandmother.

"Mr. MacGregor," I called to the man who had been

pointed out. "I'm looking for a ride to the Orkney Mainland. Your grandmother said we were to ask you."

"Did she now?" Without slowing his step, he looked at Lily, then at my hooded face. His friends looked at us with the same curiosity. "And why would my granny say that to two oddities such as yourselves?" When I could not answer, both he and the other men laughed. "I'm to do it because you did nae murder her, am I right? Do nae worry. My granny is nae murdered a good three, four times a year, and afterward she always sends the poor soul down to me. I'm waitin' with my breath held for when she realizes she's nae murdered every day of her life."

"Then you'll take us?"

"Nae today. Today we gather tangle before the tide takes it back," he said, referring to the seaweed washed up by the storm.

"Yes, today!" I said hotly. "We must get there today!" I had waited time enough and could not endure a moment longer. The vehemence of my response made MacGregor break stride. He stared intently at us, peculiar strangers who would make such demands of him.

Lily stepped forward and touched his arm. Her silent gaunt face and teary eyes were more persuasive than my temper, for his friends whispered among themselves.

"Go on, Doughall, do this boon for your granny. We'll nae be missing what you would have gathered anyway, such a wee bit it'd make nae difference."

After a moment, MacGregor good-naturedly cursed his friends, then led us to his boat.

Despite the forced nature of our coming aboard, MacGregor spoke easily the entire trip. He never asked what called us so urgently to the Mainland. He simply talked about the sea:

miraculous accounts of mermaids and mermen, the Fin Folk, and the seal people who could shed their fur skins to walk the shore as humans.

I had hoped he would sail us to the top of the Mainland to the town of Brough Head. The tiny nameless island I wanted, the island where my father had created then destroyed my mate, was about five miles off Brough Head into the Eynhallow Sound, not on any map and so far west as to be nearly in the ocean. On this point MacGregor was firm.

"As long as I'm on the Mainland, I have business I can do in Orphir," he said, "so I'm puttin' ashore at the bottom."

By now the sky was dark again and the water white-capped and choppy; at twice more the distance, Eynhallow would take MacGregor out of the natural harbor of Scapa Flow into the Atlantic, so I asked no more of him. From Orphir, it was about fifteen miles overland to Brough Head. What were fifteen miles and another day?

When we landed, MacGregor said, "Whenever you're ready to go back, I'm in Orphir most Wednesdays in the morning. Just ask for me at the market."

"Thank you," I said. "You've been very generous."

"Nae at all. I'm rightly in for two favors, I suppose," he said with a wink. "There are two of you. And neither one of you murdered my granny."

December 30

"Come, let me show you something."

Yesterday, when Orphir was some miles behind us, I led Lily onto the strip of land between the Loch of Harray and the Loch of Stenness and from which both lakes can be seen at once. With the dark sky and heavy air, one might believe the water could rise up from either side to engulf us.

"Do you see the standing stones?" I asked Lily. "I discovered them during my first journey here. There are two separate sets." Their pattern became clearer the closer we walked. "The four thin stones are the Stones of Stenness," I said. "The larger group that forms the big circle is the Ring of Brodgar. It's believed that the ancients built the Stones of Stenness as a temple to the moon and the Ring of Brodgar as a temple to the sun."

I brought Lily to the Stones of Stenness. Their sharp angular surfaces against the leaden sky hinted of menace, as if the tallest of them at five meters could call down demons on a day such as this.

"Stand here," I said, placing her in the middle.

"Why?" she asked with suspicion.

At first, I thought this remembered ritual was well suited to a woman's sentiments and hoped it might work to soften Lily—that if I first gave her a wedding of sorts, it might ensure her giving me my wedding night. Now, looking at her face implacable in the gray light, I remembered that she had already had a wedding.

"Couples pledge their faithfulness here," I continued, knowing it was now too late to stop. "The woman stands within Stenness, the man in Brodgar, and each swears an oath of fidelity. Then they come together at that stone there fallen out of the circle," I said, pointing, "called the Stone of Odin. There is a hole that pierces it. The lovers join hands through the hole and so seal their oath, which is considered binding to the death."

Lily's voice was soft: "We are not lovers, Victor."

"Have you not promised me?"

I am not my words. My limbs began to tremble—unaccountably, because for once I felt no anger.

"What would you have me do?" she asked.

I told her what to say, believing that she had to be told, that such words were as alien to her nature as they were to mine. Then I left her within the uneven square of Stenness, prisoner within the four knifelike thrusts.

The Ring of Brodgar where I was to stand formed a huge circle nearly fifty meters across. It was surrounded by a moat, dry now, carved from the bedrock. Of the dozens of stones worn round with wear, only half still stood upright.

I reached the center of the ring and nodded to Lily as a signal that we might speak in unison what I had composed while on MacGregor's boat. Because I thought it was what a woman wanted to hear, I used once more that word Biddy Josephs first used: "I give myself to you and take you to be mine. I will love you and no other, now and for always."

What spells did Lily chant instead? For, although she spoke, there was no concurrence between the movement of her lips and the words I had bid her say.

Slowly we walked toward each other, the fallen stone of Odin between us. Kneeling, I thrust my hand through the hole. From the other side Lily's hand, small and cold, slipped into mine, then quickly pulled away.

We stood up and faced each other over the stone. Behind her a single fork of lightning cleaved the sky. No thunder sounded. Without speaking, Lily pointed to Mirabella's necklace. I removed it from my wrist and fastened the little chain of charms round Lily's throat.

It did not matter whether Lily had echoed my words or not.

I knew we were both liars.

December 31

It is nearly midnight. The hour hovers between the old year and the new, in that precise moment when there is no moment, when time ceases and no man can be born or die.

I have arranged for us to be taken tomorrow to the nameless bit of rock where my father set up his laboratory. I had almost given up finding someone who would take us there. It was not that anyone recognized me from ten years ago. I had hid myself while following my father, swimming to the rock during the night and keeping to its far side when "deliveries" were rowed in. No, it was the island itself that frightened them. No seal rests, no bird roosts, no boat lands there. For more than ten years the rock has lain foul in the water, as if the whole sea could not wash it clean. It is there I go, this outcropping of Hell, on the promise of being saved and given back a life I never had.

Walton's journal:

He is close, too close for words, he rushes toward me and no longer waits to be pursued. The wind on my face is his breath; the dark sky overhead, his murderous glance. I have waited in anticipation and now I wait in fear. He is not where I expected. He is behind me now. I have overreached my mark and now the beast is at my back.

January 1

The island sits like a jagged skull emerging from black water: steep sides, cavelike depressions for eyes and nose, a strip of stony beach for a toothy grin. Above us, birds screeched warning. A tern, then a bonxie dived straight down at us. We nearly capsized the boat dodging to avoid them. The captain sailed the boat closer to the island, and the birds fell back as if giving us up for lost.

Fresh blood smeared the notes I forced on the captain. The notes were from his creditors: he was the only one in town who would take us here, and threatening his creditors the only payment he would accept. A few debts had been released unwillingly, as the blood testified. The captain's eyes shifted from water to sky to jagged rock; all the while he licked his lips. He had been drunk when he agreed to take us last night and drunker still this morning; however, the nearer our destination, the more sober he grew.

Lily pointed to the skull.

"Is the place feared because of its shape?" she asked.

The man's anger was sudden. "Are we fools to you?" he snapped.

I had to press him for the story, what the villagers thought had happened there.

Devoid of most life, the island had never been considered more than just a reference point when landing on the Mainland Orkney. Then, ten years ago, a foreigner arrived and rented one of its huts. The stranger paid well to ensure his privacy.

Huge crates from England and the Continent arrived, reeking of death and decomposition. The area's few farm animals began to disappear; others were found mutilated. Every scoundrel who went missing was believed to be on the island, dying or already dead, though none would put a name to it. Unnerved by the odors and by the sights half-glimpsed through the window at night, the island's few inhabitants left. Soon the stranger's hired brutes would only pull their boat close to shore, throw those increasingly dreadful items referred to as "supplies" onto the sand, and row away.

The town was poised between terror and outrage. Unable

to confront the man, the people left the pub and rallied round a newly arrived shipment. Our captain himself had been present that day and was one of those who had favored opening the crate. He remembered eyeing the crushed bottom corner that bore a dark seeping blotch, remembered hearing a rustle from within, a faint scratch at the boards.

He wanted to open the crate. He truly did.

"In the end nae one o' us would take a hand to it." He trimmed the sails so that we drew parallel to the island. "For all the liquor in us, we were just too scared."

One night, fishermen returning late saw the stranger in a skiff a distance from shore. The stranger waited till the clouds overspread the moon, then dumped large bundles into the water. When the deed was reported, a group of men at last sailed out. They were too late: he had vanished.

"And inside the hut?" Lily asked. "What did they find inside the hut?"

"An awful gory mess. The worst had been cleaned up, which only made you wonder what had been there before." Two days later, a head washed up with the tide. It was badly decomposed. From its long strings of hair it was presumed to be a woman's.

I pulled my cloak closer against the grisly tale. Though I myself had witnessed much of this, the story was freshly grim when told from the outside.

"You heard no more of the stranger?"

"Nae a word," said the captain. "Till you."

With a touch, he let the sail fall slack. We bobbed on the forbidding water. All was silent but for the wild cries of the birds in the distance.

"I do nae trust a man whose face I can nae see." Sweat broke out on his forehead and he wiped it away. "What's your business here?"

"You would not wish to know," Lily answered.

His eyes flicked to her. "What is yours?"

She smiled with thin, silent lips.

At last the captain let the sail fill with wind and landed us.

Now his boat grows ever distant as I sit writing this entry. Beside me on the stony beach are our few provisions: food, water, and large blocks of peat, as the island is treeless and has only bushes for kindling. On the sand, pulled up beyond the tide, is a dinghy and oars for our return trip.

Although I have had a single feverish thought the last days of this journey, I am now reluctant to go up and enter the hut. Lily said that being here will free me of the past and give me back my stolen life.

Will it? Am I not yet a man? I am already a fool. I have a fool's mind, a fool's heart, to do what I fear, what I *know* is doomed, is damned. More than appetite spurs me now. Over these last days I have seen the gentleness in Lily's expression change into a death's-head grin, but I am caught in a web. Struggle only entangles me, so I lie still and wait for the spider.

Later

When I at last put down my pen, gathered the provisions, and climbed the hill, I found that Lily had passed by the two stone huts closest to the trail and gone on to the third. There the door canted inward, attached at one rusted hinge. The thatched roof had collapsed and made a rotting veil that obscured the entrance to the inner room, which my father had made his laboratory. No furniture, no chemical apparatus, not the tiniest shard of glass from a broken vial remained to indicate his presence.

I crossed the threshold. A chill brushed me like dank breath.

"Lily?"

"In here."

Unerringly she had found the right hut. Unerringly she had found the right room. I swept aside the fall of thatch.

Inside, it was bare except for a stone block that was long enough and wide enough to hold a creature that matched me in size. Now Lily lay there, stretched out like a corpse awaiting burial, arms at her sides, eyelids lowered. With her pale shadowed skin and sunken cheeks, her death was not difficult to imagine, and I gasped. She laughed softly at the sound.

Turning away, unable to touch her so soon, I laid the peat in the hearth, then grabbed a fistful of thatch to help the blocks catch fire.

"This is like a huge altar," Lily said. "And I am the sacrifice. Or perhaps *she* was. She's still here; did you know that? I can feel her. We share a close kinship, my sister and I. Each of us is your bride."

"She was never my bride." Striking the flint, I remembered the scarred mass that had been so like me; remembered the pulpy face that already held anguish and anger before it had taken its first breath. My trembling hand betrayed my hatred of ugliness. "I did not want her. I only wanted not to be alone."

"And now it is different?"

"Yes," I said, looking at Lily, wondering how that might be possible.

She leaned on her elbow and half-rose. "Am I like her?" she asked coquettishly, a girl teasing a suitor. "Am I unnatural?"

"No!" The word came too quickly and she laughed again. "It was never a woman," I said. I stepped close to the block of stone. "It was never alive."

"And yet she is here. What would have given her life is still here, still waiting for the body she would possess. Perhaps I should let her take mine."

Lily lay back down and gave herself up to the darkness. She took my hand where its thick scar bound it to my wrist. She slipped my hand under her jacket and shirt and, sighing, held my hand against her cold breast. Although its weight and full-ness surprised me, I could number her ribs with my finger-tips; I could feel her heart beat wildly beneath my palm.

"She is in this room," Lily said. "I can feel her."

"Do not speak of such things," I whispered, hoarse with desire.

After so much waiting, fulfillment seemed suddenly too soon. Should I make tea first? Should we stroll the island like honeymooners, coyly postponing the bridal bed? Was there a way to pretend that Lily did not lie on a stone block once washed in blood?

We had both come here, if not for the same reason, then to perform the same act and, I now saw, to perform it quickly. Stretching out beside her on the stone, I felt what any oaf must feel in knowing he is too big, too clumsy, too ugly. Then I felt a greater torment. I looked at my hand and wondered what women it had touched during its first, its *natural,* life. I felt a tingling throb in my lips and wondered whose mouths they had once covered with kisses.

Did she understand?

She reached up to loosen my shirt.

"You have never let yourself be seen before, have you?" she said, misinterpreting my hesitation. "Do not worry. That day at the farmhouse when you bathed, I spied on you from the window."

"And that night you refused me."

She shook her head and uncannily echoed my thoughts: "I was made not for such pastoral settings, but for this."

She spoke dispassionately even as she half-rose at my side to bare each part of me for her inspection. Like a seamstress examining a bolt of cloth, she fingered the dramatic changes in skin texture where each limb was joined to my torso. She found on me red hair and black, brown hair and blond; a section of skin, too, curiously hairless and as smooth as a woman's. She tasted my every scar and counted each stitch that held me together.

I lay unprotesting, each touch bringing me exquisite pleasure and impossible pain. If only I had seen the smallest kindness in her face, if only there had not been such hunger . . . She stripped me in every way possible, herself remaining protected from revelation of her own soul.

I pushed aside her clothes and saw what I had only felt before: her breasts full, distended, a harsh contrast to the boniness of her frame. The diseased bloat of her stomach reminded me that the worm was with us still. The unpleasant image sent through me a powerful yet enervating thrill. Again reading my thoughts, Lily leaned over and whispered, "*She* is here, too."

"No, do not speak."

There would be no words of endearment, neither truth nor lie. I knew everything she would not say; I knew everything I feared she might. So I closed her mouth, covered it with mine, held her, and stroked in memory the soft body I had not touched before, as Lily ran along the cliffs at Tarkenville, and again, draped in purple silk at the party, as she took my arm in hers and led me into the ballroom. Once she had been the most beautiful woman I had ever seen. She was no longer beautiful, but she was mine.

The night of the party she had tossed her head and offered the sweet length of her throat to my greedy sight. Now she leaned down over me and offered it to my lips. I kissed it and felt its sweetness reduced to sharp ridges. I tasted in its hollow dirt and salt. I smelled sweat, but oh, too, I smelled the remembered scent of lavender. If I closed my eyes, she might be beautiful once again.

"Take me now," she whispered.

Humanity and inhumanity met and joined in us; I did not know which would be more changed for it.

The remembered smell of corruption choked me, and I opened my eyes. Like a graven funerary ornament, Lily was a stone angel kneeling above me, her eyes fixed at a spot beyond me. What was she thinking, what was she feeling? From every corner she gathered in the darkness. She wrapped her arms around herself, hugged the darkness close, and breathed it in like smoke.

"She is here," she whispered.

"No!" I tried to cry out. The word was unintelligible, crushed to a groan.

Afterward Lily looked down at me as from a great height and laughed.

"I have never lain with a corpse before. And now I have."

Still laughing, she pushed away and quickly dressed.

For a hellish eternity I lay on the stone willing myself to do no more than breathe. If I moved, it would be to murder her.

At last I found pen and ink and paper and set down the above, writing into existence a tether to hold my sanity tight.

Having written down my torment, writing again now hours later, I still feel violence pulse beneath my skin in the hot throb of my heart, in the steady tick of the tiniest vein. In violence I was all and everything, I was my own creation. Now, without the snapping of bones and the pouring out of blood, what am I?

A monster would have killed her. And though the coldest part of me can see that her proud armor is insanity, the larger part of me knows that a man would have left. Once I was at least one of these. Now I am neither.

January 5

Days now since I have written.

Days since my mind has thought in words.

Days and days with but the thread of silence to stitch the days together.

If Doughall MacGregor heard the silence between us, he did not remark upon it when I sought him out in Orphir to take us away from the accursed Orkneys and sail us back to John o'Groat's. Instead he filled the silence with the sound of his own voice, once more spinning tales of life on the sea. It was late by the time we landed, and MacGregor invited us to spend the night before moving on to wherever our next destination might be.

"Granny has more room than me," he said, "but in the week since I've seen you she was nae murdered twice, and I dare nae send you back to her."

With a nod I accepted, deciding that this very night I would leave the cottage as he and Lily slept. In the silence I had come as far as that, knowing I must quit Lily's presence or myself go mad. If her father's image again tried to summon up my culpability, this time I could chase it back down to darkness with the knowledge that MacGregor was a good man: I could leave her with no better protector.

After a dinner of fish chowder, which Lily did not eat— prompting a new set of tales from MacGregor about privations forced on him at sea—I stood up and said I would walk along the beach for a time. Lily eagerly ran to the door ahead of me, as if she knew my intentions and thought that this was when I would abandon her.

I set off briskly. If I could not leave this moment, at least I might so exhaust her she would sleep more soundly than usual tonight and not hear me steal away. The evening was pleasant enough for a long walk—mild, windless, and with a rare warmth. Sunset painted the air an ever-darkening red, till at last sea and sand blended invisibly, marked only by an occasional faint glimmer from a rush of foam.

"Wait," Lily called at last. Struggling in the sand, she had fallen behind. I stopped and looked backward. I could no longer see the lights from MacGregor's cottage.

"Take my arm, Victor," she said. "I am tired and ready to go back. Besides, you have ignored me all day." She spoke as easily as if we had conversed this evening and the days before it. "It is one thing to ignore me when we are alone and quite another when others are present," she said. "I would have you show me the respect I'm due. Perhaps, when my house is restored and I return home, I will find a position for you—something in the garden, I think, since you have such a fine talent for digging."

She floundered in the soft sand, then struggled to her feet, and slapped at her dirty trousers. Was she incensed because she had fallen or because I would not play at being her servant? It did not matter. Tonight all this would end.

"My *arm*, Victor." She waved it impatiently. "I need you to guide me back. I do not have your cat's eyes!"

"Now there's an ugly thought," I said. "Perhaps it's true. Or perhaps I merely see with the eyes of a man who has long had the habit of darkness."

"You see with a *man's* eyes? Oh yes," she said hotly. "That means you see nothing at all!"

Refusing to be baited, I moved past her to return to MacGregor's.

"Do *you* understand, Victor?" she asked, her voice rising. "You demanded an answer from me. Now I ask you, *Do you understand?* Of course you don't!" She grabbed at me. "You are as blind as any man, blind now with stupidity, that night blind with lust."

"Blind?"

"I offer you a position in the grandest house in Northumberland," she said, "and your silent refusal is full of contempt: 'I am too good to serve her now because I have seen her tremble with pleasure.' That night you saw only what you wanted to see. Just as you did not see what you did not want to see."

"You are right, Lily, I do not understand," I said gently, taking her arm to coax her into returning. My time with her was now short enough to count by hours, and that helped me keep my patience.

"Poor Victor. In your blindness, you did not see I was not a virgin. You did not see there was no blood to mark my purity." Her grin yielded to disgust. "I have not seen blood of any sort these past six months."

"Six months?"

"I am with child, Victor! I was three months gone when you first arrived at my estate. Did you think I would otherwise let you touch me? You didn't see my hatred, just as all along you did not see my swelling stomach." She turned on me. "Could I not have been plainer? Did I not say a thousand times how the worm battens on me like the leech it is?"

"The worm. I thought it was the bloat of disease. I thought you were dying."

"It *is* a sickness, and I *am* dying. I know what children make of a woman—nothing! I will be like our little songbird, Cassie Burke." She pressed her hands to her temples. "I drank Biddy Josephs' foul expellants. I followed *you*, enduring arduous travel, galloping on horses, starving myself to starve *it*. I deliberately taunted you that night in the cottage so you would strike me. You turned away at the last moment, and the brat is with me yet." She continued bitterly: "I had hoped the doctor in Drexham would rip it out. He would not. But the thing is small, small enough for you to have deceived yourself. Its size is my final hope—that it will not survive being born. If it does, it most assuredly won't survive its first few moments of mothering."

I sat down, my legs unable to support me.

"Who is the father?" I asked. "Surely not the man you married?"

"My parents thought the brat was yours, that you had been at Tarkenville long before you showed yourself."

"Mine?" Laughter burst from my lips.

"*That* is why my father would have killed you, because you had violated his daughter, no matter how willing she might have been, no matter how sympathetic he was to you."

"How did your parents find out you were with child?"

"I dismissed my maid as soon as I realized that she would have no bloody rags to wash when I claimed myself to be indisposed. I imagined myself growing fatter by the minute and took back from the servants my old Empire gowns. They had already been decades out of fashion when I gave them away, but they were loose and needed no corsets. I began wearing a shawl everywhere, even to the costume party. All of this was to keep eyes from what I believed was my swelling belly. All it did was draw eyes to my unexpected behavior. Lily Winterbourne dressing herself? Washing her own rags? Wearing out-of-date dresses? We betray ourselves, don't we? In the end, we have no need of enemies."

She pursed her lips, angry at herself.

"My mother guessed, and I did not deny it. She arranged a hasty wedding. She had my many suitors from which to choose," Lily said, smoothing her jacket like a bird preening.

"The man asked no questions. He was half-dead already. He believed that, at worst, he would die soon anyway, but die a happy man; at best, he might be revived for another year by such a pretty young wife."

"What of the worm?" I asked, for I could call it nothing but that.

"I planned to have a secret confinement and a stillbirth."

"A stillbirth. Ah, yes, your mothering." I raked my fingers across my scalp. "Who fathered the child?" I asked again. A dozen faces from the costume party appeared in my mind. "Did he not care what would happen?"

"I do not know who the father is, Victor, and thus he does not know." Her eyes gleamed and a sly smile tugged at her lips. "In truth, I didn't run with the hounds at night for their sport, but for my own."

Her words were beyond comprehension.

"Why have you stayed with me?" I asked. "Such a husband as you took could not really care about your virtue."

"Do not underestimate how proprietary a husband feels about his wife, especially one he has so plainly purchased," Lily said. "I was no untried maiden. That he knew—although he did not know about the worm—and that he could accept. But once I was his wife, another man's hands on me would have been an insult—*your* hands unthinkable.

"There were other reasons, too, why I remained with you." She looked out toward the sound of the ocean, as the sea was by now invisible in the dark. "When you abducted me, I had the idea of staying away till I could destroy the worm on my own. I would no longer have need for a husband. But how can a woman travel without a companion? I needed you as an escort. Also my lovely house was ruined. I needed time for the restorations before I could return and reclaim my . . . my . . . And by then, too . . ."

She stopped speaking.

"What, Lily? What other justification did your warped logic present?"

"You shall never know me!" she cried heatedly. "Never!"

"I don't want to."

As if one mask replaced another, the anger drained from Lily's face and her features settled first into calmness, then a slow smile. She crossed the few feet of sand that separated us, bent down to where I sat, caressed my cheek with a single finger, leaned closer still, and pressed her hungry mouth on mine. Hesitant, I tried to read her eyes; they were too dark, the night too dark as well. Without thought, my lips parted beneath hers. My fingers circled her waist, and I pulled her down next to me. I was repelled by her; that did not prevent my body from wanting hers.

Did all flesh betray men's souls so easily, or was it only the nature of mine, as each disparate limb battled to achieve its own will?

Her breath at my ear echoed the roar of the ocean, the roar of the blood in my veins, and she whispered, "You may now be as close to hating me, to hurting me, as you have ever been," she said, "yet you desire me still."

I shoved her backward onto the sand, shook the numbness from my legs, and returned to MacGregor's. Laughing, my eager pet followed close behind.

The cottage windows were dark, all lamps put out save one. It was not so late that MacGregor should have retired, unless he dozed waiting for us. Not wanting to startle him, I tapped on the door before opening it.

"MacGregor?" I called softly.

Beyond the unexpected darkness, nothing seemed amiss and I stepped inside.

"Doughall?"

MacGregor lay in the far corner, his burly form limp, a knife protruding from his bloodstained chest.

Lily peered from around my back.

"He's dead!"

"Yes, he's dead," said a voice from the shadows. "He said he was your friend. He left me no choice. I have no friends, so you may have none."

Two boots appeared next to MacGregor's head as a figure lurched from the shadows into the light of the dying fire. Slowly, fearfully, my gaze moved upward . . . from legs, their knees tortuously bent . . . to a hunched body . . . to the face, dry and leprous white in some places and in others, raw with scarcely healed scars that matched my own. I could almost see smoke still emanating from the burnt skin.

"I am as ugly as you now," Walton said. His eyes traveled to Lily's abdomen. "But I see I am not your first creation."

"You're alive!"

"Hatred has wonderful resuscitative powers."

Lily stepped in front of me to question her uncle.

"Has my house been restored? Did the workmen try to cheat me?"

I grabbed her shoulders from behind and forced her to her knees.

"Here stands your uncle whom we thought dead," I said, "someone with sure knowledge of your mother, and you ask about your house? Ask about your mother, Lily!"

"My sister died of a broken heart thinking *I* was dead."

Margaret dead? I had orphaned Lily and laid more guilt upon my weary shoulders. With Margaret dead and MacGregor, too, how could I leave her now? Standing behind her, I could not see if her confused mind understood what had just been said.

"Your mother died the night of the fire," Walton said.

"Did he tell you how he burned the house to the ground? I was caught in the worst of it. My clothes, my hair lit up, and I threw myself out the window to escape. My dear Margaret covered my broken body with hers to beat out the flames." His rough voice harshened: "As she lay on me, her weight sank into my burned flesh. I screamed, but my tongue was silent. I could not make a noise, I could not move, I could not breathe. She thought I was dead and died right there herself, her poor heart giving way to sorrow."

There was no candle of clarity in his eyes, only impenetrable blackness.

He was my twin, my likeness, and he was a horror.

So long a time had passed with scarcely a word between us—until tonight, this flood of insanity, scarcely minutes removed from Lily's own shocking revelations, and with MacGregor's murdered body still at my feet.

"Ten years!" I cried. "Ten years you have hunted me. Ten years you have murdered anyone who might have had so little as a soft word for me," I said, gesturing to MacGregor. "Why? For a few days' acquaintance with a stranger and a story he told, fit for a fairy tale?"

"A stranger? You robbed me of the only man who knew my soul!"

The outburst cost him, and Walton had to gasp for each breath. He limped past the body, lowered himself into a rocking chair, and put his hands on the armrests. In the light of the dying fire, I saw the empty space at his knuckles where he was missing the middle finger. With a smile he held out his gnarled hand.

"Do you keep it on you as a talisman?" he asked. "And the ring? Or did you give the ring to your whore?"

I shook my head. "Both are below the ice," I said.

"As is my ship."

"Nature sank your ship, not I."

"And was it Nature that mutilated me?" he asked. "T[hat] stole from me the pole and the world's love and forgivene[ss?] That forced me to be a saint while the demon was fruitful a[nd] multiplied?"

His eyes were blank, his tone flat, his face expressionless. This apathy, these strange words intimating carnality, were more frightening than his anger and more provocative.

"I don't understand," I said.

"You are a beast," Walton answered. "It is not in you to understand, only to kill."

Lily stepped between us.

Perhaps wishing to reclaim the attention, she kicked MacGregor stoutly and with a giggle said, "Poor Granny. It was not for herself she should have feared murderers."

Walton and Lily: such was humanity, which I would become.

I began to retch.

"See, Victor? I was right not to eat the chowder."

Laughter bubbled from my lips as I wiped away vomit. We were all mad, all those within this room, all those without— all the world, mad.

"Winterbourne warned me," I said. "He warned me of the Walton blood."

"Winterbourne is a fool," Walton sneered. "Margaret is better off dead."

I looked up sharply.

"He did not die? Lily's father still lives?"

"He is not her father," Walton said. "And yes, the fool lives."

"Did you hear that, Lily?" I cried. "Your father is alive!" I wanted to exclaim, "*My* father is alive." I did not know my full burden of grief till released from it. Dizzy, I leaned against the wall for support.

yet mine? Oh, Victor!" she cried.

's ugly face was made more horrible by
take Frankenstein's name? And you"—he
"how is it you address him so familiarly?"
lled back in revulsion, he looked at each of us,
the fire. "What you've done is far worse than
feared."

vould learn to love the monster?" Simpering, Lily
body intimately and pressed herself against me in
uction. "Yes, I do."

ved her away, saying, "You think to torment me. You
it yourself in danger!"

om *him*?"

he words were not from her lips when Walton leapt
and from MacGregor's body grabbed the knife from his
est. By the time he had wrenched the blade free from the
one, I had grabbed an iron pot from the hearth.

He threw himself at Lily.

In my moment of surprise, Walton slashed at her viciously.
He aimed at her throat, overreached, and struck high across
her cheek and tripped. As he fell, I slammed the pot across the
side of his head. He collapsed, knife still clutched in his fist.

Panting heavily, he looked up at me. His insanity lifted a
moment, giving me a view of darkness beneath a dark veil,
and he said, "Kill me now, for that is your only chance, and
hers."

The pulse of death throbbed in my fingers; still, in this single night, I had become more human than the people before
me.

Should I kill a crippled madman now, while Winterbourne
waited?

I grabbed Lily and quickly pulled her stumbling after me
out into the night.

PART FOUR

Winterbourne is alive.

I have nowhere else to go now but back to Tarkenville, back to *him*. The decision was immediate, as soon as my foot left the step of MacGregor's cottage.

After I had run a few paces, dragging Lily with me, I looked over my shoulder. There behind us stood Walton's twisted form, silhouetted in the cottage door.

"Murder!" he cried. His rasping voice splintered the quiet of the village. "Help, murder! Doughall MacGregor's been stabbed!"

Walton's voice grew louder, following us where he could not. Cottagers cracked open their windows.

"What's that?"

"Doughall dead? It can nae be!"

I pulled Lily into the shadows. Fearing she was still possessed by mania and would giggle or call out, I clapped a hand over her mouth. At once I felt her blood from Walton's knifing.

"Listen to me," I whispered. "Even now your uncle is turning the town against us. If we return to tell the truth, we will be seized, and then he will have you. You are hurt. I can tend to the wound only if you are quiet." After a moment, Lily nodded. I picked her up and, carrying her, ran to the outskirts of town where the cry had not been heard.

"He would have killed me," she said softly, her first words since the attack. There was a tremor in her voice, also anger and surprise.

"Do not talk," I said. "Press down on the wound and try to keep it closed."

Hurrying through the alleys, I hoped to find a horse for Lily, and instead found only chickens, pigs, and snarling dogs.

In an outbuilding, I found something more necessary: a tangle of fishing nets, lines, hooks, traps, and buoy markers.

From what light there was, I could see that Lily's wound required stitches. It began under her ear and from there ran across her cheek, nearly to her mouth. The fishing hooks were barbed and the line coarse. Eventually I found a supply of needles used to repair sails and tarpaulin. Even the smallest seemed a harpoon compared to my needs. I slipped back outside for a bucket of water, washed the needle, and threaded the gaping eye with a string pulled from the bottom of Lily's white shirt.

"Will it leave a scar?" she asked. She rinsed her wound with the water, which only made the blood flow so freely it seeped through her fingers.

"The cut is too deep to spare time for vanity," I said. "You are fortunate to be alive."

She never flinched as the stitching was done and even wore a grim smile as I worked.

"See how life with you changes me, Victor," she said, when I had finished. "Soon they shall be telling tales of the Patchwork Woman."

Then she fainted.

I took advantage of the level ground near the shore to run as far as I could with her. For a moment I was at last her master, holding her very life in my arms. I was also master of the worm's life. The thought aroused in me strange emotions. I hated the worm twice over—once, because it was killing Lily, even if it was she herself that denied it food; twice, because its presence, visible in her bloated stomach, reminded me of her other illness. Before I ever knew her, she was wanton. Before I ever came to Tarkenville, she was running with the hounds, waiting for whoever might pass, and now she was with child. Last month she had promised to give me back my life by giving herself to me. The promise had seemed motivated by affection or charity, perhaps even a stronger emotion. By the journey's end it was no more than another opportunity to rut.

Poor worm! I must admit that, beneath the hate, I do at last feel pity. Its only crime is its existence. Once I was as innocent, then I took life into my hands, and squeezed and squeezed, and thus learned how to sin. What will be the worm's fate if it lives past its mothering?

I stayed on the road till I thought a search party would be following, then cut directly across the rough land. The towns were so greatly separated that soon there were no lights at my back, and no lights ahead.

Where are my cat's eyes now? I wondered as I tripped on rocks and stumbled across the rugged terrain's sudden dips and rises. "Yes, I am blind. I see nothing at all."

"A hard lesson," Lily said, her head on my shoulder, mumbling with the stitches. "Have you really learned it?"

"I didn't realize you'd awakened." Nor that I had spoken aloud.

"Where are we going?" she asked.

"Where do you wish to go?" I asked. "To your father?" The thought was behind all I had done since hearing he was alive.

"No, to London." In her voice, I heard her smile. "Yes, you shall take me to London."

She had lost the mother she thought alive and regained the father she had thought dead.

Yet she would have me take her to London.

What picture dances before her closed eyes? Whatever it is does not exist.

I will take her south to her father. The direction will appease her and perhaps, with time, she will recognize that she does not belong with me, especially while there is family waiting for her.

For now, I have hidden us near the Hill of Crogodale. It grates on me to still be so close to John o'Groat's. The whole town must be hunting us as MacGregor's murderers, yet a child could walk the distance here in an hour. But Lily needs to stop. Even being carried exhausted her.

In a minute I will put aside my journal and try to coax her to come under my cloak for warmth. The idea of the worm shivering within its dark cave seems too lonely a thing. But if I said the words aloud, she would laugh and think I talked about desire.

January 15

"I must return you to your father, Lily."

Over the past days, we had been silent, though it was not the black desperation that had followed me after the Orkneys. I was silent to give all to my thoughts: I must return Lily to Winterbourne to quit my obligation; I must return myself to Winterbourne to . . .

I cannot think of what I will say when I find him. I think only of pushing Lily as far and as fast as she can walk, and when she can walk no longer, I will carry her again.

For her part, her silence has not been morose but genuinely thoughtful. Perhaps in these precious moments of calm she is at last becoming aware of the consequences of the past few weeks. Or perhaps it is only the cast of her mouth, twisted with its wound, that disguises her thoughts and gives her the mask of pensiveness.

It was because of this calm, this seeming awareness, that I said, "I must return you to your father."

"I cannot return now," she said quietly. "March, February even. Whatever shall be, shall be done by then. Though what does that matter now? The house is no longer mine and never will be. No, not Tarkenville, Victor. London."

Let her think I will bring her to London. I was an arrow and Tarkenville my mark.

January 17

Perhaps if I had read further in Walton's journal I would not have been seduced into sparing him at MacGregor's cottage:

I have seen his woman. I was puzzled by her gestures and exaggerated expressions till I realized she could not speak and must act out her desires, like a dumb animal. Of course—what else would stay with him? Such harshness is the habit of madness. Another part of me, a smaller part and diminishing by each day, says, "Leave him! Would it really harm the world so much?"

When they had both left the bell tower, I crept into his lair to see what defenses he has made against me. None! In his happiness, he has lost all sense of me. I saw their poor pretense at domesticity: broken crockery against the wall, a wilted flower in a tin cup, the single pile of rags that must be their single bed. He shall not have the contentment I cannot have!

I must take them together. If I take her first, in his maddened state of being cheated he may kill me or quit Venice at once. If I kill him first, she will slip into the crowded alleys, carrying his horror within.

January 26

At last, Walton's final entry:

I stank when I came off the herring boat at Berwick, for when the seas were bad at the crossing, they put me in the hold among the tiles used for ballast. I was ground against the sea-soaked wood till fish scales pressed themselves into my skin and made me

*silver and blue. Should I care? I was going home. I could only
wonder why he had not gone home earlier.*

*At the dock, she had a carriage waiting for me and a letter she
had given to the driver, saying how she planned a hasty wedding
for the child. Her letter summoning me had been filled with dark
hints. Now the need for a wedding said everything. She wrote of
murder, too, and violence against Winterbourne. And all these
years they thought me mad.*

*She will be astonished at what I must do. He must die, and
then . . . She will not understand . . . She has never . . . Later she
will see that I have always been right.*

And afterward?

I cannot say.

I burned the book.
And now I go home again.

Inverness
February 1

All roads meet here, even the natural passes through the
glens. At last we can leave behind the sheep tracks of the
Highlands and gain the speed afforded by the Lowlands'
more heavily used thoroughfares. More speed, too, comes
from the carriage I stole this night.

At dusk we had stopped at an inn outside the city. I had
found little shelter of late. Rather than complain, Lily was
satisfied. She hoped every extra measure of hardship would
injure the worm.

Her sentiments against it kindle sympathy in me. I understand what it means to be hated simply for existing. I may
have more in common with the worm besides, for what sort

of child will Lily have after these long months of murderous intent? She has repeated, in a fashion, my father's experiment of shaping life in artificial ways: by now she may carry an abomination, not unlike me. For that reason alone, I must look to the worm's safety, which is why I had brought Lily to the inn.

We approached from the backyard and waited outside. At length a young man in a white apron swung out from the back door, whistling and stepping jauntily as if he remembered with pleasure a previous evening's dance. He carried a bucket and was headed toward the pig sty. The open door behind him let out light and a rich oniony smell that made my mouth water. Encouraged by his cheerful manner, I stood up and pulled Lily from the shadows to stand beside me.

"Sir!" I called.

He squinted at us. "Who's there?"

"Two travelers with not a coin between us. Could you spare some slop before you feed the pigs? And a night's stay in your barn? We would be grateful."

"Pig slop? You ask little enough. Come out where I can see you."

I pushed Lily ahead of me. Her belly has grown larger daily, as if, before this, only my blindness had kept it small. The young man grunted his surprise.

"And you, sir?"

I stepped out but did not take off my hood.

"The roads carry all manner of people nowadays," he said.

"We are not highwaymen," I said, throwing back the bottom of my cloak to show I was unarmed. "Your guests are safe. We will stay in the barn."

"From where do you hail? So tall and speakin' so odd."

"It doesn't matter. The woman is English."

"English tourists have coins in their purse," he said good-naturedly. "What need does Scotland have for English beggars?"

"*He* is the beggar," Lily answered.

"And you?" the man asked, inclining his head politely.

She lifted her chin.

"I am his muse."

The young man regarded her stomach. "You amused him plenty, I see." He laughed, then made a welcoming gesture. "Tell me, have you ever tasted haggis? It's on its last day, and I'll nae be servin' it to payin' guests. Still, I warrant it's better than pig slop."

There was a sudden commotion from round front.

"The coach!" he said, letting the pail drop to the ground. The swill spilled over; now neither the pigs nor I would be eating it. "It's a bitter night. Get yourselves warmed in the barn. I've new chores now before I can see to your supper." He ran back into the inn.

Lily and I waited in the barn, both of us beneath my cloak. The close air held mixed odors of horses and cats undercut by the smell of straw; Lily brought her own essence of oil and salt. Remembering the more tantalizing aroma of cooked onions, I said I hoped the young man returned soon with the haggis.

Nestled as she was against my chest, I could not see her expression, but I heard the little sound of disgust she made.

"Haggis. You would not be half so eager if you knew what it was, Victor."

"I do not care. I am weary of slaking my thirst with snow and trying to appease my hunger with oats. Even you must desire something more," I said. "Have you no strange cravings?"

She shook her head. "I want nothing, I feel nothing. It is a lazy little worm I carry," she chided. "Or else clever, and it thinks it can hide from me by lying very still. I would scarcely know it's there but for how ill and clumsy I've become. Why, when Cook was having her baby, you could see her apron flutter and shake as if she were hiding a litter of squirming kittens."

"How sweet a description, especially as you would drown that litter; you said so yourself."

Sliding my hand to the front of her belly, I marveled on the strangeness of birth: one human emerging physically from another. Certainly *my* creation was no stranger than that. I could almost understand Lily's animosity.

There—a tiny ripple beneath my palm!

She laughed.

"You have nothing to fear from it, Victor."

"And neither have you," I said, trying to keep my voice gentle.

"*I* should feel no fear? A man's words—how quickly you're learning! The man's part in this is all pleasure. He does not bear it, birth it, nurse it. He does not watch his life get eaten away bit by bit, year by year, till there is too little left to recognize. Oh, I have been to the tenants on my estate and what I've seen among the women there frightens me. I will not be made into so small a thing."

"You are not a tenant's wife, Lily. You would have had nursemaids and servants and governesses to assist you. You only had to birth it, then turn it over." I spoke as if the worm were already dead. "You can do it still."

If she had an answer, she did not have an opportunity to say it, for the barn doors were yanked open. I leapt to my feet, thinking we would be called out as MacGregor's murderers. It was just the young man from the inn.

"I regret delayin' your supper so long," he said excitedly. "It wasn't the coach. It was a private carriage with a laird!"

Through the open doors behind him I saw in the yard a carriage more elegant and ornately decorated than any other I had seen. Its outside had been varnished to a high sheen, its doors painted so realistically with landscapes of a tropical clime I wanted to warm myself by them. All around the windows the wood was carved into delicate scrollwork. The windows themselves were draped in velvet curtains, hinting of plush cushions within. Four fine chestnut mares pawed the earth and blew smoke at the ground.

I had to have it.

"What a dear little thing!" Lily exclaimed. "I have not seen such finery since Lord Bainsbridge came to visit!"

At the young man's questioning look, I shook my head—the gesture said to ignore her—and followed Lily out. I approached the horses slowly. As though guided by my will, their nervous prancing turned the carriage back toward the road, making our escape easier.

"Were there no servants?" I asked, looking around. "What laird travels with no servants?"

"His lairdship had to leave a fancy affair in a hurry. The driver's settlin' his master in right now. Gave me an extra bawbee to brush the horses and feed them mash. He'll be down to inspect my work, he says." The young man held out the coin as proof. "Driver, indeed. Why, his uniform is better than my Sunday best, and him only—"

I covered his mouth with my great hand till he was silent.

After dragging his body into the barn, I closed the door and helped Lily into the carriage.

What a sight I must have been: a great hooded giant towering above the tiny driver's box, my cloak whipping straight out behind me as we flew down the road. Hunched forward, I cracked the whip high over the horses' heads and urged them on, whispering, "To Tarkenville."

February 4

I did not kill the young man from the inn. I am certain of that. I am certain I saw his chest rise and fall as I laid him down in the straw. I held him only till he was quiet. Surely that was not enough to do him harm! Still I am vexed by guilt. Why? Because I put my hands on him when I would not touch Walton? The young man was generous and good-natured. He would have fed us. Perhaps he would have given Lily a bed if one was empty.

I should have asked his name.

I know it is for Winterbourne's sake I feel such misgivings. I am like a bride who, walking down the aisle to her beloved groom, is ashamed to catch herself leering at the guests in the pews.

Ecclesmachan
February 11

Despite the carriage, the journey has taken far longer than I had anticipated, and even now I am only as far as this small village in Linlithgowshire, home to but a few hundred souls, as they say. Lily is often ill, and I must hide the carriage along roads as isolated as those here so she can rest, undisturbed by the bumpy ride. I delay as long as I dare. When I can no longer endure waiting, I drive away, only to see Lily's face at the carriage window as pale as a portrait in chalk, her hand knocking at the glass for me to pull over once more.

February 14

Today is Saint Valentine's Day.

"Come, Victor," Lily said brusquely. "Have you no love token for me? No flower you went to extraordinary lengths to find in this winter? No jewel, no lace, no sweets? Not even a verse that exposes the beating of your inhuman heart?"

I sighed with weariness and stretched out my hands to show they were empty of the tokens she sought. In fact, both palms were stuck with bits of hay. I had not been able to find a pitchfork and was carrying the hay to the horses in armfuls. Because the weather threatened to be inclement, we had stopped for the night in a barn, which a farmer had granted us, along with a bit of supper.

"Well?" she demanded. "It is a poor lover who brings no gifts. Perhaps I should not be surprised: you *were* a poor lover."

It was her unreason that baited me; still, I grew annoyed. Too quickly, memories of our night in the cottage below Stirling, of our time together in the Orkneys, sneered and snapped at me. Our journey had been far darker than I had imagined possible, and now I wished only to be rid of her.

"You want poetry?" I asked. "I have the perfect poem—written for a Valentine's Day wedding." I spewed out Donne's words like venom:

> *Here lies a she sun, and a he moon there,*
> *She gives the best light to his sphere,*
> *Or each is both, and all, and so*
> *They unto one another nothing owe,*
> *And yet they do, but are*
> *So just and rich in that coin which they pay,*
> *That neither would, nor needs, forbear nor stay,*

Neither desires to be spared, nor to spare,
They quickly pay their debt.

"'Rich in coin? They quickly pay their debt?' What sort of nonsense is that?"

"A good lover would understand. So perhaps I should not be surprised either."

"*Oh!*" she said, her mouth a little round of amazement. "Now I understand: *that* is your gift—to make me laugh."

I tossed the last of the hay into the stalls and brushed myself off.

"It has been Saint Valentine's all day, Lily. Why wait to torment me till we are lodged together so intimately?"

"I am bored, Victor. You have made only one joke, and now you won't argue! What shall I do for amusement?" She settled onto a pile of hay, preparing for a long complaint. "You could not entertain a child," she said. "You are as predictable as an oatcake and just as loathsome."

I opened the barn door. A blast of wind sent loose straw whisking across the floor.

"You'll be too cold out there."

"It is too cold in here."

I wandered in the yard, looking for a place to spend the night. It was fully dark, about nine o'clock, with no letup in the wind. The air was laden with moisture: before morning, no, before midnight, it would snow.

The carriage stood before the barn where I had pulled it to unharness the horses. I squeezed in. It rocked back and forth beneath my weight as I shifted positions. Much too small to provide me rest, it continued to bounce and sway until I gave up the idea of comfort and sat still.

The padding and curtains muffled sound and sight; I heard

only the velvet upholstery whispering under my movements. The air was close, the little compartment so tight I breathed back in my own breath. It was not unpleasant, yet I was annoyed being out here while Lily was within. I want to be charitable; she tries me so sorely I cannot be.

"It's not charity if it does not hurt," Sister María Tomás said to me so many years ago.

"I have done nothing to deserve *your* charity," I had answered.

"Shhh. If you did, this would be repayment and not charity. Besides, this hurts me not in the least. You have provided me with such distraction I'll have to confess it, although not until you've left," she added, her plump face red against the wimple.

"Good works must hurt? No wonder so little good is done in the world."

"More good is done in this world than you know. And much of it benefits the doer, even though it gives him nothing, even though it may even cause him pain."

"Could so pure an act exist?"

"So . . . you belong to no church then," she said.

"What church would accept a monster? No, do not answer me." I waved. "I know only too well that churches are made of men."

"Yes," she agreed. "And men do not love as God loves. Perhaps we should find you a church of women," she said, smiling broadly. "Mother would scold me for that!" She glanced over her shoulder. "Scold me, yes, then look to see where such a place existed and how quickly its current abbess could be deposed!"

"You have a sharp tongue, Sister."

"I am forever cutting myself on it."

She asked one more time about the scars on my face and

body. I trusted her, wholly and unexpectedly, but I could not tell her.

"If charity must hurt, make *this* your act of charity, and do not ask again."

Why did I not share my story with her? She would have been neither frightened nor disheartened by my existence; she would have been fascinated. Perhaps that was why I did not speak: instead of making me less than what I was, she would have made me more.

Her definition of charity pricked at my thoughts, while my body was pricked by the cramped seats and the stiff wind that shook the carriage at irregular intervals. At last I decided to return to the barn and empty my anger into my journal.

I crept inside. Lily was by now asleep. Looking at her, I remembered the mesmerizing beauty who had first appeared to me on the cliffs. Now I saw a plainly ill woman stretched flat on her back. A thread of spittle, silver in the dim light, hung from her open, snoring lips. Her hair was a snarled mess, her clothes were those of a workman, her swollen stomach rose in defiance.

Her snores ended abruptly. She grabbed her stomach as if the worm had kicked, then she tried to roll over to get off her back, a position she said caused her many aches. Her eyelids fluttered. Perhaps she was still half-asleep. Perhaps she had been having a nightmare. Her expression on seeing me was one of pure revulsion.

How easily I had silenced the young man at the inn, my hands moving of their own around his mouth, yearning to go around his neck. I watched my hands as I might have watched the hands of a stranger, which is what they are— the hands of someone else. Despite my intention to be influenced by peace, my disparate parts react with their own habits of violence.

Just now I had seen the hatred in Lily's eyes and felt my own hatred.

Was she still in danger from me?

Tarkenville
February 17

It is done. My mind is at last rid of Winterbourne, and my presence rid of Lily's.

Stopping only to rest the horses for the briefest of times, I raced to Tarkenville. Walton was close behind us—too close, too close—I felt it. I needed to get Lily back within her father's protection, for at any moment Walton might come limping after us.

Recognizing the landscape even by dusk, Lily became furious. She banged on the roof of the carriage and slammed repeatedly against the window. I had hoped that being home again, especially after being attacked, might change her mind. Instead, she was more adamant than ever. When I pulled the carriage to the side, she threw open the door and jumped into the road before the horses had come to a full stop.

"I will see no one when I am like this, no one!" she cried, stalking away.

"Only your father; that is all I ask," I said, following.

"A thousand other routes would have taken us to London!"

"I was not traveling to London. You must see your father, Lily. Perhaps he can protect you from your uncle. I cannot."

Twisting round, she clawed at my face.

"If you will not see your father," I said, coming upon an idea, "at least go see the estate. It has been several months now. Are you not curious about the repairs? So much work must have been done! So much for you to inspect!"

I could see the struggle in her eyes.

"I will not go to him," she said, pleading.

"Surely, after all that has happened, you want the comfort of family."

"I want nothing!" She turned her face and when she spoke again, it was in a soft, strangled voice: "I wished him dead to have the house. Now I should go to him?"

Could even Lily feel guilt?

"It was nothing, a selfish thought such as we all have," I said soothingly. "Your father will be happy to see you, happy to see that you need him."

Her hands encircled her stomach, and her features hardened.

"It would have been over so soon. Why didn't you wait, Victor? When I returned, I wanted to return as myself, not a mother. Now, here, even after I rid myself of the thing, I will be a mother whose child died. 'Poor Lily,' they will say. I will not be so named!"

"Shhh. Come back," I said. I tried to keep my voice soft, though I would strike the words from her mouth when she referred to getting rid of the worm. "Let me at least drive you to the manor. See that first. You must be curious."

She let herself be led to the carriage.

Circumventing the town, I drove through the woods to the estate, up the long private road that ran to the house. My first glimpse of the building was not clear, embraced as it was by the bare skeletal branches of the trees, and I thought, no, it cannot be: when we are past the woods, I will see something else.

The manor was a blackened shell. I had heard so often of the house being restored that I had come to believe it myself and had fully expected that great efforts had been made toward repairs. Instead, the building looked untouched, so freshly destroyed from the fire I expected traces of smoke to rise from its exposed, charred rafters.

No portion was inhabitable; the destruction was complete. The outer sandstone frame might someday be salvaged, but the entire inside had been turned to ash.

Where was Winterbourne? Who would know? Perhaps Reverend Graham.

Though worried about the silence from within the carriage, I did not stop, for fear conversation would provoke her rage to a point beyond recovery. I left the estate, returned to Tarkenville, and pulled up at the town's far end where the church and the parsonage stood. Both were lit against the darkness. I left Lily in the carriage and peered into a church window. In the back pew sat Winterbourne himself!

For months my thoughts had shaped themselves around this man—first in admiration, then in hate, then in unadmitted grief when I presumed him dead, and finally in passionate anticipation of seeing him again. Now he sat paces away.

He was much changed. His noble countenance was thin and as ashen as his house, his sharp eyes were dull. Seeing his transformation, I felt both sorrow that I had caused it and optimism that I had the power to restore some of his former vitality.

I turned around. The door to the carriage hung open, and I silently cursed. How could I have expected Lily to wait patiently for something she wished to avoid?

She had gone no farther than around the church and stood at a low stone wall that circled the cemetery. I approached her cautiously, not knowing whether she was dazed or enraged past words.

"My mother lies in there," she said. "It is too dark to try to find her."

"In the morning we will go together," I said. "Lily, I have found your father. He is right here, in the church."

"Will he be angry at me?"

"He will be overjoyed."

She turned her eyes to mine. Her features were settled into a rare calm. Perhaps seeing the house had forced a shred of reality on her. Her mania could not exist alongside the reality of that charcoal shell.

"Will you wait here awhile longer?" I asked. "I would speak to him alone first."

She nodded, then turned back toward the dark cemetery.

I slipped into the church and walked to the pews.

"Reverend," Winterbourne said without turning. "Did you see Barton on your rounds? This morning he pressed me again as to when I would leave here. I could not give an answer."

A cough racked his body. He brought a handkerchief to his mouth and spat.

"Reverend?" He half-turned.

"No," I said softly.

"You!" He stood up and tried to flee so quickly he tripped and again began to cough. I drew back my hood.

"I mean you no harm, sir. I never meant you harm."

Lies, even now. How dare I stand before him?

"When I heard your wife died, I was filled with . . ." I said. "And your daughter—I have brought her back."

Winterbourne looked around the church.

"Lily? Where is she?"

"Outside."

"Bring her in at once!"

"I would speak to you first." I stepped toward him, saw his body tighten, then I stopped and sat in the nearest pew. "As soon as I heard that you were alive, I knew I had to return

Lily to you. I have kept her safe for your sake," I said, thinking of the many times I would have abandoned her but for him, thinking of lying with her on that stone altar of death in the Orkneys. "Now I . . ."

"Now what? What have you done to her?"

"It is your brother-in-law. Walton tracked me down as he has always tracked me down, and when he saw that Lily had stayed with me as a willing companion—"

"Willing companion!"

"Not at first, but later when she realized she had lost everything . . . I thought you were dead. I thought I had killed you."

I gripped the pew.

"What is it you would say to me?" Winterbourne asked sharply.

How could I answer? That I never meant to hurt him, when I so gleefully set his house afire? That I never meant to hurt him, when I kidnapped his daughter? That I never meant to hurt him, when my very purpose in first coming to Tarkenville had been murder? Next to these, the one thing I *could* say paled: "I swear to you I did not kill the stable boy!"

"That is what you would tell me? Very well, you have told me."

His coldness stung. I tried to make my voice as stern and unfeeling as his.

"You must listen carefully. Your daughter is in danger. Walton now pursues her as viciously and unreasonably as he pursues me."

"Walton would never harm Lily! It makes no sense."

"She is with child. You knew as much," I said. "That's why she was being married off. Perhaps I should have brought her to her husband instead."

"Lily has no husband," Winterbourne snapped. "He died before the New Year. And it would not have mattered if he had lived. The church was his sole beneficiary in absence of a wife and heir, and he had already changed his will back. The child is yours, isn't it, and you want it for your own. That's why you took my daughter."

I jumped up and paced in the central aisle.

"The child is not mine, nor did I know of its existence when I took her."

Should I now repeat her taunts that even *she* did not know who the father was? Should I tell him that the child was in as much danger from her as from Walton? No, I had to look at myself as he did—a person not worthy of trust.

"Whether or not you believe me does not matter. Walton does not believe it. He is convinced that the child is mine and that it must be unnatural. He would kill Lily, too, for bearing it. He believes I have debauched her. He believes she has become my whore."

I looked away, unable to face the sudden dread in Winterbourne's eyes.

"You must protect her!" I exclaimed, confused by what I felt and by how he was reacting. "Her time is almost here and Walton is close behind. Do not refuse her because of my actions. She deserves far more than what you should give me."

"Why did you do it?" Winterbourne asked, slumping wearily against his seat. "Why did you come to England, why present yourself at my house, why take my daughter, why destroy my life?"

"Everything was done only to ensure my freedom. You cannot imagine my life under Walton's pursuit. I have not been allowed to be a man. I would be one, and more than a slave, too: I would be free." I faced Winterbourne, remembering how he and I had spoken of such matters at the estate. "Is freedom not worth any price? '*What we obtain too cheap, we esteem too lightly. It is dearness alone that gives everything its value.*'"

"The only thing of value here would be your death! You cannot separate fine-sounding words from the mouth that speaks them. Neither can *you* become a man by speaking like one."

Pounding my clenched fists onto the bench, I cried, "I am a man!"

"Nothing you have done proves it!" Winterbourne shouted, leaping to his feet. "Nothing! Now where is my daughter?"

"She is here, Gregory."

Both of us spun round at the voice. Reverend Graham stood at the back of the church, his arm around Lily. They had slipped in unnoticed while we were arguing.

Winterbourne fell back against one of the pews as he saw her more closely. He shook his head over and over then rushed to Lily, snatched her away, and held her tightly.

"This is how you protected my daughter? When you took her, she was a bride . . . a beautiful bride," he whispered into her hair. Pushing her back to arm's length, he stared at her bloated stomach and the ragged line of stitches across her cheek. His expression was tormented. "You took a bride. What have you returned to me? Not my daughter. A monster! A monster like yourself!"

Later

My pen ripped the page as I wrote that last word, the ink bleeding through to the pages beneath. I had returned to Winterbourne wanting nothing less than redemption. He had called me a monster.

Writing the word, I had to stop, slam shut my journal, and run. I raced down the dark country roads like a drunken fool, stumbling with my eyes half-closed, fingers pressed to my ears, as if I once more heard his denunciation spoken aloud—heard it in both his own voice and in that of my father's. The two of them have entwined themselves.

I had killed the one already. Perhaps I must do it again.

I try to make my thoughts stony. Have I done so much to save the worm only to now strike down the one man who might protect it? I cannot yield to the rage that throbs in my hands.

Now it is over, and I am at last rid of both Winterbournes.

Stupidly I had made too much of them, the father as well as the daughter. Neither was extraordinary apart from the feelings I invested in them. Neither was worth the anguish they inflicted on me. And if I have learned anything from them it is this: I was made by nature to be a solitary creature and now have become one by desire as well.

February 18

I must return to the Continent. I am too much of a foreigner in England, as if my accent were the final insult beyond my face. This morning I head south. Eventually I will cut west to Liverpool, which should be an unexpected port from which to leave the country, in case Winterbourne sends a party after me. Perhaps, too, Walton will follow me in the end rather than stop for Lily. My thoughts are far ahead of me, though, as I am still in the farthest reaches of Northumberland and have far to travel.

February 19

The door to the inn stood open to the night, letting out light and laughter, pipe smoke and cooking smells—a drunken song, perhaps, if I waited long enough. I was not hungry and could light my own fire if I wished, as bright as any that burned within, yet I did not leave. I did not want to be made to leave.

Presently a man staggered to the threshold. He paused, patted his side pocket repeatedly, and stepped down into the road with a precariously unsteady gait. Holding on to the side of the inn, he walked unseeingly toward me. I did not have to consider what to do, for he suddenly tripped. When he sank into the muddy road, he lifted his head once, then lay still. I swiftly dragged him round to where the shadows were darkest and emptied the pocket he had so considerately pointed out. Then I propped his sleeping body against the wall and walked through the open doorway.

Silence hitched over the room in starts as group after group became aware of me, and faces lifted their attention from bowls of stew or tankards of ale. Standing at my full height—no, standing tall—I surveyed the crowd with contempt, then strode to the fire, roughly shoving aside any who did not give way. At the bench closest to the hearth sat a man drawn up to a table, wolfing down a plate of sausages with no mind to what was happening. I grabbed him by the scruff of his collar, dropped him onto the floor, and sat in his place. Tossing coins onto the table, I threw back my hood, stared down the room, and dared comment.

At the clink of money, a serving girl rushed up. Her ready, thoughtless smile turned to a yelp when she saw my face. I caught her wrist and held her.

"What will you have, sir?" Her voice squeaked with nervousness.

"What's your name?" I asked, annoyed by the fear that drained her face of color except for its paint.

"Merry Osborn."

"A good choice. What are you offering? Something to make your customers merry?"

"Just supper, sir." A panicky giggle escaped her lips. "Stew's fresh today and there's meat pies left from yesterday. We most always got sausages, too."

"Two meat pies, Merry, and bread."

"Ale or wine?"

"Neither, something hot."

She bobbed me a curtsy. When she returned with the food and a mug of mulled cider, her hand shook collecting her coppers from the tabletop.

By the time I finished eating, the room had still not resumed the noisy aspect that had drawn me in from the street. Sullenly I shifted my seat toward the hearth. From behind my back came whispers.

"It's him, I tell you. Who else could it be?"

"Ask him then."

"No, you. You're the one what heard the rider."

"*I* say it's *not* him, and you do."

"He'll like as not murder the first man as what bothers him," said Merry Osborn.

"You then, you ask him," came the response. "He wouldn't murder a lady."

"No, but what about *her*?" said with laughter.

I turned my head slightly, and the voices hushed.

"I *will* ask him," said the girl, and she marched up to me with the pretense of clearing my plate. With a single glowering glance I warned her off so thoroughly she tripped and fell backward. Her tray of dishes clattered to the floor; she followed with a thud, landing on her bottom, skirts hiked over her knees. A glance from me muffled the room's laughter.

I reached out and helped the girl to her feet. Though

the rider they spoke of obviously had been sent by Walton, I should at least determine in which direction he had gone.

"What is it they've been saying behind my back?" I asked, pulling the girl close.

At first Merry flinched at my touch, then she gained courage at the sight of the coin I held out to her.

"There was a man here on horseback. Ridin' like the devil lookin' for you."

"Which road did he take?"

"I don't know. He left a message for you in case you came here afterward."

A message? This was unexpected. I asked her what the rider said. She closed her eyes and screwed up her face in concentration. "I'm to tell you that the woman says to go to Dunfield." That was a town close by to the north. "The woman will wait for you there."

"A woman?" I sat up straight. "Was her name Lily?"

"Aye, I knew there was a flower in't!" the girl said happily. "Lily says for you to go to Dunfield. She would have you there when her time comes and if you are not, you'll be sorry for it. The rider says he was to go up and down the post road with the message."

"Lily," I said with disgust. I tossed the coin to the girl, then another, and asked for a tankard of ale. I leaned back into the bench and faced the fire.

She must have escaped Winterbourne and come after me alone. Why? To see what power she could still exert over me?

"I told you it was him," a man whispered from behind. "And now a toast, laddies. Our friend here proves there's a woman for each of us, so there's hope for me yet!"

"Gorm, *he's* got money at least, if not a face or temper," said Merry.

The girl sidled up close and set the ale by my elbow.

"Yes?" I asked when she did not leave.

"Are you goin' to her?" She was braver now.

"What business is it of yours?"

"I'm curious, is all. It's such an expense sendin' a man out on horseback."

The girl's point troubled me: Lily did nothing without calculation, so what did her message signify? The only ones threatened by her childbirth were herself and the worm.

"It will not survive being born," she had said, referring to how small the worm was. *"If it does, it most assuredly won't survive its first few moments of mothering."*

I allowed myself to feel nothing. What was the worm, after all? Just a nameless, faceless thing, an insect larvae, white and wet and overgrown.

Monstrous.

No! I had protected the worm while I could. Let Winterbourne protect it now.

Another copper, another tankard. Soon I would be needing Sister María Tomás's ministrations. María Tomás . . . I saw her plump red face before me but could not read its expression. The image made me quit the inn.

Outside, carried faintly on a thin breeze, came the wail of a crying infant. Cursing, I continued south.

February 20

In the early afternoon a man on horseback raced toward me from the south. Alone on the road, I had left my hood down, enjoying the feel of the sun on my face, which meant more to me than mere warmth. Habit made me grab the cloth to pull it up. The thought made me resentful. Would men steal even the sun from me?

The distance between us narrowing, I imagined the rider

staring hard at my face even from far away. I stepped off the road to let him pass, but he reined in the animal so sharply it reared and kicked.

"It's you!" he declared. Though tall and lanky, he was little older than a boy, and he gave me a boy's wide smile, so pleased that he never once frowned at the look of me. "I've gone through four horses searchin' for you!" Jumping down, he reached inside his pocket.

"I have a message," he said.

"I know what it is," I answered curtly, walking away. "So does everyone else in the county"—including Walton. Had Lily forgotten how his blade bit into her cheek? Once she fixed on an idea, reason played no part in her actions.

"No, no, this is for you alone." He waved a letter sealed with wax. "I got paid for sayin' you was to go to Dunfield as the woman's time was come—though to my eyes," he said, dropping his voice to share this confidence, "she didn't look nearly big 'nough to be ready. I'm the oldest of twelve, so I've seen ready. Anyway that was my message and that's what I was paid to say. I get paid more for deliverin' this."

He pressed the letter upon me. When I would rip it up unread, he grabbed my wrist.

"If you read it," he said hopefully, "she'll double my pay."

I reached into my pocket.

"My coin is as good as hers."

"At least read it." He brushed back his thin hair, stringy with sweat, then dried his fingers on his trousers.

"Are your instructions to wait till I do?"

He nodded.

"Go back and say you did. She will pay you, not knowing if you did or not."

He gaped at me. "I said I would deliver it, and I said I would wait till you had read it."

"To meet an honest man so late in life," I bemoaned. For the boy's sake I broke the seal. I thought I would merely pretend to scan the contents, but the short message captured my eyes.

"First I will birth it. Then I will name it Victor. Last I will suffocate it."

I crumpled the note and squeezed tightly, wishing it were Lily's neck.

Dunfield
February 22

I continued south for several hours before thoughts of the worm slowed my pace, stopped it, then at last forced me to turn round. Unwillingly I began the journey north. Toward noon of the next day I met the rider again on the road. He did not seem surprised I had changed my course and said that the woman now wanted to know the hour of my arrival. Cursing Lily for anticipating me, I said I thought I should be in Dunfield around sunset.

"She said she'll wait in the old mill at the far edge of town." The boy shook his head and laughed. "What you're to do there I don't know. My pa always got drunk when the time come. Anyway, that's what I was to say and I've said it. After I give her your answer, it's back to the farm." He sighed, his adventure over. "Good thing it wasn't plantin' time or Pa would never have let me go."

The boy rode off, presumably to tell Lily when I would be at her side.

So short a distance now. But what would I do in Dunfield? And why did I go?

As the day cooled down, I dragged out each step till I came to the signs at a crossroads. The way to Dunfield lay along a road that hooked away from the main thoroughfare. I followed this smaller road and, by the time the sun set, could see buildings through the trees ahead. At this point I slipped into the woods and walked parallel to the road, reluctant to show myself too openly. Too many people had heard the message summoning me here; for my own safety, I should not have come.

Enough past the town so that it was no longer visible from it stood an old mill. I eyed its dark, vacant windows and half-open doors overgrown by last summer's weeds, shriveled by the winter to straw. Most of the waterwheel had rotted through, leaving the bare skeleton of its iron fixings. The waterwheel hung over a dry streambed, which explained why the great millstones had ground to a stop. Spiders would be the only workers there tonight, spinning webs from every corner, and mice the only customers, gathering up the last bits of grain.

Discarded millstones, their grooves worn too smooth to be of use grinding, had been set into the earth to make a path around the building. Still others lay propped against one another in a haphazard pile. There I sat, even after darkness had completely fallen and a single light flared in one of the windows. I told myself I was ensuring that no one had followed me and that this was not a trap laid by Walton. But long after I was certain I was alone, I remained outside. If I had thoughts, I do not remember them. I simply waited.

After a few hours had passed, I crept closer, circling the mill. In the back I found the answer to the question of how Lily had come here from Tarkenville: the elegant painted carriage I had stolen had been drawn up to a side door. Its beautiful horses were still hitched. I was surprised to see all four—that Lily had not beaten them mercilessly the way she had beaten the animals when we first left Tarkenville.

The horses snorted and shied when they saw me but did not panic.

Entering the mill from the side opposite to where I had seen the light, I let my eyes, my cat's eyes, become accustomed to the dark. I walked through the grinding room, storerooms, a smithy, an office. The building was as deserted as it appeared. Light flickered from beneath a door.

I pushed it open. This room had held cast-off tools: a bent scythe with a broken handle, a near-toothless rake, snapped barrel hoops, slivered pieces of wood, rotted sacking.

I opened the door to its widest. Only then did I see Lily on the floor next to a lantern. Head tilted, arms limp at her sides, legs splayed, she looked like a rag doll propped against the wall. Trousers and boots tossed off, she was naked from the waist down but for her stockinged feet.

A gasp whistled through my teeth.

She opened her eyes. "Sunset was hours ago," she said. "I did not think you were coming." Beneath her jacket, the farmer's shirt that she still wore was long enough that its hem dipped down between her parted legs and covered her sex. The bottom edge of the shirt was marked by a large fresh stain, and I asked: "Is it your time?"

"I have made it my time. Oh, Victor, you left me too long alone!" She lifted her hand; in it she clasped a rusted metal file. "Look what I found."

She tilted the file till the moisture on its tip caught and held the light.

"I'd have carved it out long ago. I find I am a coward even now and could make but the barest prick. Perhaps what I was wanting all along, though, was your eyes on me."

She drew up her legs as if she would once more thrust the file between them.

I did not move. I could not move.

With a half-strangled scream, she threw the file across the room and covered her face with her palms.

"What have I done?" she cried.

"No more than you promised to do in the letter."

"The letter." Her anguish was brief. "I wrote the letter while in Tarkenville right after you left. Later I regretted giving it to the boy."

"Yet you acted on it."

"You said you'd be here by sunset," she said, half beggingly.

How many hours had I waited outside while she had waited in here alone, thinking I would not come? How close had I come to leaving even then?

"We must go into town," I said, picking up her clothes. "Someone will help you."

"No, not here, not in Dunfield. He will know to look for us in Dunfield."

I did not have to ask whom she meant.

"Why be afraid?" I said cruelly. "He would only finish your work for you."

"Think of me then," she whispered. "Think of yourself." Her voice became urgent. "Now that you are here, we must leave at once! We must put this place far behind us."

Her eyes shone, their feverish glitter unhealthy against her pale face.

"How far should I take you?" I asked, recognizing her old craftiness.

"To London, Victor." Her hand flew up to the barrette. "You must take me to London."

She fell into a grinning silence. I dressed her, tearing the sleeves off my shirt to stuff into her trousers as a bandage. When I had finished, she curled into a corner and fell asleep. I was not certain whether to move her and so have written this while I wait to see how her condition fares.

The lantern burns too low for me to continue this entry. I must try to rouse her or else carry her sleeping to the carriage. I think it best that we be far from Dunfield before daylight.

February 24

I drive as a man possessed. I stopped in the first town after Dunfield. Lily refused to leave the carriage, clawing at my face when I reached in. In the next town, I beseeched an elderly woman to help her. When she opened the door to the carriage, Lily kicked her full in the chest and knocked her to the ground.

The pounding of the horses' hooves sets the pace for my thoughts. Traveling round in a groove, my mind circles in on itself. Not even my journal enables it to break free.

Why did I go back to her? Why did I not grab the file from her when she would have stabbed herself? And if I care as little for the worm as she does, if I care as little for Lily herself, why did I bring her with me?

And so I drive.

I would not stop though she pounded on the window, cried out that she was ill, and cursed me vilely. When I at last pulled over, she was scarcely out of the carriage before I accused her of the most wanton callousness.

She pushed me aside and bent double; she had not lied about being sick. Still I felt no pity.

"All your life you have had every good thing heaped upon you," I said. "How can you have come so close to killing and feel nothing?"

She straightened up and pressed her fists into the small of her back.

"What do *you* feel, Victor, when you kill? As little as you claim *I* must? Perhaps exhilaration comes only the first time."

The easy baiting in her words chilled me.

"The first time?"

"The first time one kills," she said, smiling. "Mine was the stable boy. Surely you remember the crime of which *you* were accused. It was the night I told you about the worm, though you did not understand my words. I told you someone was spying on us."

"A boy. So you bludgeoned him till he could be recognized only by a birthmark. For what?"

"He would have blackmailed me!" Lily said. "My marriage was being arranged, my land was being increased. I could not be seen with you in so compromising a way. The boy could have done me much harm if he had talked.

"And besides," she added, "isn't it what everyone wonders, what everyone asks the young soldier when he returns from war: 'How is it to kill someone?' It is a man's power, to take a life. Not *this*," she said, striking her stomach sharply. "Any bitch in heat can do this without thought."

She pulled herself back up into the carriage and settled in her seat. Then her face contorted and she clutched her sides.

"It will be soon now," she whispered. She tried once more to grin. "At least I have succeeded in shortening my sentence by a little while."

Perspiration formed on her upper lip. Her whole body shook. When she opened her eyes, they were flat and cold.

"Do not gaze on me like an idiot, Victor. Get back up and drive. Once the brat is dead, I would be in London the next day to celebrate my freedom."

Why should the worm not be meaningless to her, after all, when the stable boy—who had a name and a face, perhaps overly large ears, a fondness for marzipan, and a neighbor girl sweet on him—when this boy, whom she must have known for years, meant so little?

I asked the only thing I could: "Weren't you afraid of being caught?"

"No. I knew they'd blame you."

Without a word, I shut the carriage door and resumed my seat up on the driver's box. When I lashed out at the horses with the whip, it was Lily's face I saw before me.

Later

Again she had me stop. This time she fell to the ground, just to lie quietly, she said, away from the ceaseless jarring of the ride. A pinkish stain marked her trousers. She pushed me away when I said I would use the rest of my shirt for a clean bandage. Her pains were very sharp, yet irregular; there was no way of knowing how much longer she must wait.

"The worm has grown teeth and claws," she said, gasping. "It is trying to rip its way out. Oh, kill it, Victor, kill it!" Then, breathing more easily, she bade me help her back in and drive.

And again, later

No spasms for a while, though Lily's trousers are a sodden mess. Whenever I slow down, she screams wildly that I must not stop, that I must drive straight through to London. Instead of weakening her, the pain has given her new strength born of madness. And so I drive, telling myself that she will try to hurt herself again unless I do as she says. All the while I am listening—hoping?—for her to fall silent.

I do not know when I can write again, or what it is I will say.

March 3

It was dusk when I first heard the hoofbeats behind us. A horse and rider were racing up. Made desperate by Lily's cries, I could no longer endure my inaction.

Just minutes before, she had shrieked so wildly I pulled to the side at once. When I opened the carriage door, the smell of blood flowed thickly from the confined interior. With the setting sun I could scarcely see inside the coach; only her pale face was visible, floating in the blackness.

"Drive!" she said, her voice hoarse. "Do not worry. It is not yet time. I will do nothing without you."

What did she mean? That together we would give birth to the worm, together give it death?

Before I could snap the reins, I heard the hoofbeats.

I waved to the rider to stop. He rode past, pulled up sharply, and jerkingly circled around. Sitting far forward and askew, he swayed to the other side, then slipped down and nearly fell off. He is intoxicated, I thought. A drunkard could offer little assistance.

"Are we near a town?" I called. "Or at least a farm?"

There was a sharp crack as Lily's fist struck the window, followed by a wailing "Nooo!" As her protest dissolved into pain, her white hand opened and stretched flat on the glass.

"You can no longer refuse attention," I said, then stood up on the box and asked, "Where is the closest town?"

The man, heavily muffled against the weather, forced his horse closer, which made it rear and prance. For a moment I thought he would fall, he leaned so far to the left. The horse panted out steamy breaths as if ridden hard for a long time.

"There is a woman here in childbirth," I said.

Did the sound of Lily crying out at that very moment distract me, or did the scarf round the man's face make his voice too soft for me to hear more than the words?

"Your wife?" he asked, riding closer.

"Yes." Any other response would give rise to questions I had no time to answer.

"Then I am right to kill you both!"

Another crack. How loudly Lily struck the glass, I thought as the horses leapt and I sat down hard on the box. Then I saw the pistol in the man's hand, saw the puff of smoke rising from its barrel. At the shoulder, my cloak bore a hole, immediately ringed with blood. Terrible cold rushed through me, only to be burned away by a hot stabbing flash.

The man struggled to reload. I threw myself from the box, fell onto his horse's neck, and knocked the man half off the saddle. As the horse bucked, he slid down away from me, still working the gun. The horse reared full up and threatened to trample us. I grabbed its mane and held on, too stunned to do more than let my weight drag the animal to a stop. In the time this took, the stranger had found his feet and finished reloading.

Scarf fallen to reveal his face, Walton aimed his pistol at me again, his lame, burnt body in the crooked stance I had mistaken for drunkenness.

"Victor! Victor, now!"

Lily's voice, harsh and guttural, made us both turn. A flash of white appeared at the window. Immediately Walton shifted his aim and fired. The bullet shattered the glass.

Again the horses leapt, and this time, without my hand to stay them, they bolted down the road, jerking the carriage after them. I tried to mount Walton's horse. He jumped at me, his grotesque body as horrible as a nightmare. I swatted him, pulled myself into the saddle with my good arm, and galloped after Lily.

Walton's horse, already exhausted and now carrying the weight of a giant, could not overtake the carriage. Instead we trailed behind at greater and greater lengths. *"Victor! Victor, now!"*—Lily had cried. But after the second shot, only silence. I slapped the horse and urged it onward with shouts.

Far away to the south the road curved downward into a

valley, leading to such an unnatural glow that the sky itself burned, it seemed, as it burned on Lily's last night in Tarkenville. Traveling down the curve, the carriage disappeared from sight. My heart hammered and I could not breathe.

"Faster!" I shouted. Trying to spur the horse on, I nearly slid from the saddle, my own strength sapped by fiery pain. I wrapped my arms around its neck and held on.

Columns of smoke rose up in that strangely lit sky. Soon I was close enough to see the underside of the clouds orange with reflected fire. An inferno was before me: I was chasing Lily into Hell. I felt my flesh being consumed, starting with my shoulder.

Night cast its darkness like a net that would draw me in and trap me; it was dark, all dark, save the weird light in the distance made more vivid by the surrounding night. The light pulled me in, pulled me down the road; I descended quickly, willingly, racing on and on toward damnation till I fell from the saddle. Fingers knotted in the reins, I was dragged along till the horse at last stopped.

The ground beneath me beckoned: Close your eyes, give up.

"*Victor, now!*" I heard, or maybe it was the mute scream of the worm.

I pulled myself to my feet. If I once more mounted the tired horse, I would prompt no speed from it, so I gave it the only rest I could by trotting alongside.

Down and down the road led till finally, rounding a bend, it passed under a great bridge like the gateway to the underworld and opened onto a scene that displayed the horrors of man's art.

Before me lay a river and on the riverbank an ironworks, a huge vaulted building whose inside was open to view. The furnace dwarfed the men who walked its top to feed it barrow after barrow of coal to make iron. Next to it sat a tremendous bellows powered by chutes of water to provide a continual blast of air. The bellows wheezed as if a great dying beast were encased in its leather flaps. With its every breath the furnace burned more hotly, flames shot up from the top, and thick black smoke billowed out. The river itself was ablaze as the water's reflection held the fire captive.

Everywhere men rushed back and forth. Panting with their labors, they breathed smoke into the frosty air and so burned themselves along with the coal. They looked up as I passed, a giant running alongside a horse, then they looked down upon their work once more. Had they dismissed Lily as easily, an out-of-control carriage of less importance than their drive to keep the furnace in blast, hour after hour, day after day, till the river dried up and the ore was mined out?

Shoddy row houses lay beyond the ironworks: cracked slate roofs, crumbling brick walls, undrained alleys between, and privies—far too close, and far too few.

The carriage had not stopped here.

"Faster," I whispered to the horse. Even at this weary trot, it breathed as noisily as the bellows, its energies drained by the double chase, first Walton's, now mine. I tried to walk a little faster myself. The raw ache in my shoulder flashed down my arm and up my neck; around the bullet hole my cloak was soaked with an ever-widening circle of blood.

Up ahead the houses ended and the town spread out into places of commerce: taverns and stores, potteries with kilns attached, a blacksmith, a brewery, a bakery, a school, and a church. Some distance beyond this, still below the road but also crossing it to engulf the other side, was a colliery, another hellish engine of human art that did not close for the night.

Before the road had passed by the trade shops, it had forked; the branch closest to the river ran directly through the colliery, the other veered to the right as if to circumvent it. Just a few yards along the upper path, deep ruts marked the road, and it was there I found the carriage. It had lost a wheel and overturned, dragging one horse down with it. The animal lay on its side, legs flailing; the other horses pulled at the harness in a frenzied effort to free themselves. I began to run and called out Lily's name.

How she had found the strength, I do not know, but she had crawled out of the wreck and sat against its side, her legs drawn up, her chalky face contorted. One hand, pressed to her heart, was pierced as by a saint's stigmata. It bled profusely, and I realized it was not her face that had been the flash of white I had seen and at which Walton had shot.

I tried to gather her into my arms to carry her to town.

"There is no time," she said, her voice almost too weak to be heard.

One of the mares reared, bumping the carriage, and Lily screamed and swore. I unharnessed the animals to keep them from jostling her again. Before I thought to tie them elsewhere, the three mares ran down the road, followed by Walton's horse. The horse on the ground had broken its leg and lay there whinnying, rolling back its lips and showing its teeth.

"Help me," Lily said. I took off her boots, then trousers. The soaked cloth peeled away, making my hands slick with blood. With my cloak I covered her nakedness. She complained of its smell, but her voice was thin. Another cramp seized her. Howling, she writhed against the carriage.

"You must push, Lily, even I know as much."

"I cannot."

"Push it out," I said. "It is the worm. You hate it, you despise it. It is a loathsome parasite feeding on your flesh. It has invaded your body, it has ruined your life. Push it out! Push it out so you can kill it!"

She grabbed my hand and squeezed. My whole arm caught fire and I remembered the bullet in my shoulder.

"Push," I whispered. I slipped my other arm around to cradle her back. The fallen horse moaned so loudly I raised my voice: "Push, and you will be rid of it!"

When she finished, there was no final triumphant yell. She simply let her head drop back against the carriage.

"Is it alive?" she asked.

I looked at the mess that lay between her legs, so covered with blood I could scarcely see it in the darkness. Too much blood. Had Lily not said the worm had grown teeth and claws and was ripping its way out? Surely it had done so, and that was why Lily was still bleeding.

But there were no claws. It was as weak a thing as I ever saw that yet lived. I pulled the tiny body up by its slippery feet and laid it in my palm. It gave a hiccuppy cough, took a small gulp of breath, and opened its eyes, but it did not cry. Sticking my great finger into its mouth, I cleared out some mucus and, with the edge of my shirt, wiped the blood from its head. It was very small, with an odd shriveled face as if an old man possessed its soul. One leg was withered and shorter than the other.

I hated it fully and at once, with a physical revulsion that made my stomach clench. Did I despise the thing because it was ugly? That made me no better than the rest of the world, no better than my father.

"It is a boy," I said.

"It is the worm. Give it to me."

"No," I said, holding it close, away from her reach. "It is feeble and will die of its own soon. Let this not be on your conscience as well."

"Give it to me, Victor," she repeated. She gasped; her body clenched with a spasm.

"Push again," I said. "There is more to come."

She had no strength left, and the blood still flowed from her. Because she had not passed the afterbirth, she was attached to that which she hated. So I cut the cord, using the sharp edge of a rock. I was surprised at how the thing resisted me, forcing me to bring the rock down again and again.

At last Lily and the worm were separated. I ripped a strip from my shirt, tied the cord, and coiled it on the worm's stomach. Noticing how it quivered, I took my shirt off entirely. The one side of it was stiff with my own blood; I folded that to the bottom and wrapped the clean side round the worm. Fighting my hatred, I held it close till I felt its breath on my face, so faint it would not make a feather stir. I pulled the cloak over the three of us, then took Lily's hand, gently squeezing back in answer to the slightest movement of her fingers.

"Is it dead now?" she asked. She could not see that I held it.

"Yes," I said. "It is dead."

"Then I am free." Her body convulsed. In a little while, the pain passed and she looked up at me and smiled. "When shall we arrive in London?"

Against my legs, the cloak felt wet where it had soaked up her life.

"Tomorrow," I answered.

"Tomorrow? Foolish Victor, I am teasing you. I shall die soon."

"No, I will take you to London."

"However will you live without me?"

"Tell me," I asked. "Tell me truly. Why did you stay with me all this time?"

Countless expressions passed over her pale face: pity and cunning, anger and hate, and finally, such gentleness as I have never before seen. Would she lie or would she be truthful? And would I care? Not if she said she loved me.

She never spoke, only closed her eyes and rested her head against the carriage. Her breathing became very slow; the pressure of her fingers against mine, the barest tremble. Such shallow breaths, such a slight tremble, that in the end I did not know when she had breathed her last. Waiting to hear she loved me, I held on to her cold hand tightly, as if it were possible to keep her. Needing to hear she loved me, I held on to her cold hand tightly, as if it were possible to follow.

Where was Winterbourne this very moment? I wondered. Did he suddenly feel his heart fill with unaccountable grief? In the church I said I had protected her, kept her safe for his sake. And in the church he rejected me. Had I let her die because of it?

I pulled Lily close. The feel of her body limp against my arm reminded me of Mirabella, how I had held her, too, after she had been shot. Two women, one leading to the other, both dead, and for no better reason than that they both stayed with me for a little while.

After cradling the worm on my lap, I shakily removed the necklace I had given Lily, Mirabella's necklace. I fastened it back around my wrist where it belonged, next to the bracelet Lily had fashioned for me. Two women, two gifts, two deaths. The little charms tinkled as I moved, and the worm turned its head toward the noise.

The worm: Winterbourne's grandson. If he had a choice, he would take this pale wrinkly thing over me—another reason to hate the worm. Still, I lifted the little thing up to my chest and pulled the cloak over us again for warmth.

Minutes passed, or hours, or days. Someone drew close, carrying a lantern. Walton, I thought, come to finish what he had begun. I did not lift my head.

"There's been murder done here!" a man shouted.

From farther away: "Another joke, Darby? We'll be late for the shift."

"'Tis a man and a woman, both of them dead. There's blood everywhere. My God! His face!"

Stirring, I raised my eyes to see blunt features framed by bushy black hair and a beard. Part of the man's cheek had been scooped away, an old wound, long healed. The rest of his skin was deeply pitted with strange bluish marks. When I looked up, he cried out, "He's alive!" He pulled the cloak away. "And there's a baby! That's alive too!"

A dozen voices filled the air.

"Settle down," Darby said. "Cooper, Sheffield, Smith—help me carry him to town. It'll take at least three of us, maybe four. Why, he looks twice bigger than old Tom Humphries! The lot of you should go meet the shift. No need for all of us to be docked, and no need for Paxton's crew to be sent back down again."

As Darby picked up the worm, I whispered, "Get rid of the thing. *Get rid of it!*"

When the men lifted me, an explosion of pain pulled the night crashing down till I at last knew nothing. Oblivion was dark and sweet, but I was too soon forced to wakefulness by a howl so loud God himself must have gone mad.

I awoke with a violent start and found myself on my back, lying on the floor in a dark room. From the ceiling hung smoked meats, thumping into one another as they swung wildly. Crockery had fallen and shattered; on the shelf, a lone unbroken bowl spun itself dizzy. The air was powdery, like someone had just run through sawdust.

What had happened?

My ears hurt. At first I thought only noise had wakened me—an enormous, astonishing boom that still echoed inside my head. But the meat swung and the bowl spun and the floor I lay on vibrated.

A moment of silence, not half-a-blink long, then—

Shrieks from the next room. And from the road, names, instructions, wails overlapped in a single cry of agony.

I bolted up to a sitting position, was immediately crushed back by the fierce pain in my shoulder. I gritted my teeth and used the other arm to push myself up. I sat, then I knelt, then I stood.

A tunic had been made for me from sackcloth, two or three flour bags split open and stitched together to make a loose sleeveless shirt. Beneath it was a dressing on my shoulder, which had soaked through. While I watched, the bottom edge dripped. Instantly all the blood of all the world fell from the heavens. Standing bowed beneath this steaming cataract, I remembered.

Lily was dead.

And Walton was still alive.

Another blast! The ground convulsed: the earth itself shifted, as if the turmoil trapped in my soul had burst free. I staggered out, tripping where the floor had collapsed and dirt and stone had thrust upward. The main room was a tavern, empty now, half-filled mugs and smoking pipes abandoned on the counter. I ran out into the road. People raced by me unseeingly. Men struggled to button trousers or to pull coat sleeves onto their bare arms as they ran by. Women with tear-soaked faces dragged children by one hand, clutched babies with the other.

Down the road at the colliery, a pillar of flame spewed into the air, so huge as to transform night to day. A bell clanged over and over; another bell from the town soon answered.

Someone grabbed me from behind. Thinking it was Walton, I swung round and seized his throat, then recognized the man who had found me on the road. I let him go. He rubbed his neck and winced.

"What did you think? That I was your wife's murderer?"

"What happened?"

"An explosion in the mine."

"Hurry, Darby!" someone called.

"What of you?" Darby asked. "You're up, though I never thought you'd be on your feet so soon. Will you come?"

"You would ask *me* for help?" I said in wonder.

"I'd ask the Devil himself to go into the mine for us. Maybe I *am* asking him."

My chest grew thick with the strange discomfort of putting aside my anger. Nodding, I followed him to the colliery.

The fire was at the rear and issued from the upcast shaft, which was used for ventilation, Darby explained, pointing as we ran toward the site. The furnace on top that created the draft had exploded, followed by another explosion down in the mine.

The winding gear stretched across the main shaft, a massive wooden frame of pulleys and drums powered by an engine to lower the men and pull up the coal, both in an iron cage. The explosion had split the upright timbers and crossbars. Repairs had already begun.

"That's my shift down there, my friends." Darby's eyes met mine, then moved away. "I don't know whether to curse or thank the luck that had me stop for you."

The men could not wait till repairs were finished. A rope was attached to the drum of a smaller engine used for sawing wood, then hooked to the cage to lower rescuers. Darby insisted on being the first to go down the shaft. I went with him, although there were quiet arguments whether I would bring bad luck into the mine. After all, it had exploded just hours after I had been found. Darby reminded them I was helping even as I mourned my wife. The others turned away, shamefaced.

I ducked down and squeezed myself into the interior of the cage. It was aptly named, for I felt trapped by the iron bars.

"Now we'll see if the little engine will hold," Darby said, grinning.

As soon as we were in place and a safety lamp was handed to each of us, the engine was started. It played out the rope and, with a loudly creaking effort, lowered us into smoky blackness. The silence was uneasy, so I asked, "What do you think caused the explosion?"

"Reynolds will say there are as many reasons as miners."

"Who is Reynolds?"

"The new mine boss." Darby spat in disgust. "He refused us more props to support the mine ceilings. Said it was dead work settin' props, as there's no profit in't. Now Reynolds will know about dead work for sure."

He looked up the shaft, the circle of light at the top slowly waning.

"In the tavern we sing a song about him. I hear it began in the city, but it suits. Here's the part I like best."

Still looking upward, his face as earnest as a penitent's, he started to sing.

> And may the odd knife his great carcase dissect,
> Lay open his vitals for men to inspect
> A heart full as black as the infernal gulph
> In that greedy, bloodsucking, bone-scraping wolf.

Poetry was different for the miners, just a hard song about their hard boss, sung by lips so grimy after their shift that they drank coal dust with each sip of ale. Darby broke off the song and laughed, at himself it seemed. He extended his hand awkwardly.

"Tell me who you are."

"I'm Victor Hartmann." How easily my lips now spoke the name, how easily I took his hand. "I know you are Darby."

"John Darby, yes. You are good to put yourself in danger for us, bein' a new father as well as mournin' your wife, and I thank you."

Mourning. Twice now he had said the word. My fingers found the bracelet Lily had made for me.

"It's nothing you yourself are not doing," I answered.

"But I'm a miner and you're not. You have a dozen good reasons to stay above. I wouldn't have begrudged you, even though I'd asked. Besides, I still don't believe that you're up. I saw what the bullet did to your shoulder. I know how much blood you lost."

I looked away.

"Most of it was hers," I said, my voice rough. I remembered telling him to get rid of the worm. "Where is . . . ?"

"I brought it to the baker's wife. She's a wet nurse." Darby patted my arm. "'Tis common to hate the child that killed the mother. But a son is a son, cripple or no. You'll feel differently in a month."

In a month, Lily would still be dead.

Our descent stuttered to a halt, then the cage dropped in free fall. A jerky stop sent my head crashing against the cold iron bars. The cage itself banged against the sides of the shaft as round and round it twisted on its cable. Long dizzying moments passed, then once more we slowly, fitfully descended.

Darby looked up at the pinprick of light that was the shaft's opening. "I do hope she holds," he said. "This is only the first trip. 'Twould take too long to lower the cage by hand."

From below I heard a rushing noise.

"What's that?"

"There's a sump at the bottom. An engine pumps the water to the top. See this?" He held up his lamp to illuminate the wall of the shaft. A pipe appeared to run its length. "The explosion must have cracked it," he said as the noise grew louder.

"What does that mean?"

"The mine will flood without repairs, but not so fast you need worry. Worry about fixed air chokin' you, firedamp explodin' in your face, cave-ins buryin' you alive."

He laughed grimly.

Just before we passed the break in the pipe, he had us turn our backs to protect the lamps from the water. Deeper and deeper we dropped, like bait on a hook dangling in the darkest ocean. The air grew thicker with smoke. Darby coughed for several minutes, then suddenly yanked a scarf from his pocket and tied it over his mouth and nose.

"I should have put this on up top. I hope that's the last mistake I make this night. You'll need something too." He started to unbutton his shirt, meaning to rip off some of the cloth. I closed my hand over his and shook my head. It would not bother me.

We hit bottom with a thump. Darby did not notice how I sucked in my breath with pain, or else he would have sent me back up. Stepping out of the cage, he shook a hand bell that was tied to one of its bars. The rope ceased to fall.

"Will! Will Cobb! Pete?"

No one answered. Darby motioned me out, then rang the bell again. The cage began to return to the surface.

We were in a large, low-ceilinged chamber that had been carved out of the rock. Although our lamps were dim, my uncanny eyes saw far beyond their small circle of light. Several tunnels led into the chamber. Within each tunnel was a set of wooden railroad tracks leading straight back into the darkness. A stub switch had been built in this main chamber so that a straight line of tracks was able to curve around, cross the other tracks from the other tunnels, and then merge with them to make a single line. In this manner the coal carts could run from each tunnel to the cage and then be brought to the surface.

Narrow spikes had been nailed into the walls as hooks. On the ground lay all sorts of tools: spades, hammers, wedges, and drills. There were long-handled picks, short-handled picks, and some with no handles at all, just double-pointed heads. Each had its use, depending on whether the miner had room enough to stand or had to crouch low or had to wriggle on his belly into a space so narrow all he could do was chip away at the rock.

"I'm glad the lamps didn't go out," Darby said. "I couldn't risk striking a flint." He showed me the screen encircling the wick. "Don't ever let the flame pass beyond the mesh. There are more gases down here than names for them. Blackdamp and chokedamp and afterdamp. If the flame dwindles, get back where you can breathe. If it flares, drop to the ground. There's firedamp at the ceiling. It can explode, though sometimes it'll just burn up. Coal dust can explode, too, when there's enough of it and it has a mind to. Doesn't need a spark, doesn't give you warnin'. It's like a hotheaded woman with a toothache."

I nodded. Lily had taught me at least one thing I could share with other men.

"By now you're wondering if there's anything down here that can't kill you." Darby grinned. "The answer is no."

"What should I be looking for?" I asked.

"Follow the main track so you don't get lost. Call out, see

if anyone answers. Ignore the pit ponies for now, but remember, each has a driver somewhere close."

The ground vibrated beneath us and a low rumble thundered from far away.

"Sounds like a cave-in," Darby said, swearing vehemently. "Reynolds has been scantin' the props in the waste rooms as well: those are the rooms where the coal's been worked out. Or maybe she bumped in one of the back tunnels."

"Bumped?"

"That's when the ground shifts and the floor bumps up to meet the ceiling. It's like a mouth clampin' shut, but no miner wants to find himself between *those* lips. Go on now. Keep as low as you can, though I see you're already bent over. At least hold the lamp down. There's more gas for sure with this last bit of business."

He strode away into the darkness.

I waited, watching his light fade, listening to the gurgle from the sump and the faint noise of the lift at the top of the shaft. From within the darkness here, Darby called out to any who could hear him.

I entered the tunnel opposite the one he had taken. Holding the lamp low, I walked past rough-hewn walls and timbers of supporting wood. Up ahead, part of the track curved away toward a wood-and-canvas door, fit snugly into an earthen archway. I opened it and called out. My words echoed, hinting at the depths within. No one answered.

From behind me I heard voices and realized the lift had returned with more men. I had been dreaming, struck by all I saw, and now hastened my step. There was no time for delay.

For a while I stayed to the track, but there were doors beyond the main ones. I grew frustrated, imagining miners trapped behind each. When I opened perhaps the fifth or sixth, I stepped inside. Another closed door stood at the back.

Without thinking, I lifted my lamp to better see the supports. Too late I remembered Darby's caution. At once the flame of the lamp swelled as if oil had been spilled on it, and with a sharp crack the ceiling ignited. I dropped to the ground. In an instant the whole ceiling burned with a roiling pool of flames. I stayed a moment, held by the awful beauty, then crawled out backward. The effort set my shoulder aching, and blood soon flowed steadily from beneath the bandage.

Quickly I returned to the main tunnel. Fireflies of light pricked the darkness, marking more men from above. Knowing the others could better search the warren of rooms behind the doors I had passed, I continued down the main track. Smoke gathered at the top of the tunnel and I bent even lower to find the sweeter air.

The next door had been torn off its frame with tremendous force, and its boards scattered across the tunnel, one driven into the wall itself. Stepping into the room, I found an empty coal cart knocked off the tracks. Just beyond that was a pit pony slumped against the wall. Between the two, head and arms resting on the pony's back, was a boy no older than twelve. Both boy and animal looked to be asleep. They were not.

Though expected, the sight of this first body stunned me. Sweat crept across my skin as I lifted the boy up and laid him in the righted cart. I did not know if the force of one of the explosions had killed him or the smoke that clouded my eyes. It was only after a few moments had passed that I realized his presence here must indicate a work site.

"Can anyone hear me?" I called out. "Is anyone there?"

Silence.

I followed this branch set of rails till I came to another door, also torn off. There I found the body of a younger boy on the ground beside it.

Finally I understood that most of the work would not be a rescue.

I went back for the coal cart and pushed it along the track to this second door. I laid the younger boy alongside the first and pushed the cart into the next room.

In here shovels and picks were scattered about, as well as empty wooden tubs with curved bottoms like the runners on a sleigh. Among the tools lay two men in loose-limbed positions. I put them at the bottom of the cart and repositioned the smaller bodies on top.

Off this room ran several smaller tunnels, just now being worked, each only a few feet high. Getting down on my knees, I held my light to the first tunnel and caught the shining gleam of a thin seam of coal and the sight of a man's booted foot. I grabbed onto it and tugged. Rocks spilled out: the tunnel had caved in. I cleared away chunks of coal and loose dirt. The body came free and I laid the man in the cart.

In the next tunnel, the lamp revealed a girl of about six, her little face blackened with coal dust. I took her under her arms, expecting to pull her out easily, but could not. This tunnel had also caved in. I dug around her body. Straps and chains around her waist led to a heavy object, and it was this that had been buried. The narrowness of the tunnel prevented my undoing the straps, so I just gripped the chains and dragged the weight from the earth that covered it. When I pulled the child clear, I saw she had been harnessed to one of the curved tubs like a pit pony.

This body seemed the heaviest of all. I laid it atop the others. A tear glittered on the girl's cheek. My blood raced, then I realized the tear was not hers.

This is what it meant to be human—to die.

And I, who had been made of death, still had no part in humanity.

I leaned against the cart and gripped its sides for support. Compared to what I had just seen, my own existence, which I had always deemed miserable, was a riotous celebration of freedom. I had counted myself unfortunate without knowing what the word might mean to some.

The tightness in my chest squeezed my heart and I gasped. The room had grown darker; the lamp was nearly extinguished. The air in here was bad, but I had not noticed the dimming flame. I pushed the cart along its rails back toward the main tunnel. Suddenly the ground beneath me shook more violently than before.

At the movement came a low moan.

"Hello?" Perhaps the vibration had stirred someone to waking. "Where are you?" I asked. I had too little breath to speak more loudly than a whisper. I extended the lamp and hoped its flame held for a moment longer.

"Here . . . here . . ."

It was a boy, along the track just beyond the next shattered door, thrown back against the wall behind a cart. The cart must have shielded him somewhat from the explosion, though he was dazed and his face was bloody from a gash that ran the width of his forehead.

"Shut the door," he said weakly as I carried him through the archway. The doors throughout the tunnels directed the path of ventilation, Darby had told me, and were open and shut by children who sat in the dark, waiting for a cart to pass. The boy panted out his words: "Benny said I'm never . . . to leave it open. . . . Shut the door."

I whispered to him that I had.

Though I hated to put the living among the dead, there was no place for the boy other than the cart. Fortunately his eyes were closed, and he did not realize who his companions were.

At that moment the light failed.

Using the rails as my guide, I pushed the cart through the darkness. The load was heavy with bodies, and though the burden was made lighter by the one who yet lived, the effort proved a terrible strain. The foul air that had extinguished the light made my lungs burn and sapped my strength. By the time the air had grown sweeter and I had pushed the cart into the first room, my legs felt rubbery and boneless, and I was slumped over it in exhaustion.

Faraway voices floated toward me. I realized I did not have to do this alone. I gathered up the child, felt my way down the rest of the line till I passed the final archway into the main tunnel. With what was surely my last breath I called out, "Down here . . . a boy . . . alive."

I rested against the wall. Circles of light danced as two men hurried toward me. One would have taken the boy, but I would not give him up.

"I can walk," I said. "But there's a cart with bodies just beyond the door. That's as far as I could push it."

They set one of the lamps on the ground by my feet, then brought out the cart. It took both men; they were amazed that I alone had pushed it as far as I did, especially with the bad air and my bleeding wound. They did not look into the cart, only at the boy.

"It's Tommy Sutton," one man said. He peered up at me. "You're Darby's Devil!"

"Is that what they're calling me?"

"That and more. You'll find out on top." He pointed to my

shoulder. At some point the bandage had fallen off. The open wound was ugly. "The doctor's arrived," the man said. "Get that dressed when you bring the boy up."

They pushed the cart back to the lift for me while I held the child in the crook of my arm, his head on my shoulder. The farther we walked, the more his breathing eased. At last his hand stole round my neck as if he were home asleep, pulling his pillow close. From time to time we passed other rescuers, each of whom asked who the boy was.

The lift was not there when we arrived, but its low growl echoed in the shaft. Safety lamps had been hung on the wooden supports, lighting up this room where the main tunnels intersected. One of the men brought me a dipperful of water from a barrel.

"No need for us to wait with you," he said. "Just ring the bell when you're in the cage and ready to go." He followed the other man back down the tunnel.

When the cage came to a stop, the two men inside it pushed out an empty cart. They looked at mine with its heap of bodies, nodded, and pushed it into the cage without speaking. I squeezed in behind it, still holding the boy, and rang the bell.

How much time had passed since I had made the journey down with Darby? I could not guess. The lift moved at a dizzying rate, suggesting that the winding gear had been repaired. I held the boy close and waited for the light.

When I reached the top, dozens of women cried aloud at the sight of the child and reached out. Only one of them found comfort.

With a fearful glance, she seized her son as if I meant him harm, then immediately faltered. "I never thought to be blessin' the Devil," she said. "Thank you." She hurried off. Someone led me in the same direction to the doctor.

The crowd parted before me. From both sides and behind, the whispering began: "Darby's Devil," then hushed murmurs. I was too exhausted to be angry. I followed my guide to the doctor. Only the boy I had brought up needed to be treated before me; no other survivors had yet been found. I let the doctor change my bandage, refused to answer his astonished questions about "my condition," then rode with an empty cart back into the hole.

I worked for hours, sometimes alone, sometimes not, unburying the dead and trying to make the breathless breathe. I carried the bleeding till their blood soaked my wounds. I carried the burned till I wore their ashes like penance. The worst: to sit with a miner as he wept over the body he had just found, his own son or daughter.

While I was making another trip to the shaft, Darby passed by, stopping to clap me on my back. I did not know his sooty face until he spoke: "'Tis the work of three men you're doin', Victor Hartmann, but you haven't the sense of one. I hear you're diggin' out bodies where the coal is still fallin'."

Not answering, I pushed the cart into the lift, stepped in beside it, and rang the bell.

"Grief can make a man careless," he said. "Do not make me feel guilty for havin' asked you down here. Don't forget that you're a father."

He reached between the bars of the cage. I took his hand and pressed it. The lift jerked once, then ascended. With a wave, he disappeared down the tunnel.

Up top, I was amazed to see the sun when I had come from such dark work. I blinked hard against its brilliance, but it was still night in the hearts of everyone here. Seventy-eight bodies had been brought up thus far, I was told. I had thought to have my bandage changed again while I was here, but the line for the doctor was long, all of them men injured during the rescue. Not wanting to delay while there was work to do, I returned to the shaft. When the cage came up, it was Darby pushing a cart this time. A long, swelling gash along his hairline bled down the side of his face. I half-carried him to the doctor. When I returned, the cart had already been emptied. I rode down alone.

After the harsh sunlight, the dark, quiet shaft would have been a comfort had I not known I was being lowered into a tomb. I leaned my head against the bars. I could not recall the last time I had rested or the last time my shoulder did not burn as if it held live coals within. Weeks and months and years seemed to have passed.

And yet, just a day ago, Lily had still been alive.

The grisly work had numbed my mind. What would happen when all the bodies had been brought up? What would I do when I had the time to think?

When the cage hit bottom, I walked across the rails to the farthest tunnel. I meant to go back to work, but pain and fatigue at last overwhelmed me. I leaned against the rocky wall, slid down, and sat. From far away a rescuer called over and over, his voice fainter each time. The sump murmured as gently as a brook. The supports creaked once, twice. At last it was so quiet I thought I could hear the whisper of coal dust as it fell.

"They are calling you a widower. So, she's dead."

Walton.

He had come upon me while I dozed, although I should have heard his scraping limp as he dragged one bent leg behind the other, using a pick like a cane, leaning heavily on its head for support. How many injured men had he passed by searching for me?

I thought I would be enraged seeing him again. After such a night as this, I felt only weary recognition.

"What did you do with your spawn?" he asked.

"The child isn't mine," I answered.

"Where is it?" He limped closer. "I will find it anyway in the end."

"As you found your niece?"

"My niece?" A smile cracked the scabs on his lips. "I did not spare my own daughter to see you dead." With demonic speed, he yanked up the pick and slammed the point into the bullet hole in my shoulder. "My own daughter!"

Lily.

I screamed—body and soul shattered in the same instant.

Agony ripped through every muscle, thought, feeling. Who Walton was, what he had done, hammered at me. I barred my mind against him. I had a monster's strength. *I would not let the horror in!*

But it burst in anyway. And the screams became tears.

Poor, poor Lily. To have had such a father—a madman, at a distance, but still a madman. Such a mother—who swung between love and shame. And such as me—whatever I was to her.

I was right. Death stalked her, and it had done so from her very conception.

Walton watched me suffer through the revelation.

"Say I'm mad and I'll not deny it. I am *all* madness now," he said softly. "Only Margaret would say otherwise, but she is dead." He pressed the pick harder into my shoulder and twisted it. "Where is the child? Tell me!"

"You're its grandfather. Would you also be its killer? But then, that would be the same for you."

His laughter was immediate and hearty, and in laughing he unwittingly eased the pressure on the pick by a fraction. I knocked him backward and the pick to the ground. At once he leapt forward and wrapped his fingers round my throat.

The choking sensation incited in me a strange joy, the teacher recognizing his influence upon the student. Walton's fingers tightened. He had a strength born of insanity while I was at my weakest. I staggered to my feet, though still stooped beneath the low ceiling.

Like a dog I shook back and forth, and like a dog he held on. I rushed forward and rammed him up against a wall to knock him loose. He would not let go. Over and over I slammed him till coal dust rained like black snow. The fight exhausted me. When I finally broke free, I slipped to my knees, whereas he at once attacked again. He jabbed at the bloody bandage. Still on my knees, I seized his fists and thus locked we pushed and pulled, swaying absurdly, foolish children playing at a game.

Walton's face, cracked and scarred and twisted, had become a mirror to mine. He was my brother, my twin, closest kin to my soul: it was he and I who were inexorably linked, not he and my father as he so passionately believed. He was the horror that lay beneath the mere scars and deformities of my body, a creature whose violence had grown to match my own. And so I fought with myself, wanting both to kill the monster and to let it live.

Unable to break loose from my grip by tugging backward, Walton instead rushed forward and butted his head into my shoulder. With a howl, I let him go and doubled over, one hand limp, the other clutching my battered arm.

As soon as he was free, he grabbed the pick and, tottering, raised it high over his head as I knelt before him, my head low, a condemned man before the executioner. Just when the pick began its descent, my good hand shot out and shoved him. He tripped backward over the tunnel's rails even as he swung the pick down and forward with the last of his maddened strength. The pick point pierced his own shin, shattered the bone, and struck the metal rail beneath with a crack whose echo was drowned by his sudden wild scream.

At my feet, the poor demented man writhed, his twisted leg now ruined forever, the bottom part nearly hacked off. Even if he survived the shock and blood loss of this amputation, he would never be able to hunt me again. Yet had I not thought as much at other times?

My whole body shook. I could no longer tolerate the uncertainty of the past ten years. I burned with the desire to snap his neck and be done with him.

But what did my desires matter? Had I not seen enough death this night?

Slowly I pulled myself up, holding on to the timber supports.

Walton's eyes were half-closed, and his face was slack and graying. If I left him here like this, he would not survive. Yet neither would he survive if I had to carry him into the lift and hold him in my arms and feel the filth of his hate against my skin.

I used the pick to tear a hole into my grainsack tunic, then ripped off a long strip. I tied a tourniquet around his thigh, avoiding touching him as much as I could while pulling the strip of cloth as tight as it needed to be.

Suddenly hatred returned to his eyes and he threw out his hands to claw at me. I had done all I could and now began to back away down the tunnel. Walton grew still, his eyes on me so penetrating I wished he would lose consciousness or that the lamps hung along the wall would extinguish so that I would not have to see his stare.

Impossibly, he rolled over onto his stomach, hoisted himself up onto his elbows, and began to drag himself after me.

By the dim safety lamps set along the supports, I saw when

the bottom part of his leg flopped loosely over the rail; when the bare shred of skin gave way, leaving the foot behind; when the blood streamed over his chin as he bit down against the effort.

"Lie quietly," I said. "I will go up top and fetch the doctor." I should carry him into the lift with me right now, I thought again, but knew that my resolution not to kill him could not withstand his hatred for as long as the journey to the surface.

Like an awful crawling reptile, he continued to advance, following me slowly.

At last I reached the lift. I rang the bell and stepped inside.

"You're not going to kill me?" he asked. "Why? Because you still hear Winterbourne's voice whispering in your ear?"

"No . . . I have been a monster of my own making," I said wearily. "It has taken me far too long to see it. I will be a man of my own making instead. I have *decided* to be a man."

"Well, you're a fool as well as a monster," Walton said, and he drew the pistol from his shirt, "for men kill, too. This time I will kill us both."

"No!" I cried, but too late.

The crack of the pistol was followed by a great whoosh and a thunderous roar, as the spark of the shot ignited a huge fireball. The hellish globe surrounded Walton and consumed him, then rushed down the tunnel toward me. Gases burned, coal dust exploded, each propelling the fireball faster and faster till the great force shot under the rising lift and hurled the cage upward. Thrown to my back, I lay helplessly as the lift ricocheted up the shaft. The metal beneath me grew red hot. It burnt through my clothes and into my skin and branded me with the mine's own mark. Above me the light swelled from a pinpoint, to a flame, to an all-engulfing sun, as I was thrown clear, up into the sky.

March 15

It has taken me a week to set this all down, recounting everything from the time I first met Walton on the road till the final explosion in the mine. For days after the blast I lay in darkness, Darby said, and for days after awakening I did naught else but write, till he was convinced I had gone mad. There was not ink and paper enough in his house, and he had to fetch it in town wherever he could: sheets of brown wrapping, backs of old letters, endpapers of family Bibles, and such. Even now, cushioned by pillows, I lie on my stomach on the floor of Darby's row house and write. As always, what was chaos when lived has order when written down.

What can I do otherwise? The burns across my back and legs thus far prevent me from walking more than a few yards. I will be scarred for life, the doctor said solemnly. In the silence that followed I began to laugh. I laughed until the tears flowed, and then I laughed some more, until Darby understood the absurdity and joined in.

The greater danger had come from my shoulder. When Walton jabbed the pick into the bullet hole, the bone fractured and the doctor had to dig out the splinters. The wound then became infected, and they expected me to die, or at the least to need amputation almost to the collarbone. But I lived. I will always have a "bad arm," the doctor said. Somehow, that makes it more mine. Despite this, I am thankful I do not write with the hand on that side, or else I would be wild.

I have not yet been able to visit Lily's grave, though Darby's wife says the view is a pleasant one, facing away from the colliery and the ironworks and west toward the hills. At night, when Darby and his wife and children are asleep, I think of

Lily in her grave and wonder if everything I have done since first seeing her on the cliffs has been meaningless. Then the dawn breaks and Darby's children gather and play about me, pretending I am an elephant or a pirate ship or an unclimbable mountain (unclimbable because the burns on my back are still raw). More people have shown me kindness than I ever allowed myself to believe; and many others gave begrudging tolerance. Despite it, Walton or my own violence always forced me to leave, and I never discovered what might have happened if I had stayed where I had been accepted and tried to live peaceably. Now my injuries *force* me to stay—at least for a while—and a child on one side of me stares transfixed at every word I write, a child on the other side weeps piteously because I have not yet told him today's story, and Mrs. Darby is enough at ease to yell at me for dropping crumbs on her newly swept floor.

And what of Lily? Must I discount our days together as meaningless because she was mad? I never knew happiness with her, but I glimpsed its possibility. And, in the end as she lay dying and later as I worked in the mine, I felt pity. I felt forgiveness. I felt . . . even love?

For a monster, such emotion is itself a prize to be treasured.

EPILOGUE

Letter from Anne Todd to
Lizzie Beacham

My dearest Lizzie,

I should have given you news before this, I know, but the rector, who usually writes my letters for me and is so kind as to correct my grammar besides, has been too busy with his duties to spare the time. By now you've heard about the dreadful accident in the mine last month, one hundred forty-nine lost and only twenty-one brought up alive. The rector has gone from burying the dead to comforting the living to helping the widows and orphans. His work is not yet done, but he is sitting with me now over a cup of tea and has consented to put up with my talkative tongue and write down my words. He says he would teach me to write myself but then I wouldn't have such a chance to visit with him and gossip.

Again I'm thankful I'm the wife of a baker and mother of his own apprentices, for it is dreadful enough just to watch such tragedy without having one's husband go down below. George's cousin, whose shift had just come up, was badly hurt when he'd gone back down to help, for a final explosion killed almost as many rescuers as men working the shift. George's cousin will be out of the mine for several weeks, the doctor has told him, which I say is more blessing than curse. At least there will always be bread for him and his family.

Though you may have heard about the accident, you have not heard, I wager, about my part in it, for I did help in a way. The very night it happened, just a few hours before, who should come to my door but John Darby, carrying the most pathetic infant I have ever seen. It was tiny and weak and had a leg that looked like a thin twist of dough. It didn't cry.

Later, when it was hungry, it gave a faint squeak like a mouse caught in a trap.

"Its mother is dead, poor thing," Darby said, "and the father's been shot and is lying up in the tavern. Can you nurse it till we know what to do?"

I felt peculiar to be given a stranger's babe to nurse, and not someone from town I've known all my life, but how could I not take it in with its little wrinkled cheeks and crippled leg? Later I found out the father recovered enough to go below and help. He was a wonder to see, they told me, as big as a giant in a fairy tale and working a fairy tale's deeds, but with so ugly a face they were calling him Darby's Devil by night's end. Of the twenty-one survivors, he alone brought up seventeen, going into the most dreadful and dangerous places to find them. The last explosion hurt him badly. As he lay at Darby's house for days without talking, the stories of what he'd done spread through the town and so excited everyone they wanted to see him. Little Tommy Sutton, Peggy's youngest, was for staking a claim on him, saying the man should be called *Tommy's* Devil, for it was Tommy what he brought up first. As everything became known, the miners started calling the man the Black Angel instead, for all that he did, but not even an angel could stay white down in the mines.

The rector says we must stop calling the giant so many things, as we will confuse him as well as ourselves, and at every name, strange or not, we will all run out into the square and bump into one another.

When he was well enough to walk, the first place he came after seeing his wife's grave was right here. He had to stoop low and sideways to get through the door, and then couldn't straighten up when he got inside. I was so shocked, with him being so tall and having such a dreadful face, that I blurted out, "It's such a start you gave me, your being so ugly, sir. It's you, isn't it? The Black Angel. I swear, you look like you've been in a hundred explosions before this one, I mean, like bits of a hundred miners come together in you." My face was red with shame but my mouth still wouldn't stop. "I swear, I pity anyone who runs up against you in a dark alley." At last I had the sense to keep still.

He pretended as if he hadn't heard a word, or maybe he really didn't, with explosions still ringing in his ears. He said he was Victor Hartmann, and that he'd come to see the boy and maybe to bring him over to Darby's to show him round, as it was a warm and sunny day.

"What have you called him?" I asked, for I've been nursing the lad the whole while without knowing his name.

The man smiled, which in itself was something to see as it pulled his scars every which way. The smile was so sad it made me teary.

"She used to call him 'worm' so often I'm of a mind to call him that myself," he said.

I nodded. "It was that way with my last. I called him 'lump.' He was near three months old before I began to call him Kevin. And yours—he looks like a wiggly white worm, doesn't he, sir? Well, I'll fatten him up soon enough, that is, if you're going to leave him with me."

"Leave him?" he asked. "If I leave him, he will end up in the mines, won't he?"

"I think he should be weaned first, no? And grow a tooth or two?" I tried to make a joke, he was frowning so much.

"Of course," he said. "You mean, leave him with you for now."

"Yes, just for now. Later you'll be wanting to take him back home to your family."

"I have no family."

"Your wife's then," I said quickly, for he still looked so sad.

"Surely there's someone who'll be glad at the sight of him. What of your wife's parents?"

"I don't know. I would want her father to be glad to see the boy, but after all that has happened . . . He doesn't know that Lily is dead." He was talking more to himself, not me, as if I'd left the room. His big hand touched a straw bracelet around his wrist, which sat right next to another of little bells. It seemed to comfort him and to help him think. "I should try, though, shouldn't I?" he asked. "To bring the boy home? I should at least try."

"Yes," I said quickly, as he was about to go melancholy on me again. I could see he was the type to brood and would like as not see a sunny day as only what happens in between the rain. "No one can resist a fat new baby," I said, giving him the boy. "And he *will* be fat by the time you leave, I promise you."

When I said that, he reached into his pocket and pulled out a hair barrette with jewels in it as big as summer peas. "They are real," he assured me. "Are they enough for payment?"

"Why, to be fair, if I pried out one and gave you back the rest, I'd still be paid a thousand times over. Even so, you shouldn't talk about payment," I said. "For what you've done, I guess I can spare a bit of milk."

"Take it anyway," he said, pressing it into my hands. "Along with my thanks. I suppose you will see me often, now that I am well enough to visit the boy, though I'm not sure where I'll be staying. I think I've imposed on Darby too long."

I laughed at him and said there were at least seventeen families that would take him in that minute if they knew he was wanting a roof.

"Then you think I might be welcome in this town?" he asked.

"Aye, more than welcome. We're grateful to have you."

He looked down at the boy for a long time, then said something very peculiar:

A fairer Paradise is founded now
for Adam and his chosen sons.

The rector just told me this is poetry by Milton. I am a great respecter of words, having none, and said I would give Wally Milton an extra cake for his. And now the rector is laughing at me as he writes this and says no, he doesn't mean Wally.

Anyway, after the giant said his bit of poetry, he lifted his enormous hand like he was going to touch the little boy under the chin, but he stopped and didn't do it. The baby grabbed his finger, or tried to grab it since it was so big—and oh, the look on him then! Like he didn't know grabbing fingers is what babies do. Like he was the first father in all the world and this was the first baby.

He was making me teary again, so I shooed him out, saying, "Be off with you. Black Angel or not, you're just a man and like any man you're underfoot. Let me get back to my work."

"What did you say?" he asked.

"I said I must get back to my work."

"No, your words before that."

"I said you're just a man, and like any man you're underfoot."

I cannot describe the expression that came over his face, so fast did it change from one feeling to another. Then he suddenly held the baby close, as if something dreadful would snatch it away, and he left to go to Darby's.

I must end here, for the rector has just interrupted to say this is the fifth time I've used *dreadful* and do I want to go back and strike some out or leave my words as they are. I say leave them, but I'll not repeat myself again, nor go on to a new sheet of paper, so I will end here with my love to you and your new husband. Do write back and tell me when we may expect a visit, but remember, it is the rector who will be reading your words, so do me no mischief when you put your thoughts on paper.

Your cousin,
Anne

ACKNOWLEDGMENTS

I'M ENORMOUSLY GRATEFUL to the many people who helped me birth the Monster, including—

My tireless agent, Steven Chudney, who on the inhale can extol the wonders of a new manuscript and on the exhale say, "Now cut 20 percent, rewrite the rest, and *then* let me see it— and *where is that other book I'm waiting for?*"

My editor, Heather Lazare, whose insights into the characters and suggestions for the story gave the novel a much deeper and truer emotional heart.

Fellow writers Susan Taylor Brown, Laura Salas, Bonny Becker, and David Caruba, who kept me sane throughout.

Friends and family members, who have always generously given me their help.

Readers, past, present, and future, who patiently allow this author to tell tales.

And my husband, Michael, who has supported and encouraged and loved me as a writer, from the very first line of my very first picture book, through the books that followed, to *Frankenstein's Monster*. Despite new stories already littering the house and possessing my mind, he loves me still—and, for that, mere gratitude is a pale, pale word.

◇

Works by other authors are quoted throughout the book. Some quotations are unattributed to maintain the flow of the scene. Some have been changed to better express Victor's emotions at that moment. For questions regarding these or anything else—or to just stop by for company—please visit my website: www.susanheyboer okeefe.com.

Frankenstein's
MONSTER

◇

READER'S GUIDE

1. Each of the main characters in *Frankenstein's Monster,* especially Victor, makes a journey. Their physical journeys are clear. What are the emotional and psychological journeys for Victor? Lily? Robert Walton? Gregory Winterbourne? Who reaches their "destination" and who doesn't? Whether yes or no, why? Which of the other characters makes his or her own journey?

2. Victor's journal is bookended by a captain's log and a letter. What are the differences between the log and the letter? The similarities? Which differences and similarities seem to be a true impression of Victor and why? How do the differences and similarities reflect the character of Walton and of Anne Todd?

3. Victor's overall movement in the book is his attempt to change from monster to man. Is he truly a monster at the beginning? Truly a man at the end? If he is not a man at the end, why? What else must he do to find his humanity? If yes, at what point does he stop being a monster, and why? What made or *will* make him human?

4. *Frankenstein's Monster* begins ten years after Mary Shelley's *Frankenstein*. What do you think happened during those ten years for Victor? For Walton?

5. Over the course of the book, Victor is bound to two women: Mirabella and Lily. Which did he have stronger ties to? Which one would have proved better for him in the long term? What would be the advantages and disadvantages of each relationship? Would either relationship last? Who would be the one to leave, and why?

6. Victor quotes from essays, poems, and scripture to describe or emphasize his feelings at certain points throughout the book. What does reading mean to him? What does reading mean to you? What would a life without books be for Victor? For you? Which was your favorite quotation in the book, and why?

7. A key scene in the novel is Victor and Lily's overnight stay at the cottage. Lily leads Victor on, then spurns him in the worst imaginable way. How did you interpret and feel about Lily's behavior when you read the scene? How do you see it now? In the same scene, after she so brutally rejects him, Victor runs into the woods and commits an act of bestiality. Did it offend you? Did it make you feel more sympathy toward Victor or less?

8. At the beginning of the novel, the monster is nameless. About a quarter of the way through, he takes his father's first name, and then Lily gives him his surname. What is each name's significance? Does either one's significance change over time?

9. There are many references to God and religion throughout the book. How are they used? How are they depicted by the characters? Which reflect and/or influence Victor and in what ways? Did you believe them to be fair and accurate both in their depiction and in Victor's perception of them?

10. Four different settings and groups of people encounter Victor: beggars, "civilized society," the clergy and religious, and coal miners. If each group had accepted him, which would he have felt most comfortable with? Least comfortable with? If there was an ideal group or setting for Victor, who and what would it be? If he existed today, how would he be perceived? What are the possible kinds of acceptance and rejection he might face?

11. How would you have reacted to Victor? How would your reaction to him differ if you were a member of each of the above groups? If you had the opportunity to know him over time, how would that initial reaction stay with and influence you? Would you ever be able to see beyond the nature of his creation? His physical ugliness? The ugliness of his past behavior? Which would be the most difficult to accept?

12. The author has said that, while the idea was not used as a theme, today's scientific work in cloning, genetic manipulation, the use of animals in the treatment of humans, and so on, might be discussed in light of *Frankenstein's Monster*. How? Do you agree with Victor that the creator must take responsibility for what the creation does? Does this responsibility extend to humanity as a whole? To God? Can and should a creation become independent of its creator? If yes, what are the consequences? If no, why not?

13. *Frankenstein's Monster* is shaped in many ways by the fairy tale "Beauty and the Beast." How do you see that evidenced in the book? Where does it depart from the fairy tale? What other fairy tales, myths, archetypes, and so on, do you see in the novel? How did they shape your understanding of the book?

14. Victor displays varying degrees of violent behavior many times. Which were the most shocking to you? Why? How did

these incidents influence your perceptions of him? Were any of them physically necessary? Emotionally justified? Is violence ever justified?

15. In the coal mine, Walton makes a startling revelation that changes how Victor has perceived all that came before it. Was the revelation a total surprise or did you see hints of it throughout? How did it change your perception of Margaret, of Walton, and especially of Lily? What did you think of Victor's reaction to the revelation?